The
Bride of Stone

A Novel

Thomas Williams

Revell
Grand Rapids, Michigan

Published by Fleming H. Revell
a division of Baker Publishing Group
P.O. Box 6287, Grand Rapids, MI 49516-6287
www.revellbooks.com

Printed in the United States of America

Library of Congress Cataloging-in-Publication Data
Williams, T. M. (Thomas Myron), 1941–
    The bride of stone : a novel / Thomas Williams.
        p.   cm.
    ISBN 0-8007-5861-7 (pbk.)
    1. Blind sculptors—Fiction. 2. Princesses—Fiction. 3. Scars—
Fiction. I. Title.
PS3573.I45562B75 2004
813′.54—dc22   2004011021

To the Jernigans:
Terry, Cynthia, Candace, and Seth

The Seven
Kingdoms

NARROW SEA

MERIDAN

Maldor Castle
Forest of
Maldor
Garvane
Dormagan
Mountain
Rynde River
Plain of
Moribume
Northmere
Lenshaw
Evenshire
Middlemoor
Estate
Rallenstone
Hallifax
Rokestrand
Leverton
Parandor
Sothemer
Newfrith
Kerrigorn
Reddway

Corenham
Braegan
Wood
Ironwood Estate
Ironwood
Kemstead
Farandale
Llewenham

Stenholm

RHONDILAR

Sunderlon

Sunderlon River

Ridgedale
Surrifax

Ensovandor
Tarnbury
Souport

VENSAUR

DRAGONTOOTH
MOUNTAINS

Dunnestan
Levonwicke

ORANTH

Kenmarl
Estate
Engleham
Gorth
Brancester
Greenmeade

Soucroft
Norfeld
Lorganville

Ironwood

Rennet River

SORENDALE

Mithrach

Faranburgh
Wallenton
Laverton

Sunderlon
River

LOCHLAUND

Furthing
Blaiseburn
Kranthar
Widdcroft

GRAYSTONE
MOUNTAINS
Morrowton
Macrennon

Kellenwood Forest
Black
Mountain
Blackmore
Forest
Valthorne

VALOMAR

Part 1

Perivale

1

The tall warrior spurred his horse and loped toward the top of the rise. When he reached it, he wheeled the stamping charger around three times as he looked in all directions across the Plain of Moriburne. His sword, gripped in his powerful hand, gleamed red with blood. Finally he reined the great stallion to a halt. Its sides heaved, and its black body was lathered with sweat and spattered red, as was the knight himself. He took a corner of his cape, tattered and splotched as if the skies had rained blood, and wiped his blade clean before sliding it into its sheath. He removed his helmet and set it on his saddle before him. The tumbled waves of his sweat-soaked hair glimmered like burnished gold in the waning sunlight as he wiped his hand across his brow and looked out across the battlefield, now stretching gray beneath him in the lengthening shadows of the Dragontooth Mountains.

The battle was over. The warrior watched as the soldiers on the plain began to sheathe their swords and wander among the bodies strewn about like shapeless rags dropped from a washerwoman's basket. When they came upon one of their own who showed signs of life, they carried him to the camp set in a grove of trees near the river at the edge of the plain. The warrior nudged his horse and began to descend the rise. As he passed from sunlight into the shadows, he came upon one of the fallen bodies of the enemy. He shuddered. Where did Morgultha find such monsters? The torso was human, as were the arms and hands, though the naked flesh was gray and mottled. But the head was that of a wolf and the feet and legs apparently those of a bear. A few yards away another body lay twisted and broken, its torso covered with reptilian scales. The hands and arms were human and the head that of a wild boar. Next to the creature lay the crumpled body of a warrior from Meridan, fully human and fully armored. The sparse, fine growth on the corpse's chin marked him as a stripling who would never reach his twentieth birthday. The tall warrior dropped his head in anguish as he passed by. He did not yet know how many men had perished in the terrible battle, but he knew the number would be staggering.

As he reached the base of the rise, a warrior on a roan charger broke from a cluster of knights at the edge of Braegan Wood and trotted toward him. The rider had removed his helmet, and blood matted his hair and streaked his face.

"Sir Perivale," the rider said. "What shall we do with the bodies?"

"We will bury our own here on the Plain of Moriburne," Perivale replied. "Their sacrifice will hallow this soil. As for these hellish monsters, build a fire and burn them."

"Our men don't want to touch the creatures," the horseman said. "Though they be good soldiers and will obey your word."

"I don't want any man to touch those bodies. Indeed, I forbid it. They must use rags, ropes, poles, discarded clothing, or whatever they can find to avoid contact with that vile flesh. Carry the bodies to the fire in carts, and then burn the carts. When the field is clean, every man must bathe in the river before returning to the camp."

"It will be done, sir," the horseman said as he turned and trotted away.

Perivale rode slowly about the battlefield, brooding deeply as the soldiers carried out his orders. The mound of hideous corpses grew to the size of a haystack as the men emptied cart after cart upon it. Soon writhing tongues of flame began to lick about the pile. When darkness descended, the blaze lit the plain with a sheen of lurid red. A column of smoke, oily and black, rose hundreds of feet into the air, the underside of the billows glowing orange like the roof of hell. Perivale looked into the blackness of Braegan Wood, from where the creatures had launched their attack. He wondered if any man or woman would ever again feel safe in that forest.

As he sat pondering, three more captains rode up to him, led by Sir Everedd.

"Sir Perivale," Everedd said, "it is now too dark to see the bodies clearly. Many are hidden by the brush and tall grass. I say we should quit gathering corpses for the night and resume in the morning."

"No," Perivale said, "you must continue. Give the men torches. Be sure they search every inch of this plain and inspect it when they are done. I don't want a single one of Morgultha's abominations left unburned tonight, nor do I want a single body of our own warriors left on the field. Work the men through the night if you must. They can take their rest tomorrow."

"Where in the devil's name could she have got such a monstrous army?" Everedd said. "I've never even imagined that such creatures could exist."

"It seems she has patched them together from the limbs

and organs of whatever creatures she could find," Perivale replied. "Most are part human, especially the hands and arms. It's likely she robbed graves or murdered men on the highways or in the forests. Many of the parts are from wolves, boars, stags, and crocodiles. I even saw one creature that seemed to have the legs of some huge fowl. What dark enchantments or unholy spirits brought them to life I hardly dare to imagine."

"Whatever they are, they fought with the strength of oxen and the fury of hell," one of the captains said.

"The only good thing about them is that they apparently don't hold life well," said another. "Though it was hard to wound them, it seems that almost any wound they took proved eventually fatal. I saw one dying near the edge of the woods with nothing more than a gash in its arm. It was gasping like a winded cur as it crawled toward the trees."

"That is a blessing," Perivale said. "I would like to think that if any escaped into Braegan Wood, they will perish of their wounds. Though I would not send any man into that forest tonight, tomorrow we must search at least the edge of it. I don't want even one of Morgultha's hell spawn left alive. They are an abomination to the earth and an affront to the Master of the Universe."

The captains' faces turned ashen beneath the orange glow of the fire as they considered the prospect of following the monsters into that black wood.

"How many men did we lose?" Perivale asked.

"As best we can tell, just over six thousand dead and another seven thousand wounded," Everedd said. "Of the wounded, I fear we will lose a third before the night is over."

Perivale closed his eyes, grimaced, and turned away.

"That means we have lost two-thirds of all the armies of the Seven Kingdoms. A fearful price to pay."

"Yes, a fearful price, sir. But we had no choice. Had Morgultha won this battle, the entire island would have been hers," the captain replied. "And she certainly would have killed any of our warriors who survived."

"True enough." Perivale sighed. "But the thousands of newly made widows and orphans will grieve as deeply as if we had been defeated. In a single day an entire generation has been decimated." He sat quiet for the space of seven breaths as the captains waited in silence. "Let me know the moment you find the body of Morgultha."

"We will do it, sir." The captains wheeled their horses around and returned to their grisly task.

After circling the field twice more, Perivale turned his stallion toward the camp on the bank of the River Crynnedd. Once he reached the cluster of tents and wagons, he dismounted. A groomsman took his steed, and he walked to his tent, where his aide, Crandon, joined him. Perivale lifted his weary arms as the man unlaced and removed the plates of dented and splattered armor that protected his torso and the chain mail that covered his arms and legs. He stripped off the rest of his clothing and walked to the river to bathe. Torches set on oaken poles lit the riverside, and at least two score soldiers already splashed about in the water while that many more milled about the bank, drying themselves or removing their clothing in preparation for their bath. A hush came over the men as their new commander approached, and many cast awe-filled, sidelong glances at his towering form as he stepped into the water among them. After scrubbing himself and soaking his bruises in the cool water, Perivale returned to his tent, where Crandon applied salve to his wounds and bound the worst of them.

Perivale donned a robe, eased himself onto a stone just outside his tent, and leaned his sword against a nearby barrel of ale. He began to eat the roasted hare Crandon had brought him. A sudden clamor of voices sounded in the distance in the direction of the great fire. He looked up to see a bobbing mass of bodies moving toward him, silhouetted by the firelight from the burning monsters at their backs. Perivale stiffened and reached for his sword, then relaxed and waited. Apparently, the approaching huddle posed no threat, for the soldiers near the camp parted and allowed them to pass. As the party drew near the torchlight, Perivale made out the faces of two of his own men, grasping between them the arms of a tall, slender human form. A black robe covered the captive from the top of the head to the booted ankles. Not even the hands were visible. Behind these three walked another half dozen men, their faces wary and their swords ready should the black-robed prisoner attempt escape.

The party stopped ten feet in front of Perivale. One of the men reached up and pulled back the hood from the captive's head, revealing a woman's face, thin and pallid as the moon. Framing her face were long locks of straight, black hair falling to just below her shoulders. The woman glared at Perivale through eyes pale and cold as winter frost.

Perivale did not rise from his stone but returned the gaze without expression. "You have failed to conquer this island, Morgultha," he said. "Yet your attempt has brought terrible grief upon us. Our kingdoms were at peace. They were prosperous and content. The people were ruled well, and they were happy. Why did you bring such destruction upon us?"

"The answer is simple, Sir Perivale." The woman's voice was hard as iron and almost as deep as a man's. "I am more fit to rule this land than any of its seven kings. I, and only I, have the knowledge to lead this sleepy little island to become the envy of all the earth. I could have transformed it into a civilization rivaling the ancient nations of the east."

"And you would impose your vision for this island on its people against their will? You self-centered, arrogant witch!" Perivale's eyes flashed, and his voice rose with passion. "The people wanted no part of your bloated ambitions. They were content before you came, and after their grief is spent they will be content again."

"They are content only because they are ignorant of what I could have offered them," Morgultha replied. "I have lived among the ruins of the city of the ancient Nephilim. I have studied their arts—the art of leading men, of war, commerce, metallurgy, astrology, occultism, and spiritual power—arts that have been lost to mankind since the great flood. I could have—"

"The Master of the Universe sent the great flood to destroy the Nephilim because of their unholy knowledge," Perivale said. "The Seven Kingdoms want no part of such abominations."

"For all the glory of your victory, you are no better than the rabble that makes up these kingdoms. You are all slaves to this spirit you call the Master of the Universe. He hides great truths from you, yet you fear to reach out and grasp knowledge that could make you equal to him. I sought only to free you from your blind bondage to this close-handed master."

"The Master of the Universe withholds from us nothing that is good," Perivale said.

"Oh, you little man," Morgultha replied with a laugh as brittle as ice. "The spirits of the Nephilim have not departed from the earth. I have discovered channels by which I can speak with them. They have revealed to me many secrets your master hides from you, such as the secrets of life by which the titans of old lived many centuries, secrets that have enabled me to live on this earth more than three hundred years, secrets I would gladly have imparted to every citizen in the Seven Kingdoms if your own fear of what you do not know had not thwarted me."

"You lie. Only the Master has the power to grant life."

"Then how do you explain the creatures that made up my army? They are of my own devising, knitted together from the flesh of reptiles, animals, birds, and men, animated by spells I learned from the Nephilim."

Perivale said nothing. As he looked into the woman's eyes, hard, cold, and baleful as the gaze of a basilisk, he was inclined to believe her. He was certain that the creatures of her army could not have come from the hand of the Master of the Universe. Only a corrupted mind could have spawned such monsters—a mind in rebellion to the order of creation. There were issues here far beyond his understanding. He would think more on them later.

"The people of the Seven Kingdoms had no wish to become vessels to display the wisdom of the Nephilim," he said wearily. "I will bring you to Maldor Castle, where you will stand trial before the council of Meridan."

"And no doubt your little laws will find me guilty and warranting death," Morgultha replied, contempt dripping from every word. "All because I wanted this island to become something more than a lazy farmer's paradise. What blinders you cravens wear!"

"My blinders do not hide the death and destruction you have wrought—especially the death of a great king who did us only good."

"Surely you can see that King Landorm's death has brought great good to you, Sir Perivale. Not only are you now head of his army, but for the moment you are head of the combined armies of the Seven Kingdoms. If you are not chosen to replace him as king of Meridan, then I am not a prophetess."

"That is preposterous!" Perivale spat. "King Landorm's nephew Lord Fenimar will ascend to the throne of Meridan. I will return to my estate and take up my life with my wife and children."

Morgultha thrust out her long chin. "Say what you will. I predict that you will soon sit on the throne of Meridan."

Perivale noticed that the woman's right hand had remained hidden in her robes throughout the encounter, and as she shifted her position, a metallic flash shot from within the folds. Immediately he rose to his feet, wary that she was concealing a weapon. "What do you hide in your robe? Show me your hand."

Morgultha neither replied nor moved her hand but glared defiantly at Perivale.

"I said, show me your hand—now!" he demanded.

Still she stood immobile, and Perivale nodded to the men holding her. They gripped her arm and tried to pull it from the black folds. She resisted, turning and twisting and clutching her right arm with her left. The woman was surprisingly strong, but in moments they wrenched her right arm from its hiding place and held it outstretched toward Perivale. Clutched in her fist was a crown, shimmering gold in the torchlight. The crown was of circlet design, with a rim a little over an inch high that rose to three peaks in the front, the center peak a half inch taller than the two on either side. In the center of each peak was set a single stone. The stones in the two side peaks were identical rubies, while the center stone was larger and shimmered with colors impossible to name. No eye looking on had ever beheld such colors—colors that wavered

15

and flashed with each movement of the crown. The hues were not of the earth's natural spectrum, and every man in the camp stared in utter fascination.

Perivale himself gazed with wonder, his eyes held fast by the fluid flashes of unearthly light. "What is that?" he asked.

"It is a crown," Morgultha sneered.

"I can see that it is a crown, but whose crown is it?"

"The crown is mine," Morgultha replied. "I have possessed it for many years. It is of no particular importance."

"Then why do you carry it with you, and why were you so careful to hide it?"

"It is made of gold," she replied. "I could not risk it becoming a spoil of war."

"Do not believe her, Sir Perivale." The voice rose from the crowd of men who had gathered about. Everyone turned as King Telagorn of Valomar stepped forward. "I know of this crown. It is the fabled Crown of Eden, so called because it bears the Stone of Eden, which was the talisman of Adam's charge to rule the earth."

Perivale stepped toward Morgultha. "How did you get this?" he asked.

She did not answer but glared at him.

"Give the crown to me," he commanded, his open hand extended before him.

"I will not." She struggled against her captors to pull back her hand.

"Take it from her," Perivale commanded.

Two soldiers stepped up and grasped the woman's hand, intending to pull her fingers from the crown. But after a few minutes of futile prying, wedging, and pulling, her fist remained clenched as firmly as the talons of an eagle. One of the men slipped out a knife and tried to wedge the blade between the rim of the crown and the woman's fingers. Trickles of blood began to seep from between her fingers as the soldier worked the blade back and forth. He pushed the knife outward, expecting the pressure to lift the fingers from the rim of the crown. To the surprise of all, the blade bent and then snapped, but Morgultha's grip remained intact.

"We cannot open her hand, Sir Perivale."

Perivale picked up his sword and drew it from its sheath. "Morgultha, you will give me that crown, or I will cut off your hand."

Still she did not relent. Her fingers remained knotted in their viselike grip as she glared at him with unmitigated hate.

"Hold out her arm," he said. The soldiers complied, and he lifted his sword to strike. "I ask you one last time to give me the crown. I do not want to maim you, but if you continue to defy me, I will do it."

Morgultha opened neither her mouth nor her hand. After the space of three breaths, Perivale brought down his sword in a swift arc, and the hand fell to the grass, where it lay bleeding, still clutching the crown.

Morgultha made no sound and did not even look at her severed hand or the blood gushing from the stump of her wrist but continued to glare at Perivale.

"Bind her wound, then remove the hand from the crown and bring it to me," he said.

But the men found that removing the severed hand was no easy task. It still gripped the crown as tightly as it had when attached to Morgultha's body. Their only recourse was to cut away the fingers joint by joint. When the grisly task was done, they washed the blood from the crown and brought it to Perivale.

Perivale took the crown and turned it slowly in his hands, marveling at the clear imprint of Morgultha's fingers in its golden rim. Though he had heard legends about the Crown of Eden, he had not known until this moment that it actually existed. But he could not deny the evidence before him. The stone's unearthly colors gripped his eye as firmly as Morgultha's hand had gripped the crown. If the legends about this stone were true, as he now suspected they were, he held in his hands the talisman the Master of the Universe himself had given to Adam to signify man's dominion over all creation. With some difficulty he tore his eyes from the stone and wrapped the crown in his ruined cape. He instinctively knew it was perilous to behold such a thing and determined not to look at it again.

"Place the woman in a tent and post a guard of six men around it. Tomorrow we will strike camp and march to Maldor, where she will stand trial."

"It will be done, sir."

As the soldiers took Morgultha away, Perivale entered his own pavilion and collapsed on the furs and pelts that covered the ground inside. For a while he stared unseeing at the glow from the ghastly fire dancing in a frenzy of orange ripples on the translucent fabric of his tent. He rubbed his eyes as if to wipe away the images of death the flame brought to his mind. But the grim pictures would not leave—men of strength and vitality, once so full of life, laughter, and love, now gone from the earth forever. Many of the dead he had known, some quite well. The faces of his slain friends, with the hellish monsters of Morgultha's army looming in the shadows behind them, paraded relentlessly through his thoughts. It was long past midnight before he slept.

The first rays of the sun barely touched the peaks of the Dragontooth Mountains when Perivale awakened suddenly to the urgent call of his aide. "Sir Perivale, you must wake up."

The commander sat up and looked at the alarmed face peering through the tent flap. "What is wrong?"

"It's the witch Morgultha, sir. She has disappeared. She is not in her tent."

"Not in her tent? Impossible! I posted a guard of six men on her."

He arose, threw a cloak around his shoulders, and stepped out into the crisp morning air. He walked toward the men clustered about a small tent some hundred paces away, his aide following nervously behind.

"What has happened?" he asked as he approached the tent.

"We don't rightly know, sir," Sir Ashmond replied. "The men tell me the guard of six was posted as you commanded, and nothing happened until in the dark of the morning when one of them saw a blue glow within the tent and wisps of smoke curling out from the seams. He alerted the other guards, and two of them approached the tent opening while the rest stood about it with ready swords. The moment they opened the flap, a huge blackbird rushed out and flew into the woods. The furs inside the tent still smoldered, but there was no longer any flame. Morgultha was not inside. They looked beneath the furs and probed every corner, but she simply was not there. We don't know what to make of it, sir."

"I think I know what has happened." All turned to the voice of King Telagorn. "Either she turned herself into the blackbird or, more likely, covered herself with the illusion of a blackbird and escaped. Such things are not uncommon among those who traffic in the black arts."

"Shall we pursue the bird, sir?" one of the guards asked.

"No," Perivale replied. "It is still too dark to see, and she has been gone too long. I fear she is lost to us for now."

"I am very sorry, Sir Perivale," Ashmond said. "I will have the guards duly punished."

"No, they are not at fault. None of us knew Morgultha could do such a thing." He looked toward the site of the great fire, now merely a black mound of smoldering embers. "Have all the enemies' bodies been cleared from the field?"

"They have, sir. And the field has been checked three times for any we may have overlooked."

"Good. As soon as you have enough light, send men a hundred yards into Braegan Wood to be sure none are left there. At noon we will strike camp and return to Maldor Castle."

2

Perivale's task was now finished. He rode alone, sitting astride his charger, with a loaded packhorse tethered close behind. He followed the forest road southward from Maldor Castle toward the central region of Meridan. He had spent three days making his report to the council of the kingdom's elders, an emeritus body that advised the king and Hall of Knights in times of peace and functioned as caretaker rulers in times of war when the members of the Hall were away at battle. He had also delivered to them the Crown of Eden. Immediately the council and the Hall had recognized the danger of the legendary relic falling into the wrong hands. They had voted to lock it inside the great vault of the kingdom's treasury, deep in the hidden bowels of the castle. A double guard was posted day and night.

The council grieved over the loss of good King Landorm and briefly considered the matter of his succession. It quickly became apparent that the discussion would be factious. Landorm had died childless, and many in the Hall thought the king's nephew, Lord Fenimar, should take the throne. Others insisted that the Hall consider other candidates before endorsing the succession. The Hall had voted to table the issue and convene a special council to take it up again in one month and one day.

None of these thoughts lingered long in Perivale's mind as he left Maldor Castle and rode toward his estate, Middlemoor, which lay two days southward from Maldor. He spent the first day and half the next riding through woods and highland hills dotted with white sheep and grazing cattle. Shortly after noon on the second day, he emerged from a thick wood, and a wide vista of patchwork fields opened before him. His heart warmed at the sight of cottages nestled in the groves of oaks and conifers that tufted the rolling landscape, and for the first time in weeks, the heaviness in his heart began to lift. He was nearing home. Soon his beautiful wife, Rianna, would be a warm reality enfolded in his hungry arms and not merely a dream of exquisite longing that tortured him waking or sleeping.

The face of his son, Rhondale, rose in his mind—wide-eyed, innocent, and full of wonder. Even at the age of six, the boy had a creative bent and a warrior's spirit. Perivale smiled as he remembered the day he had heard the voice of his son bellowing behind the feed barn. He had run toward the sound, thinking the boy was in danger. He would never forget the sight that had met him as he rounded the corner. Little Rhondale was armed with a wooden sword and a shield he had fashioned from a stiffened scrap of discarded leather. He slashed and thrust at a dragon made of piled stones topped with a green gourd painted with fierce red eyes and a mouth filled with jagged teeth. Perivale had watched silently as his little son moved in on the monster and lopped off its head, sending the gourd bouncing across the grass. The boy had the makings of a fine warrior.

Perivale's smile softened as another face rose in his mind—the face of his daughter, Avalessa. He was in utter awe of this little seven-year-old creature, wondering at the lovely gentleness of her spirit and the promise of great beauty already evident in her features. He rode on, lost in his happy reverie until he came to the stone cairn that marked the border of his land. His heart leapt as he turned his horse onto the road toward his manor. He would be home within half an hour.

Avalessa sat at the window of the highest tower in the manor, her chair positioned where she could see the road that stretched from the manor until it disappeared into the line of trees some two hundred paces from the gate. She sat at the small table her father had made for her and her Chrissy, the wooden doll he had carved and painted with his own hands and for which her mother had fashioned a gown fit for a princess. Chrissy sat facing her across the table. Avalessa had taken this position five days ago after a messenger had ridden to the estate and told her mother the war had ended. The king was dead, but the army had rallied and won a great victory for the Seven Kingdoms. Avalessa remembered her mother's face when she had heard the news—soft and full of anticipation, radiant as the little girl had never seen it before.

"Your father will be home soon," Rianna had told her son and daughter, drawing them to her side and hugging them as she gazed down the road. "Possibly within the week."

Immediately Avalessa had taken up her post by the tower window and looked often toward the road emerging from the line of oaks and elms. "He will come today, Chrissy, I know he will." She had spoken the same words to her doll every day since beginning the vigil. She poured her little friend a cup of imaginary milk, then settled back in her chair to watch the road. The day was warm, and Avalessa was still, and soon her head nodded and fell forward. Golden waves of hair formed a curtain around her face as she slipped into a doze.

She started suddenly and looked around the room. She did not know what had awakened her, but she felt that something had. She looked out at the road and saw a tall man astride a great, black charger, leading a laden packhorse close behind. For three or four seconds she thought she was dreaming. As the truth penetrated the fog of her drowsiness, she jumped up and cried, "Papa! Oh, he's here! He's here! Look, Chrissy, Papa has come home!"

She ran out of the room and down the stairs, through the great hall, and out into the road. She did not stop running until she was beside the horse, jumping up and down, squealing, and looking up into her father's smiling face. The big man reached down and swept her up into his arms, holding her as if he would squeeze her into himself. Avalessa cried, kissed his neck, and giggled with delight.

"Look, Papa," she said when at last he released her from his embrace. She spread her mouth in a wide grin, showing the gap where her front tooth had been.

"You lost a tooth!" Perivale said.

"Another one is loose," she said, putting her finger to the mate of the missing tooth and moving it back and forth.

"Here, I will pull it for you now," Perivale teased, reaching toward her mouth.

"No, Papa!" she cried, fighting his hand away. "It's not ready yet. We have to wait until it's looser."

"You mean wait until it falls out," her father said, laughing. "Oh, my little girl is growing up. Soon you will be a lady and some thief of a boy will steal you away from me. What ever will I do?"

"I could never leave you, Papa," she replied soberly.

"Ah, but someday you will. It's the nature of things, my little princess."

He placed her on the saddle in front of him, where she sat in quiet ecstasy, delighting in her father's strong arm holding her snugly against his broad chest as they rode toward the manor. She felt utterly secure and immensely valued that this important man should care so much for her.

When they reached the flat cobblestones at the door of the manor, Perivale dismounted and lifted Avalessa from the saddle.

"Father!" A joyful yell came from inside the hall as Rhondale burst from the door, running toward Perivale with arms spread wide. The knight took the boy in his arms and embraced him, swinging him about in a circle.

"How tall you've grown!" he exclaimed. "You're getting to be a little man."

No sooner had he spoken than he felt another presence at the door of the manor. He set the boy down and looked at his wife, Rianna, gazing at him as if her eyes would never get their fill. He stood still for a moment, his heart pounding at the sight of her golden hair and eyes the color of the sea. They stepped toward each other, slowly, deliberately, impelled by deep yearning long denied. For another moment they stood facing each other, inches apart, the eyes of each held fast by the gaze of the other. Then Perivale reached his arms around her, drew her off her feet, and kissed her deeply in a long embrace. The two children grinned and squirmed where they stood, stealing embarrassed glances at each other and stifling giggles.

When Perivale finally released his wife and eased her back to the ground, both were trembling gently. Perivale wiped his moist eyes with the back of his hand and turned again to the children.

"Let's see what we can find on this packhorse," he said.

They stood on either side of him, watching eagerly as he untied the ropes and pulled away the tarp. He lifted a long, thin bundle wrapped in sacking and handed it to Rhondale. All watched as the boy peeled back the layers of cloth to reveal the scabbard of a sword, half the length of a warrior's weapon. A carved hilt protruded from the top of the sheath, and little Rhondale's eyes grew wide as sunflowers. Eagerly he grasped the hilt and drew out the sword. The blade of tempered steel gleamed bright and clean. Perivale took a child-sized leather belt from his pack, tied the scabbard to it, and strapped it about his son's waist.

"Now you look like a real warrior," he said.

"I am a real warrior. Yesterday I killed a snake in the chicken yard with my wooden sword."

"He really did," Rianna said. "Though I told him he must never get that near a snake again."

Perivale beamed with pride and grinned as he watched the boy thrusting and slashing with his new weapon. His son would make a fine warrior. After a moment he looked at Avalessa, who gazed expectantly at him. He smiled and turned again to the packhorse.

"Let's see if this old horse brought anything for you, my little princess."

He took from the pack another bundle wrapped in sacking cloth, thin except for a rounded bulk at one end. He gently handed the package to his daughter. She sat on a nearby stone bench, and when she peeled away the sacking, a mandolin lay on her lap.

"Oh, Papa, thank you!" she said as she gazed with delight at the instrument.

She had wanted a mandolin ever since a snowstorm

26

had confined the minstrel Falladin to the manor for five evenings in the winter of last year—five evenings of ballads, stories, and folk songs. She strummed the strings, and the sound came alive in the deep wooden chamber. She tried to hold the instrument as she had seen the minstrel hold his, but she could not get the beautiful chords that had come so effortlessly to him.

"I have seen the minstrel Falladin, and he is coming to this country not more than a month from now," Perivale said. "He has promised to stay with us a week and give you lessons. In the meantime, he sketched out finger positions that will show you how to make the five basic chords." Perivale went again to the pack and drew out a small piece of folded yellow paper. He knelt beside the bench and opened it for his daughter. "He says you are to practice these before he comes. It will make the lessons easier and toughen up your fingertips."

"Thank you, Papa," Avalessa said, beaming as she laid aside the mandolin and threw her arms around her father's neck.

Perivale stood and turned once more to the pack on the horse. He drew from it a wooden cask a little larger than his hand. He went to Rianna and placed it in her palm. She undid the brass clasp and opened the box. Inside on a scarf of blue silk lay a golden chain of delicate links, each half the size of her littlest fingernail. Hanging from the chain was a golden pendant, oval in shape and carved with leafy filigrees. In the center of the oval shone a bright, many-faceted stone, flashing colors of emerald green, brilliant purple, golden yellow, and lightning blue.

"It's beautiful," she whispered as she lifted it from the cask. "I've never seen anything like it."

"It's called a diamond," Perivale said. "Mined on the dark

continent to the south of the Southern Sea and shaped by secret processes."

He stepped behind his wife, drew the chain around her neck, and fastened the clasp. Then he reached his arms around her and drew her to him, kissing her neck as she closed her eyes in ecstasy, both of them oblivious to the shouts of the young warrior slashing at an imaginary troll and the cacophonic plucking of mandolin strings.

That evening the family dined together for the first time in nine weeks. It was a memorable night. The meal was sumptuous, and the servants were diligent to see that every plate and mug remained full until the diners could hold no more. Stories abounded throughout the meal. The children told of adventures in fields and forest, while Rianna filled her husband with details about the planting and growth of their crops, all handled efficiently by the overseer, Wolderand. Perivale told of incidents on the road and at inns, though he avoided speaking of the war. Laughter and high spirits cheered the evening until Rianna called the nurse to take the children up to their beds. Then the couple left the table to the servants and moved to Perivale's grand chair in front of the hearth.

He sat in the chair as Rianna snuggled on his lap, resting her head upon his shoulder. Both gazed contentedly at the low flames in the hearth as he stroked the golden softness of her hair.

"The Seven Kingdoms are through with war," he said after several minutes.

"That would be wonderful if it were true," Rianna replied, "but how can you be sure?"

"Morgultha has been thoroughly defeated, and I'm sure she cannot rise again in a generation or more. The cost was great, but out of it grew a great thing. The Seven Kingdoms united as one against a common enemy. Having learned of their collective power, they will not be easily defeated again."

"With no more wars to wage, what will you do?"

Perivale smiled and gave her the answer he knew she wanted to hear. "I will stay home and manage my lands. I will develop our herds and sow crops in rotation to get the most from the fields. I will indeed beat my sword into a plowshare."

Rianna snuggled deeper into his bosom, and he continued to stroke her hair as long, contented silences alternated with quiet conversation. After the last flame flickered and their faces glowed warm in the reflection of the red embers, Perivale stood, took his wife in his arms, and carried her up the stone stairway to their chamber, where they lost themselves in each other for the rest of the night.

3

Lord Reddgaard, vice-regent and hallmaster of Meridan, stood at the side of the great hall in Maldor Castle, his aide, Sir Danward, at his elbow. He gazed all around at the lords and knights of Meridan who had been summoned to the assembly. Some milled about the hall, and some sat on benches, while others stood in clusters talking quietly as they awaited the call to order.

"Lord Fenimar just arrived, sir," Danward said. Reddgaard looked toward the door to see the nobleman enter, dressed as usual in rich finery and trailing a billowing red cape. Accompanying him as always were his cousin Lord Ashbough and Lord Kramad Yesenhad, a dark-skinned lawyer from the seacoast town of Kerrigorn.

The three new arrivals came directly to Reddgaard, and after exchanging greetings, Fenimar said, "Please forgive our tardiness, my lord. The inn was late with our breakfast this morning."

Reddgaard said nothing. Fenimar had never yet arrived before the beginning of a meeting. He derived some sense of power from his ability to disrupt procedures with his late entrance.

"We will assemble shortly," Reddgaard replied. "Your tardiness is of no consequence for once, as other lords and knights have not yet arrived."

"Oh? For whom do you wait?" Fenimar looked about the room, quickly counting heads. "It appears to me that everyone is here."

"All are here but two," Danward replied, "and one we are loath to start without."

"And just who would that be?" Fenimar asked.

"Sir Perivale has not arrived. Of all Meridan's noblemen, we want him here today."

"Of course, we want to render proper worship to the hero of the hour, do we not?" Fenimar replied.

Reddgaard did not miss the sarcastic lilt of his voice.

"If I know Sir Perivale," the hallmaster replied, "fear of the honor we would do him is enough to keep him away."

"Perhaps he has more than honor to fear in this hall." Fenimar raised an eyebrow as he spoke. Then he bowed and walked away, his two companions following.

Reddgaard watched as Fenimar and the two knights who were his shadows approached Sir Grenvar and ushered him to a far corner, where they engaged him in earnest conversation.

Reddgaard turned to Danward. "A fear is creeping upon me, Danward. I suspect that Lord Fenimar is hatching some scheme."

"You can be sure of it," his aide replied. "Fenimar is singling out knights and lords who owe him money and reminding them of their debts. Were he to call in those debts, half the nobles of the land would become paupers overnight. Few in the Hall have any love for Fenimar, but if he tries to leverage himself to the throne with threats, as he is sure to do, he has a fair chance of succeeding."

"May the Master of the Universe protect us from such a fate," Reddgaard said.

At that moment, one of the two missing members of the Hall entered. Sir Everedd stepped through the doorway and walked purposefully toward the hallmaster.

"Greetings, my Lord Reddgaard," he said as he bowed before the venerable statesman. "I beg pardon for my tardiness. I began my journey three days back, but on the first morning a messenger met me on the road to summon me to the manor of Sir Perivale. I obeyed the summons, then rode through the night to get here. I bring tidings from Perivale."

"Your friendship with Sir Perivale is well known, Sir Everedd. What is the message?"

"Perivale will not attend the council, my lord. He begs your pardon and bids you proceed without him."

"He will not attend?" Reddgaard replied. "Is he ill? Is anything amiss with his family? Does he protest some action of the Hall?"

"No, my lord. All is well with him. Indeed, I think I have never seen him look more content and at peace. He has sent a letter that explains all." Everedd handed Reddgaard a small roll of parchment tied with a leather thong.

The hallmaster unrolled the sheet and silently read the few words written upon it, then looked up at Everedd. "You know what this says, don't you?"

"I do, sir. Perivale asked me to read it when he gave it to me."

"He has resigned from the Hall," Reddgaard said, absently tapping the rolled parchment against his hand as dismay darkened his ancient face.

"But not from his duty to the kingdom," Everedd said. "You know that for all his courage, patriotism, and battle prowess, Perivale is at heart a quiet, private man and a

32

peace-loving one. He hates war, and he fights only by necessity. He desires nothing more than to improve his farmlands and live in peace with his family. Note that he says he will always come to the aid of Meridan in times of need, but he chooses to relinquish his duties as a standing member of the Hall."

"I understand that perfectly well," Reddgaard snapped, "but a man cannot so easily escape the hand of fate." Before Everedd could ask the meaning of his words, the hallmaster turned to Danward and said, "We need wait no longer. Call the meeting to order."

Danward sounded the call. It took several minutes for the forty or so knights and lords of the kingdom to quit their conversations and make their way to their seats. As the Hall fell silent, the knights stood in front of their carved oaken chairs, which were set against the walls of the two long sides of the hall and facing the open floor in the center. The throne, set atop a two-tiered dais at the end of the room, was empty except for the helm of King Landorm resting on the cushion. Reddgaard took his seat at a table set in front of the dais facing the great door at the far end of the hall. A scribe and a historian sat flanking him at the table. As Reddgaard rapped his staff against the polished flagstone floor and called the assembly to order, only the first chair on the right of the hall—Perivale's chair—remained empty.

"Lords and knights of Meridan," he began, his still-powerful voice resonating in the rafters. "We have assembled here for a strange mix of purposes: to mourn, to celebrate, to honor, and to fill the now-empty throne of our kingdom. We mourn the loss of our great King Landorm, the noblest of men, who courageously laid down his life for the people he served so selflessly. The ceremonies we have already observed at his passing comfort us, but we shall mourn him for years to come. Yet we celebrate the great victory we have won in his name—victory over an evil so powerful and so insidious that none can doubt that the hand of the Master of the Universe must have come to our aid. And we honor the man who took up King Landorm's fallen banner, brought courage and order to our disheartened and disarrayed troops, and turned the tide of the battle, leading the armies of the Seven Kingdoms in the resounding defeat of the invader Morgultha. May she never rise again."

"May she never rise again." The men of the Hall repeated the words in ritual unison.

"I had hoped we could honor Sir Perivale in person today, but I regret to announce that he has chosen not to participate in this assembly. Indeed, he has resigned his chair in the Hall in favor of a life of peace in Meridan's middle country." A murmur of surprise rippled through the Hall. Reddgaard held up his hands to quiet the men. "Do not misunderstand. Sir Perivale has not turned his back on Meridan. He assures us that he will come when true need calls. He will do his duty by his kingdom, and gladly enough. But he wishes to retire from public service to attend to his growing crops and growing family."

Again murmurs ran through the Hall, expressing understanding on the part of some, dismay on the part of others, and on the part of a few, clear relief.

"Now we move to the central matter before the Hall. Since King Landorm died childless, it falls to us to determine who will sit on the throne of Meridan. As you know, the law provides for succession by a king's direct descendants, males first in order of age, females if there is no male heir or if the male is unsuitable to serve. If the king leaves no heir, the Hall of Knights must determine succession. I now call for proposals on how this Hall can fill the throne of Meridan."

Ashbough stood and faced the hallmaster. "Speak, Lord Ashbough," Reddgaard said.

"In your recounting of the succession law of Meridan, you overlooked one thing, my lord," Ashbough said. "When the king dies without issue, the Hall must turn to his near kin for succession."

"That is not written law but merely custom," Reddgaard responded, "though it is true that the Hall has often turned to next of kin in filling Meridan's empty thrones."

"It is a custom that has served the kingdom well," Ashbough continued. "King Boromaine was a cousin to his predecessor, and King Carldane an uncle."

"You are correct in your history, Lord Ashbough, but a custom is not a law, and the Hall is not bound by it."

Sir Gorlac rose, and the hallmaster recognized him. "Yet the Hall has followed this custom for more than six generations. There comes a point when good customs become law by mere usage. I believe we have passed that point. We should admit that succession by next of kin now carries the force of written law."

Everedd rose and spoke. "I agree with Sir Gorlac only to this extent: As he says, good customs should become laws by continuous usage. Customs become good customs when they serve us well. But I disagree that succession by next of kin is an innately good custom. Kings Boromaine and Carldane served the kingdom well not because they were kin to their predecessors but because they were good men. Their election to the throne was due more to their character and ability than to their bloodline. Our duty is to choose the best king, not the nearest kin."

Several of the knights and lords rumbled their agreement as Everedd resumed his seat.

"By Sir Everedd's logic, even direct succession by a son would be in question," Ashbough replied. "He is proposing that we undo the right of succession that every kingdom in the world has observed throughout history."

"I proposed nothing of the kind," Everedd said. "I do not question direct succession by an heir, because that is the law of the kingdom. I question the right of custom to supplant good judgment."

Sir Agramont stood, his ruddy features made even darker by the scowl on his face. "We all know why Lord Ashbough is manipulating history to pass off this custom as law. He wants to force the Hall to place Lord Fenimar on Meridan's throne. And I, for one, will have none of it."

Murmurs erupted throughout the Hall.

"Your prejudice against Lord Fenimar is well known, Sir Agramont," Ashbough replied. "I presume that cooler heads harboring no such personal vindictiveness will prevail."

Sir Baldorne rose and fairly shouted, "Lord Fenimar has well earned the prejudice many in this Hall hold against him. I will not place on the throne of Meridan a man who has cheated me out of eighty acres of fine cropland."

Fenimar rose and spoke calmly. "I did not cheat you out of anything. I bought the land at an agreed price from your father."

"Yes, you bought it for one-tenth its value when he was on his deathbed, too ill to understand your offer. He had willed that land to me."

Lord Greyhorne, Meridan's minister of justice, stood. "I also object to Lord Fenimar's ascension to the throne. Rumors grow daily that in defiance of the laws of the kingdom, Fenimar has deflowered most of the new brides of his male servants, invoking the cruel Right of the First Night as a condition for newly married servants to remain on his lands."

"Since when have mere rumors become the basis for the judgments of this Hall?" Fenimar shouted. "I deny the rumors and demand that Lord Greyhorne retract his objection."

"The accusations are more than rumors," Greyhorne replied. "Five such complaints against Lord Fenimar have been lodged in Meridan's high court, and three others are in process."

"I demand to know who has lodged such complaints," Fenimar shouted.

"So you can expel them from their cottages?" Greyhorne replied. "I will not reveal their names while Meridan's throne is empty. When they are under the protection of a king, you will have their names on a summons to defend yourself before the throne."

Grenvar rose. "I know nothing of Lord Fenimar's ethics or his morals. I do know that he is a fine military strategist. He plotted and planned many victories for King Landorm. Had Sir Perivale not usurped his place, I have little doubt that Fenimar would have rallied the armies himself and won victory over Morgultha. I support his ascension to the throne."

Sir Waldrone spoke from his seat near the center of the hall. "Perhaps Lord Fenimar is a great military strategist. Perhaps he has cheated some of us. Perhaps the betrothed maidens on his holdings are prudent to hide from him. But my objection to him is simply his cowardice. He may be a great planner of battles, but he is never in the forefront of any of them. He always stays well to the rear, observing and commanding, but drawing a sword only when he is in a superior position to a weakened opponent."

Fenimar arose and strode angrily to face Waldrone. He glared at the offending knight as Ashbough drew up beside him, removed his gauntlet, and cast it at Waldrone's feet.

"Sir Waldrone," Fenimar said, "I will not abide such an insult before my peers. My champion challenges you to a duel to the death to avenge this assault on my honor."

"You prove my point, Fenimar," Waldrone retorted. "You will not even fight your own battles. Your henchmen must fight them for you. I will not deign to pick up Lord Ashbough's gauntlet, for I have no quarrel with him. But if you will drop your own, I will take it swiftly and gladly."

"You mistake prudence for cowardice, Waldrone," Ashbough replied. "A strategist as brilliant as Lord Fenimar must not risk himself in battle. His skills are too valuable to the kingdom. Your refusal to pick up my gauntlet has shown the Hall who the real coward is."

"Fenimar! Ashbough! Waldrone!" Reddgaard shouted, standing and rapping his staff on the floor. "This is no occasion to air private vendettas. You will return to your seats and resume the business of the Hall."

Fenimar resumed his chair, and Ashbough followed, glaring hard at Waldrone as he scooped his gauntlet from the floor.

Danward stood. "As an alternative to Lord Fenimar, I put forth the name of Sir Everedd as worthy successor to the throne of Meridan."

Reddgaard watched the members react to the nomination, many turning to their neighbors, nodding and murmuring in affirmation, while others remained quiet and looked at their hands.

But before his name could be affirmed, Everedd stood and spoke. "Noblemen of the Hall, I am greatly honored by Sir Danward's confidence, but I fear it is misplaced. Many men in Meridan are more worthy of the throne than I am, and one is more worthy than any of us." He paused as all faces turned expectantly toward him. "I propose that we offer the throne of Meridan to the one man who can lead this kingdom in peace and prosperity for years to come. I propose that we make Sir Perivale our new king."

Suddenly the Hall came alive with all voices speaking at once. Many affirmed the proposal, a few opposed it, and several remained quiet.

After a moment Fenimar rose and shouted over the din, "I object! We cannot place on our throne a man who cares so little for his kingdom that he will not even attend the council to select its king."

"How can you say that the man who united the Seven Kingdoms in battle against a common foe cares little for his kingdom?" shouted an unidentified voice.

"And how can you say that a man who usurps such authority for himself can be trusted?" Ashbough retorted. "What powers would he assume next?"

Knights now spoke in rapid succession.

"Our armies were like headless chickens until Perivale rallied them. We were retreating and stumbling all over ourselves while Morgultha's beasts ran us down right and left. Restoring order and courage was a Herculean feat."

"Perivale did what had to be done, and no one else was doing it. He is a true hero and the best man in the kingdom to take the throne."

"He's not even here to perform the more humble duty of selecting a king. Why should we think he would accept the greater duty of being the king?"

"Surely such a man would not deny the hand of providence."

"Now you speak as if the throne were Perivale's destiny," Fenimar shouted. "I strongly object to such language. You prejudice the minds of the Hall."

"It appears that we must choose between a man who doesn't want the throne at all and one who covets it like a drunkard craves his ale."

Shouts followed each other in rapid succession until the hall became a din of angry noise.

Reddgaard pounded his staff on the floor, and his voice boomed over the chaos. "Noblemen of Meridan, cease this shouting and take your seats!" When the hall quieted, Reddgaard continued. "I know that many of you have strong convictions about who should rule this land. Each conviction will have opportunity for expression, but we will do it in an orderly fashion."

Again he opened the floor for discussion. As the knights spoke, Reddgaard noted that while over half the men supported Perivale, perhaps a quarter remained ominously silent. Finally, when the hallmaster was satisfied that every man who wished to speak had said his piece, he called for the ballot.

"The names of two men have been placed before the Hall as candidates for election as king of Meridan: Lord Fenimar of Grangefield and Sir Perivale of Middlemoor. As I call each name, the supporters of that candidate will please stand forward. I place before you the name of Lord Fenimar of Grangefield."

Several lords and knights stood at their chairs and took one step forward. Reddgaard noted that most of the men who had refrained from participating in the discussion were among those standing. The clerk walked down the hall between the two rows of seats, counting the supporters of Fenimar. He wrote the number on a small parchment and bowed as he handed it to Reddgaard.

"Lord Fenimar has in his support seventeen members of the Hall," Reddgaard announced. "I now place before you the name of Sir Perivale of Middlemoor."

Again the clerk walked among the balloters to conduct his count. After recording the number, he handed the parchment to Reddgaard, who announced the result.

"Sir Perivale has in his support twenty members of the Hall. A tally of the numbers shows that we have three abstentions and that neither candidate has achieved the two-thirds majority required for election. We will again open the floor for a discussion of one hour, after which we will once more call for ballots."

At that moment the great oaken door at the far end of the hall swung open, and the herald stepped inside. Behind him stood three men, regal of bearing and dressed in richly embroidered surcoats, golden rings, collars, and floor-length capes.

"Noblemen of the Hall," the herald cried, "it is my honor to present to you King Telagorn of Valomar, King Brodderand of Oranth, and King Macrendall of Lochlaund."

The members of the Hall stood in surprise and bowed as the three kings entered and walked toward the table where Reddgaard stood.

"You do us great honor, Your Majesties," Reddgaard said, bowing low as he spoke. "And as friends and allies of Meridan, we welcome you to the assembly of our Hall. May I be so bold as to ask what good fortune brings you to us?"

Macrendall stepped forward. "The three of us met in the hall of King Brodderand days after the final battle with Morgultha. We discussed matters relating to the fate and defense of the Seven Kingdoms. We have reached a conclusion, which we wish to share with Meridan's Hall as you deliberate on King Landorm's successor."

"We will hear you gladly," Reddgaard replied. He called for pages to bring chairs for the three kings, and after they were seated he gave them leave to address the Hall.

Telagorn stood and faced the assembly, his trim, blond beard and lean, aristocratic face framing steel-blue eyes that gazed with confidence over the Hall. "Lords and knights of Meridan, we thank you for hearing us today. As King

Macrendall has said, the three of us met shortly after the defeat of Morgultha to assess the implications of our victory. We agreed on three observations: First, while each of our individual kingdoms is vulnerable alone, the strength of the combined armies of the Seven Kingdoms is formidable. Second, your great warrior Sir Perivale saved us all from certain defeat by taking bold command of our armies and leading them to an astounding victory. Third, we find deep meaning in the capture of the fabled Crown of Eden. From these observations we formed a conclusion. Before we tell you of it, I beg you to heed the words of King Brodderand."

Telagorn took his seat, and Brodderand rose. Unlike Telagorn, the king of Oranth was a little shorter than average and somewhat rotund. His round face had the look of a cherub. "Late on the night before the three of us were to meet, I sat alone in my chamber, about to retire. I snuffed out the candle, but strangely, the room did not go dark. I first thought I had failed to extinguish the flame, but the candlewick was blackened and gray wisps of smoke were curling from it. Perplexed, I looked about, and to my astonishment, I saw standing before me not three paces away a man, white haired, white bearded, and robed in the colors of the forest. Though his eyes held the wisdom of the ages, his skin and features were anything but old. He looked so fresh faced and healthy that he almost glowed. And, inexplicably, my chamber door was still shut and bolted.

"You would think that on seeing such an intruder, my first impulse would be to call the guard. But somehow I felt no alarm, though to this day I don't know why. Something about the man bespoke peace and goodwill. He addressed me by name and told me not to fear. He bore tidings that I would find useful in the meetings with my fellow kings. Give heed to what he told me."

As the king paused, all eyes were on him, some filled with curious anticipation, others with sidelong skepticism.

"The ancient man said that a leader of great strength and courage had arisen in Meridan. Were the Seven Kingdoms to unite under this man, whom the Master of the Universe had raised up, peace and great prosperity could rule on this island for generations to come. He spoke simply and without elaboration, but each word sank deep into my mind like an arrow in the heart of a stag. After delivering his message, the man left my chambers. I did not see him leave, though I gazed straight at him in wonder. He did not fade away; he did not open the door and walk out; he did not pass through the walls; he did not suddenly vanish in a puff of smoke. He was simply gone, as if I had closed my eyes and missed his departure, though I assure you that my eyes were far from closed.

"The next morning when I awoke, the image of the man and his message rose immediately in my mind. I asked myself if he had been a dream, but the question would not stand. I know the difference between a dream and reality, and this was no dream. As I met with my brother kings, I found my thoughts troubled all the while by the strange man and his message. Though I strongly desired to tell them of it, I could not bring myself to do it. Surely they would think I had gone mad.

"However, we had not met long before it became apparent that each of us felt uneasy, often speaking distractedly as if holding back some unspoken thought that begged for expression. As the meeting progressed, my nighttime visitor and his message became the total focus of my mind, and finally I could hold it no longer. I told them of it.

"As I recounted my experience, the expressions on the faces of my colleagues alarmed me. I expected hidden glances and subtle attempts to hide their reactions to what they would perceive as my madness. But instead, their eyes grew wide and their jaws dropped. I wondered if I had indeed gone mad. Though I thought I was speaking calmly and sensibly, perhaps I was screeching, drooling, and clawing the air. But soon I learned the reason for their wonder. I will now sit and let King Macrendall explain it to you."

Macrendall arose from his seat, a burly man with reddish hair, a beard and eyebrows bristling like gorse bushes, and clear, blue eyes set deeply above ruddy cheeks. He looked out over the knights and lords of Meridan. "I will tell you the reason for our wonder at King Brodderand's words. Both of us had shared his experience. The same white-haired man had appeared to each of us, giving each the same message, delivered at very near the same hour."

A low rumble of voices filled the hall as many of Meridan's noblemen looked at their fellows, some in wonder, others in disbelief.

"As a result of this common vision appearing separately to each of us," Macrendall continued, "we, the kings of Lochlaund, Valomar, and Oranth, are convinced that we bear witness to the voice of the Master of the Universe. To preserve the prosperity and peace of the Seven Kingdoms of this great island, we advise the Hall of Knights of Meridan to place on your throne the one man among you who has demonstrated strength, courage, and bold leadership beyond any man in the Seven Kingdoms. We urge you to elect Sir Perivale of Middlemoor as your king."

Fenimar jumped to his feet, his eyes flashing fire. "Who gave you the right to meddle with the internal affairs of Meridan? We will choose our own king without unsolicited advice from beyond our borders."

"We understand your position, Lord Fenimar," Macrendall replied. "Indeed, we would never presume such a thing had not the Master laid the message upon our hearts. We do not come to force anything upon you. We presume only to deliver the message as it was given to us. Yet for the good of the Seven Kingdoms, we urge you to heed it."

"You urge us to heed the tale of a man seen in a vision and a voice heard in the night? How easy it is to conjure up such mystical experiences to give your own desires the authority of the Master! This Hall will base its decision on reason, not on visions induced by an evening awash with wine and mead."

Telagorn arose, tall and straight, glowering at Fenimar. "Under any other circumstance, my gauntlet should lay at your feet for such slander. But today my cause outweighs my honor. Yes, Lord Fenimar, it would be easy for us to conjure up a vision to deceive you into believing our message is from the Master. However, the three of us are prepared to give you ample reason to know that we believe his voice is in what we have seen and heard. We have agreed—and we have the backing of our Halls of Knights—that if you crown Sir Perivale king of Meridan, we will submit our own thrones to his. We will unite in federation with Meridan as independent nations under a single rule—that of King Perivale."

The din of voices rose to the point that Telagorn could not continue. Reddgaard stood and rapped his staff on the floor until the noise subsided. Then he turned to the king and said, "This is a most astounding announcement, Your Majesty. Can you tell us why you would be willing to submit your thrones to our king?"

"I can," Telagorn answered. "As monarchs, we are the servants of our people. We are bound by oath to dedicate ourselves to their welfare. We believe that the promised peace of the Seven Kingdoms under the reign of Sir Perivale is in the best interest of our nations."

Fenimar replied, "I commend the three of you for your dedication to your people. And I beg forgiveness for my premature judgment of your motives. I had not yet seen the selflessness of your hearts. However, I fear that your proposal is fatally flawed. As you can see, Sir Perivale is not even present at this assembly. Furthermore, he has sent a message announcing his withdrawal from active public life. Nevertheless, we see merit in the heart of your proposal that the Seven Kingdoms unite under Meridan's king. That king simply will have to be someone other than Sir Perivale."

Brodderand stood. "The proposal was of a piece. The condition of our uniting with Meridan is the placement of Sir Perivale upon your throne. He must be persuaded, or we remain separate kingdoms."

"Then we must object," Ashbough said. "Again we perceive that you are trying to manipulate the internal affairs of Meridan."

"We are manipulating nothing!" Macrendall boomed. "We are merely delivering the word of the Master as it was delivered to us. What you do with it is your own affair."

"Why should you of other kingdoms be chosen to bear the word of the Master to us?" Fenimar asked. "If he had a word for the Hall of Meridan, why didn't he deliver it himself?"

"We do not prescribe the ways of the Master, and we do not defend the veracity of our vision," Brodderand said, frowning. "We are here merely to deliver it and depart in peace. But insults from such as you make that increasingly difficult."

"And what of the kingdoms of Rhondilar, Vensaur, and Sorendale?" Ashbough asked. "Have they no say in this uniting of the Seven Kingdoms?"

"We cannot speak for them," Telagorn said. "We have

sent messengers to their kings declaring our intention. They can respond as their Halls dictate."

Fenimar rose and said, "Fellow knights of the Hall, however noble the motive or inspired the message, we who are responsible for the welfare of Meridan cannot allow outside interference to shape this most important decision. I urge you to disregard the proposal of our neighboring kings and elect a king who is willing to serve Meridan."

"Lord Reddgaard," Danward said, "I believe we have heard all we need from both sides of the issue. I urge you to proceed with the next ballot." A chorus of ayes rose from many of the knights of the Hall.

"Very well," Reddgaard said. "We will now conduct a second ballot to choose between the two men whose names have been placed before us as candidates for the throne. All who support Lord Fenimar of Grangefield as king of Meridan, please stand now."

Four knights stood at their seats—Ashbough, Kramad Yesenhad, Grenvar, and Fenimar. Fenimar glowered at several knights who had supported him on the first ballot, but none returned his gaze, looking rather at their own feet.

"All who support Sir Perivale of Middlemoor as king of Meridan, please stand now." The remaining thirty-seven knights stood, and the clerk did not even bother to count. "I announce to you that the Hall of Knights of Meridan has elected Sir Perivale of Middlemoor as king of the realm of Meridan."

Great shouts arose in the hall as the thirty-seven knights drew their swords and pledged their loyalty to the new king. Fenimar stood for a moment amid the din, his face dark as a thundercloud. Then he turned and strode rapidly to the great door of the hall with Ashbough, Grenvar, and Kramad Yesenhad following close behind.

4

Perivale sat astride his horse and looked out over the rolling field he had helped clear with his own hands. He smiled as he remembered the surprise of his workers when he had stripped down to his breeches and helped them cut down the scrubby oaks, harness oxen to unearth the stumps, and carry stones from the land to build the lichen-speckled wall that now enclosed the field. His steward, Wolderand, had been appalled. He had urged his liege to leave the field to the workers and return to the more lordly pursuits of overseeing and planning. But Perivale would hear none of it. He loved his land, and the closer he could get to it, the happier he was.

As he sat reminiscing, he saw movement in the distance. He watched as a horseman topped the rise on the far side of the field and approached at a fast trot. Soon Perivale identified the rider as Wolderand.

"Sir Perivale," the steward said as he drew rein, "you have guests at the manor who require your presence." The look on Wolderand's face was odd.

"I am expecting no guests," Perivale replied. "Who has come?"

"A delegation of knights and lords from Maldor's Hall. Seven of them, sent by Lord Reddgaard and led by Sir Everedd and Sir Danward."

Perivale felt his stomach tighten as a vague foreboding fell upon him. "Has the Hall elected a king?" he asked.

"They have, my lord."

"And did they tell you the name of this new king?"

"They did, my lord."

"What is his name?"

"I think you know, my lord."

Perivale sat for a long moment as he looked toward the distant forested hills. "Wolderand, you know the meadow just south of the Sun Mound. I have been thinking we could clear at least twelve acres of it and have a new field as rich as this one. Let's ride over and look at it."

"But, sir, your guests . . ."

"These are not guests. They are invaders who have come uninvited for reasons of their own. I need not talk with them. I must be about my own business." He wheeled his horse and began trotting south along the stone wall.

"Sir Perivale, you cannot refuse to see them," Wolderand called. The overseer spurred his horse and caught up to his liege lord. "You can't do this, my lord. Sir Everedd and Sir Danward are your friends. You cannot dishonor them by denying your hospitality."

"They are dear friends and battle mates. But today I fear them, Wolderand. I fear they wish to set me to a task for which I am unfit."

"At least do them the courtesy of hearing them, sir."

"Sir Danward is a persuasive man. He weaves words like a spider weaves webs, and one soon finds himself trapped within them. I must not listen to him. I must attend to my field." Perivale kept riding south.

"My lord, I am but a servant, but if you will not listen

to Sir Danward, you must hear me at least. You cannot escape your destiny by losing yourself on this farm. You ride on to your field if you will. I shall ride back and tell the delegation where you are. You cannot hide from the Master, Sir Perivale."

Wolderand wheeled his horse about and galloped toward the manor as Perivale continued southward.

A half hour later Wolderand walked into the manor hall, where the seven knights waited at the table with Rianna.

"Did you not find him?" Rianna asked.

"I found him," Wolderand said. "But he would not return with me. He knows why you have come, though I did not tell him. And though you know the love and respect he bears for each of you, he will not hear your supplication. He bids you to avail yourself of his hospitality tonight. Feast at his table, drink from his kegs, and rest in chambers we will provide for you. But he will not see you. I am sorry, my lords."

"We will not return to Maldor without completing our mission," Everedd said. "Will you tell us where he is?"

"That I will. My master knows I will have no part in his attempt to hide from you. He is in the south of his lands, not a half hour from here. I will lead you there."

"Then let us be going," Danward said, rising from his seat. His six companions rose with him.

"I will go with you," Rianna said.

She led the delegation to the stables, and when they had all mounted their steeds, Wolderand led them across the estate and past the walled field. He swept his hand toward it as they rode by. "Perivale's own sweat watered this land," he said proudly. "And his own hands placed many of the stones in this wall. He intends to clear another such field, and when I left him he was riding toward it."

They continued south through alternating patches of forest and open meadow until they reached a place where the ground rose into a large mound, upon which stood seven vertical monoliths, each three times the height of a man. Four of the stones stood straight, while the other three leaned, one precariously. Across two of the vertical stones lay a horizontal slab six yards long. Many more stones of similar size lay strewn about the mound. As the party followed Wolderand up the mound and through the stones, they could see that they had been arranged in a large circle.

"This is the Sun Mound," Wolderand said, "built ages ago by we know not whom. Yonder lies the field where Sir Perivale said he was going."

The men and Rianna rode onto the field, littered with natural stones, scrubby oaks, and a few conifers. Perivale was nowhere to be seen. They rode into the woods adjacent to the field and up the ridge beyond it, where they could see into the next valley. But they saw no trace of the knight.

"I should have known he would not stay here," Wolderand growled. "He knew I would betray him to you."

"We can spread out and ride over his entire lands," Danward said. "He can't escape us all."

"You don't know the length and breadth of Perivale's estate," the overseer said, sweeping his hand over the landscape. "It contains dozens of forests, fields, crevasses, streams, and even caves where he could hide. Though you spent days searching, he could easily evade you."

"But we must make the attempt. Where else does he often go?"

"Possibly to Dragon's Head Ridge, a high point from which he sometimes surveys his holdings."

"Lead us there," Everedd said.

Perivale was not on the ridge, nor at Herron Lake, nor with the shepherds on the north slopes. When Wolderand led them to the elder oak, an enormous, gnarled tree with spreading branches that could easily have sheltered thrice their number, the sun hovered above the treetops of the forest to the west. The knights sat on their horses, looking about them as they deliberated on what they should do.

"I know where he is," Rianna said. All heads turned toward her.

"He's at the Trysting Spring," she said.

"How do you know that?" Danward asked.

"I don't know it with certainty, yet I think I know it."

"Then lead us there," Danward said, prodding his horse forward.

"No, I will go to him alone. Return to the manor, receive your dinner, and take to your beds. I will bring my husband to you in the morning."

Rianna watched until Wolderand and the seven knights rode out of sight, and then she turned her palfrey eastward and crossed the meadow, now streaked with the lengthening shadows of forest trees, and entered the woods beyond. Though no trail was visible, she rode with sureness among the great boles until she came to the base of a cliff half covered with vines and glistening with water seeping from internal springs. She rode along the cliff until she came to a cleft within it thrice the width of her horse. Turning her mount into the cleft, she rode some fifty paces in the dim light before emerging onto a carpet of tall grass. She slowed her horse to a walk and moved silently among the willows that sheltered the turf. Soon she saw her husband's horse cropping grass some thirty paces ahead, and she halted her palfrey beside it.

Rianna dismounted and walked quietly forward, brushing willow fronds away from her face until she came to the stream that ran through the grove. Just ahead, on a stone beneath a spreading cypress tree, sat her husband. He stared absently into the stream where it widened into a pool. She went silently to the stone and without a word sat beside him, placing her hand on his shoulder. For a long while they sat in silence, the only sound the muted rippling of the water over the stones where the stream fed the pool.

Finally Rianna spoke. "What are you hiding from?"

"From those who seek to bind me to a task I do not desire," he answered.

"Sometimes duty must rise above desire," she said.

"I do not see this task as my duty. You know I am a simple man. I never even wanted to be a member of the Hall of Knights. We seldom attend functions at Maldor Castle because I despise the court games one must play there. Everything I want is right here in Middlemoor—a good parcel of land and a family to enjoy it with. I have no taste, no inclination, no experience, and no talent for ruling a kingdom."

"Until today I might have agreed with you. But your fellow knights spoke of things you have hidden from me." Rianna looked reproachfully at her husband.

"What have I hidden from you?"

"You did not tell me how Morgultha was defeated. You told me of King Landorm's death and of the final battle at the edge of Braegan Wood, but you failed to tell me who rallied the troops of the Seven Kingdoms, who brought order out of chaos, and who led them to victory."

"I told you the essentials. The details were unimportant."

Rianna laughed. "That's like saying you found a pot of gold without mentioning that you had to slay a dragon to get it. Had Sir Danward not told me the full story, I might accept your declaration that you have no talent for leading. But the entire Seven Kingdoms see what you did as an astounding feat that no other man could have accomplished, one that demonstrates that you above any other should become king not only of Meridan but of the entire Seven Kingdoms."

"No. Meridan cannot presume to extend its rule beyond its own borders."

"It's not Meridan that urges it. Sir Danward told me that the kings of Valomar, Lochlaund, and Oranth have already pledged to join in confederation with Meridan if the Hall will name you king. You do not realize the height to which the defeat of Morgultha has raised you."

"It's a height I fear. I could easily fall from it." Perivale turned to his wife. "Did Sir Danward tell you about Morgultha's crown?"

"He mentioned it but said little about it."

"It's the legendary Crown of Eden, the ancient talisman of Adam's dominion over the earth. I must tell you the truth, Rianna. It's not only that I feel unworthy to rule the kingdom; I fear what that crown might do to me. When I first saw it in Morgultha's hand, it drew my eye as if it were enchanted. It was all I could do to look away. On our return to Maldor after the battle, King Telagorn told me more about this crown. It has elevated, enhanced, and amplified the good of many kings, but it has also destroyed others. Morgultha herself could not let go of it. We had to destroy her hand to free it. And when I held it in my own hand, I felt a strange mixture of fear and desire. I knew I must get it out of my sight. I had it wrapped and bound in leather, yet I found myself reluctant to give it up. I often think about it even now."

"You wouldn't have to wear the crown. Take the throne, but wear Landorm's crown instead."

"That's a fine thought, but surely the people will expect their king to wear the Crown of Eden. And I'm not sure it would be right for a king to take the throne without risking the crown, considering the good it could draw out of him. But even if I chose not to wear it, could I resist it? I fear what may happen if I have access to that crown. It's best for me to stay right where I am and let Meridan choose another king rather than take the risk."

Rianna sat quietly, thinking hard on her husband's words. "You are right," she said. "Taking the crown is a risk, and a great one. Yet it seems that the Master of the Universe himself has chosen you to wear it, and I don't see how you can escape his call."

"Even if it means self-destruction?"

"It need not mean that, Perivale. The crown won't force you into ruin. Only your own choices can do that."

"But the path of prudence is to avoid entirely what you know you may not be able to control. You know the old maxim: 'The only moth that survives the night is one that keeps the flame from sight.'"

"The path of duty often veers from the path of prudence," Rianna replied. "You cannot walk both. Meridan calls you, and you must choose between duty to your people and your own safety."

"You want me to do this thing?"

"No, of myself, I do not!" she replied emphatically. "With all my heart I wish this call had never sounded. I would happily cling to you and our life in this beautiful country, far from Maldor. But to do so would be selfish of me. You are clearly destined for greater things, and I must not hold you from the task to which the Master calls you."

For a long moment the only sound was the rippling of

55

the stream and the croaking of frogs. Finally Perivale spoke. "You are right. It would be cowardly and self-serving to turn my hand from the field the Master would have me plow. Yet I feel a strong foreboding."

"I know. I feel it too. We cannot avoid the danger, so we must be vigilant against it."

Perivale embraced his wife, enfolding her in his great arms as if he would press her into himself. Then he stood and drew her up beside him. Willow fronds caressed them as they walked hand in hand toward their horses. Rianna began to laugh softly.

"What a strange man you are!" she said. "How many men would kill to wear a crown? And here you are hiding from it like a scullery drudge in a cupboard corner." She stopped and turned to him, her face now solemn and her voice earnest. "You won't be alone, my dear husband. As long as you make the Master of the Universe your master, the crown cannot master you. And I will always be beside you. I will help you in every way I can."

They walked on in silence, his arm about her slender waist. He stopped at his charger as she began to walk toward her palfrey. But he took her arm and drew her back. He mounted the charger and lifted her up, setting her on the saddle in front of him. He spurred his horse, and they loped toward the manor, the palfrey following close behind.

5

The beginning of King Perivale's reign was filled with hope and promise. It was generally known that the king did not want the crown, which endeared the hero to his subjects all the more. Indeed, behind his back he was often called King Perivale the Reluctant. Within a fortnight of his coronation, Kings Telagorn of Valomar, Brodderand of Oranth, and Macrendall of Lochlaund came to Maldor Castle and pledged allegiance to Perivale as their high king above kings. Within three months the kings of Rhondilar, Sorendale, and Vensaur made identical pledges, uniting all the seven kingdoms of the island under the rule of the high king.

Perivale had been ceremonially coronated with the Crown of Eden, and he had worn it throughout the feasts and festivities of coronation week. But after all the celebrations ended, to the surprise of everyone and the displeasure of some, he placed the crown inside an oaken chest reinforced with metal bands and locked it deep within the vaults of the castle treasury. He and no one else held the key to that vault. Many of the knights wondered why their king did not wear the fabled crown, and when those close to him queried him about it, his answers were vague and unsatisfactory.

Yet the crown often stole unbidden into Perivale's thoughts like a cat into a buttery. But he was vigilant to thrust it out again, refusing to let the colors of the stone tease his imagination. He knew how easy it would be to dwell on the crown, to picture himself with it on his brow, and to bask in the glory emanating from the stone like beams of starlight. He would not speak about it or even think of it.

A year later, at the first assembly of the delegations from the seven kingdoms, a lord from Rhondilar proposed that the confederated kingdoms adopt a single name—the Isle of Perivale. The hall rang loud with acclamation, but Perivale would not hear of it, giving new life in the inns and alehouses to the name King Perivale the Reluctant and further endearing him to his people.

A sense of well-being settled over the island. Trade began to increase with the nations across the Narrow Sea, and the Seven Kingdoms prospered in every way. Even the seasons seemed to endorse the new king. Rains came in torrents after planting and returned at regular intervals throughout the summers. Then the clouds withheld their riches at harvest, giving farmers time to reap their abundant crops. Game became so plentiful that no household, however humble, lacked for meat on the table.

Perivale began to build roads throughout the island so that trade increased among the kingdoms. And he put knights on constant patrol of the roads, keeping them clear of thieves and highwaymen.

Soon the Seven Kingdoms became renowned throughout all the nations on the great continent between the Narrow Sea and the Southern Sea. Travelers streamed to the island on trade and on tour, bringing even greater prosperity to the land's already burgeoning fortunes.

Perivale ruled the kingdoms well; his judgments, decrees, and diplomacy were deemed to be just and wise. He opened his hall to the people, and a steady stream flowed through the great door like water through a sluice gate, bearing grievances, suits, requests, or reports. He was kind and patient with all supplicants, but he instructed his seneschal to close the doors each day at the hour of four. He spent the next two hours in conference with his ministers and advisors. Precisely at the hour of six, he left the hall and went directly to his chambers, where his family awaited him. On evenings when ceremonial or diplomatic dinners required his presence, Queen Rianna always accompanied him, and Avalessa and Rhondale often did as well. Perivale's family adored him. Rianna, always beautiful, glowed in his presence like the moon to the sun.

As their daughter, Princess Avalessa, grew, the promise of great beauty that had graced her form and features from birth moved toward extravagant fulfillment. She grew in knowledge as well as in beauty, taught by the best of tutors in languages, literature, history, and philosophy. But her real love was music. Before she was ten she became accomplished on the mandolin her father had given her. She learned scores of songs from traveling minstrels who entertained at Maldor Castle, and she often sang them sitting at the window of her second-story chambers. Strollers in the castle bailey marveled at her clear and lovely voice floating on the chords of her instrument like a bird on a summer breeze.

Prince Rhondale gave up playing swords and dragons long before his voice began to crack. Considerably smaller than the sons of nobles and knights of similar age, he could not compete in their games. By the time he was twelve, it became apparent that he would attain neither his father's height nor his strength. The wise Wolderand, who often came to Maldor to report on Perivale's estate, took notice of the prince's deficiency and led him to Lord Reddgaard, who took the boy to the library and introduced him to the world of books. Rhondale fell in love with reading. He loved most the legends and tales of the ancient days when the island was riddled with dragon lairs and infested with seafaring warriors wearing yellow beards and horned helms. As long as the prince had a book in his lap, he was content.

In short, the king, his subjects, the land, his wife, and his family were happy and prosperous.

The change came slowly. Many marked its beginning in the seventh year of Perivale's reign. Twelve months before the anniversary of Morgultha's defeat, the Hall of Knights met to deliberate on how they should commemorate the event. All thought it should be a festive occasion. They would invite the kings of the six other nations, as well as emissaries from many countries beyond the Narrow Sea. A week of feasting, carnivals, and entertainment, as well as solemn ceremonies, would mark the event.

"The Seven Kingdoms must show themselves at their best," Sir Everedd insisted to the assembled Hall. "Trade with the nations on the continent is good now, but it shows signs of expanding well beyond what we can imagine. To inspire confidence in our trading partners, we must present to our visitors a city and country brimming with strength and prosperity."

"What do you propose, Sir Everedd?" Reddgaard asked.

"We must scour the city. Repair the cobblestones and clean the streets. Each hosteler and tavern keeper must clean and repair his establishment to high standards we will set in this Hall. And we must inspect them all to ensure that they measure up to the standard."

"We must build a stage for the mummeries," Sir Danward added.

"And double the number of lamplights in our streets," Sir Baldorne said.

"And we must repair the jousting field. It is high time we hosted a Seven Kingdoms tournament," Sir Agramont added.

"We must lime the stones of Maldor Castle," one knight said.

"And fly banners from the ramparts," said another.

One by one the knights added to the list of repairs and improvements. All proposals were duly debated and many of them adopted. The meeting was moving toward a successful close when Lord Fenimar, who had remained silent, rose and turned toward Perivale, who was seated on his dais at the end of the hall.

"I presume that for such an auspicious occasion, the king intends to wear the Crown of Eden, does he not?" he asked. A murmur of approval rippled through the hall.

Perivale shifted uncomfortably. "No, I do not intend to wear that crown."

"May the Hall know why?" Fenimar asked, every word tinged with a hint of sarcasm. "The crown is a symbol not only of your victory but also of the unity of the Seven Kingdoms. Furthermore, it signifies the Master's blessing on its wearer. The crown will inspire awe in our many visitors. I urge you to wear the crown, Your Majesty."

Lord Ashbough stood. "I agree with Lord Fenimar, Your Majesty. The Crown of Eden has an unparalleled history. It has come to you from Adam through Melchizedek, David, Solomon, Cyrus, and many other great men in history. The fact that it now belongs to the Seven Kingdoms is portentous. It is your duty to wear the crown, sire, not to bury it like a corpse in a casket in the bowels of Maldor Castle."

A spontaneous chorus of affirmation arose from almost every throat in the Hall. Perivale did not answer immediately but sat with his fingers laced beneath his chin.

In that moment of silence, Reddgaard stood. "Your Majesty, in the six years you have been our king, you have chosen not to wear the Crown of Eden. Though we are not privy to your reasons, we must trust that they are as sound and wise as your rule over us has been. We do not need such a symbol to flout before our sister kingdoms. The peace and prosperity of this island are much more solid expressions of our worth than a piece of gold and stone. I urge you not to yield to the Hall in the matter of the crown. Trust your own wisdom, not the desire of the Hall for a bauble to show."

Immediately over half the members of the Hall were on their feet, shouting against Reddgaard's caution and urging Perivale to wear the crown.

"Silence!" The king stood and held up his hand. The din of voices ceased. "I will consider wearing the Crown of Eden at the celebration of our peace. I will give you my answer at the next meeting of the Hall. Today's business is concluded. You are dismissed." He turned without another word and left the hall through the door beside the throne.

As the knights dispersed, Danward fell in beside Reddgaard and spoke in a low voice. "We have witnessed a great wonder today. It seems that Lord Fenimar has finally accepted Perivale as king."

"Do not be misled, Danward. The man's honeyed words conceal a poison," Reddgaard replied. "Fenimar's proposal that King Perivale wear the Crown of Eden is more deadly than anything he has yet done. I fear he has discovered the seam in Perivale's armor."

"What do you mean?"

"Just this. I suspect that Perivale fears the Crown of Eden, and perhaps rightly."

"Fears it? Why?" Danward walked beside his mentor, accommodating his pace to the shorter steps of the venerable man.

"I remember well that night on the Plain of Moriburne six years ago when the crown was cut from Morgultha's hand and Perivale first held it in his own. I saw the look in his eyes. It was a look of hunger, even lust. He stared long at the shimmering stone, and he had to force his eyes away from it. His reluctance to let the crown out of his sight was apparent even as he wrapped it up and put it away. He has never once looked upon the crown since the week of his coronation. He fears it, and with reason. It has often been unkind to its wearers, withering them, driving them insane, bloating their pride beyond control, transforming them into bloodthirsty tyrants, ravenous lechers, or cowering puppets."

"But if Melchizedek, David, and Cyrus wore the crown, why did it not work its evil on them?"

"You misunderstand the nature of the crown." Reddgaard stopped at a stone seat near the door and eased himself down with a grimace. He motioned for Danward to sit beside him. "The crown has no evil to work. Its nature is to amplify tendencies that lie sleeping at the center of a man's soul—tendencies with titanic power that could dominate the man if they were ever awakened. A man whose center holds a burning passion for good will find that good drawn out and ignited by the crown. A man hiding a dormant vice or impurity will find that evil awakened by the crown. The crown gives opportunity for the expression of tenden-

63

cies that have been denied occasion to show themselves, whether good or evil."

"But the heart of Perivale is good. His reign has amply demonstrated it."

"The heart of no man is truly good," Reddgaard replied. "Within each of us lies a raw self—vile, evil, lawless, depraved, and destructive. All that keeps that self from having sway over us is the presence within of a higher self that is not our own but given by the grace of the Master of the Universe. It is a copy of his own nature. Our own wills decide which self will dominate our lives. The crown presents almost irresistible opportunities for both selves to act, and only the man who has buried that raw and lawless self so deep that the voice of the crown cannot reach it will survive the wearing of it."

"And that is why you think King Perivale fears the crown?"

"I think he fears his own longing for it. His brief gaze at the light of the stone momentarily lit the dark places of his soul, and he saw sleeping dragons he had not known were there. Having glimpsed what the crown could awaken, he has shunned it. Now I fear that Lord Fenimar has aggravated the longing Perivale stifled that day on the field of victory."

"How could Lord Fenimar know that the crown might undo Perivale?"

"He may not know with certainty. Perhaps he has heard that the crown has undone kings in the past, or perhaps he has dark sources of knowledge that tell him such things. Whichever it is, he could hardly have done anything that has more potential to destroy Perivale's rule and the prosperity of our kingdoms. As you petition the Master tonight, do not fail to remember King Perivale. We are in grave danger."

6

The seventh anniversary celebration of Perivale's victory over Morgultha was an enormous success. Not only did the kings of the nations on the island attend, but kings from five countries on the great continent did as well. Maldor Castle and the surrounding town shone with whitewash and goodwill. The days were alive with games and feasts, the evenings with entertainments and dancing. All the inns were filled at the beginning and all the kegs emptied at the end. The reputation of the Seven Kingdoms swelled mightily in the estimation of the guests. And the merchants of the island had visions of the Narrow Sea becoming even narrower, with ships making more frequent crossings to export their goods.

King Perivale presided over the event magnificently. On his brow rested the legendary Crown of Eden, and its stone shone forth like a star. Queen Rianna sat beside him, her beauty and radiance compelling as much awe as the crown. The celebration continued through the week, and then all the guests left the city and returned to their homes, sated and marveling.

On the morning following the last feast, Rianna would easily have slept another hour after the rigors of the week.

But dimly, through the haze of her exhaustion, she heard Perivale stirring softly about the chamber. Every move was muted. He eased open the wardrobe door, drew out his robes, and slipped them on with little rustling or bumping of furniture. Obviously, he was trying not to awaken her. On any other morning after such a week she would have accepted his gift of another hour and snuggled deeper into the covers. But something seemed amiss. Some quality in her husband's movements made them seem not only quiet but furtive. She kept her eyes closed and listened. She heard the soft crackle of the brush pulling the night's tangles from his hair, then the muted contact of leather and brass as he buckled on his sword. After a moment of silence—in which she was almost sure he was looking directly at her—she heard a faint creaking, which she knew immediately. It was the iron hinge of the oaken cask that held the crown. She opened her eyes just enough to see what he was doing; then suddenly they went wide with alarm. Perivale was placing the Crown of Eden on his head.

"Perivale, surely you don't intend to keep wearing the crown."

He started at her voice and almost dropped the cask.

"I think we have exaggerated the dangers of it," he replied with a smile intended to disarm her fears. "I have worn it for a week now with no ill effects. In fact, as the days went by, I often forgot it was on my head."

"That means nothing. The danger wouldn't show itself at first. It would build slowly, and you wouldn't notice it."

"That is true, my love." Perivale set the crown aside and came to her and sat on the bed and took her in his arms. He kissed her on the cheek and neck. "But I will be wary. I will stay attuned to the crown, and at the first hint of evil I will put it away forever."

"You miss my point," Rianna replied, pulling away so she

could see his face. "You wouldn't feel the evil creeping upon you. Remember the frozen fish in the moat last winter? Before the freeze they stayed near the surface, watching for the floating carcasses of the fall's last flies. They became so accustomed to the slow cooling of the water that they saw no need to swim to the warmer depths. And we found them the next morning frozen in the ice, victims of their capacity to adjust to the creeping cold."

"I am not a fish, Rianna. I will see any approaching danger."

"Perhaps you will; perhaps you won't. Why risk it? You've ruled well for seven years without the crown. Why wear it now?"

"The knights of the Hall were right. The crown came to me for a purpose. The people want me to wear it. As you said yourself when you urged me to accept the throne, shall I put my own wants before the desires of my people?"

"But Perivale, I am afraid. The crown has ruined many kings."

He arose from the bed and picked up the crown, lifting it to his eye and gazing at it not with his former awe and longing but as a familiar companion. "I too have feared the crown, but I am now convinced that my fear was needless. We must remember that it hasn't ruined all its kings; it has enhanced the reigns and increased the good of many. Shall I let my fear keep such blessings from my kingdom?"

He lifted the crown over his head and lowered it into place as his wife stared in wide-eyed dismay. With a smile intended to brush away her fears, he went to her, took her head tenderly in both hands, and pressed a gentle kiss to her brow. Then he turned and strode from the room, his robes billowing wide as he closed the door behind him.

From that day forward Perivale wore the crown every day that he was in the city. He wore it from the time he arose in the morning until he returned to his chambers in the evening. The only times he did not wear it was when he journeyed from Maldor. On such occasions he left the crown in the castle, fearing it was more at risk on the road than inside the vaults of Maldor. Nothing about his rule changed; his decisions continued to be just and wise. Nothing about his nature changed; he remained humble, even tempered, courteous to his associates and subjects, and loving to his family. Rianna, deeply apprehensive at first, often urged Perivale to lock the crown again inside Maldor's vaults. But after a few weeks her fears diminished. When six months had passed, neither she nor the king ever gave the matter any more thought.

When the first cloud appeared, it was so small and thin that no one even knew it was a cloud—no one but Lord Reddgaard, who kept a vigilant watch on Perivale's heart. It was near the end of a long day, made longer by an endless line of emissaries and petitioners. Though Perivale remained even tempered and courteous, it was clear to Reddgaard, watching from the table at the side of the dais, that the king was tired. The aged hallmaster glanced over at the seneschal's list, and he was pleased to find that only one supplicant remained on the day's agenda, a merchant named Renalleo from a peninsular country in the Southern Sea.

Reddgaard watched as the merchant was announced and approached the throne. The man was heavy and dark skinned, with a black beard that covered half his chest. At his elbow walked an assistant who carried a package about the size of a man's head, wrapped in gray linens. The merchant approached the throne, his shimmering green robes almost dragging on the floor.

"Your Majesty," he said, bowing low and touching his

forehead with his fingers. "May your kingdom prosper and your reign never end. You honor me greatly by granting me this audience."

Perivale acknowledged the greeting but stifled a yawn. "We welcome you to our land, stranger. What is your business with us?"

"O worthy king of the seven nations of the unnamed isle, your fame has spread throughout the world. Its echoes reverberate even in my distant country. To witness for myself the truth of the reports, I attended the celebration of your seventh year of peace, and I must say that I was overwhelmed by the beauty, the fertility, and the prosperity of your realm."

"We thank you for your praise," Perivale replied. "What is your petition?"

Reddgaard could see that the king was in no mood for flattery or prolonged speeches. He wanted the man to quit gnawing the fat and get to the bone.

"I have no petition, Your Majesty. I have come simply to do you honor. As I said, the might and prosperity of your land is legendary. Only one thing is lacking, and it's a thing I can supply."

"We have a lack that you can fill?" The suggestion annoyed the weary king. "And just what do you think that is?"

"Art, sire. The palaces of the kings in the south are filled with art—sculptures, tapestries, paintings, murals, earthenware. Art is the mark of civilization. It is the sign that a kingdom has risen above its barbaric roots and turned its attention to the souls of its citizens."

"In our kingdoms the kirk supplies the needs of the soul," Perivale replied. Reddgaard nodded in silent approval.

"Of course, Your Majesty," Renalleo replied. "The kirk does attend the soul by subjecting man's will to the Master of the Universe. And there is immense value in such a discipline, but—if I may be so bold as to say it—little joy. While the kirk disciplines the soul, art liberates it. Art gives expression to man's innermost feelings and longings."

"Man's innermost desires and feelings usually need to be harnessed rather than expressed," Perivale replied. "The soul finds its joy when liberated from the tyranny of self."

Those listening in the hall nodded and murmured their agreement. Reddgaard began to relax. The king was handling the merchant well.

"True enough, Your Majesty. Much that we desire would destroy us. But what about the desire for beauty? Must that also be suppressed? The artist says no. Beauty should be affirmed, expressed, and displayed for the inspiration of all."

"Have you found no beauty in our island that you think we must bring it in from afar?"

"Your Majesty rules a land of wondrous beauty. The shimmering sea, emerald lakes, golden fields, green forests, majestic mountains and glens—it hardly has an equal."

"Then what need have we of art? The Master himself is our artist. We need no other." Perivale made a move as if to rise and end the audience, but the merchant detected his intent and spoke quickly.

"Yet—forgive me for speaking plainly, O worthy king— something is lacking in the Seven Kingdoms. The Master gave Adam and Eve trees bearing fruit for food, but he also gave them a garden to tend. He created nature to meet their needs for survival, but he intended that their hands should enhance nature and bring greater beauty to it. Your gardens have color but no accent. Your castle walls are thick and strong but bleak and bare. Your chambers are warm but without elegance. Your library is well appointed with scrolls and books, but no carven bust or figure inspires the reader's mind to soar. Your kingdom is prosperous, but its attention is turned downward, toward the earth. Your people till their fields, they herd their cattle and sheep, they hunt, they fish, and they run their hounds. They feast and dance and woo and wed. But their center is their belly and their loins—their immediate animal needs."

"My kingdoms are prosperous, and the people are happy," Perivale replied. "What more can they need?"

"Yes, you are prosperous, Your Majesty. The star of the Seven Kingdoms is rising, but none who visits will think you great among the nations. After the ancient civilizations established their boundaries, built their cottages, and fenced their fields, they turned to art to proclaim their greatness. After beating their swords into plowshares, they beat their plowshares into sculptor's chisels. They left the world a legacy of art. What will Meridan leave? No kingdom stands forever. In time the wind and rain will turn your fields to wilderness. Your cottages will rot. Your castles will crumble into piles of stone. But art endures. The Seven Kingdoms need art, Your Majesty."

Perivale did not reply, and Reddgaard looked up to see him sitting with his fingers laced beneath his chin as he looked toward the merchant. But Reddgaard knew the king's mind was seeing something else. Had Renalleo's arrow reached Perivale's heart? The hallmaster hardly breathed as he awaited the king's response.

"I have brought a gift for the king," Renalleo said as he turned to his assistant and nodded.

The two men approached the throne, and Renalleo lifted the linen covering from the thing in his assistant's hands. The king's eyes widened slightly, and his lips parted in wonder. He looked into a human face made of stone but with features as real and natural as a living man. The form of the head was perfect, even to the whorls of the ears and the curling waves of close-cropped hair. The only flaw was the base of the neck, which was jagged and broken. A brass fixture mounted the head to a pedestal of polished oak.

"It is utterly beautiful," Perivale said as he took the sculpted head in his hands. "I have never seen anything like it."

"Your pleasure honors me, Your Majesty," the merchant said, his white teeth gleaming in a broad smile. "This head is all that remains of a complete statue of the god Hermes. It is a mere sampling of the wonders that litter my land, where the ruins of an ancient civilization lie everywhere. I am a broker of such art. If you like this piece, I can bring others even more beautiful. Not only mere heads but entire figures of gods and goddesses, fauns and dryads, satyrs, warriors, courtesans, rulers, and philosophers. And I can bring pottery, tapestries, wrought gold, and paintings. I can fill your castle, your gardens, and your parks. Tell me what you want, and I will find it for you."

Perivale looked up from the image now resting on his lap. "This is indeed a fine gift, Renalleo. I thank you for it. Yes, I want to see more. And whether you bring sculpture, pottery, painting, or tapestries matters little. Bring what you can, and I will pay you well."

The merchant bowed low to the king. "I thank you, Your Majesty. You will not be disappointed." He turned and left the hall, and the guards closed the great door, ending the audiences for the day.

Perivale spent an hour with his ministers before retiring to his chambers, taking the sculpted head with him.

After the king departed, Sir Danward helped Reddgaard to his feet. They walked slowly toward the door, Reddgaard hobbling as the tap of his cane echoed in the hall.

"It appears that culture is coming to the Seven King-doms," Danward said.

"It appears that sorrow is coming to the Seven Kingdoms," Reddgaard replied.

"What? Importing art will bring sorrow? Surely you don't shun art as the kirk's austerites do."

"No, I value art," Reddgaard replied. "Art is an instrument whereby man can imitate his creator and expand the Master's beauty as an echo expands a song. But like any other good, art can be a path to perdition when it is wrongly used."

"Art can be wrongly used?"

"Indeed it can. Instead of reaching out with art to touch the secrets of eternity, man often turns art inward to display pride in himself."

"Are you not passing judgment before the sin has been committed? Perivale has not yet purchased any art. What makes you think he will use it wrongly?"

"Didn't you hear him today?" Reddgaard wheezed, breathing hard in spite of their slow pace. "He had no interest in what the merchant offered until the man appealed to his pride. The king was content with the natural beauty the Master has lavished on this island until Renalleo caused him to step outside and look at his kingdoms through the eyes of others. No longer content with what the Master has given, he now wants history to see his greatness and remember his name. I fear that his pride has been awakened."

"It has not happened yet. Perhaps it will not," Danward insisted.

"No, it has not happened yet, but the seeds have been sown. The question is, Does King Perivale have the will to uproot the shoots when they sprout? Or will he let them grow until their thorns snag and choke him? I fear for the Seven Kingdoms, Danward. I have feared for them since the day our king first began wearing the Crown of Eden."

7

On the morning following Renalleo's visit, Perivale delayed
his first appointments and made his way through Maldor's
halls toward the library. He carried the carved marble head
the merchant had given him. He could have assigned the
placing of the sculptured fragment to the seneschal, but
he wanted to place it himself. All through the evening, the
merchant's words had echoed in his mind—*Your chambers
are warm but without elegance. Your library is well appointed
with scrolls and books, but no carven bust or figure inspires
the reader's mind to soar.* The king's head was filled with
visions of white sculptures accenting the great hall, tapestries adorning the stone walls, and paintings hanging
in the galleries. The fragment he now held was the mere
vanguard of many more to come.

He reached the library door, and to his surprise, it was
unlocked. He dropped the key into his pouch and entered
the room. A lone figure sat at the long table in the center,
a large book of wrinkled yellow leaves open before him.
The reader looked up as he entered.

"Rhondale!" Perivale said in surprise. "What are you
doing here?"

"Reading, Father. I am reading the legends of the Nephilim. They are said to have built a mighty city far beneath the surface of Lochlaund."

"But it is the second hour of the morning. Why are you not on the practice field with Sir Rudmore?"

"I chose not to attend today. I come here often. You know that."

"Yes, I know that. But you should not be here when duty calls you elsewhere. You will be king after me, and your training as a warrior is of utmost importance. You cannot skip sessions. Daily practice is absolutely necessary to maintain your skill. Now, put that book away and get down to the field."

"I . . . I have no skill to maintain, Father. I'm not like you. I have no aptitude for warfare."

"That is not so. I well remember when you were only five or six, killing gourd dragons with the little sword I gave you. You handled it well."

"I was a child then. I am almost fourteen now, and my adversaries have changed. They fight back. And you can see that I am short and thin—smaller than all the other boys training under Sir Rudmore. I cannot compete with them, and there's no need to waste his time or mine by trying."

"It's a matter of will, son. You can do what you decide to do. In fact, you must. A king must lead his army. You must become expert in weaponry, tactics, strategy, and command."

"But since you have brought peace to the land, the next king need not be a warrior. The island will need a king who can build on your strength—a scholar king. I will follow you as Solomon followed David. Lord Reddgaard says I have the makings of a scholar."

"Peace is achieved with swords, not books. It does not last when weakness is evident. You must show yourself formidable or your enemies will overrun you like a stampeding herd over a nest of doves. Now close that book and go."

"But Father—"

"No more words! I said go." Perivale glared at his son.

Rhondale closed the book, placed it on the shelf, and hurried from the room. Perivale set the sculpted head on a central shelf where light from a high window fell upon it. He scrutinized the lifelike face from several angles and found himself pleased with its prominence in the room. He left the library and took his throne in the great hall.

On the next morning before taking his throne, Perivale went first to Sir Rudmore's practice field, where the sons of knights and noblemen drilled under the eye of the seasoned veteran. He approached unnoticed behind a low wall and stopped at the gate, where he waited until the trainer called his son's name. He watched as Rhondale took the sword and held it low and wavering. Its weight was too much for him. When the duel began, it took only three strokes for his opponent to trip the prince and place his sword point at the boy's heart.

Perivale frowned and clenched his jaw.

"You must raise your sword, Your Highness." Rudmore spoke gently and courteously, obviously aware that his pupil was of royal blood. "And if you please, you must feint more quickly. Now, try again, if you will."

Again Rhondale's opponent attacked. The prince's awkward stance and slow handling of the weapon left an opening that his adversary exploited immediately, laying the prince in the dust. The trainer hurried to Rhondale, helped him to his feet, and dusted off his clothing. The boy fared no better on his third duel, and disgust marked the faces of the other trainees, though they dared say nothing.

As the next pair of duelers began, Perivale called for

Rudmore to come to him. "You are coddling the prince, and it's not helping him learn," he said.

"But he is the—"

"He is just another young man learning battle craft. Treat him exactly like the others. Don't even address him by his title. Don't pick him up when he falls. Bellow at him when he errs. He will never make a warrior if you keep treating him like a princess."

"But, sire, he can hardly—"

"I don't want excuses. The boy will learn; do you hear me, Rudmore?"

"I do, sire. It will be as you say."

"Good. I will look in on you each morning, and I expect to see progress."

As good as his word, Perivale did watch the budding warriors practice from behind the wall each morning. Rudmore, aware of his monarch's presence, did as he was commanded and gave the prince no quarter, bellowing and cursing, urging the boy to perform to the standard of his fellows. But it was to no avail. After two weeks of watching, it was clear to Perivale that his son had made no progress at all.

"He's too small," Perivale muttered to himself on the morning the trainees began jousting practice.

He watched as Rhondale struggled to mount his charger and had to grip his lance with both hands. Even then it wavered and bobbed in his struggle to keep it level. The prince barely managed to spur his horse to a trot, and as he met his opponent, his lance dipped to the turf and stuck fast, tumbling him into the dirt.

With his jaw clenched and his brow furrowed, Perivale turned away from the wall and walked swiftly toward the kitchen. He called the chief cook from his hearth and got from him a list of foods thought to stimulate growth and bulk. He told the cook that from this day forward, those foods should be on the table at each of the royal family's meals.

That evening at the family table, Perivale himself prepared his son's plate, loading it to capacity with the foods the cook had prepared.

"What is this?" Rhondale asked when his father set the plate before him.

"It's your new diet," Perivale replied. "A banquet fit for a king-to-be: beef, potatoes, pheasant, pork, nuts, dates, fruits, and—"

"But Father, I can't eat all this!"

"Of course you can! Why, when I was thirteen I ate everything in sight and still felt I could swallow an ox. Eat up, son. It will help you grow."

"But I don't even like—"

"What you like is not the issue!" Perivale thundered, banging his fist on the table and glaring at his son. "Do you want to be an inept skeleton the rest of your life? Now eat!"

Rianna and Avalessa looked up, wide-eyed and open-mouthed. Rianna laid a gentle hand on her husband's arm. "Now, Perivale, we don't want to—"

"Are you going to coddle the boy too?" he shouted. "He will be the next king. It's time he grew to the task."

Perivale began to eat his meal as if nothing had happened. The others sat stunned. They had never before seen him lose his temper. Rianna's heart pounded, and her thoughts roiled in confusion. Rhondale, his head bowed, stared in dismay at his heaped plate. Avalessa's eyes remained wide in unabated shock, and her lips began to quiver. After a moment tears burst forth, and she ran sobbing from the table. Rianna got up and followed her. Perivale ate his meal in silence as Rhondale picked at his food.

That night when Perivale removed his crown and retired, Rianna was already in bed, her back turned toward him, asleep. He left her alone. Remorse swept over him, and he could not bring himself to enfold her in his arms as he always did. He knew he had behaved badly. Rianna would think it was the crown, of course, but he was simply concerned about his son. He had a duty to mold the prince into a king. He must do what must be done, but he must do it without hurting his family. Avalessa's face loomed in his mind, her eyes wide with dismay. He had never hurt her before, and the remorse he felt at hurting her tonight tore at his heart.

The king tossed and twisted all through the night and arose two hours early the next morning. He dressed, slipped out of the room, and stole silently down to the chapel, where he spent an hour in penitent tears as he confessed his wrong before the Master of the Universe. He arose, heaving a sigh of relief, and went out to perform the duties of the day. That night he apologized to his family and tearfully embraced each of them. The embraces of Rianna and Avalessa were warm and sincere, but Rhondale's body felt tense and resistant. Perivale gave it little thought; he was sure the boy would come around.

At Rianna's urging, Perivale no longer watched the young warriors in training. "It is hurting both him and you," she had said. "Your presence only increases his humiliation and your frustration. Let him learn in peace." However, the king insisted on regular reports from Rudmore. But the reports were unsatisfactory, filled with generalities that told him little about his son's progress.

A fortnight later Wolderand arrived at Maldor to give an account to Perivale of the affairs at Middlemoor. After leaving his horse with the stabler, the overseer walked toward the keep.

"Wolderand, wait. I must speak with you," Rudmore called.

"What is it, Sir Rudmore?"

"Come with me; I have something to show you."

Wolderand followed Rudmore along the wall to the practice field where the trainees were at their drills.

"Watch Prince Rhondale," Rudmore said, pointing to the slight figure in padded armor, trying to wield a broadsword with two hands.

Wolderand watched. Clearly the sword was too heavy for the boy. He could hardly lift the point from the ground, much less duel with it. His opponent quickly knocked it from his hands as the prince lost his balance and fell into the dirt.

"What are you doing to the prince?" Wolderand glared at Rudmore. "Can't you see he's too small to be a warrior?"

"Exactly!" Rudmore said. "He hasn't the size, the strength, the grace, or the aptitude. Yet King Perivale insists that he can will himself into competence."

"You must tell the king," Wolderand said.

"I have tried, but he will not hear me. He is intent on remaking his son in his own image. But it can never happen. Lord Reddgaard says he has an aptitude for scholarly pursuits, but the king pulled him from the library and forced him onto the drill field. Something must change or the boy's spirit will be beaten into the earth, not to mention his body."

"What have I to do with this?"

"You must tell King Perivale to take Prince Rhondale out of training. Everyone knows he listens to you when he will hear no one else. He knows you speak only the truth and speak it whether or not it's to his liking."

"Very well. I will tell him."

Wolderand met with Perivale in the early afternoon, and

after giving a full accounting of the burgeoning prosperity of Middlemoor, he looked his master straight in the eye and said, "Your Majesty, you must take Prince Rhondale out of battle training."

All goodwill left Perivale's face, and he glared at his overseer. "Who has bought your tongue: my queen, my son, or Sir Rudmore?"

"No one buys my tongue, Your Majesty. Not even you. I say what I know to be true. Your son will never make a warrior, and your insistence that he try is destroying him."

"If he doesn't make a warrior, his enemies will destroy him. A king must lead his army. A little discipline and a few hard knocks will not destroy him. Adversity will make him stronger."

"It will make him stronger if he has the capacity to get stronger. But, sire, you must know that Rhondale hasn't the build to be a warrior. He can hardly lift a broadsword. He can never accomplish what his body is incapable of doing. Continual humiliation before his peers and the disappointment of his father will crush his spirit, possibly beyond repair. You don't want that for your son, sire."

Perivale looked hard across the table at his overseer. "Wolderand, because you have been with me for so long, I choose to overlook the audacity of your intrusion into my private affairs. It is not your place to tell me how to raise my son."

"Someone must tell you, sire. If no one else will do it, then it falls to me. I've known the boy since he was born. He's a good lad, smart as a fox and wise as an owl. He can make a good king without being a warrior. Other men can lead his armies. The king himself need not—"

"Wolderand, you will cease speaking this instant!"

The overseer sighed and stood at the table. "I will cease,

Your Majesty. I will return to Middlemoor and muster the men for harvest. But I pray you, listen to what I've—"

"I told you to cease speaking! You flout my command as if I were neither your king nor your liege. You will return to my estate only to pack your belongings and leave it forever. I need an overseer who will stay with his assigned tasks and not meddle in affairs that don't concern him."

Wolderand showed no shock at Perivale's words. He looked at the king not in anger but in sorrow—not for himself but for his master. "It will be as you say, sire. I will leave your employ. But I fear that some great doom is descending upon you. Look to your heart and scour it until you find the thing that is gnawing away your humanity; then cut it off—even if it be your own hand."

Perivale said nothing but turned red as he watched his most loyal servant and friend leave his life forever.

8

Rhondale now spoke little at the family meals. He ate what he could of the fare Perivale continued to set before him and endured in sullen silence his father's ceaseless urging to eat more. Rianna begged her husband to ease the pressure he put on their son, but Perivale held fast to his insistence that the prince become proficient at arms. He remained blind to the truth that was clear to everyone else: Rhondale would never be a warrior.

Lord Reddgaard noticed other changes in the king. He spent less time in audience with supplicants, and occasional flares of impatience broke into his controlled disposition. One afternoon he returned from his midday meal two hours past the time set for a meeting with Lord Kalthane, land minister of Valomar. Other appointments forced his time with Kalthane to be cut short, deeply offending the diplomat and cooling relations with Meridan's strongest ally. On another afternoon the king's eyes became heavy, and he nodded more than once as an emissary from Oranth read a quarter-hour proclamation honoring the king for repairing his country's central highway. Often Reddgaard could see that Perivale's attention drifted from his supplicants, as he stared right through them with eyes glazed over and his mind far away.

The one visitor who always brought the king to his old alertness was the merchant Renalleo. The art broker had returned to Meridan twice after his initial visit. On his first trip he had brought two full-size marble statues, one a dying warrior and the other a patrician nobleman. Both were chipped and cracked and stained from weather and lichen. The patrician was missing a hand and the warrior both hands and one foot. But nothing like them had ever been seen in the Seven Kingdoms, and Perivale had bought both with little haggling. He had set them in the great hall and instructed Renalleo to bring more, and soon. On his next trip the merchant had brought three large carts loaded with eight sculptures, six rolled tapestries, and a painting of an ancient family in a hillside villa overlooking the Southern Sea. Perivale had bought the entire selection and urged Renalleo to return quickly with more.

The merchant knew he had found in Meridan a nest of golden eggs. He made Perivale his major patron and brought on his next trip a train of carts loaded with sculptures, paintings, wrought gold, tapestries, and earthenware. Perivale bought every piece.

One of the sculptures stirred a controversy. It was a life-size image of a dryad—a lithe and gracefully formed female nude with the head and hands missing. Perivale placed the piece prominently at the door to the great hall. The ever-watchful Kirk of Lochlaund had been observing Perivale's accumulation of artifacts with growing disapproval, and the display of the dryad prodded the bishop to act. He wrote a letter of protest condemning the statue as evil, sure to incite lascivious thoughts among the men of the Seven Kingdoms. Seven Lochlaund kirkmen, led by the bishop's accorder, delivered the letter and awaited the king's response.

That evening as Perivale's advisors sat at the council

table, the angry king dictated a reply as he paced back and forth. His letter gave no credence to the bishop's viewpoint. He asserted that the beauty of the dryad's form had its source in the mind of the Master and that any illicit thoughts it spawned were begat by the depravity of the viewer. Furthermore, he suggested that the bishop of Lochlaund should refrain from imposing his religious views upon the rest of the Seven Kingdoms.

Reddgaard urged the king not to send the letter. "You released your anger in the writing of it; now throw it into the fire and draft another more conciliatory."

"Then you agree with the bishop?"

"Absolutely not!" Reddgaard replied. "In fact, I concur with the substance of your letter. The Master originally intended the beauty of woman not to be hidden beneath clothing but to be displayed for delight. Didn't the poetry of the ancient Solomon praise the naked body of his Shulamite maiden? It is part of our tragedy that man can no longer gaze upon the best of the Master's creation without arousing appetites he can hardly resist. We must cover living human bodies now to quiet those appetites. It is only in art that we can now appreciate the beauty of the body without the complication of lust."

Sir Danward spoke up. "But like our primeval parents, we also are fallen. Doesn't a nude sculpture arouse such appetites in us?"

"A nude image may incite a surge of sensual pleasure," Reddgaard said, "but I question whether this is illicit. Art incites pleasure in beauty uncomplicated by the intent to consummate carnal desire. In the presence of an actual unclad woman, desire overpowers the appreciation of beauty and demands fulfillment. Treating a person solely as an object of pleasure is at the heart of the sin of lust. But because a work of art has no personhood to be violated, one can appreciate its beauty objectively. Art can do for beauty what a filtering cloth does for milk, straining out the impurities but passing on the nourishment. Art enables us to see beauty without interference from the turmoil of contaminating lustful responses."

"Since you and I are in accord, I see no need to modify my response to the bishop," Perivale said. "We are right, and he needs to hear the truth."

"At times one should speak the truth strongly without regard for the consequences," Reddgaard replied. "And I applaud you, sire, for your willingness to speak it. However, at other times one must be conciliatory and respect differing views when others have not yet reached your enlightened conclusion. This is such a time. My counsel is to write another letter respectfully acknowledging the bishop's view and stating your own with less fervor."

But Perivale would not hear of it. He ordered the letter sealed, to be sent the next morning with the accorder of the Kirk of Lochlaund. After the discussion he continued to pace the floor, his anger still seething. Reddgaard caught Danward's eye and gave a slight nod toward the door. The knight understood and made his exit, leaving the king and the hallmaster alone.

"Your Majesty," Reddgaard said. "Those of us who are close to you can see that something is amiss."

"What? You too?" Perivale said. "My wife, my overseer, my battle trainer—and now my hallmaster!" The king punctuated his words with emphatic gestures. "Has everyone around me conspired to tell me how to rule my kingdom?"

"I have no such intention," Reddgaard replied. "My concern is not your kingdom but you. Never until lately have you reacted to opposition in anger as you are reacting now. Never have you—"

"Reddgaard, I am in no mood to hear a catalog of my faults," Perivale warned.

"Your Majesty, I am well into my eighth decade. You can ignore me as you do Sir Rudmore or dismiss me as you did your loyal Wolderand. It matters little to me. But I will speak whether or not you will it. Something is amiss. Perhaps you are exhausted. Perhaps some dilemma eats at your heart. Perhaps the weight of the crown rests heavy on your head."

"It is not the crown." Irritation tightened the king's voice.

"I spoke metaphorically, sire. I did not refer to the wearing of the Crown of Eden. I meant only that the burdens of ruling seven nations must at times try even the hardiest constitution. Perhaps if you and your family took a holiday—a month in Souport or Reddwar would do you a world of good."

Perivale let out an explosive sigh and dropped into the nearest chair. He lifted the crown and ran his hand through his hair, then settled it back on his head. "The last thing I need is a month of doing nothing," he said. "I had fought in many wars before conquering Morgultha, and I thought it a fine thing that her defeat would end all wars for this island. I hated war. Or I thought I did. But now I find that peace brings no challenges, no firing of the blood. I will admit, Reddgaard, that at times I find myself wishing for a good battle—even a little skirmish—something to conquer or win by my own hand. I'm chained to that throne, performing a cycle of trivial acts that mean nothing and accomplish nothing—stroking an endless parade of emissaries, mediating petty rivalries among nobles, arbitrating suits about water rights and land encroachments, and smiling through endless festivities and balls. It's all tedious and frivolous activity, hardly fitting for a king and hardly the stuff of greatness."

"It is the small, mundane things men do that accomplish greatness," Reddgaard replied. "In books of romance and history we read only of the heroic acts, the momentous encounters, the ringing victories, the earthshaking decisions. But at best these events occupy only a tiny fraction of anyone's life. It's inside the daily humdrum that we live the bulk of our existence. The trivial details become the bricks from which great nations are built. And how we handle them determines our own greatness."

Perivale sat quiet for a long moment, picking at a splinter in the oaken table. "You're right," he said. "But I often think I'm miscast as king. I feel like a fish in a bird's nest. I was happy at Middlemoor. I could see my accomplishments in the reshaping of the land, in the crops, in the breeding of my herds. Here I seem to accomplish nothing. I merely maintain what is."

"No single twig a beaver brings to its dam seems worth the effort," Reddgaard replied, "but after weeks of cutting and applying such twigs, the beaver eventually turns the course of the river. By your daily tedium, you are surely turning the course of this island."

"But I need to see the result of what I do." Perivale slapped the table in frustration. "There is nothing concrete, nothing visible, nothing I can point to and say, 'That is what I accomplished.'"

Reddgaard saw the problem clearly. The ugly head of pride was beginning to push its way into Perivale's heart. His focus was shifting from service to the people to the visibility of his own accomplishment. But the wise man knew better than to confront the king in his present state of mind. It would only erect a barrier to the possibility of his seeing the truth later. Instead, the hallmaster thought he saw a way to lead the king toward a path that might meet his need for visible results yet refocus his efforts toward selfless service.

"Do you remember the parchment drawing the merchant Renalleo brought to you on his last visit?"

"The ink sketch of the ruins of the aqueduct?'

"That's the one. He explained the design of the aqueduct and told you that such ruins lay in his country. Have you considered building aqueducts for Meridan? As near as Maldor is to the river, it could be done. The people would have water right at their doorsteps. And you could build baths and—"

"Yes! And fountains and parks with pools," Perivale said, suddenly sitting straight in his chair. His eyes glowed brighter than Reddgaard had seen them in months. "We could build an amphitheater and stages for mummeries and plays. And with the sculpture I am importing, we can turn this country into a showplace of civilization."

"I was thinking more of utility than show," Reddgaard said. "Aqueducts would relieve your people of cumbersome daily burdens. In addition to aqueducts, you could build—"

"Thank you, Lord Reddgaard." Perivale rose from his chair with new energy. "I needed to view the valley from a different mountain. You have helped me greatly. You have given me ideas that will certainly revitalize my reign." He left the room and bounded up the stairway to his family's chambers.

Reddgaard sighed and shook his head. He had miscalculated. Hoping to turn the king's attention back toward selfless service, he had apparently only fed the man's growing hunger to leave a legacy. Though aqueducts and baths would ease burdens and enhance the health of the people, Perivale saw them only as potential monuments to his own accomplishments. Again Reddgaard feared for Meridan's future.

9

After dinner, when Avalessa and Rhondale had retired to their rooms, Perivale and Rianna sat in a chair in front of the hearth, she on his lap as in older days, watching the embers burn low. Perivale was more relaxed than Rianna had seen him in months, and more open as well. He told her of his angry response to the bishop of Lochlaund and of his complaint to Reddgaard about the tedium of daily ruling.

"The man found the answer to my unrest, my love."

"That you put away the Crown of Eden?" Rianna replied, hope rising in her voice.

"The crown has nothing to do with any of this," Perivale said with only a touch of irritation. "He gave me an idea that will define my reign and give it meaning. I will build aqueducts, baths, gardens, parks, pools, and fountains. I will make Maldor the flower of the Seven Kingdoms. History will remember that I was king."

"Lord Reddgaard wants you to build these things as monuments to your reign?"

"He wants my reign to serve the people, as I do."

"But you do serve the people. Your monument is the peace these kingdoms enjoy and your rule of justice."

"But you cannot see peace or touch justice. When I am gone, these virtues will not remain as legacies. Aqueducts, parks, monuments—such things will endure as long as the kingdom lasts."

Rianna stared silently into the glowing embers. After a moment, Perivale spoke. "You don't seem pleased."

She turned to him with a look both tender and troubled. "My dear one, do you remember our last night at the Trysting Spring? Both of us were wishing that the call to Meridan's throne had never sounded. We preferred to live our lives far from Maldor in peace on our beautiful estate. But we knew that you should not refuse the task the Master had placed on you. We feared the danger of the Crown of Eden, but we agreed that we would be vigilant in our watch for its effects."

Perivale started to speak, but Rianna placed her fingers on his lips. "Please let me continue, my dear one. The crown has begun its work on you, Perivale, and it is not a good work—no, you must let me continue. Your attitude toward your reign has changed. No longer are you Perivale the Reluctant. You have begun to be conscious of your reputation and seek to enhance and preserve it. Please, Perivale, lock the crown in the vault again. It has begun to destroy you."

Perivale looked at his wife with reproach but spoke calmly. "Yes, the crown has begun to affect me, but not with destruction. It has opened my eyes to wisdom I couldn't see before I wore it. We were naïve at Middlemoor, Rianna. I am a better ruler because of the crown. I have been restless because the crown has inspired me to do greater things, but I hadn't found the answer to the desire it was planting in my heart. Now, thanks to Lord Reddgaard, I have found it. The crown will increase my power to accomplish great good."

"Was it a great good that you discharged your loyal Wolderand? Was it a great good to pick a needless quarrel with the Kirk of Lochlaund? Is it a great good that you continually torture our son?"

Perivale reddened as he fought down a surge of anger. "An effective king must disregard personal emotions and make hard decisions that sometimes tear the heart from his own breast. Far from destroying me, the crown has given me strength to make such decisions and endure their consequences."

"The crown has blinded you to its own danger. But those around you see it clearly—Rhondale, Lord Reddgaard, Wolderand, Sir Rudmore, and Avalessa. You must listen to those who love you, Perivale. You must let us be your mirror, since the crown has fogged your own."

"It is painful to have you divided from me in this matter, Rianna, but I cannot help it. It is the sad burden of the crown that only he who wears it can see the truth about ruling a people. And naturally, those who lack such insight cannot understand. Each new revelation brings new burdens. My burden now is that my own wife misunderstands me."

Perivale set Rianna aside, arose from the chair, and took a step toward the door. She clutched his arm.

"We are not divided, my love. I am fully one with you. I simply want you to step back from the brink before it is too late. Please listen to me. Or if not to me, listen to Reddgaard, to Wolderand, or even to our son. Please, Perivale."

Perivale looked at his wife with eyes hard as stone and wrenched his arm away. "How can I listen to those who will not understand?" He turned and walked out of the room. She saw him no more until the next evening.

Within the week Perivale summoned a renowned architect from Valomar and a master builder from Corenham. When they arrived, he gave them houses of their own near the castle. He ended all audiences at two o'clock each day and spent the remaining time in a room furnished with tables and drawing boards where he explained his vision for Maldor to the two men and their assistants. On some days he dispensed with audiences altogether, leaving to Reddgaard and Danward the task of stroking emissaries and appeasing supplicants. On these days Perivale took his planners on tours of Maldor and the surrounding farmland. They looked at sites for parks and fountains and plotted the path of an aqueduct from the river to the town. He showed them his statuary and tapestries on display in Maldor Castle, as well as those filling a storage room, awaiting places to be set.

"There is no more room in the castle," he told the builders. "These pieces must find homes in our parks and fountains."

The planners spent another fortnight making sketches as Perivale looked on or visited frequently to monitor their progress and make suggestions. When the drawings were finished, the men again toured the city to help the king visualize how their structures would be set within the landscape. At the top of a low rise just outside the town, Perivale and his planners sat on their horses, looking back on the thatched roofs of the cottages surrounding the castle. He held the sketches and studied them thoroughly, often looking up at the village and the castle. The king's silence and stern countenance told the others that he was not al-together pleased.

"What is wrong, Your Majesty? Have we failed to capture your vision?" the architect asked.

"You've done it as well as it could be done," Perivale answered. "But I am coming to realize that we can do only so much with this castle and this village. The castle is not large or particularly distinguished. The village is small and poor. The countryside is flat and unimposing. Much of the ground is marshy and unstable. And, as you can see, the castle is not strategically located. It has no natural defenses; it depends solely on its walls and battlements. I wonder if we are wise to expend our efforts on such a dismal site. It's like dressing a plain woman in a lavish gown with jewels and ribbons. The adornment only makes the plainness more apparent."

"Perhaps you are right, sire, but we must work with what we have. We will do our best."

"What would you think of building an entirely new castle on an altogether different site?" Perivale asked.

The builders looked at each other in wonder. "What are you thinking, Your Majesty? I know of no better sites in this area."

"I'm not thinking of building in this area. In fact, I have been thinking that Maldor is too far from the center of Meridan to serve well as its capital. We need a site more central and strategic."

"And do you have such a site in mind, sire?"

"Indeed I do. In the war with Morgultha, we fought one of our fiercest battles on the Plain of Moriburne just north of Corenham. From that field, one can see in the distance the massive rock known as Morningstone Hill."

The architect began to grin. "I know the place, sire, and

I begin to see your mind. Morningstone Hill would be a wondrous site for your castle."

"It's a toe-and-bluff hill of solid marble," the king said. "Perfect for defense and solid enough to last till the sun burns cold."

"Indeed it would be strong and magnificent," the master builder said. "But raising a castle on such a hill would take seven years, at least."

"I want it done in five," Perivale said.

"Five years? But, sire, that would take an army of stone-masons, carpenters, blacksmiths, carvers, and laborers."

"You shall have your army. Remember, we are seven kingdoms now. We can draw the best skills and talents from each nation. And we can buy talent as we need it from across the Narrow Sea."

"But finding skilled workmen is not the only obstacle, sire. There's the problem of sufficient stone. Where will you quarry so much? And how will you get it to Morning-stone?"

"An arm of the Dragontooth Mountains juts into Braegan Wood just to the west of Corenham," Perivale replied. "We can quarry from those mountains and have rough masons cut the stone on site. Then we can cut a road through the wood and cart the stones to Morningstone, where master masons will dress them for placement. The trees we fell in the making of the road will become the castle beams, gates, and scaffolds."

Before the end of the day Perivale convinced the master builder that the task could be done, or that it had best be done if he wanted to retain the king's patronage. The men made a journey to Corenham to survey the hill and the site of the quarry, and a month after their return they presented drawings to Meridan's Hall of Knights. The Hall affirmed the project, but the vote was close. Several of the knights voted reluctantly, some swayed by loyalty, others by Perivale's insistence that the castle must be built. In the end, a few feelings were bruised, but Perivale merely sighed and said that diminished loyalties were the price visionaries paid for stepping into the future.

For the next few weeks, the castle project kept Perivale so occupied that he virtually abandoned all audiences in the great hall, leaving most decisions in Reddgaard's hands. The king spurred the architect and builder to a frenzy of speed. In four months all castle plans were drawn and the builder had secured all the best craftsmen from over the Seven Kingdoms by doubling their wages. This drawing of crucial skills from the allied nations caused some grumbling among their monarchs. Since prosperity had come to the island, all the kings had their own building programs. King Agrilon of Rhondilar had his own castle halfway finished when Perivale called the Rhondilar workmen to Meridan. Agrilon sent a strong letter of protest, which Reddgaard brought to Perivale in his planning room. "Answer him any way you wish," the king said, "as long as we get our workmen."

"But, sire, remember that Agrilon has another quarrel with us. He has disputed dominion over the border town of Sunderlon ever since the river changed its course and put the town on their banks. I'm sure he is smarting from your refusal to hear his case on the matter. To anger him again could jeopardize his willingness to remain in the Seven Kingdoms, which is tenuous at best."

But Perivale merely shrugged. "Such misunderstandings are the price we pay in the march toward greatness."

With all design and building plans complete and the cornerstone for Morningstone Castle laid, Perivale found himself with little to do. The building of the castle was now in the hands of others, leaving him feeling hollow and dry. Reddgaard urged him to resume giving audience to the people. "They loved you for your personal care of them," he told the king. But the castle project had fired Perivale's blood and lifted his imagination to new heights of grandeur, and he could not endure the tedium of audiences again. He traveled often to Corenham to check the progress of the building, much to the dismay of the architect and master builder. With each visit the king expressed his frustration that the project was not further along. He always found details that dissatisfied him and insisted that they be changed.

When in Maldor, Perivale continually searched for ways to spend his time. He hunted, flew his falcons, shot arrows at hay bale targets, rode about the land, ran his dogs, and sometimes even took a sword and joined Sir Rudmore in the training yard. When those diversions wore thin, he often went to the room where he and his builders had done their planning. He tacked the drawing of Morningstone Castle to the wall and placed a chair before it, where he sat and stared at his dream. Often he came into the room as early as midafternoon and remained staring long after the sun had set and the room went dark.

10

Avalessa sat in her chair near the window of her tower room, singing and strumming her mandolin as she often did in the afternoons. She looked down on the bailey, its grass now a luminescent green with the coming of spring. Her song was of spring as well. She had always loved spring above all seasons, but somehow this spring touched her differently. In addition to the promise of new life and bursting color, a longing for something she could not define hovered about her. The feeling, though vague and somewhat melancholy, was not unpleasant. It seemed to hold a promise, but a promise for she knew not what. She could feel it in the breeze that rustled her curtains and caressed her cheeks like a lover. She could see it in the pair of cardinals that briefly alighted on her sill, chirping and nuzzling each other with neck feathers ruffled like winter collars.

Avalessa was happy, perhaps the only one of her family who was. Her brother, Rhondale, had grown sullen and distant and usually kept to his chambers. Her mother, Rianna, though deeply troubled by the change in the king, covered her worry and kept the dinner table bright and congenial. Whatever changes others saw in the king were hidden from Avalessa. Because she was the one person in his life who did not make demands or badger him with warnings, the love between father and daughter remained intact, with none of the stresses that threatened the king's other interactions.

Avalessa put her mandolin aside and gazed out her window as she idly twisted a ringlet of her golden hair. She sighed deeply for no reason she could understand. She watched as two young washerwomen, chatting and giggling, walked from the keep to the well, buckets in hand. Three noblemen strolled along the stone path leading to the stable, talking together as they walked. Two of them she recognized as the architect and master builder who were constructing her father's new castle. Their presence reminded her that tonight was the night of the banquet, which the king always gave when the two men made their monthly report. Soon after the three disappeared, a tall young man she had never seen before stepped from the door of the keep into the sunlight. His hair was the color of a chestnut, his bearing straight, and his tights and tunic rich and elegant. As nearly as she could judge from the distance, the youth was about her own age. She watched as he strolled across the bailey, whistling a tune she did not recognize. When he disappeared through a gate in the stable wall, she strummed her mandolin and began to sing.

> "Do spring's caresses stroke the air,
> Or could it be love's first sweet kiss?
> Is that a lark with song so fair
> Or love's dear words of whispered bliss?
>
> "Does sunlight sparkle on the lake,
> Or is that gleam within love's eyes?

Do flowers tremble, dance, and quake,
Or is that love's deep longing sighs?

"What promise fills the tingling air
In each aroma, sound, and sight?
What magic bathes my dreams so fair
And touches me with wan delight?

"My wakened body and my heart
With longing sighs for something yearn.
That lies beyond all song and art
And makes my soul within me burn."

As Avalessa sang she looked out at the white clouds and the blue hills on the horizon, taking no more notice of those strolling below. When she finished the song, she glanced again into the bailey and saw the young man standing directly beneath her, staring up in rapt attention. She blushed deeply and moved away from the window, her heart beating like the wings of a bird. Several minutes passed before she dared to look out again. The youth had left. She laid her mandolin aside and paced restlessly about her chambers. She knew she should work on a Latin text her tutor had given her to translate, but she could not bring herself to do it. Not today. Instead, she filled the rest of her afternoon reading a romance of Galleson the troubadour.

As the sunlight faded at the window, Lady Elowynn and her maidservants came into Avalessa's room to light candles and dress her for the banquet. An hour later the princess entered the banquet hall and sat beside her mother, who was seated on the king's left. The architect sat to the right of the king, and next to him sat the master builder. Avalessa looked down the table at the other guests, which included a few of the knights and lords of the Hall and five of the master builder's best craftsmen. Near the end of the table sat the young man who had stood beneath her window in the afternoon. He was gazing straight at her. She blushed and looked away. Although she was growing accustomed to men gaping at her, she found herself unaccountably nonplussed by the gaze of this young man. She stole furtive glances at him several times during the banquet, and more than half the time she found him looking at her.

The two seats across from the king and to his right remained empty until the middle of the first course. At that point all heads turned toward the door as the master mason entered with a young woman on his arm. What turned the heads of the banqueters was not so much the girl's beauty, though she had beauty enough, as her dress, which was of a shimmering red fabric, tightly fitted to every contour of her body, with a neckline of a daring sweep revealing a bosom to incite the envy of a barmaid. The two approached the table, and the mason introduced his daughter Bloeudewedd to the king. She smiled and lowered her eyes as she curtsied and took the seat beside her father.

For the rest of the evening the king seldom turned to his queen or to anyone else. He engaged the architect in continual conversation, which kept him facing the girl. She looked at him often, each glance accompanied by smiles and a fluttering of her kohl-darkened lashes.

Lord Fenimar, sitting near the opposite end of the table, missed none of this. He turned to Lord Kramad Yesenhad and nodded slightly toward the king. His friend watched for a moment and understood. He spoke low in Fenimar's ear. "At last we see a crack in our king's armor. If that girl can enter it, perhaps we can follow."

Avalessa did not notice the woman's flirtations. She was concerned for her mother, for she noticed that the queen looked pale and distraught. Rianna ate little and spoke less, though her words were kind and gracious to those who spoke to her.

"Are you ill, mother?" Avalessa asked.

Rianna smiled and clasped her daughter's hand. "No, but I suppose I am a little weary." She looked at the princess through eyes distant and sad. "You look utterly radiant tonight," she said, turning the conversation away from herself.

"Thank you, Mother. Somehow, I feel radiant. I don't know why or even exactly what I mean when I say it. But I feel something inside me calling for something I can neither identify nor define."

"It's spring, my child. And you are sixteen and beautiful. Life blossoms in the spring, not only in the sap of the trees and the nectar of the flowers, but in the blood of youths and maidens as well. Spring is a wonderful time but a dangerous one."

"Dangerous? What do you mean, Mother?"

"I mean that the warming of your blood can urge you onto paths you should not yet walk . . ." The queen's throat tightened, and she could not speak. Her eyes welled with tears as she remembered the spring afternoon when she had first met the young Perivale beneath a willow on her father's estate.

"Mother, what's wrong?" Avalessa was alarmed.

Rianna dabbed at her eyes and shook her head. "Nothing . . . No, that is not quite true. But I cannot tell you of it now. Yet I must speak of it to someone. Come to me tomorrow, and we will talk."

After excusing herself, the queen arose from her chair and left the hall. Soon Perivale and his builders also left—after the king had kissed the hand of the blushing Bloeudewedd. The three men went to the planning room to review the progress of the castle construction. The band in

102

the hall began to play a galliard, and many of the remaining guests arose from the table to dance. Avalessa was left alone to ponder her mother's disturbing words.

A voice at her ear startled her from her reverie. "Would the princess care to join me in a dance?"

She turned to see the young man standing beside her chair.

"Please forgive me, Your Highness," he said, bowing. "We have not been introduced, but I hope you will excuse my boldness on the grounds of our fathers' closeness."

"Who is your father, and who are you?" Avalessa asked.

"I am Kaldor son of Kalmor. My father is your father's architect. I heard your voice from the bailey this afternoon, and I was entranced. I had to see if you were as lovely as your music, and I must say that I am not in the least disappointed."

Avalessa blushed lightly but smiled and stood. "I will be pleased to dance with you, Kaldor son of Kalmor."

She took his extended arm, and he led her to the floor. He was an excellent dancer, every movement filled with grace and poise. After three or four rounds, Avalessa suggested that they rest. Kaldor had a servant pour two glasses of mead, then followed Avalessa to a pair of chairs beneath the window.

"That song you sang this afternoon," Kaldor said as he sat beside her, "it was more beautiful than anything I have heard. Where did you hear it?"

"I didn't hear it anywhere. I often make up songs for my own enjoyment."

"You compose such songs yourself? The muse is certainly with you. I would like to hear more."

"Oh, I don't write them down. I remember most of them, though not all. Those that escape my memory are

103

likely better off gone. But what about you? Will you be an architect like your father?"

"I will. I am apprenticed to him even now. I work on-site at Morningstone and travel with my father when he reports to the king. So I will be coming to Maldor at the end of each month until the new castle is completed. I will be at these banquets on each visit. I hope I can see you again."

"I am expected to attend these banquets. No doubt we will meet again."

After another hour of talking and a few more dances, Avalessa left the hall and went up to her chambers. She slept well, her dreams filled with the tall young man with eyes of gray and hair the color of a chestnut.

On the next morning the princess took breakfast alone. After dressing she descended the flight of steps to her mother's room. She knocked lightly and entered. Rianna was still in bed.

"I often lay in bed another hour or so after your father is up," she explained. "There was a time when I couldn't wait for the day and the wonders it would bring, but now . . ." Her voice trailed off and tears welled in her eyes.

Avalessa was sure her mother had grown thinner. Her cheeks were beginning to look sunken, and the bloom on them had paled. The princess sat beside the bed and took the queen's hand in her own. It felt small and cold.

"I know something is amiss, Mother. Please tell me what it is."

Rianna closed her eyes and sighed deeply. "It's the crown, my daughter. The Crown of Eden is destroying your father."

"The crown is destroying him? What do you mean?"

"Have you not heard the legend of the crown?" Rianna asked.

"I've heard a little. In fact, I just read about it in a romance of Galleson. The crown enhances the power of good or evil in a ruler, whichever he allows to dominate his will."

"That is the essence of the legend," the queen said. "And I can attest to its truth. Ever since your father began to wear the crown, he has become more prideful and self-willed. He is little like the gentle and humble man I wed."

"But I thought the stories about the crown were only legends. How do you know it's the crown acting upon Father?"

"His behavior began to change as he began to wear it. For the first seven years of his reign, he kept the crown locked away. He feared it because he was inordinately drawn to it. But after the seven-year celebration of his victory, he began to wear it every day, though he removed it for sporting events or informal occasions. But now he never removes it until he comes to bed at night. The only time he doesn't wear it is on journeys away from Maldor. But I'm sure that on at least two of his journeys, he has taken it with him, though he didn't wear it and didn't let anyone know he had it in his keeping."

"And his behavior changed only after he began to wear the crown?"

"Yes. The longer he wears it, the more pronounced the changes. He and Rhondale do not speak to each other. He now spends only a fraction of his time in audience with his people. He browbeat the Hall of Knights into building Morningstone Castle. He is absent from most of our family meals now. He talks little to me and resents it when I suggest the crown is leeching away his humanity."

105

"But perhaps it isn't the crown. Couldn't there be another explanation?"

"I haven't told you all," Rianna replied. "When he first began to wear the crown, he would take it off at night and place it in the cask he had made for it. Later he began to leave it on the table next to his side of the bed. And now he not only sets it on the table but takes care to place it within reach. One morning as he was dressing, I picked it up merely to look at it. He watched me intently the whole time, and I could see that he was uneasy with me handling it. One night a few weeks later, he was in a cheerful mood, and as he undressed for bed, I lifted the crown from his head to set it in its usual place. He gripped me by the arm, spun me around, and wrenched it from my hand. With fire in his eyes and hostility in his voice, he told me never to touch it again. On many mornings now he is clutching the crown when he awakens, often so tightly that his fingers are stiff and sore when he releases it."

Avalessa was astonished. "I had no idea of any of this. My only hint of anything amiss was the night months ago when Father lost his temper with Rhondale. As alarming as that was, when Father apologized I thought it was over."

"Has he ever mistreated you?" the queen asked.

"Never. He shows me nothing but kindness and love."

"He dotes on you, Avalessa. He would cut off his hand before he would hurt you. You have always been his pride and joy."

"But he loves you as well, Mother. I have never seen a couple as close and loving as you and Father."

"That was true once, but you do not see us after you return to your chambers in the evening. In times past we sat close by the fire and talked every evening. Now he sits alone and broods. Often I must speak twice to get his attention, and even then he hardly hears and answers absently if at all."

Rianna dabbed at her reddened eyes with the corner of the bedsheet as Avalessa leaned over and clasped her in her arms. "I'm so sorry, Mother. What can I do?"

"I know of nothing. I didn't call you here to resolve the problem. I confess that it was to ease the burden I've been bearing. Your father is in danger, Avalessa. I know you love him as I do. He needs us now more than ever. If we can do nothing else, we must love him."

Avalessa promised to do that and more. She held her mother close, then returned to her own chambers, her mind reeling with what the queen had told her.

She closed her chamber door and leaned against it. She was shaking. When she got herself under control, she would find some way to help her father. However, for the moment it would have to wait; her tutor would arrive in minutes. She sat on her bed and tried to calm the turmoil in her heart. By the time the tutor arrived, she breathed normally and her heart no longer pounded. The elderly scholar Giffering listened as she read Latin texts until one o'clock. She had intended to take her midday meal in the garden with her mother, but a page brought a message that the queen was not feeling well and would not eat today. Avalessa sent a message to the chief cook, instructing him to prepare a light meal of cold meats, cheeses, and wine, and send it to the queen's chambers. Then she went to her mother and insisted that she eat. Her bright talk and girlish exuberance cheered the distressed woman, and after the meal the princess brought out her mandolin and sang the song of spring she had composed the day before.

"It's beautiful," the queen said. "Your father once loved music, but he hasn't listened to a minstrel in many months. And strangely, he seems not to miss it."

At once an idea came to Avalessa. She knew how she could help her father. After her mother had finished her meal and began to doze, the princess returned to her room. She spent the next hour playing and singing her song of spring, honing it to perfection. As evening approached, she placed her mandolin in its case and took it to the great hall, thinking the king would soon be ending his audiences.

"King Perivale has not been in the hall today," Lord Reddgaard told her.

"Perhaps he is with Kalmor the architect?" the princess suggested.

"Lord Kalmor left today for Morningstone," the hall-master replied. "The king may be on the falcon field. He has gone there often since the coming of spring."

She did not find her father at the falcon field, nor had the stabler seen him. The gamekeeper told her the king had not run his dogs in many days. It was almost dark when she returned to the keep. As she walked down the corridor, now lit with torches, she passed the door of the room where she knew the king and his architect reviewed plans for the new castle. She tried the door. It was unlocked. Slowly she pushed it open, its hinges groaning as if in agony as she peered into the darkness. She was about to close the door when she started and gasped. Against the darkening gray of the sky that filled the window, she saw the black silhouette of a man's head and shoulders. He was absolutely still and hunched forward, his head bowed with his chin resting on his hands. The outlines of the crown shone dimly on his head.

"Father?" she said softly.

Perivale did not answer.

"Father?" she called a little louder, a fearful tremor in her voice.

Slowly the head turned toward her. "Who are you? What do you mean coming here? Go and leave me in peace."

She realized that she was silhouetted to him against the torchlight from the corridor, and he could not see her features. She took a candle from one of the tables and stepped out of the room to light it at the hallway torch. "Are you well, Father?" she asked as she returned.

Perivale said nothing but dropped his head again. Silently Avalessa sat in a chair, took out her mandolin, and began to sing.

> "Do spring's caresses stroke the air,
> Or could it be love's first sweet kiss?
> Is that a lark with song so fair
> Or love's dear words of whispered bliss?"

She sang through the song, and before she finished the last verse, her father dropped his hands to the arms of the chair and raised his head a little. Avalessa immediately began another song. As she sang, she could see the king's fingers softly tapping out the rhythm on the arm of his chair. She finished with a lively ballad she knew to be a favorite of his—that of a seafaring warrior wearing a horned helmet who rescued a flaxen-haired maiden from the lair of a dragon. She finished the last bar with a flourish of dancing chords, then laid her instrument aside and smiled broadly at her father.

Perivale smiled in return. He stood and came to where she sat, drew her to her feet, and kissed her on the forehead. "Thank you, my daughter. You have drawn me up from a dark pit."

"A dark pit, Father?"

"Yes," Perivale sighed and resumed his chair. "I feel the weight of the kingdom heavy upon me these days. The burdens of office are greater because fewer help me bear them. The people don't understand where I am leading them, and they are reluctant to help shoulder the load. Sometimes the weight presses me deep into a darkness that blackens my soul. But your songs have lifted me back into the light."

"I'm glad, Father. I'm sorry for the weight you carry. We could help you—Mother and I—"

"I want to show you something," Perivale said, deflecting the direction of her thought by standing abruptly. He took her arm and led her to a table stacked with parchments and papers, some rolled, others laying flat on the surface. He lit another candle, then shuffled through the parchments and pulled one out and spread it before his daughter. "I was planning to surprise you with this, but I want you to see it now. It's what I am building for you in the new castle." He traced his fingers over the drawing as he explained. "Here are your chambers on the second floor of the keep. Here is your own room, and beside it a smaller chamber for your wardrobe, and your maidservant's quarters adjacent to it. These three arched windows look out over your own private garden. A stone stairway descends from your window balcony to your garden, which is completely enclosed. A fifteen-foot wall protects your privacy from the bailey. These steps take you to a balcony at the top of the garden wall overlooking the bailey. From here you can see all that goes on in the yard. No one but you has access to your garden. The only entrance is from your chamber or through the gardener's door, to which you will have the only key."

"It's beautiful!"

"All the trees in the drawing actually exist. We designed the garden around them."

Avalessa was overwhelmed. "I can hardly believe you're doing this for me. Mother would love such a—"

"You needn't worry about your mother," Perivale said. "She will have her own private garden."

The king showed his daughter several more drawings of the castle, and then they left together and ascended the stairway to the family chambers. The queen joined them in their evening meal, and for the rest of the evening Perivale was much like his old self.

Avalessa often sought him out and sang for him in the days that followed. And for a time some of the darkness that had begun to descend upon the family lifted, and Rianna regained a little of her former glow.

11

The builders completed Morningstone Castle two months and eleven days short of the five-year mark Perivale had set. Workmen returned to their homes throughout the island, and the other kings resumed their own projects. The castle was magnificent, by far the largest on the island, with many towers and turrets thrusting skyward from its thick walls. Set as it was on the pinnacle of Morningstone Hill, travelers could see the structure for miles around. The stones gleamed white as ivory in the sunlight, and the banners flying from the spires gave it life. It was the first object in the valley to catch the morning sunlight breaking over the peaks of the Dragontooth Mountains. Perivale was immensely pleased and gave the architect and master mason bonuses, which made them wealthy men.

The move from Maldor to Morningstone took most of three months and tied up most of the carts from the merchants and tradesmen of Corenham. Perivale ignored their grumbling, again shrugging it off as a lack of vision. On the day after the last cart was unloaded, he announced to the Hall of Knights that a grand, three-day celebration of the opening of the castle would be held in sixty days.

He ordered that all furnishings, tapestries, and statuary be in place by that date. And he insisted that the new suit of armor he was having made should be ready. The celebration would include feasts, dances, music, games, and other entertainments. For three days the castle would be open to all, and the pages and squires would conduct tours. He expected all the lords and knights to attend.

After the meeting of the Hall in which Perivale announced his celebration plans, Lord Fenimar rode out from the gate of Morningstone Castle with Lords Ashbough and Kramad Yesenhad mounted on either side. As they reached the base of the stony hill, Kramad Yesenhad reined his horse to a walk and called the two men to draw near.

"In spite of all the king's new pomp and show, we have known for some time that the man has a weakness. And I now see our opportunity to exploit it. Come to my manor tonight, and we will discuss it."

His friends agreed and rode away.

Shortly after sunset the three men arrived at the new manor Kramad Yesenhad had built at the edge of Corenham. Soon they were settled into their chairs with mugs of ale in their hands.

Fenimar looked at the lawyer and said, "What is this weakness of the king, and how will it help us?"

Kramad Yesenhad smiled, his white teeth gleaming from his black beard like a cyclops's eye. "Though our king seems to enjoy the favor of the gods, the truth is, his world is falling apart. He thinks himself a misunderstood visionary forced to drag his people into his dream of glory for the island. He does not see that his central desire is for his own glory, a craving that now grips him like a claw.

Morningstone Castle is an example. The building of it has consumed him. He has neglected his duties, his family, and his people. There is trouble within his own house, not only with the queen, but with his son as well. But he hardly notices. He is driven by his need for adulation and grandeur. His desires are out of control.

"Among those desires is one that many have begun to notice. Even Queen Rianna knows of his growing attention to the master mason's daughter, Bloeudewedd. He sees that she is invited to every event at the castle, and he always seats her just near enough that he can leer at her but not near enough to arouse suspicion."

"But she was wed to Lord Weathereld a fortnight ago," Fenimar said.

"It doesn't matter. Everyone knows her marriage to Weathereld is in name only," Ashbough said. "The important thing is that Perivale can't keep his eyes off the girl."

"This woman is just what we have been looking for," Kramad Yesenhad continued, his smooth voice seeming at home in the shadowy corners of the room. "She can take the reins of Perivale's desire and lead him by the nose. She can lure him on and withhold her favors to get what she wants. We can pay this woman to lead him into the trap we set. She can be our Delilah to his Samson."

"Has the king acted on this infatuation?" Fenimar asked.

"He has not," Kramad Yesenhad said. "I have several pages in the castle under payment. They have eyes that see past every door, day or night, and they assure me that Bloeudewedd and the king have never been alone together. But I believe he is precariously balanced between desire and propriety. If we can nudge him over the edge, we can make his indiscretion known and bring him down."

"Are you sure that exposure will bring him down?"

Fenimar asked. "Other kings have taken mistresses and remained on their thrones."

"Only under certain conditions," Kramad Yesenhad replied. "They remain on their thrones when their indiscretion remains hidden or when their power overshadows the law. We will see that the indiscretion is not hidden, and the kirk will see that the king does not place himself above the law."

"Actually, we may not even need to bring Perivale down," Ashbough said. "Think of what we could accomplish if we use what we know to blackmail him. We can threaten exposure unless he follows our every instruction. We could rule the Seven Kingdoms from behind the curtain."

"No!" Fenimar shouted. "I won't hear of it. The throne of Meridan is mine, and I mean to have it. I will not be a shadow king or the king's puppeteer. I will settle for nothing less than the title of king as well as the power."

"Of course, of course," Ashbough said. "It was merely a thought."

"How do we implement our little plan?" Fenimar asked.

"We approach the girl with the proper price and get her to seduce the king," Kramad Yesenhad replied.

"What if she refuses? She may want nothing to do with our plans, having wed Lord Weathereld."

"She won't refuse." Kramad Yesenhad laughed dryly. "Lord Weathereld is old enough to be the girl's grandfather. And she is a lively lass with hardly the temperament to stay by his hearth. Look at the way she displays her charms. Look at the way she casts her eyes at the king. It is apparent that she has already marked him as a conquest. I assure you, Ashbough, this girl is more than ready for the venture we have for her."

"Perhaps," Ashbough said, "but have you noticed Lord

115

Weathereld when she is around? He watches her with the eyes of an eagle."

"And he is wise to do it. But we can take care of Weathereld," Kramad Yesenhad said. "I have access to potions that can make the old man sleep for hours."

"Also, Weathereld is known to pinch a farthing until it bends," Fenimar said.

"All the more to our advantage," Kramad Yesenhad replied. "Lady Bloeudewedd will be in need of money. She will listen to any plan we propose."

12

The celebration opening Morningstone Castle outshone that of the seven-year anniversary of Perivale's victory over Morgultha. A grand parade through the streets of Corenham set the tone of it, with Perivale leading his mounted knights and lords, all in full regalia. The king looked magnificent—some said like a god—astride a great white charger and wearing his golden-hued armor made especially for the occasion. People lining balconies tossed down flowers, and adoring young women ran alongside the mounted king, reluctant to let him out of their sight. The parade ended at the gate of Morningstone, and the king and knights entered the hall where the grand feast and ball would shortly begin.

When a page knocked on Avalessa's door to announce the arrival of the king and his knights, she left her chambers with her lady-in-waiting, Elowynn, by her side and made her way toward the hall. At nineteen Avalessa more than fulfilled the promise of exceptional beauty that had graced her features from birth. Before she had turned seventeen, the men in Perivale's court had suddenly noticed that the bud had blossomed into an exquisite rose. Already many had pressed the king for her hand, but he had refused them all. Though scores of young and not-so-young knights and nobles lavished attention on the princess, none edged from her heart the first young man who had awakened her to the charm of the masculine. Avalessa saw Kaldor often, and a tingle of anticipation thrilled her as she thought of seeing him tonight.

She stood at the top of Morningstone's grand stairway. The blended sound of voices and laughter filled the air below as Lady Elowynn brushed and fluffed her lavender gown one last time. "There, you look perfect, Your Highness—utterly breathtaking. You will steal the heart of every man in the hall tonight."

Avalessa stepped down the stairway with the grace of a descending swan. Several of the guests caught sight of her and could not turn their eyes away. The princess blushed lightly at the attention as she scanned the upturned faces for Kaldor. She saw many of the suitors who had pressed her father for her hand, and near the center of the hall stood the king, watching her descend with a look of unambiguous pride. As she neared the floor, she caught sight of Kaldor standing near the far wall, gazing at her entrance. Her smile widened, and her blush deepened. When she reached the floor she made her way toward her young friend, but immediately a dozen knights and sons of lords pressed about her, each vying for her attention. She could do nothing but stop and smile, making pleasant talk as the circle of admirers imprisoned her.

She glanced beyond them and was pleased to see Kaldor working his way toward her. She continued the trivial conversation but watched from the corner of her eye as he approached and wedged himself into the circle.

"Good evening, Princess Avalessa," he said, bowing low.

"Good evening, Kaldor," she replied, extending her hand, which he took and kissed.

The other young men stood nonplussed, and their faces darkened. She had offered her hand to none of them. Soon they began to fall away to find other, more receptive women. Kaldor gave the princess his arm and led her through the crowd until they stood near the infamous image of the dryad at the door of the hall. For a moment he looked at her, openly enthralled, until she blushed and lowered her eyes.

"I have something to give you," he said. He drew a small piece of folded parchment from his doublet and placed it in her hand. "I cannot sing or play an instrument as you do, but I have often written verse, feeling a sort of music as I write. This poem came to me not long after I first stood beneath your window and heard you sing. I thought you might put it to music and play it for me sometime."

Avalessa unfolded the parchment and read the rhyme, blushing yet again as the words left her lips.

"Kaldor, it's beautiful," she said softly. "I will certainly put it to music."

"When can I hear it?" he asked.

"Do you know where my garden is?"

"My father designed this castle, remember?"

"Of course. When I have completed the music, I will send a note telling you when to come to the wall of my garden and hear your poem as a song."

The two young people talked of many things, and each delighted in the newly discovered joy of the presence of the other. Avalessa had begun to understand the nature of her undefined longings, and those vague desires that had arisen like mist from her heart began to take a masculine form. Everything about the young man seemed to quicken all her senses. She delighted in the timbre of his deepening voice, the depth of his clear, gray eyes, and the strong outlines of his face. As they talked she forgot all else, and for that eternal moment of enchantment, the hall filled with milling people did not exist.

"Avalessa." A voice behind her broke the spell.

"Yes, Father?" She turned and addressed the king.

"You must come with me." Perivale's voice was stern as he glared at Kaldor.

"May I come later? I want to—"

"No. You must come now."

She excused herself from Kaldor but whispered to him, "Come to me after the feast, and I will dance with you." She took the arm of her father, who led her through the crowd.

"Who is the young man you are with?" he asked, scowling.

"He is Kaldor, son of your architect Kalmor."

"I am now taking you to meet a man who is no mere architect; he is a king. King Agrilon of Rhondilar has seen you this evening, and he has asked to meet you. He is recently widowed and looking for a new bride."

"That is all well and good, Father. But I am not looking for a husband."

"No, but a husband of suitable stature for the high princess of the Seven Kingdoms will not be easy to find. A mere count, lord, or earl will not do. Nor are many princes available. We must be open to good opportunities that present themselves."

"I would be perfectly happy to wed a count or a lord or a herdsman if I loved him. And I would be perfectly miserable with a king if I did not."

"It isn't that simple, Avalessa. You are a princess, and you cannot escape the duties of royalty. The interplay between kingdoms is often complex and tenuous. Rhondilar

120

is not altogether happy under the rule of Meridan. They are disputing possession of a border town, and Agrilon is unreceptive to our position. Often a marriage will bind nations together when diplomacy fails."

Avalessa felt a surge of panic as her father's purpose in this introduction became clear to her. Her eyes darted about the room as if looking for deliverance. "Is Mother here? I haven't seen her tonight."

"She didn't feel well and couldn't come down."

"Very well. I will meet this king, and then I will go to my mother and see to her needs."

"Your mother's needs are met. I left her in the care of her closest servants. I have arranged for you to sit beside King Agrilon at dinner. And I want you to dance with him afterward."

A sudden coldness gripped Avalessa's heart. "Are you saying you intend to wed me to King Agrilon?"

The king looked down at her and smiled. "I would not force you to wed anyone against your will, my dear one. All I ask is that you give the man a chance. Compare this king of a nation to those beardless green fops who have been badgering me for your hand these many months."

At that moment they approached a thickset man dressed in a leather suit and boots. A rich blue cape, clasped at his neck with a cluster of golden chains, flowed to below his knees. His thick, black beard was riddled with gray, and his black eyes peered at her from beneath a bush of eyebrows at the base of a craggy forehead.

"King Agrilon, I present to you Her Highness, the Princess Avalessa," Perivale said.

"Greetings, Your Highness," Agrilon replied in a voice deep and heavy. He made as if to reach for her hand, but Avalessa did not extend it.

After exchanging a few pleasantries, Perivale left his

daughter with Agrilon. The king of Rhondilar said nothing but paced slowly back and forth, looking her up and down as if she were a prize mare on an auction block.

"You appear to be a strong, healthy woman," he said. "Are you prone to sickness or weak spells?"

"I'm as healthy as a horse," she replied. "Would you like to see my teeth?" Though she spoke in jest, the look of the king made her wonder whether he wouldn't act on the offer.

The steward rang the bell for dinner, and Agrilon ushered her to the banquet table. He took the seat immediately to her left and began to fill her ear with tales of the riches and wonders of Rhondilar. The chair on her right remained empty. As the toasts and speeches began, Agrilon ceased his talk and gave his attention to the hallmaster. Avalessa looked around the hall for Kaldor, but she saw him nowhere. She reminded herself that the guests numbered over seven score and many were not visible from her table.

"I know where he sits," whispered a voice in her right ear.

Avalessa started. Intent on finding Kaldor, she had not seen Rhondale take the empty seat beside her. "You don't even know who I'm looking for," she whispered.

"You're looking for the architect's son."

"How did you know?"

"I make it my business to know many things that people don't see—and some things they choose not to see. He's sitting just behind the column on the far side of the hall to your right."

"Who does he sit with?" she asked.

Rhondale grinned smugly. "What if I told you he sat beside Sir Everedd's beautiful daughter Gwenellen?" He watched with satisfaction as Avalessa went pale and her eyes widened in dismay. He laughed softly. "Never fear, dear sister. Your young friend sits with his father."

"But so far from the king's table? I thought the architect of this castle would be an honored guest tonight."

"It seems that our dear father quickly forgets his debts," Rhondale whispered as the speeches droned on. "He has reserved the high seats for kings and princes from outside the Seven Kingdoms. The obligations of the past mean nothing to him. He lives only in the future."

"I don't understand," Avalessa replied. "The master mason sits almost directly across from our father."

"Surely you know the reason for that," Rhondale said. "Look at the mason's daughter, Bloeudewedd, sitting right beside him, her rounded young bosom heaving and over-flowing her gown as she blushes demurely and flutters her lashes at our dear father."

"Oh, Rhondale, surely you don't believe for a moment that Father would even look at such a woman. He loves mother dearly."

"Of course he does," Rhondale replied, sarcasm evident even in his whisper. "That's why his architect sits insulted in a corner threatening to stalk out of the hall with his son, while the lowly master mason sits at the table with kings."

"Kaldor may leave?" Dismay clouded Avalessa's face. "Rhondale, you must do something for me. Please go to Kaldor and ask him not to leave with his father. I will have a carriage take him home. Tell him I must dance once with King Agrilon but afterward I will dance with him. Will you tell him that for me, Rhondale?"

"Your wish is my command, my princess," the prince whispered. "I shall do it before the feast is ended."

Avalessa turned from her brother and glanced at Agrilon. He sat impassively until the speeches ended, then loaded his plate from the roast pig set before him. After filling his mouth, he turned to the princess. "Has your father told you that I am widowed?"

"Yes. I am very sorry for your loss," Avalessa replied.

"May the Master rest her soul," Agrilon said, his voice muffled by the pork he chewed. "She bore me six daughters but no sons. A king needs sons, Your Highness—many sons to carry on his name and rule his kingdom and provinces."

"But daughters sometimes ascend to thrones. In Valomar a generation ago when King Volthring died without sons, his daughter Branwilda assumed the throne."

Agrilon frowned at her. "Yes, it has happened, but it should not. What kind of kingdom allows a woman to rule it? It is not according to nature, and I will not subject the men of Rhondilar to such a humiliation. In Rhondilar we do not educate our royal women in such things as kingcraft requires—Latin, history, literature, or mathematics. It is a waste of time. A woman's task is to fulfill the duty for which she was born, which is to bear and raise children."

"Nevertheless, since the Master has blessed you with six daughters, perhaps you should begin grooming one of them to take your crown."

"One cannot consider six daughters to be blessings."

"Surely you don't believe your daughters are curses."

"Indeed I do. My late wife was born in the land of the Frankens, across the Narrow Sea. When we were wed she was unfamiliar with the rituals we observe in Rhondilar. At our wedding feast when the cup of fertility was given her, she drank only half of it, not knowing that unless she downed it all, she would bear only daughters. Later in the evening her lady told her of her error, and immediately my bride had another cup poured and drained it in a single draught. But it was too late. The propitious moment had passed, and thus she remained forever unable to bear sons, much to her sorrow."

"Rhondilar wives must feel very fortunate to live in such an enlightened kingdom," Avalessa replied.

As the meal progressed, the princess learned much about the women of the court of Rhondilar. They were essentially drudges, given little attention by their men and expected to maintain the mundane functions that kept the castle running. They attended few royal events and saw little of their husbands, living in quarters with their children, while their mates had private chambers. The king and his lords were often away from the castle at war, on hunts, or on diplomatic missions, or often merely gathered at lodges, spinning tales and quaffing ale.

Rhondale, listening silently to the conversation, smiled wryly. As Agrilon explained to Avalessa how his queen had died giving birth to her seventh child—a stillborn daughter—the prince slipped away from the table and made his way to where Kaldor sat.

Rhondale took the empty seat beside him and said, "Where is your father, Kaldor?"

Kaldor turned to him, his eyes forlorn and listless until he recognized the prince. He stood quickly and bowed. "Greetings, Your Highness."

"Oh, sit down," Rhondale growled. "I see that your father isn't here."

Kaldor's face darkened further. "He has left the banquet," he replied.

"He left the banquet?" Rhondale's voice expressed great surprise. "Why would the king's architect leave the banquet that celebrates his greatest accomplishment?"

"He . . . uh . . . he was tired and not feeling too well."

"Too bad," Rhondale replied. "I feared it was because the

king had failed to give him due honor. It seems a terrible affront that your father was not seated at the king's right hand tonight. No one deserved honor more than he did. And why the master mason should be given a high seat while your father was not is a great mystery. Look at him up there, sitting smugly across from the king, eating the choice beef and drinking the finest wine in the hall. Did your father notice?"

"Yes, he noticed," Kaldor said bitterly. "In fact, I'll be frank, Your Highness; that is why my father left."

"I am so sorry," the prince replied, shaking his head. "It may console you to know that many of us in the royal court have noticed the slight and share your hurt. May I ask why you remain at the ball?"

"I . . . I hoped to see your sister again. She promised to dance with me."

Rhondale looked at Kaldor through eyes feigning infinite sorrow and laid a sympathetic hand on the boy's shoulder. "I fear I must add to your unhappiness, my young friend. The princess cannot dance with you, tonight or ever. You see, she has promised to wed King Agrilon of Rhondilar, at whose side she now sits. Tonight she will dance only with him."

Kaldor's eyes grew wide in disbelief. "She has promised to wed King Agrilon? Why has she not told me? Why would she show me such attention? Why would she promise to dance with me?"

Again Rhondale shook his head and looked at the young man in solemn sympathy. "You have much to learn about women of royal houses. Though they wed only men of high position, they often toy with others who take their momentary fancy. And though it pains me to say it, I fear that my sister is no exception."

Kaldor stood, his eyes and face set hard as stone. "I

thank you, Your Highness, for teaching me a hard lesson about the ways of royal women." He bowed stiffly, turned on his heel, and strode swiftly from the hall.

The meal ended, and the band began to play for the dance. Agrilon turned solemnly to Avalessa and said, "My princess, let me be frank. I am looking for a strong, healthy young wife who can bear me many sons."

"It is hard to imagine that any woman would resist such an offer," Avalessa replied. "I wish you well in your search."

"Your father has given me to understand that you might—"

"That I might like to dance?" the princess said as she stood. "He is right; I love to dance. If I could have one dance with you, Your Majesty, I would be greatly honored. Then I will meekly withdraw to chatter with the women about nursing, colic, and the price of potatoes in Sorendale while you kings polish up your crowns."

"Ha!" Agrilon grinned. "I knew it! You have the makings of a woman of Rhondilar."

"I can't tell you what kind of honor it is to hear you say it," Avalessa replied as she grabbed his hand and dragged him to the floor to fulfill her father's command.

She endured one galliard, during which the heavy king trod on her toes at least three times. She would have bruised toenails tomorrow. As she danced she heard the ringing laughter of Bloeudewedd and looked to see the woman dancing in her father's arms, her red dress hiding little of her charms and the citron scarf in her hair flying like a banner as they whirled about the floor.

When the dance ended, Avalessa curtsied to Agrilon, praised him for his grace, and left him to search for Kaldor. She looked all about the hall as well as in the corridors outside it and on the balcony, but to no avail. She looked for Rhondale to ask whether he had delivered her message, but he was nowhere to be found. As she scanned the hall, she saw Agrilon walking toward her with determined purpose. She quickly slipped through the crowd, now looking for her father to tell him she was leaving to tend to her mother. But Perivale was not in the hall either. "He probably went up to check on mother," she thought. Again she spied Agrilon lumbering toward her. She slipped through a door and walked swiftly toward the stairway.

13

Avalessa ran up the stairway and down the corridor toward her parents' chambers. She knocked at the door, and Lady Rhoenda, her mother's lady-in-waiting, admitted her. Rianna was sleeping, Rhoenda told her, and no, the king had not been up since before the ball. No, she did not know where he might have gone.

The princess walked on down the corridor to her own chambers. The clock had not yet struck nine, but the evening was ruined. She had attended the ball tingling with the anticipation of seeing Kaldor. Though he had left early, she might have enjoyed mingling with her friends and guests were it not for the relentless pursuit of King Agrilon. She could not go back and face more of the man's scrutiny. For all she knew, he might start measuring and weighing her.

A low fire already burned in her hearth, and candles were lit about the room. Avalessa did not send for Elowynn, who was still enjoying the ball, but undressed herself and slipped into bed with a book of Coreddan, the great storyteller of the Seven Kingdoms. The princess hoped the book's legends of the giants, dragons, dwarves, and elves that lived on the island before the coming of man would dispel the disappointment of her evening.

But the dragons in the book could not defeat the dragons in her mind. She tried to read a story of an enormous giant terrorizing the villages of the island. Her eyes scanned the lines, but her mind retained nothing. Why had Kaldor left the ball? She thought she knew the answer: loyalty to his father. The architect had been snubbed, and his son could do no less than support him in his humiliation. But why had her own father not honored the architect on the occasion of his greatest accomplishment? She would not accept Rhondale's suggestion that the king had displaced Kalmor in order to seat Bloeudewedd near him. Whatever the reasons for her father's action, she was certain they must have been sound.

She thought of Agrilon and shuddered. What was her father thinking even to suggest such a marriage? No doubt he had known she would refuse the match. Perhaps that was it. He was playing a diplomatic game. Merely offering her hand to the neighboring king would show Perivale's goodwill and do much to mend damaged relations even if she refused to comply. Surely that was her father's strategy. Yet she remembered the coldness in his eyes when he glared at Kaldor. Why would he object to Kaldor? The young man was titled, courtly, and educated.

Such thoughts chased each other through the labyrinth of her mind as she tried to follow the stalking giant through the pages of her book. But finally her eyelids grew leaden and closed, and the volume fell across her breast. In her dream she still held the book before her and read the story. Gradually she heard from its pages a vague, dull thudding that became louder as she read on. Soon the thuds rattled the leaves of the book; shortly afterward they shook the bed and finally the walls of her chamber. Then she seemed to enter the pages herself, where she stood facing a rolling horizon that shuddered with each thud, now booming like distant thunder. Soon she saw a dark head appear over the crest of a hill, then the shoulders and torso of an enormous giant. The creature was clad in leather studded with brass and hung with golden chains. The face that grinned out from its grizzled beard was that of King Agrilon.

Avalessa tried to run, but her feet seemed rooted to the soil. The giant came ever closer, each ponderous step shaking the ground like an earthquake. Finally the monster stopped, looming over her like a mountain and grinning from ear to ear. For the first time she noticed that he carried what appeared to be a bag made of a white sheet. With a gesture of disdain, he flung the white thing to the ground before her. As the bundle rolled to a stop at her feet, the sheet fell away, and she could see the body of a young woman, heavy with child, curled up to hide her nakedness, her hands covering her face. The body was smooth and lustrous, the hair soft and blond, tumbled in chaotic waves across her bare shoulders.

A great dread descended upon the princess as she looked down at the woman. She tried to draw back, but something impelled her toward the poor creature. She had to look at that face. Slowly she reached forward and brushed the hair away. Then with trembling fingers, she drew the woman's hands from her face. Avalessa started violently. The face was her own. She awoke panting hard and crying out.

"Is anything amiss, Your Highness?" Elowynn entered holding a candle, concern showing on her face.

"N—no, nothing, thank you. I just had a terrible dream."

Elowynn brought Avalessa a cup of warm milk, took the book away, and helped her settle back into bed. But the princess slept fitfully the rest of the night as the giant with the face of King Agrilon chased her across the countryside. And she could hardly run because she was naked and heavy with child.

On the morning she awoke late and got out of bed slowly, her muscles sore and stiff as if she had actually run all night. She took her breakfast in her own rooms, then dressed and went to her parents' chambers. Perivale had already gone, and when the princess saw her mother, a surge of fear passed through her. The queen lay asleep in her bed, her head propped up by pillows. Her face was pale and her cheeks sunken. As Avalessa picked up her mother's thin hand and held it in her own, Rianna slowly opened her eyes and smiled wanly at her daughter.

"Mother, you are not well," Avalessa said.

"I'm very tired, my darling," the queen replied. "It seems that I stay tired most of the time these days. All I want is sleep." Her eyes began to close even as she spoke.

The princess did not try to awaken her but pressed her hand and returned sadly to her own chambers.

After a page delivered a message that the tutor would be delayed until early afternoon, she unfolded the parchment bearing Kaldor's verses. Her blood quickened and the day brightened as she read them again. She got her mandolin, sat on the terrace overlooking her garden, and began to sing. She was surprised at how quickly a melody formed, seeming to emerge from the character of Kaldor's words. She added chords to enrich the tune, and an hour before noon the song was finished. Any further embellishment would diminish it just as too many jewels diminish rather than enhance the beauty of a woman.

She wrote a note to Kaldor bidding him come to the balcony wall of her garden at two o'clock tomorrow afternoon to hear their song.

With a renewed lightness of step, the princess again checked on her mother and found her still asleep. She took lunch in her own chambers, and after a brief nap, awoke to the knock of her tutor.

Two hours later the tutor left and Elowynn handed her a note. "This came while you were studying."

Avalessa broke the waxen seal and unrolled the parchment. Her mouth opened in dismay and her eyes began to water as she read:

Princess Avalessa:

Last night your father dealt callously and shamefully with my father. However, I chose to attend the ball, thinking it unfair to ascribe to the daughter the character of the father. But last night you showed yourself to have inherited the family trait of treachery. I learned through your brother that you have treated me falsely. You did not tell me you were pledged to King Agrilon but trifled with my affections as if my pain meant nothing to you. I will not humiliate myself further by hearing my song from your false lips. Those words from my heart are mere sport to you. If you have any decency, you will burn my verses and bury the ashes beneath a bitterroot vine.

Kaldor Son of Kalmor

Avalessa dropped the letter to the floor, buried her face in her hands, and sobbed. How could Kaldor think such a thing? Rhondale! The answer was in the note itself. She felt heat rise to her face, and her temples pulsed with the angry beat of her heart. She bolted from her chair, walked swiftly from her room, and descended the stairway with lightning-quick steps. She reached Rhondale's door and pounded on it. When her brother's face appeared, Avalessa pushed the door open and brushed past him into the room.

"My dear sister," he said. "What induces you to honor me with a visit?"

"What did you tell Kaldor last night?"

Rhondale grinned and sprawled in a nearby chair. "Everyone thinks you are the most beautiful woman in the Seven Kingdoms. Ah, but if they could only see you when you are angry—the blush on your cheeks, the fire in your eyes, the feline grace of your poise, ready to spring upon your prey—they would fall into a trance of rapture. Anger becomes you, my sister."

"What did you tell Kaldor?"

"I merely told him the truth—at least it was mostly the truth."

"You did nothing of the sort. You promised to deliver my message. I trusted you. Instead, you drove him from me with a vicious lie. Why, Rhondale, why?"

"I did you a great favor. I told the boy the truth, though you may not yet know it to be the truth. You will wed King Agrilon whether you want it or not. Our dear father will see to it. Last night I merely spared you the agony of breaking it off with your young suitor."

"I certainly will not wed Agrilon. I detest the man. Father assured me that he will not force me to wed against my will."

"And you believed him? You are much too innocent and trusting, dear sister. I happen to know that he has already promised your hand to the king."

"It cannot be true. Even if it were, how would you know of it when he hasn't told me?"

"He didn't tell you because he dotes on you. He thinks that because Agrilon is a king, you will choose to wed him of your own free will. As to how I know such things, I told you last night that I make it my business to know many things that others don't see—and some things they choose not to see."

Avalessa felt a cold hand gripping her heart. "Father would never do such a thing to me."

"You think you know our father well, do you? Do you want to hear what he did after he left the ball last night?"

"No. I'm not interested in more of your lies. I will go now and repair the damage you have done to Kaldor." She started toward the door, but Rhondale blocked her path. "Get out of my way," she said.

"No, you will hear this whether or not you wish it. Sit down." Rhondale gripped her arm and guided her to a chair, where she sat stiffly, her hands folded in her lap. Her brother sat facing her and said, "Last night our father was unfaithful to our mother."

Immediately Avalessa jumped up and walked to the door. "I will not listen to such lies."

"Did you see who he danced with last night? Did you see either of them after the first dance?"

Avalessa's hand was on the latch, but she didn't lift it. "That proves nothing. No doubt they left separately and for different reasons."

"They were together. I followed them."

Slowly the princess turned and took her seat, where she remained silent as her brother told of what he had seen.

"Even before the dance Lady Bloeudewedd played up to our father. She listened with rapt wonder to all his stories, laughed delightedly at his jests, and prodded him into telling of his heroic exploits, which Father was all too happy to do. Then during the dance she moved closer and closer to him, moving her body against his as she gazed at him with those doelike eyes. And soon he could look nowhere else.

"As the dance ended he whispered in her ear, and she smiled and nodded. Moments later she left the hall by the door into the corridor that leads to the guests' chambers. Father spent a moment talking with Sir Everedd but glanced often toward the door. After about five minutes he left by the same door. I followed quietly at a distance, keeping him within my sight. Do you need to hear more?"

"Lady Bloeudewedd may have gone to her chambers and Father to check on Mother or to get a breath of fresh air—or to the privy, for that matter."

"He could have, but he didn't. I watched him from behind the statue of Heracles—those sculptures do have their practical uses—as he approached the door to one of the guest rooms. He hesitated for a moment and looked down the corridor in both directions, then drew out a key and entered the room and locked the door behind him. I crept to the door and listened. I will spare you the details of what I heard, but I assure you that our father was unfaithful to our mother."

"You tell a convincing story, Rhondale. But you also told a convincing story to Kaldor last night. Why should I believe you?"

"I thought you might ask." Rhondale grinned. He reached inside his tunic and drew out a citron-colored scarf. "You should believe me because of this." He reached into his tunic again. "And because of this." He held a small opal toward Avalessa. "Do you recognize this?"

Avalessa took the gem and looked at it. "Yes, it's the stone from the pendant Mother gave Father on their fifteenth anniversary. He always wears it beneath his tunic."

"The next time you see our dear father, ask him if this stone isn't missing from its setting. I hid in the corridor until the lovers left the room almost an hour later. Then I went into the room and found these items. The scarf was beside the bed, and the stone was in the bed. Our father is a bit careless, don't you think?"

Avalessa was stunned. She couldn't help but believe her brother's story, yet she found herself unaccountably angry at him for telling it. "You have a vendetta against our father."

"And you think it's without reason?" His voice tightened with bitterness. "Haven't you noticed that Father treats me much differently than you? You have your beauty. You are an asset to him, a source of pride, even a bartering medium to achieve his grand visions. I have nothing he values, nothing to make him proud. I am small and weak, with no aptitude for any of the skills that in his eyes make a man. When I was a child, he loved me. But as I grew older he became ashamed of me and made my life a living hell, trying to reshape me into his own image. When he found that my clay was too soft to hold his shape, he simply forgot me. When he looks toward me, he sees nothing."

"Oh, Rhondale, I am so sorry. I'm sure Father loves you. He just doesn't know how to show it."

"Spare me your sympathy. You will soon need it for yourself. Though you don't see it yet, his love for you is turning into something hideous. Once he loved you for yourself. Now he loves you for himself—for what you can do for him. He will barter you to the highest bidder without remorse if he thinks it will add one beam to his glory."

"Rhondale, you are slandering our father. Whatever his faults, we are his children, and we owe him filial honor and respect."

"Respect!" Rhondale snorted. "Once I respected my father. I adored him. He was not only the hero of the Seven Kingdoms but my hero as well. But no more. I hate the man. I hate him for bullying me. I hate him even more for ignoring me. After last night surely even you know he isn't worthy of our respect. Many a serf living in a thatched hovel has more honor than our father."

137

"It isn't our father who is doing these things, Rhondale. Some monstrous evil grips him. What can we do for him? How can we help him overcome this thing that is leeching his soul?"

"You do what you want, but I won't lift a finger to help him," Rhondale replied. "I am long past caring what happens to the man. Whatever doom awaits him is no less than he deserves."

Avalessa shook her head sadly. She felt her world crumbling about her. Her father was sinking into some hideous pit, her mother's life was ebbing away in deep sorrow, a wall of deceit estranged her from her first love, and her brother was infected with a malignant bitterness that isolated him from his own humanity. She took her leave and returned to her own chambers.

14

Avalessa sat on the terrace overlooking her garden, her mind a whirlwind of chaotic thoughts. What could she do to prevent the unraveling of her family? Should she confront her father with his infidelity? Would he listen to her? Should she tell her mother? Could the queen bear the news? Or did she already know? Maybe everyone knew. Such news had a way of getting around. What was the old proverb? "Bad news fills the air like cottonwood seed, while good news drops like an acorn." Perhaps she should seek counsel. Wolderand or Lord Reddgaard would know what to do. But would she be right to tell them what she knew without going first to her father? Such thoughts chased each other like hounds after hares until she realized a clear course of action would never present itself. She would simply have to choose one and make the best of it.

In the end, she decided she must confront her father. And having made the decision, she did not want to delay the dreaded act. Dinner was almost two hours away; she would find him and get the duty done.

But first she had another task. She took a quill and parchment and wrote a note to Kaldor explaining her

139

brother's malicious deception and assuring him that she was not, nor would she ever be, pledged to King Agrilon. She asked him to come to the garden balcony at two o'clock the next afternoon to hear his song. She sealed the parchment and gave it to Elowynn for delivery. Then, with dread churning her stomach like writhing serpents, she took up her mandolin and went to find her father.

Because it was late afternoon, Avalessa did not even check the great hall but went straight to the architect's room. Slowly she opened the door and saw the crowned silhouette of the king slumped in the same chair and shrouded in the gray shadows. Without a word she lit the candle, took out her mandolin, and sat in a chair a few feet away from him. Softly she began singing the familiar songs her father loved. Soon he sighed heavily and began to stir. She continued to sing until the slackened muscles of his face regained their manly character and his eyes the look of life.

"Greetings, Father." Though she trembled a little, she laid aside her mandolin, went to him, and kissed his cheek.

"Thank you, my little Avalessa," he replied, smiling. "You always know exactly what I need."

"Oh, I wish I did know what you need." She drew her chair close to his, took his hands in her own, and drew a deep breath. "I must speak with you about a most unpleasant thing. Will you listen?"

"Of course I will listen to you, my dear daughter. I think you are the only one left who has my best interests at heart."

"You must believe that I do, Father, for I would rather tear out my tongue than to speak of what I now must." She swallowed hard and continued. "I will not dance around the hat. I . . . I have heard that last night you and . . . you and Lady Bloeudewedd were together in a locked room for

140

over an hour. And that you . . ." Her voice quivered, and she could not go on.

"Lies! Vicious, malicious lies!" The king glowered, and his face blazed like a hot coal. "Who told you such a thing? I will have the varlet hung."

"Are they lies, Father?"

"Of course they are lies. Someone bearing a grudge obviously made up the story. Where is their evidence?"

"Have you looked today at the pendant Mother gave you?"

"What does my pendant have to do with this?"

"Just take it out and look at it," Avalessa said.

Perivale unlaced the top of his tunic, reached inside, and drew out the silver chain that held the pendant. He turned it over in his hand. "The stone is missing. How did you know?"

"It was found in the bed where you met Bloeudewedd," Avalessa replied, tears now streaming and her voice a quavering wail. "How could you do this, Father? How could you do it to Mother?" She broke down and sobbed uncontrollably as Perivale looked on, his face now cold and impassive.

"There are some things you cannot understand," he said. "You don't know what it's like to come home each evening to a cold wife."

"She wouldn't be cold if your love still warmed her," Avalessa replied.

"How can I love someone who continually badgers me to curtail the good I would do for my kingdom and diminish my power to do it?"

"You mean she wants you to quit wearing the Crown of Eden, don't you?"

"I didn't want to become king, but your mother shamed me into it. She said if I ran from the task I would be a coward. So I took the throne and found ruling seven kingdoms to be a crushing burden. I found that wearing the Crown of Eden gave me the strength and wisdom to rule. But she fears it and urges me to bury it in the vault. She pushed me to the throne, then tried to deprive me of the strength to rule."

"She knows the crown is ruining you. We all do. Can't you see it? You aren't the loving husband and father you once were. You drive people away and throw them aside. Look at what you did to Lord Kalmor last night. Why wasn't the architect of your castle at the high table sharing with you the honor of its opening?"

"Do you know what honors and riches I have heaped upon Lord Kalmor? I gave him a title, lands, cattle, servants, and enough gold to last three lifetimes. What more could the man want?" Perivale leaned toward his daughter, and his eyes narrowed. "I think I see what is behind this little confrontation of yours. You are trying to leverage my sin against me for your own ends. You want me to withdraw my offer of your hand to King Agrilon so you can wed the architect's son."

"No, my wishes have nothing to do with this. I am concerned only about you and Mother. She is killing herself with worry, and you are killing yourself by wearing that horrid crown. All I want is—"

"Silence!" Perivale thundered, slamming his fist against the arm of his chair. "You are just like your mother. The two of you are conspiring against me. But it will do you no good. Do you hear? None at all! You will not strut in here acting as my judge so you can continue your dalliance with the architect's brat. I forbid you to see him again. Do you understand me? You will obey my word and marry King Agrilon."

"Last night you said you wouldn't force me to wed

142

Agrilon against my will. I hold you to that promise. I cannot wed such a man, and I will not wed him."

Suddenly Perivale drew back his hand and struck Avalessa full force on the right side of her face, knocking over her chair and sprawling her to the floor. She looked up at him in terror. He stood over her. His face turned beet red, and his eyes glared. He stepped toward her. Pushing desperately with her feet, she scrambled backward on the floor, shielding her burning face with her arm. She reached the wall and could go no farther, but still he came. As she opened her mouth to scream, he dropped to his knees, tears streaming from his eyes. He gathered her in his arms and held her to his breast and sobbed like a child.

"Oh, my dear little Avalessa. I am so sorry. How could I have done this to you? I am so sorry, my little one . . . so sorry. I don't understand. I would never hurt you. I . . ." Great, wrenching sobs convulsed the man.

After a moment's hesitation, Avalessa stroked the back of his head. "It's all right, Father. I'm not badly hurt."

Perivale arose from the floor and lifted his daughter to her feet. Looking haggard and miserable, he turned her face upward toward his. "Can you ever forgive me, my little love?"

"Of course I forgive you," she said, trying bravely to smile. "But can't you see now what the crown is doing to you? You have never in your life struck me. You couldn't have done such a thing before you wore the crown."

"Or it could simply be the burdens of ruling seven nations and the fact that I am very tired."

"No, Father. Can't you see that—"

"You need not say more about it, Avalessa. I promise to give the matter serious thought."

"Thank you, Father," she said, still trembling. "The future of all of us depends on it. Now you must go up to Mother.

She needs you desperately. Go to her and love her. Nothing but your love can save her from the grave."

Perivale nodded solemnly, and after clasping his daughter once more, he left the room and walked unsteadily down the corridor toward the stairway. Avalessa gathered her mandolin and returned to her chambers. She trembled so much that she could hardly fit the key to her door. She would not dine with her parents tonight. She was not sure she could stop either her trembling or her tears. Besides, her mother must not see the bruise that was already swelling her face.

When Avalessa awoke the next morning, the right side of her face from cheek to jaw had turned a blackish purple. Elowynn was horrified and packed the princess's face with a soothing poultice. She was curious as well, but the princess would not explain, and the loyal lady did not press her.

A feeling of impending doom hung about Avalessa from the moment she awakened. Elowynn sensed her sorrow, and as she served breakfast she did her best to cheer the girl with talk of the grand ball—who met whom, who said what, and who cast eyes at whom. The two young women were near the same age and more like sisters than princess and servant. Avalessa listened, and several times she smiled and even giggled in spite of the pall that overshadowed her. The arrival of the tutor lifted her a little more. The familiar simplicity of an old routine seemed to tell her that sorrows are momentary interruptions. In spite of them life goes on and always will.

After the tutor left, Elowynn brought Avalessa a small rolled parchment. She broke the wax seal and read it. The note was from Kaldor. He expressed sincere regret that he had acted so hastily in believing a rumor. He would be honored to stand beneath her balcony, entranced at her beauty and the loveliness of her voice as she sang their song. Avalessa's spirits lifted even higher. She thought for a moment of her father's command that she see Kaldor no more, but the king's contrition after striking her seemed genuine. She was certain he would no longer force her to wed Agrilon. She felt a tingling in her heart as she took up her mandolin and began to strum the melody.

Suddenly she stopped and touched her bruised face. Kaldor could not see her like this. Yet she was loath to postpone the meeting, especially after the misunderstanding at the ball. She would not play from the balcony. Instead, she would sit in the seat beneath it as he listened from the other side of the wall. They could talk to each other through the small, vine-covered gardener's window through which servants passed their tools, but she would allow nothing more. He must not see her bruised face.

Elowynn brought lunch, and the two women dined together as Avalessa told her about the coming of Kaldor. After clearing away the dishes, Elowynn said, "It's a cool day, and the stone bench will be cold. I will light an oil brazier and place it beside the seat where you sit."

After firing the brazier and setting it in the garden, Elowynn left for the afternoon to run several errands. Avalessa took her seat on the stone bench beneath the balcony of her garden wall.

When the castle clock struck two, she began to strum her mandolin and sing. Her voice had never been clearer, nor had she ever put such feeling into her tones. The foreboding she carried opened her heart to her deepest emotions, and her song lifted them above the garden and over the wall like a dove on the wing. It seemed that time paused until the last note shimmered in the air. When she had finished,

Avalessa laid the mandolin aside and looked toward the vine-covered window in anticipation.

After a moment she heard a voice—not from the window but from the top of the wall. "That was unspeakably beautiful, Your Highness."

She looked up to see Kaldor standing on the balcony. Quickly she wrapped her shawl about her head, hiding the sides of her face. "Kaldor! How did you get up there?"

"By climbing the vines, Your Highness." He walked along the top of the wall toward the steps that led down into the garden.

"No! You are not supposed to be here," she cried as he descended.

"I had to see you. Why didn't you sing from the balcony as you said you would?" He reached the garden path and began walking toward her.

"I—I can't tell you now. But I—"

He clasped her in his arms and smothered her words with a kiss. She resisted for a moment but yielded to the bliss, and slowly her arms encircled his neck.

Suddenly a bellow of rage split the air, and Kaldor was jerked away, causing Avalessa to reel backward. She would have fallen, but rough hands grabbed both of her arms and kept her on her feet. She found herself in the grasp of two castle guards, while her father clutched Kaldor by the neck of his doublet and shook him unmercifully.

"What do you mean dallying with the royal princess?" Perivale shouted, his face contorted with madness. He cast the boy to the pavement and turned to a third guard behind him. "Take this dung bag to the dungeon and have the barber rip away his manhood in the morning. Give him the night to think about what he is losing."

"No, Father, please!" Avalessa cried. "I beg you not to do this."

"What right have you to beg for anything," Perivale shouted. "You accuse me of infidelity while under my nose you play the whore."

"No! We never did anything wrong. We would never have—"

"Silence!" the king bellowed. "Take the carrion away," he ordered the guards.

He turned again to Avalessa, who was wailing softly as tears streamed down her face. "You scheming little vixen," he raged. "No wonder you wanted Kalmor honored. You defy me and refuse to wed Agrilon so you can make a garden nest with this fuzz-cheeked boy. Tomorrow morning that game will be over. He will be useless to you. I will have the contract drawn for your betrothal to King Agrilon.

"I will never marry Agrilon!" Avalessa cried through her tears.

"You *will* marry Agrilon!" the king thundered.

"I will not!"

The king's face turned livid, his lips curled into a snarl, and a guttural cry tore from his throat as he picked up the burning brazier and flung it toward the princess's face. Caught in the grip of the two guards, Avalessa could not dodge, but she managed to turn her head as the hot oil seared the bruised side of it. She screamed with the pain, but Perivale clamped his hand over her mouth, and the three men dragged her moaning and twisting into her chambers. They seated her on a chair, but she slid to the floor, writhing and clutching at her face. Perivale dismissed the guards and stood impassively over her.

"Let this be a lesson to you, Avalessa." He spoke as coolly as if he had done nothing more than switch her across the hand. "I am your father, and I will not be defied. You will obey me. From this day forward, you are not to leave

147

your chambers without my permission. I will have a lock fitted to the outside of your door. I will also post a guard there. You will play the wanton no more in my castle, nor will you spy on me and spread false rumors." Ignoring her moans, he turned and left the chamber.

15

Later in the afternoon Lady Elowynn returned to Princess Avalessa's chambers to find an armed guard posted at the door. "What has happened?" she asked the sentry.

"The king has ordered that Her Highness be confined to her chambers, my lady. Only you, the king, and such servants as are required will be allowed entrance and exit. No one else may see the princess without the king's permission. You must give up your key. After you enter I must lock the door behind you. When you need anything sent or when you need to leave, knock on the door, and I will open it."

"Why is the king doing this? Is the princess ill?" she asked.

"I know nothing of the reasons," the guard replied.

Alarmed, Elowynn gave the guard her key, and he let her into the chambers. Elowynn gasped as the door closed behind her. Avalessa was lying in the floor, moaning softly, holding her shawl to her face.

"Your Highness! What is wrong?" She knelt over the princess, and with some effort pulled the girl's hand away from her face. She cried out in shock at what she saw. The right side of Avalessa's face was a massive burn. The skin was blackened and curling, and it glistened with seeping fluids. "Oh! My princess! What has happened? Why has the physician not come?" Quickly Elowynn went to the water ewer and soaked a towel and applied it to Avalessa's face. Then she helped the girl to her bed and ran to the door, forgetting it was locked, and tried to wrench open the latch. She pounded and yelled for the guard to open it.

"Send for Manwold, the royal physician," she cried the moment the door opened. "Have him bring poultices for a burn and a draught to ease pain. And be quick about it."

The guard assented, and when the door closed Elowynn returned to the princess with a fresh wet towel. "What has happened, my princess?" she asked. But Avalessa simply shook her head as tears streamed from her eyes. Somehow the lady knew that some inner pain wrenched the girl—a pain even greater than her ruined face.

"Kaldor. We must save Kaldor," Avalessa moaned. "Father is going to wound him grievously." She whimpered and sobbed. Her pain was so great that she spoke in a near delirium, and Elowynn had trouble making out the words.

"Your father is going to wound Kaldor? What do you mean?"

"Unmanned. He's in the dungeon now."

"Kaldor has been unmanned?"

"Not yet," Avalessa moaned. "In the morning."

The lady began to form a dim picture of what might have happened. Apparently, the king had learned of his daughter's interest in Kaldor and had caught the boy listening to Avalessa's song. In one of his rages, which were rumored to be growing more frequent, the king had ordered the young man emasculated.

"What happened to your face, Avalessa?" Elowynn asked gently.

But the princess merely moaned and turned away as a fresh flood of tears streamed from her eyes. At that moment the chamber door opened and Manwold entered, carrying a wooden chest. Elowynn stepped aside, and as the physician attended the princess, she went to the door and called to the guard. When he opened the door, she stepped into the corridor and closed it behind her.

"The princess tried to tell me that Kaldor, the architect's son, has been sentenced to a horrible fate," she said. "I don't know whether it was true or whether her pain was speaking. What can you tell me?"

"She spoke the truth," the guard replied. "Kaldor is chained in the dungeon. In the morning he will endure the barber's knife."

"And what then?" Elowynn asked. "Will he remain a prisoner?"

"No, my lady. He will be released."

"And does his father know?"

"Kalmor the architect left the city the night of the ball."

Elowynn thanked the guard and returned to the princess's chambers. She waited while Manwold dressed the girl's wound, using poultices, wrappings, and salves from his chest. He mixed a powder in a mug of water, held up the princess's head, and put the draught to her lips. After settling her into bed, the physician turned to Elowynn and shook his head sadly.

"The wound will heal, but burns heal slowly. This one is large and deep. It will take weeks."

"Will she . . . Will her face . . . Will she heal completely?"

Again the physician shook his head. "She will regain

151

health and be free of pain, but she will be scarred for life. I am sorry." Elowynn's eyes filled with tears as Manwold continued. "I have given Her Highness a potion that should dull the pain and help her sleep. The poultice must be changed twice each day. I will return to change it myself in the morning. At that time I will teach you how to do it."

"Thank you, Manwold. I have one other question. We hear that Kaldor son of Kalmor is to be eunuched in the morning. Will you be the surgeon?"

The physician drew himself up and said, "My lady, I am a healer, not a butcher. The king calls for the barber Hineson to perform such outrages."

Manwold packed away his instruments and left the chamber. After the door closed behind him, Elowynn heard moaning from the princess's bed. She went to her mistress and leaned over her.

"Kaldor . . ." the princess murmured weakly. "Must save . . ."

"I promise to do what I can, my princess. You get still and sleep. I will return as quickly as possible."

Elowynn left the chambers and hurried to the stable. In the name of the princess, she demanded that a small coach be outfitted and a driver secured to take her immediately into Corenham. As soon as the coach was rigged, she instructed the driver to take her to the shop of Hineson the barber. It was dusk when the carriage descended the stony road into the city. The street was filled with carts and mounted riders and pedestrians carrying lanterns. The driver weaved his way through until Elowynn saw ahead the barber's red-stained rag hanging on a shop door. The coachman halted the horse, and immediately the lady went to the barber's door. She found it locked, so she pounded until it opened.

"D'ye mean to wake the dead, woman?" The voice came

from a sour, grizzled face with bleary eyes peering at her from beneath a mop of tangled hair.

"I am Elowynn, Princess Avalessa's lady-in-waiting. I have business with you in the name of the princess."

The barber's eyes widened, and he opened the door for her to enter. "How can I serve ye, m'lady?" he said.

"I am told that in the morning you are charged to maim Kaldor, the architect's son."

"Indeed I am, m'lady."

"What fee does the king pay for such butchery?"

"Nothin' more than what I be always gettin'—a half crown."

"The princess is prepared to pay you ten crowns if you will not perform the surgery. I will write you a bill to be drawn from the exchequer at Morningstone." She drew from her bosom the seal hanging from a chain about her neck. "You see that I carry the seal of the princess to confirm the draft. What do you say?"

The barber grinned, showing several gaps in his yellowed teeth. "Nay, m'lady. I'll not be defyin' the king even for a thousand crowns. When he found out, I'd be sufferin' the boy's own fate."

"The king will not find out."

"To be sure, he will find out. I've got to be showin' him the evidence of the surgery."

"I have already thought of that. Listen to me. Kill a large hog tonight and take its male parts, along with a quart of its blood, with you in the morning. When you go into Kaldor's cell, smear the blood on his clothing. Instruct him to scream and continue crying out and be doubled over in pain when the guards come to release him. Then you take the hog's genitals to the king. He will not look at them carefully. There is no reason why this will not work. You will be saving a young man's future."

153

"It's my own future I be worryin' about," Hineson replied. "'Tis a fine plan, m'lady, but I'll not be riskin' it even for—"

"Twenty crowns," Elowynn said.

The barber hesitated and scratched his chin. "Thirty crowns."

"Tweny-five," the lady replied. "And the princess will pay for the hog."

Hineson laughed, a raspy sound with no humor. "Done!" he said. "I'll get ye a parchment and quill."

When Elowynn returned to Avalessa, she found the girl sleeping fitfully, often calling out Kaldor's name. She leaned over the bed, put her lips close to the princess's ear, and said, "Kaldor is saved, my poor one. You can rest. He is saved." The princess seemed to hear and relax somewhat, though she slept fitfully throughout the night as Elowynn sat by her bed and held her hand.

Just after sunrise on the next morning, the guard at the dungeon ushered Hineson through the gate and walked with him toward the cell where Kaldor was held. Wrapped in a bloody napkin deep inside Hineson's bag was the grisly false evidence of his surgery that he would show to Perivale. Inside the same bag was a parchment imprinted with the seal of Princess Avalessa that he would take to the exchequer after seeing the king.

When the two men reached the darkened cell, the guard turned the key in the lock and swung open the creaking door. He held a torch before him as he stepped inside with Hineson following at his heels. Suddenly the guard stopped, and the barber bumped into his back. Hineson looked up to where the man was staring, and his eyes widened in horror. Swinging slowly before the two men was a pair of legs. They looked up to see the rest of the body, naked to the waist and hanging by the neck from the shirt tied to the rafter above. The guard felt the dangling hand and found it cold and stiff.

Kaldor was dead.

16

Avalessa's wound healed within three months, though the right side of her face from her ear to the corner of her mouth and from her eye to the line of her jaw was a massive scar. The once-velvety skin was now creased and ridged like eroded stone. The scar would have stiffened into a hard mask had not Lady Elowynn spent a half hour three times each day massaging the princess's face with a soothing balm Manwold had given her.

While Avalessa's face healed, her soul did not. On the morning after her wounding, Elowynn had gone to the barber Hineson to learn the outcome of her plot to save Kaldor and found that the young man had chosen death over Perivale's punishment. Avalessa was crushed by the news. For several days she brooded and wept as she lay in her bed or huddled in a dark corner of her room. Elowynn did what she could to cheer the princess, but the girl's losses were too great to be assuaged. She grieved the loss not only of Kaldor but of her loving father as well. This man who now bore her father's face and name was a cruel and tyrannical stranger. Often scenes rose in Avalessa's mind of happy times from her childhood when she had basked in her father's tender love and protection. Then the horror of his raging face intruded, livid and fiendish as when he had dashed the brazier at her, and she broke down and sobbed.

For days these losses so overwhelmed her that she thought little about her wounded face. But as the physician changed the bandages daily and Elowynn tenderly applied the healing ointment, she began to ask when her wound would heal. By the gloom of their expressions and the evasiveness of their answers, she came to realize that she would be permanently disfigured. Once the most desirable woman in the Seven Kingdoms, she would forever be a horror to look upon—an object of pity and compulsive stares. Her loss of beauty and desirability took its place among the other shadows that darkened her life.

For the duration of Avalessa's healing, Perivale strictly enforced his command that the princess should not leave her chambers or garden. He successfully kept her scarring secret. He had the guards who had witnessed the event falsely accused of treason and executed. He warned Elowynn to keep the matter to herself, threatening exile if she did not comply. The lady never would have consented, but she knew that if she were banished, Avalessa would be left in the care of a stranger or, worse, would have no one to care for her at all. Therefore, she swore to the king that no one would ever hear of the princess's scarring from her lips.

When Queen Rianna questioned her daughter's absence from the evening meals, the king explained that she had taken a vow of isolation to draw closer to the Master of the Universe. She would not be present at family meals for several weeks. The queen made no comment, but in her heart she knew that something was amiss. She tried twice to visit her daughter in her chambers, but each time the guard turned her away. Something had gone wrong, but she could not discover what it was. Both her husband and son were already estranged from her, and now she feared the same of Avalessa. After her third trip to her daughter's rooms, the queen returned to her own and crawled into her bed, where she remained, no longer attempting to rise. Servants brought meals to her, but she ate little and grew continually thinner and weaker.

The courtiers and suitors who had flocked about Avalessa at festivals and balls began to question her absence. Perivale explained that the princess was fulfilling the terms of a vow of isolation. But as they continued to clamor for her, he realized that he could not keep her imprisoned much longer. When Elowynn reported to him that the princess was healed, he had her veiled and ordered her to begin attending court balls and feasts. He always sat her at his own table, across from him but down a few chairs, where he could watch her. He surrounded her with older ministers and courtiers he knew and trusted. And when she left the table, he kept her under the escort of a guard who took her directly to her chambers, thus preventing young men from speaking with her at all.

Avalessa begged to see her mother, but Perivale denied her request. One evening as the guard knocked on her door to escort her to a ball honoring a delegation from Vensaur, Avalessa refused to go. "I will not attend another ball until the king allows me to see my mother."

The guard reported her refusal to the king, who came into her chambers himself and sternly commanded her to accompany him.

"I will not go. You must take me to my mother," she insisted.

"Then we will force you," the king said, nodding to his

guard. The guard hesitated, reluctant to manhandle the princess but equally reluctant to disobey the king.

"Won't that make a pretty spectacle?" Avalessa said. "Your soldiers dragging a screaming girl before ambassadors you are trying to impress. Go ahead. Try to take me."

"I will make you sorry for this, you wench!" the king growled, his face growing livid.

"What will you do to me, Your Majesty? Do you think you can hurt me more than you have? I care little what you do to me now. I will attend the ball only if you first take me to my mother."

For a moment the king looked as if he would strike her, but he relented and said, "Very well. I will give you a quarter hour with your mother. You will wear your veil, and you will say nothing about your wounding. I will remain in the room as you speak with her, and I assure you, if you violate my terms, I will indeed make you sorry."

Perivale himself escorted Avalessa to her mother's bed and remained in the room as the two women embraced and wept in each other's arms. For the moment Avalessa was glad of the veil, for it hid her shock at her mother's appearance. The woman was thin to the point of being skeletal. Her eyes were sunken, and the skin of her face was gray and pasty. Under the threatening glare of her father, Avalessa explained the veil as the second stage of her vow and evaded her mother's question as to how long she would wear it. She could tell by the look in the queen's eyes that she did not believe the vow explained the veil. Avalessa sat on the edge of the bed and held Rianna's bony hand. For all their long absence from each other, the two could say little under the watching eye of the king, and most of their talk was of things of little consequence. But they found nourishment in the touch of each other's hands and the sound of each other's voices.

When Perivale announced that it was time to leave for the ball, Avalessa bent down for a parting embrace. Rianna withdrew her hand from Avalessa's, and with surprising quickness lifted her daughter's veil.

"Oh, my poor daughter!" the queen wailed. "What has he done to you?"

Avalessa could not speak, but her face contorted into a mask of grief, and she reached for her mother's comforting arms and cried like a child. Immediately the king's hand gripped her and jerked her from the bed. Both women cried in anguish, and their arms stretched toward each other as Perivale forced the princess from the room and slammed the door.

"I met my end of our bargain, now I will hold you to your promise," he said as he gripped her arm and forced her, stumbling and crying, down the hallway. She could not stop her tears as the image of her mother's anguished face seared her mind. On reaching the door of the great hall, Perivale jerked her to a stop and turned her to face him. "You will now stop your whining and enter that hall as the daughter of a king. You gave your word, and I hold you to it."

Avalessa composed herself and stepped into the hall on her father's arm, glad that the veil hid her swollen eyes and tearstained face. She sat at her usual place, with the usual ministers and courtiers and their ladies surrounding her. As the diners became sated with meat and turned to their cups, the king rose and made his way down the table, greeting the various guests with a few pleasant words. When he reached the end of the table, he mixed with lesser guests, always working his way toward the door at the east end of the hall. Avalessa watched him. When he reached the door, he looked briefly about the hall and disappeared into the corridor. Three minutes later Bloeudewedd excused herself with a headache and left the hall by a door to the north. The pattern had become familiar to Avalessa, for she had seen it repeated many times since her brother had told her of their father's infidelity.

With the king gone, several other guests left the hall, including Lady Meliorre, wife of Sir Everedd, who had sat to the right of the princess. Moments later Rhondale came and sat in the empty chair. She had not seen him since the day after his malicious trick on Kaldor.

"Well, my sister, am I not a prophet?" he said.

"Get away from me, you snake! I will have nothing to do with you."

Rhondale grinned but made no move to leave. "Did I not tell you that our father's love for you had turned into something hideous? You would not believe me then, but perhaps now you see the wisdom of my words."

Avalessa stiffened but remained silent. Did Rhondale know what their father had done to her? Surely not. He was certainly speaking of the outrage against Kaldor.

"Does the veil hide your voice as well as your vaunted beauty?" he continued. "Or is it truly even beauty that the veil now hides?"

"What do you know of this?" she blurted, her voice betraying her fear that he knew her secret.

"I make it my business to know many things that other people don't see—and some things they choose not to see," the prince replied. "I wonder if you still defend our father's honor so adamantly."

"I hate my father," Avalessa replied emphatically through gritted teeth, shocking herself as well as Rhondale. She knew the burning acid searing her heart was hate, but she had never until now uttered the word. "He is the author of all our woes. He has killed an innocent young man who cared for me, he has estranged you from the family, he has robbed me of all hope of love, and now he is killing our mother." She looked at Rhondale through the haze of her veil and saw his mouth spread into a mocking grin.

"At last, my dear sister, at last you and I have something in common." Rhondale rose and bowed, then left the hall.

At that moment, Queen Rianna, lying prone on the bed in her chamber, drew in a deep breath broken by convulsive sobs. As she exhaled, her lips formed Avalessa's name. Her tears went dry, her eyes went sightless, and she did not breathe again.

17

The king's elaborate devices to keep Avalessa isolated to protect his awful secret were unnecessary. She had no desire either to be seen or to endure company. She would not be an object of pity or a monster causing children to scream and run for their mothers. She would not endure young men who once could not keep their eyes off her now glancing briefly and then turning away in embarrassment. Had King Perivale not locked her door from the outside, she would have locked it from the inside.

Indeed, her heart was now locked from the inside. It, as well as her face, had been scarred, and she could never allow it to hope for love. She knew her disfigurement would repel men. She closed her heart to all expectation of happiness and hardened it against any blow the future might bring. The scar on her heart would be a shield against more of the kind of pain she already endured.

For many days after her mother's death, Avalessa spent her hours brooding in the darkness of her room with curtains closed and candles snuffed. No visitors came to comfort her. Lord Reddgaard, Sir Danward, Sir Everedd, and many of the princess's friends in the court paid calls, but the guards turned them away at the door. When Lady Elowynn found the princess brooding in the darkness, she would open the curtains to flood the room with light. At other times she would insist that the princess walk with her in the garden. On such occasions Avalessa would stroll listlessly about the paths, oblivious to the trees, foliage, and fountains that had so delighted her before misfortune clouded her life. She did not wear the veil while within the walls of her chambers or garden but took care that it concealed her entire face whenever she attended balls and banquets at court. For a while Perivale demanded her presence at almost every event, but as the days wore on, he began to forget her and seldom sent for her unless the occasion was great enough that her absence would be questioned. She complied with these demands merely because she could not find the will to refuse. Nothing seemed worth the effort required to do it. She would not have bothered even to eat had not Elowynn set plates before her and nagged her until they were at least half empty.

Soon her infrequent appearances and the unexplained mystery of her veil bred speculation among the men of the Hall. The hiding of her face made the exceptional loveliness of her form even more apparent. Word began to spread throughout the Seven Kingdoms and across the Narrow Sea that the princess of Meridan possessed beauty so great that it must be hidden, for to look upon it would drive men mad. When these rumors reached the king, he was greatly relieved and encouraged them. Apparently, no one suspected that the goods were damaged, and he reveled in the additional fame the mystery brought him. The rumors also strengthened the plans he still harbored to wed his daughter to the advantage of his reign. Emissaries to Rhondilar told him that King Agrilon still wanted to wed the princess, but he was occupied with border uprisings and could not presently pursue the match.

One morning about a month after the queen's death, Elowynn looked out the chamber window to see Avalessa sitting unveiled on the stone bench in her garden. As usual, the princess merely sat and stared at the paving stones. An idea came into the lady's mind. She found Avalessa's long-abandoned mandolin and took it to the girl.

"Play a song for me," she said.

Avalessa shook her head and turned away, but Elowynn sat beside her and placed the instrument in her hands.

"Play Galleson's 'Peasant Dance,'" she said. "I haven't heard that song in years."

"No, Elowynn, I can't. I simply can't."

"Of course you can!" the young lady said brightly. "It's as easy as this." She picked up Avalessa's limp left hand and clamped it onto the frets of the mandolin, then picked up the princess's right hand and raked her fingers a few times across the strings.

Avalessa smiled wanly in spite of herself at the clumsy noise. After a moment she began to form a few chords as she softly strummed. She picked the opening notes of the peasant dance but played so slowly that it dragged along like a dirge. She paused for a moment as she plucked several strings and turned the keys until she was satisfied with the tuning. Then she began the minor chords of "The Knight's Lament," a ballad about a king's warrior who died in battle on his wedding day. On each full moon the spirit of the slain knight appeared in the chamber where his bride slept and sang a haunting lament that he was forever sundered from his love.

"Well, that's not quite the song I'd hoped to hear, but it's a beginning," Elowynn muttered as she left the mandolin with the princess and returned to the chambers.

From that day forward Avalessa spent two or three hours each day in her garden playing ballads of lost loves, dirges, mournful laments, and passages from requiems. Visitors to Morningstone, whose route from the castle gate to the great hall led them past Avalessa's garden wall, often paused, enchanted by the sound of the melancholy voice and haunting chords that met their ears.

On an afternoon not long after, Perivale grew weary of the petty squabbles, grievances, and wrangling among the knights in his Hall. As he sat on his throne, he began to feel a familiar dull pain encircling his head, as if the crown were contracting like the coils of a serpent. The pain grew steadily until he could not focus on the words of Lord Ashbough, who seemed to be saying that village ordinances should be bifurcated according to the adjudication of courtly infiltrations. As Ashbough droned on, the light from the high windows became unbearable, and Perivale excused himself, calling on Reddgaard to complete the meeting.

The king left the hall and went to the chart room, where he closed himself in and drew the curtains. He dropped into the chair in the corner and began to feel a sickening sensation as if he were falling into a bottomless pit of darkness. Fear rose in him as hideous voices railed at him from all sides, some shrieking like tormented spirits, others growling deep as thunder. As he fell he flailed about for a ledge, a rope, or anything he could grasp to stop the never-ending descent into utter madness. Avalessa! He needed Avalessa's songs. The bright sweetness of her voice would draw him from the pit. Where had the ungrateful girl been these past months? He had given her a fine mandolin and a magnificent garden, yet she hadn't the gratitude to sing her father out of the pit. Was she so selfish that she no longer cared for the father who had given her life? Had her frivolous dalliances with tradesmen's sons caused her to forget her high duty to entertain the king? He must hold the girl to her duty. With the shrieks of demons and spirits echoing in his brain, he struggled from the chair and stumbled to the door. After shouting into the corridor for a page, he staggered back to his seat and dropped heavily into it. Moments later a towheaded boy stood at the door, bowing low and asking what the king desired.

"Send the Princess Avalessa to me," he moaned, "and have her bring her mandolin. A guard must accompany her," he added as the page left to do his bidding.

When Avalessa entered, Perivale looked up and started violently. He had forgotten that the princess now wore a veil, and for an instant he thought she was the dead Rianna, shrouded as he had seen her on her bier. "Light a candle," he told her. He did not want to sit in the gloom, staring at the ghastly blankness of that veil. Why did the fool of a girl wear a veil, anyway? Without a word Avalessa lit the candle. But the light on the white linen chilled the king's spine. "Remove that veil and sit down," he said. Without a word, Avalessa removed the veil, and when Perivale saw the scar that covered the side of his daughter's face, he remembered what he had done.

"It always pains me to have to discipline you, my daughter. But you know it is a father's duty. As the old proverb says, 'The switch prevents the witch.'" He beamed a fatherly smile. "I hope you have learned your lesson and will behave better in the future. Now, let's put this little incident behind us and get things back to the way they were." Avalessa said nothing but kept her eyes on the floor as Perivale settled back in his chair and looked dreamily at the charts on the wall. "Do you remember when I used to take you on my lap and read to you from the tales of Lleweddan?" The king smiled warmly at the recollection, but Avalessa said nothing, and her expression did not change.

"Well, what will you play for your dear old father today?" he said, turning his eyes back to her. Avalessa took up her mandolin and began strumming the mournful chords of "The Knight's Lament," but Perivale stopped her and with irritation in his voice said, "I am the high king of the Seven Kingdoms. I would think you would do me more honor than to sit with the bad side of your face toward me. Turn the other way so I won't have to look at that horrible scar."

Avalessa turned and began the song once more. This time she got halfway through the first verse before the king stopped her again.

"What kind of song is this?" he demanded. "I don't want to hear dirges and laments. Play something happy."

She paused for a moment and began to strum. After a series of minor chords, she began singing in low tones "The Death of the Maiden" from Galleson's ballads.

After five lines the king shouted, "Silence! Why do you defy me, daughter? I told you I don't want dirges and laments. Give me a sprightly jig, or if you must sing a ballad, make it a happy one."

Once more Avalessa strummed her instrument and sang. But once more the song was of death and mourning. Suddenly Perivale reached out and grabbed a water pot from the table of parchments beside him and hurled it at the princess. She dodged to the side and felt the ewer brush her hair and then shatter against the wall behind her.

"Get out of my sight," Perivale said. His teeth were clenched, and his hands clutched the arms of his chair as he struggled for control.

Avalessa calmly stood, donned her veil again, and left the room. The guard waiting outside escorted her back to her chambers. From the moment she had left her door to the moment she entered it again, she had not spoken a single word.

18

The death of Queen Rianna ruined the plot of Lord Fenimar and his supporters. They had planned to expose the king's infidelity and depend on the moral outrage of the people to depose their monarch, leaving the throne open to Fenimar's claim. But when the conspirators leaked rumors of the affair to some of the knights of the Hall, they did not get the reaction they anticipated. Sympathy for the recently widowed king diffused the outrage. Infidelity to a mate was one thing; a lonely widower seeking solace in the arms of a beautiful woman was another. While many felt dismay at the king's immorality, few felt constrained to move against him.

The rumors reached Perivale's own ears. He did not cease his dalliance with Bloeudewedd, but the couple became more cautious and secretive, making it easier for those who did not want to force the issue to turn their heads the other way.

"I fear that our prosperity has buried our morality," Lord Reddgaard said to Sir Danward and Sir Everedd as they sat at their noonday meal. The two knights had come to Reddgaard proposing that they confront the king and demand that he give up his paramour. "The entire Hall now knows of it, and only we three care enough to do anything about it."

"You are right," Danward replied. "The men of the Hall simply don't want any stones falling onto their road to riches. Some are even taking measures to keep the people from knowing about the king's indescretion. They fear that his fall would destroy the Seven Kingdom alliance and their prosperity would come to an end."

Another turn that Fenimar and his conspirators did not anticipate was the ambition of Bloeudewedd. Her aged husband, Lord Weathereld, had recently become gravely ill. He was now confined to his manor without memory or control of his bodily functions, and his physician said he would not last a fortnight. With the king now a widower and her own husband dying, Bloeudewedd saw herself as the next queen of the Seven Kingdoms. Therefore, she began to hold herself aloof from Fenimar's plot and returned to Lord Kramad Yesenhad half the money she had taken to seduce and betray the king.

The holes she had probed in Perivale's armor for the sake of the conspirators she now exploited for herself. She massaged his pride with the oil of flattery and admiration and missed no occasion to garnish his wit with cascades of laughter. She oozed sympathy for the loss of his queen and scorned those who would not understand his desire to lead the Seven Kingdoms toward unprecedented glory. At her urging he began to have scribes record the history of his victories and accomplishments.

On a morning several weeks after his wife's death, Perivale, avoiding audiences with supplicants in the great hall, left the keep through the scullery door and walked about the bailey. As he neared the low wall of the training field, he heard the voice of Sir Rudmore bellowing at the young squires dueling with blunted swords. "Get that shield up, Jorgen. Do you want Bromont to split your skull? There, that's better. No! No! Bromont! A sword is not a club. Thrust with it! Don't swing it like you're hacking down briars. Jorgen, push him away with your shield. It's a weapon too. No! No! Keep your sword up. You've got to keep both moving at all times. Sometimes I think you goslings should take up knitting."

Perivale watched, grinning as he rested his arms on the top of the wall. The two young swordsmen were not doing badly, but Rudmore's warrior eye missed no fault in their style.

After a few minutes the king opened the gate and walked over to the assisting page. "Bring me a blunt," he said. "I'm a bit rusty, but I can still show these lads how it's done." A page brought him a blunted sword, a shield, and a breastplate. "This is all I need," the king said, taking the sword but refusing the shield and armor.

He stepped into the circle and faced Jorgen, keeping one hand behind his back. The squire attacked, using his best technique, but Perivale disarmed him in a few strokes. The young trainee attacked twice more, and both times the king penetrated his defense and pointed him with little effort.

"Keep your shield closer to your body," Perivale said as they met a third time. "Move it only to deflect blows you see coming from your left. Use your sword to deflect those from the right."

Jorgen heeded and stayed in the battle a minute or so longer before Perivale again put his point to the boy's chest. Bromont and the six other trainees also matched swords with the king, all with the same result. Perivale stepped out of the circle grinning and gave his sword to the page.

"You have not lost your touch, sire," Rudmore said.

"I needed that, Rudmore," Perivale said as he wiped a

cloth across his sweating brow. "I feel like a caged hawk in that castle, listening to peasants droning on about neighbors' cows trampling their turnips or complaining about the pittance of a tax we levy on their farms. I miss the feel of a sword in my hand, drinking the blood of an enemy. Sometimes I long for a foe to fight, a real battle to be won. When you read of the great wars of such kings as Boromaine or Carldane, you forget that those campaigns took only a few months out of reigns that lasted decades. Most of a king's life is spent in tedium."

"But it's a fine blessing to be at peace, sire," Rudmore said.

"True enough." Perivale sighed. "But I never realized peace would be so hard to endure."

He left the trainer and walked to the well, where the page drew him a bucket of water as he removed his tunic. He poured the water over his head and bare chest, then made his way back to the keep as he slipped into his shirt.

When he walked into his chambers, Bloeudewedd sat near the window, combing out her chestnut hair. "You should not still be in this room," Perivale said. "You should have left before dawn."

"Oh, you worry too much," she replied, smiling. "Everyone in the castle knows about us, and few care what we do."

"But those few could cause trouble. Reddgaard, Danward, Everedd—"

"What can they do? They are three against forty."

"I know. But it bothers me for them to know. We must not be so open. It's too late for you to leave now without someone seeing you. You will have to stay here the rest of the day."

"Is that such a terrible thing?" Bloeudewedd stretched provocatively and gazed at him through half-closed eyes.

"You need not even go back to the hall today. We can have our meals sent up."

"I don't want to spend the day cooped in this room like a bull in a pen." Perivale began to pace the floor. "I need to be doing something—not just sitting on that throne all day or attending balls or signing parchments. I need to do something I can see the result of."

"I have an idea," Bloeudewedd said, standing and walking toward him. She ran her fingers through his still-golden locks, let them run down to his wide shoulders, and drew them across his massive chest. "From the window I watched you sparring with the trainees this morning. You were magnificent."

"They are just stripling boys," Perivale said.

"But even against boys, your strength and skill stood you like an oak among saplings. And when you removed your shirt and splashed water over yourself, glistening in the sun like bronze, I almost swooned. It's a shame you must keep this magnificent body of yours hidden. Here is my idea: You must commission a statue of yourself—a majestic one on a high pedestal—and set it in a prominent place for all to see. It will keep you in the memory of the Seven Kingdoms for hundreds, even thousands, of years."

"We have no sculptors in the Seven Kingdoms capable of such a carving."

"Have Renalleo hire one from the countries around the Southern Sea."

"Such a sculpture could take a year to complete. I can't take a year from the throne and spend it sitting in a studio on the Southern Sea."

"You don't have to leave Corenham. Have Renalleo bring the sculptor to you and set him to the task here."

Perivale thought on Bloeudewedd's suggestion all that day and into the night. When he awakened her before dawn and sent her home under the escort of a guard, the idea kept him awake until the sun's first rays beamed into his window. He arose and looked out over Corenham, its golden-thatched cottages gleaming in the dawning light and pearl-colored smoke curling upward from stone chimneys. The tall projection of marble at the edge of Cheaping Square cast a shadow over the roofs of six cottages. Perhaps he could place his image at the base of that stone. But immediately he rejected the idea. The stone would overshadow the sculpture, making it seem small and insignificant. Suddenly a thought hit him. Could his image be carved into this stone itself? Even if the sculptor could utilize only half of it, such a statue would still be enormous. The stone towered above all structures in Corenham except for Morningstone Castle, standing four times the height of the cottages around it. He had passed near the stone many times and knew it to be solid and free of cracks and fissures. Yes, this stone would become his monument.

He knew Renalleo had come to Corenham the day before and would have stayed the night in the castle. Immediately he sent a page to awaken the merchant and have him meet the king for breakfast in the little hall. Renalleo arrived in the hall just after sunup. He had dressed hurriedly, and his cap was askew as he was ushered to the table where Perivale was already seated.

When the merchant had settled into his chair, still panting from his swift walk, the king turned to him and said, "Renalleo, I am ready to offer a commission for a monument that will make the name of some artist live until the end of the world."

Renalleo plunged his fork into the bacon on his plate. "It will be my honor to find you such an artist. What is the nature of the monument?"

175

"You know the marble stone at Cheaping Square? I want that stone carved into my likeness."

"The stone at Cheaping Square?" Renalleo almost choked on his mouthful of bacon. "That would be a colossal sculpture. You have seen the work I brought from the sculptors in my own country. I will see if any of them are capable of such a monument."

"No. I do not want some grotesque deformation like the trash you have brought from the sculptors of your own country. I want it to match the beauty of the carvings of the ancients."

"But, Your Majesty, I know of no such sculptor. The work being done today matches the sculpture of the ancients like a mud hut matches Morningstone Castle. But it's the best that's available, and I feel sure I can induce some sculptor from Hrombulous to carve your monument."

"You do not hear me, Renalleo." The king's voice carried a touch of impatience. "I want beauty, majesty, realism. Find me such an artist and induce him to come here."

"But, Your Majesty, you ask the impossible. If mere wanting such an artist could cause him to materialize from thin air, I would have a dozen working for you already. No one since Hrombulous fell has learned the art of the ancient stonecarvers. The quest is futile."

"Renalleo." The king looked sternly into the merchant's eyes. "For the past year you have brought me little worth having—chipped and broken fragments of stained marble. Each piece is more battered than the last. And the misshapen, amateurish junk your sculptors pass off for art today sickens me. You begin to tire me. Either you find the artist I want for my monument, or you will not enter my presence again."

"But, Your Majesty—"

"This audience is over. You may leave now," the king said.

Renalleo looked ruefully at the unfinished bacon and honey cakes on his plate, then rose, bowed, and left the hall.

All through the day Perivale's mind churned with thoughts of his monument. He did not send for Bloeudewedd that night. At dusk he went to the chart room, where he lit a candle, took up a quill, and began to sketch the rough outlines of a park at the base of the great stone. It would be a small matter to clear away the several cottages clustered about it. He drew on several parchments, impatiently discarding each before he finished. He had little skill at drawing, and his hands could not form the image in his mind. As his frustration mounted he began to feel the crown tighten around his skull. His head began to throb, faintly at first and then more persistently as he angrily ripped apart yet another failed drawing. Soon the pain grew so intense that he could no longer focus on his work. Finally he snuffed out the candle and sank back into the gray darkness of the room. He felt himself descending again into the horror of the bottomless pit. But before the darkness could engulf him, he struggled to his feet, and holding his head between his hands as he grimaced in pain, he stumbled toward the door. After fumbling for the latch, he managed to open the door and call to the page standing in the corridor.

"Send for Princess Avalessa," he groaned. "Have her bring her mandolin." The king reeled back to his chair and fell into it, where he sat moaning and clasping his head.

Moments later he heard the door open. He did not look up but called out in desperation, his voice a hoarse whisper. "Avalessa, you must play for me. You must. Give me songs of sunshine, dancing, and love. You must lift me up from this pit of terror that draws me into hell."

"I am not Avalessa, but I can help you escape the pit," said a masculine voice rich as the ringing of a great bell.

"Who are you? How did you get past my guards?" Perivale cried, straining his eyes toward the door but seeing nothing in the darkness.

The figure at the door lit a candle and set it on the table. The king looked on in wonder. Before him stood a tall man robed in the muted greens and grays of the forest. His hair and beard were long and shimmered white in the candlelight. His eyes shone deep and clear and reflected an infinite store of wisdom, which gave Perivale the impression of age beyond reckoning. But when he looked at the man's face, he amended his impression. The man was young. The skin was fresh and smooth, glowing with perfect health. Yet he sensed that the man was surely ancient, existing perhaps before the foundations of the world.

"I have many names," the man replied, "but you may call me Father Futuras. I have lifted the curtain of your heart, and I know the hideous monstrosity that lurks within it. You harbor a demon that has begun to devour your humanity. And it will consume you utterly unless you kill it, and quickly."

"What is this evil, and how can I kill it?" Perivale moaned through his pain.

"It is an evil that has lain sleeping deep in your heart, as it lies within the heart of every son of Adam and daughter of Eve. You kept this evil bound in its shroud and buried beyond reach, even keeping vigil over its grave until you wore the Crown of Eden. The crown weakened your vigilance, allowing this monster to emerge and rule your life. It grows ever stronger as you grow ever weaker. Now more of it lives within you than of you yourself. If you allow it to grow any stronger, it will smother you entirely."

"How can I stop it from growing?" Perivale pleaded.

"The only way to stop it is to kill it."

"Yes, I want to kill it," Perivale said, hope now lifting his voice. "I want to kill the monster. How can I do it?"

"You cannot kill it. I must do it for you. Do you truly want me to kill it?"

"Yes, I really do. Please kill the monster for me, Father Futuras."

"Very well. You must do as I say."

"I will. I will do anything. Just tell me what and I will do it."

"Give me the Crown of Eden," Father Futuras said, holding his open hand toward the king.

Perivale sat silent and unmoving for a long moment. "Give you the crown? What good would that do? How would that kill anything?"

"You said you would do whatever I asked. I ask you to give me the crown."

"But I thought you would ask for some great act of penance—to trek to Lochlaund's Black Mountain to cast a sacrifice into the cave of the Devil's Mouth, or to wear rags and ashes and pray hourly to the Master of the Universe for a month, or to fast for forty days, or to suffer flogging at the hand of the kirk's accorder, or to wear a crown of thorns pressed down upon my head like the Son of the Master. Indeed, I will do any of these things, all of which are more difficult than merely handing you this crown."

"I do not ask for deeds great or difficult or painful. I merely ask for what is necessary. I ask you to give me the crown. If you find that you cannot give it to me, then ask me to take it, and I will do it. But I will do nothing against your will."

"I would do as you ask were it not for the inanity of it," Perivale replied. "How can it make any difference in my heart whether a piece of metal rests upon my head? The thing eating away at me is a disease of the spirit. Removing this bit of metal and stone is a physical act. It makes no sense. Besides, this crown is not really mine. It belongs to the kingdom—the people of Meridan. I cannot rightly give it away, especially since giving it up is unlikely to resolve anything."

"King Perivale, I will not force you. But know this: If you do not give up the crown, your doom will be great. You will die a lunatic and a coward, and the thing you fear the most will be yourself. Your own image will drive reason from your mind. Your island empire will shatter, and Meridan will become a poor and common kingdom. The monument you plan to your own glory will stand as a monument to your shame. I tell you one last time, you can avoid this doom and live under the protection of the Master if you will simply give me the crown."

Perivale's eyes narrowed, and he peered at Father Futuras with suspicion. "Why do you burn so to have the crown? Would you use it to build your own empire? Perhaps you are in league with Morgultha, and this is a ploy to trick me into surrendering my kingdom to her."

As the king spoke, the outlines of the man at the door began to blur. Yet Perivale rattled on, and the robe and face of the strange man slowly became transparent until he was no longer visible. Perivale stopped short and looked about in horror. He felt the crown tighten, and his head throbbed with unbearable pain. He felt himself sinking into the black pit, and the hideous voices began to thunder, groan, wail, growl, and screech, resounding and echoing hideously in the dark chambers of his mind. He grimaced and clapped his hands over his ears but to no avail. Downward he plunged, flailing for anything that might stop his fall. The voices grew even louder and closer, until finally the only way he could bear them was to scream, long and loud, at the top of his lungs.

Part 2

The Sculptor

19

Far to the southeast of Meridan, across the Narrow Sea and beyond the land of the Frankens, lay the great peninsula of Appienne, thrusting far into the Southern Sea. At the time of Perivale's conquest of Morgultha on the Plain of Moriburne, a boy of seven played in a muddy street in the village of Paziona. The boy was beautiful. His dark, curling hair framed a perfectly formed face set with an elegant nose and full, sensitive lips shaped like Cupid's bow. But it was his eyes that enthralled everyone who looked upon him. Deep brown and flecked with gold, they gazed with solemn openness from a rim of dark, curling lashes, thick and long, that were the envy of many a budding maiden. The boy was tall for his age but well formed and graceful of movement.

Unlike the other urchins, who splashed naked in the puddles after the spring rains, the boy sat on the wet earth, his feet hidden in the muddy water of a fresh wagon track. His eyes focused intently on the activity of his fingers as they kneaded and stroked a gray-green lump of clay. On the ground beside him sat a little image of a lion, turning chalky gray as it dried in the sun. Oblivious to the squeals and laughter of the children playing tag about him, he did not look up or flinch as they splashed happily through the puddle where he sat, speckling his sun-browned skin with flecks of mud and water. He wiped a rivulet from his forehead and went on shaping the thing in his hands.

"What are you making?"

Davian turned in surprise. Screams and laughter could not break his concentration, but the gentle voice of Lavia could. The girl, a year older than Davian but no taller, gazed in awe at the thing in the boy's hands.

"It's a unicorn," he said, holding the figure toward her in his open palm.

"A unicorn? I never heard of such a thing."

"Papa told me about them. They live a thousand miles away, up north where dragons that breathe fire fly around eating cows, and huge serpents live in lakes, and giants and goat-men called fauns have caves in forests. But no one can see a unicorn."

"Then how does anyone know there is any such thing? And how do you know what they look like?"

"Well, only virgin girls can see them. I guess virgin girls told other people what they look like."

"What's a virgin girl?" Lavia asked.

"Um, I think it's a girl who is beautiful and never does anything wrong."

"It looks so real." Lavia's eyes were wide with wonder. "How do you make such beautiful things?"

"Would you like to have it?" Davian held the unicorn toward her.

"You would really give it to me?" she said, obviously pleased.

"Yes. I think you're a very virgin girl." He blushed deeply. "It's still wet, so you must hold it in both hands."

The girl cupped her hands, and Davian placed the little

184

image in them. She smiled warmly at him, then before he knew what she was doing, she kissed him quickly on the cheek and walked down the narrow lane toward her home, carefully holding the unicorn before her.

Davian watched her for a moment, then scooped up another handful of mud and began to make a faun. By the time the sun touched the broken-tiled roof of his family's cottage, the faun was set aside, finished, even down to such details as pupils in the eyes that glared from its gargoyle-like face. He gathered another handful of clay and began shaping it into the serpentine coils of a dragon when he heard the approaching creak and clatter of a rickety cart, punctuated by the muted clop of hooves in the muddy street. He dropped the dragon and ran toward the sound.

"Papa! You're back," he cried as the cart slowed to a stop. The burly man on the board dropped the reins and opened his arms toward the boy.

"Ah, my Davian," he said, ignoring the mud that streaked the child's skin as his son leapt onto the wagon and into his arms. "My dear little mudwright. Look at you! I've been gone hardly a week, but I'm sure you've grown three inches." He held his son at arm's length and gazed at him. "Where are your brothers and sisters?"

"The little ones are playing tag. Michelo and Carlini are feeding the chickens, and Mariona and Genida are in the house with mother."

"You don't miss a thing, do you? When you have clay in your hands, you seem totally absorbed, but you know exactly what goes on around you."

"Papa, let me show you what I've made." Davian leapt from the cart and ran to the puddle where he had spent the afternoon. He picked up the faun and carried it to his father as the weary man eased himself to the ground. "It's a faun,

185

like the ones you told me about from the country where Mama was born. This afternoon I made a unicorn."

Gently, almost reverently, Dantioni took the little image in his hands. The creature looked exactly as he had described it to his son. He marveled at the detail in the two tiny horns, the furry texture of the goatlike shanks, and even the clefts in the hooves. Where did the boy get such talent? A deep sadness clouded his eyes, and he seemed to age visibly.

"Don't you like it, Papa?" Davian asked.

"Yes, son, I like it. I like it very much." He gave the faun back to Davian and looked toward the cottage. "How fares your mother?"

"I'm sure she's much better. She got out of bed today and sat under the oak for almost an hour. Then Mariona helped her back inside. That does mean she's better, doesn't it? Some days she can't get out of bed at all."

Dantioni nodded but said nothing as he started toward the door of the cottage. "Call Michelo and Carlini to put up the wagon and horse." His voice sagged as much as his shoulders. "I will go in and see your mother."

"I will come with you, Papa. Mama hasn't seen my faun. She likes the things I make. They make her smile."

"I know they do, son. And I'm grateful to you for it. But you stay out here for a while and make another creature. I need to speak to your mother alone. You can show her your faun tonight."

The sagging wooden steps creaked as Dantioni wearily climbed them and opened the weathered door. The house had only three rooms: the kitchen, the bedroom where the eight children slept, and Dantioni and Felice's room, barely large enough to accommodate their bed. The bricks within the walls showed in many places where the mud daub had crumbled away. He entered the room and looked at his wife, lying still on the bed with her eyes closed. Despair swept over him. She was thinner even than when he had left, and dark circles surrounded her sunken eyes like the beds of parched moats. Her once-flaxen hair had lost its luster and lay lank about her ashen face. He stood for a moment, remembering her vibrant, young, and full of laughter when he had brought her back from the kingdom of Rhondilar on the great island in the Northern Sea. He bent to kiss her forehead, and her eyes opened.

"Dantioni," she said in a voice weak and raspy as he reached his arms about her and clasped her to his breast. "I'm so glad you are home. Did your journey go well? Did you . . . Did you . . ."

"Yes, all went well," Dantioni answered. "I got what I went for."

Tears gathered in the woman's eyes and she shook her head slowly, but all she said was, "That is good. Tell me all about it."

Dantioni sat on the bed and took his wife's hand. "It's a strange city, Hrombulous," he said, speaking in her native tongue. He knew it was easier for her since she had become ill and exhaustion had taken its toll. She had taught all their children the language and often used it when speaking with them inside the home, though she strictly forbade it in public. "Great, fluted columns and blocks of stone pocked with time and streaked with weather lie everywhere like the bones of the city's past. Elaborate fountains, now dry, boasting huge images of horses, gods, and goddesses adorn every major street. All are cracked and decayed. Ghosts of marble haunt the ruins—broken, weather-stained sculptures of heroes, emperors, dryads, and goddesses, most missing limbs or heads.

"Yet among these ruins, shops, stables, inns, villas, churches, and civic buildings now sprout like flowers on graves. And the people mill about their business, completely ignoring the bones of the past strewn about them. Indeed, the past doesn't exist for them, and neither does the future. Their only concern is today's food and tonight's bed."

"How did you find the studio of Myronius?" Felice asked.

"It wasn't as easy as I expected. Hrombulous has a district where artists live and work. Most of them band together in ateliers and share the rent as they work under a master. But not Myronius. He works alone."

"Why does he work alone?" she asked with a hint of apprehension. "Does he not get on well with people?"

"No, it's the nature of his art. His work is different from the others. He strives for what he calls idealism, while all the others do stiff and blocky images. They want no part of him. I heard one artist accuse him of slavishly copying nature because he has no inner inspiration. But to tell the truth, I think they envy his talent." Dantioni did not tell her that the bishops of Hrombulous disapproved of Myronius and his art. He knew she would abandon their plan if she knew the sculptor was at odds with the ecclesium.

"But you found him, and you showed him Davian's images."

"I did. But when I told him who had made them, he wouldn't believe me. He insisted that no child of seven could do such work. However, when I wouldn't change my story, he began asking questions. What training had the boy had? Where did he live? What was his temperament? Was he healthy? Did he love making the clay images? When I was sure he believed me, I told him why I had come—that I was looking for a sculptor to whom I could apprentice my son."

"Will he take him?"

"First he asked why I had chosen him. I said my son was

188

already a better artist than any other I had found in Hrombulous. For a moment he just sat there, stroking Davian's little centaur. Then he said he had long thought of taking an apprentice. He's getting older, and he has spent his life trying to revive the sculptural techniques of the ancient Hrombulans. If he doesn't pass on what he has learned, it will die with him. The other artists say that man's art should look forward and shouldn't try to emulate the tired work of the past. He thinks that—"

"You exhaust me, husband, with your lessons on art. Just tell me whether he will take our son."

"As I was about to say, he wants an apprentice, but not a child of seven. And he isn't quite convinced that seven-year-old hands molded these images. He wants proof. He wants the boy to come to him and mold two or three figures in his presence. Then he will make a decision."

"So you didn't strike a bargain with the man."

"It's as good as done, wife. When he sees the magic of Davian's hands at work, how can he fail to take the boy? I will take our son to Hrombulous in seven days, and I know Myronius won't let me bring him back."

"Oh, my beautiful little Davian, I will never see his angel face again." Felice began to sob until a fit of deep coughing gripped her. Her husband looked on helplessly, sadness clouding his eyes. "But it must be done," she said, dabbing her eyes with the corner of the sheet, "and for Davian, no better future is possible. You did well, my husband. What arrangements have you made for our other seven jewels?"

"Mariona will work in the vineyard of Guillina. She will do well as a vinedresser. You know how she loves growing things. Genida will work as a maid for the prefect. Michelo will apprentice to Carilliano the stonecutter. He needs a big, strong boy to load stone onto his carts. Carlini will work with me delivering coal. As for the younger children, your sister Mariella will take the twins, and my sister will take Gavrenia. So you needn't worry about any of our darlings, my love. They will be cared for."

"Thank you, my Dantioni. You have been a good husband. Life has been good to me but not to you. You made a bad bargain when you gave up your dream to bring me back from Rhondilar. You would have been a fine scholar in the university. You wasted your education when you defied your father and wed me. When I leave, you will have nothing."

"Don't talk like that!" Dantioni spoke sharply. "You have been the joy of my life—my love, my home, my comfort. How can you say I will have nothing? You may leave this world, but you will never leave my heart. And I have the eight fruits of our love. I will see you in their eyes every time I look at them or even think of them."

"But they will be scattered hither and yon. How can you still be a father to them?"

"I will see each of them every Sunday," he promised. "And Davian I will see twice every year."

Felice closed her eyes and sighed, and Dantioni knew she was content.

Seven days later he packed all of Davian's belongings in a single hopsack bag and took the boy to Hrombulous to meet the sculptor Myronius. After four more days had passed, Felice heard the slow, uneven clop of the horse and the heavy groanings of her husband's cart. She looked out the window as it stopped at the door of their cottage. Dantioni was alone. She could not help but notice that his shoulders sagged a little more and his movements were heavy and slow as he eased himself down from the cart. She turned her head away, and all that was left of her tears was a moist place on her pillow.

20

Myronius ran a brush through his iron-gray hair. It did little good, for the thick waves merely sprang back to their gorse-bush shape. He splashed his face with water from the clay basin on the unpainted table that stood in the rudely framed compartment that served as his bedroom. Ferato's rooster crowed again, and Myronius looked out his window. The rim of the sun glowed red behind the clusters of daub-and-wattle cottages filling the hillside that formed his horizon. It was time to wake the boy. He walked out into the high-roofed hall that was his studio and wound his way around the scaffolding frames, tables, ladders, and marble blocks that filled the space.

He grimaced as his shin hit something hard and unmoving. "I wish that boy would put things where they belong." He shoved aside a wooden platform. An instant later he stumbled into the cart and remembered that he had moved the platform himself to make room for the vehicle. He had brought it into the studio the day before to load the beams and chains they would need for today's task. The cart was stout and heavy, with solid oaken wheels rimmed with half-inch metal bands. Myronius worked his way around the cart, his muscular bulk bumping and rattling in the darkness like a blind bull. As he approached the far corner, he saw by the dim light from the window the long table on which rested the various shapes the boy had carved or molded—horses, goats, dogs, and children, as well as centaurs, dragons, sphinxes, and other fabulous creatures. Some were of clay, others of wood or soapstone. He neared the corner where a cot and a small table made up the boy's home. A shadow stirred in the darkness.

"Good morning, Myronius." The sculptor noted that the boy's voice had definitely deepened. He no longer sounded like a girl.

"Good morning, Davian," he boomed jovially. "If you're up and dressed, we can be on our way. Oh, and be sure to bring your life-size cartoon of the gladiator."

"Why do I need to bring that?" Davian asked.

"Don't ask questions; just bring it."

Myronius unbarred the doors, and together the man and boy swung them open, revealing a sky just beginning to glow orange on the horizon. Myronius lit a lantern, and they walked to the stable, where each brought out one of the horses. Davian secured the bridles on their heads as Myronius rigged and hitched them. The big man mounted the board and drove the cart from the building. He stopped as Davian closed the doors and then climbed onto the board beside him. The boy was fourteen now and growing tall and strong.

"Did you bring the drawing?"

"I brought it. But why do we need it?"

"You will know soon enough."

The red sun bloomed like an opening flower on the horizon, and cottage windows began to glow with hearth light as the ponderous cart lumbered along the rutted road. Davian shivered and drew his cloak about his ears as his

192

breath fogged the air before him. "Why do you always go to the quarry for your own stones?" he asked. "Hadrianni, Flaviel, and all the other sculptors have theirs delivered."

Myronius snorted, a great puff of steam shooting from his nostrils like smoke from a dragon. "For the kind of work they do, it hardly matters what kind of stone they get. Limestone would do well enough. Indeed, I don't think they care. They decide how to carve after they see the shape of the stone. I must have a stone that fits what I want to carve."

"Why do you hate them so?" Davian asked.

"I don't hate them at all. I say nothing against them as men. But their art, ah, that's another matter. It's a foul odor in the Master's nostrils, as is virtually all the sculpture that has come out of Hrombulous for the last five hundred years."

"Perhaps you don't hate them, but they hate you. I heard one of the stonecutters at the quarry say that you are riding into the future sitting backward on your horse. They say you look only to the past. Is that true?"

"I am aware that the other artists in the city hold me in contempt. I hear the same gossip you do. They disdain my work because it reflects a style of art that is five hundred years old. They think I am tied to a past that no longer exists—and to their minds, shouldn't exist. They think anything old is by definition bad, that only the new and novel has worth."

Davian sat quietly, watching the bobbing of the horses' heads as he reflected on what his master had said.

"But why do people buy more of their work than of yours?"

Myronius sighed. "The main reason is the ecclesium. The bishops adorning their abbeys and cathedrals will not commission the kind of idealistic forms I create. They want all figures to be plain and devoid of beauty—almost to the point of grotesqueness. They condemn any work patterned after the old, idealistic art, which frightens many people from buying it. Then others don't buy it simply because they want only what everyone else has."

"Why do the bishops want their art plain and ugly?"

"They mistrust the physical world." Myronius's hands were as expressive when he talked as when he sculpted. He held the reins with his left hand and carved his arguments in the morning air with his right. "The bishops point to the ruined beauty lying around us in the sculptures and buildings of old Hrombulous and say it was preoccupation with beauty that brought down the city and its empire. They say that beauty enticed people to seek pleasure instead of the spiritual ideals of the Master of the Universe. So when they began to rebuild a new civilization on the rubble of the old, they insisted that art must shun physical beauty. The faces and figures they approve must be plain, severe, angular, even crudely rendered and devoid of detail. They believe that by removing the distraction of beauty, art will reflect the spiritual instead of the physical."

"But I don't understand, sir. Are crude and ugly things more spiritual than beautiful ones?"

Myronius laughed. "Your mind is as nimble as your fingers, boy. No, ugly things are not more spiritual. The Master himself never created anything that was not beautiful or meant to be beautiful."

"But he made people, didn't he? We're not all beautiful. In fact, I've never seen a form or face that was quite perfect."

"The Master is the source and essence of all beauty, and originally, everything he created reflected his own nature. He infused mankind with beauty, joy, and love and intended our lives to be filled with nothing else. You know how

194

things went wrong. The enemy contaminated all creation, infecting it with ugliness, evil, hate, and sorrow."

Myronius reached behind the board and drew out a stoppered jug of warm mead wrapped against the cold in heavy sacking. "You'll find two cups beneath the board," he said as he handed Davian the jug. "A drink will stave off the morning chill."

Davian poured the mead and sat huddled in his cloak as he enjoyed the warmth of the cup in his hands. "If the Master intended everything to be beautiful but it got contaminated, why do the bishops want to take away what beauty remains?"

"Like I said, they don't trust it. They think it lures people away from the Master."

"But they are wrong, aren't they?" Davian asked.

"Yes, they are mostly wrong, but they do have a point. In this world where men and women are slaves to inner cravings and determined to get all their itches scratched, yes, beauty can lure them into raw sensuality. But it's a danger inherent in all creation, because everything the Master made is infused with beauty. If we try to reduce the risk by shutting our eyes to beauty, we deny the heart of all creation and fail to praise the Master for his finest gifts."

"But if beauty leads men and women away from him . . ."

"It's not beauty or the desire for it that's the problem. It is desiring to possess a beauty that doesn't belong to you, or indulging in more of it than you need, or worshiping beauty instead of its source, or craving it inordinately, or pursuing it for your own pleasure while ignoring the needs of others.

"The bishops think my sculptures lead people to seek the beauty of the world instead of the Master. Where in thunder do they think the beauty of the world comes from?" The big man's voice rose, and he shook his head in exasperation. "Can't they see that the beauty of the world expresses the nature of the Master? It declares his glory. The highest purpose of art is to help others look beneath the blight of the fall and show how the beauty of creation reflects the Master, whose nature is beauty and perfection. Ugly, crude, or distorted art can show nothing about him."

"Then how can the bishops say that artists must subordinate physical beauty in order to show the spiritual?"

"It's a confusion of the mind." Myronius punctuated his assertion with a flick of the reins, causing the horses to pick up their pace. "We mortals cannot know anything of the spiritual except as it is displayed in the physical. Everything we know, whether spiritual or physical, comes to us through our five senses. The physical world is all that is available to those senses. Therefore, all art is sensual—even ugly and distorted art—simply because the only way we can experience art is through our senses. But then all knowledge and experience is sensual for the same reason. Though we artists strive to show the inner truth of the soul, we have nothing to work with but the outer appearance. We show the spirit by how we present the body. We must plumb the soul and create a body that reflects the inner truth of it."

"So art that shows nature at its truest is good?"

"That's close to right, boy, but not quite. If by 'showing nature at its truest' you mean freeing nature from the effects of the fall and showing it as close to the Master's intent as you can, then the answer is yes. But an artist can follow the forms of nature accurately with no intent of leading the viewer's thoughts to the Master."

"I don't understand."

At that moment the road approached a field littered with lichen-covered fragments of weather-streaked sculptures and broken, fluted columns lying among the weeds like bones on an ancient battlefield. Here and there among the ruins a few columns remained upright, some still supporting fragments of roofs.

"Do you see the figure of the man over there?" Myronius pointed to their left at a mottled statue of a male nude. Its head and left arm were missing. "Look at his poise. See how straight he holds himself. His muscles are well defined but not overwrought. They show strength but not brutal force. His chest is broad and powerful, yet he seems relaxed and confident. We can see in this image more than just a man. We see the spiritual qualities of strength and nobility. We see something of the dignity of man in this piece because its forms and attitudes are focused and idealized, whereas in actual people that glory and dignity is often hidden beneath the distorting effects of the fall."

When the cart had lumbered another fifty yards, Myronius pointed to another statue just ahead of them, this one a female nude. "Now, this artist was equally skilled in carving an ideal image. The woman is well formed and perfectly modeled, but the artist's intent was altogether different."

"How can you know his intent?"

"It's quite clear by what he emphasized in the form and attitude of the figure. Look at the exaggerated amplitude of the hips and breasts. And her pose is not at all noble and unaffected like the male we just saw. See how she puts her weight on her right leg, emphasizing the outward thrust of her right hip and the rise of her left shoulder? Her pose greatly exaggerates the undulating curvatures of her body, especially those parts that differentiate her sex. Everything about this image is voluptuous. It is designed not merely to show pristine beauty but to incite feelings of desire."

"But aren't feelings of desire also from the Master? Otherwise how would the race continue?"

"Good thinking, boy!" Myronius grinned and hit Davian's shoulder playfully with the heel of his hand. "You are right, of course. But those feelings are so strong that they don't need encouraging, especially since the fall, which so weakened our wills that we now find lust difficult to contain."

"But maybe all nude statues have this effect simply because they are nude, whether or not the sculptor intended it," Davian said.

"There's a kernel of truth in what you say. Some people will always have voluptuous reactions to any ideal work of art, whether or not the artist intended it, just as some men will always have voluptuous feelings about any beautiful woman. You cannot stop men and women with impure minds from lusting after the Master's creation. But when an artist creates a statue like this female, his intent is obvious and such a reaction is inevitable.

"That female was carved some two hundred years after the male, and it reflects the kind of decline that prosperity tends to inflict on a culture. As people prosper, they tend to descend from idealism into pleasure seeking, and from pleasure seeking into license. When individuals resist all limits to their pleasure, nations lose the mortar that holds them together, and they collapse. Then leaders of the ecclesium rise from the rubble and seek to reestablish stability by denouncing all pleasure, including the enjoyment of beauty." He put his fist to his chest and frowned as his voice took on the stentorian tones of an ecclesiastic orator.

"Is there no good at all in the icon art the ecclesium endorses?"

"Well, it does give sculptors with little talent a way to make a living," Myronius grinned, "and it's much easier to become a sculptor with such unexacting standards. You

198

will apprentice with me for ten years before you are ready for your own commissions. Apprentices to Hadrianni and Flaviel can be as good as their masters in three or less."

Myronius stopped talking and watched the road ahead, which was now sparkling like a field of diamonds as the rising sun infused each drop of dew with a little copy of itself. They were nearing the quarry of Penoa Mountain, and ahead they could see glaring in the sunlight the white, craggy bluff that supplied marble to the sculptors of Hrombulous.

As they approached the gate, Myronius looked over at Davian. "Did you bring your drawing?"

"Yes, I've got it in here." Davian patted the leather satchel in his lap. "But I still don't know why you wanted me to bring it."

"Because today we shall select a stone to fit that drawing. It's time for you to carve your first real marble."

21

Myronius walked around the stone gladiator, still set on the wooden platform where Davian had carved it. This warrior was no brute thrown to lions on an emperor's whim. His stance expressed courage and readiness, yet his face reflected an untroubled acceptance of his fate with no trace of anger or despair. Even the eyes, stone though they were, met the danger before him with confidence—confidence not in victory but in his own well-being in spite of the outcome. How had Davian managed to get hard marble to convey emotions so delicate? How did he get the skin so velvetlike? The boy had rare genius. Somehow every seed Myronius dropped into the young man's mind germinated and spread to his hands like living tendrils. Myronius knew his pupil's ability would soon surpass his own.

"I wonder if my own masterpiece will be not something I've carved but the boy himself," he muttered.

At that moment the side door swung open, and Davian entered carrying a pail of water. He set the bucket down and looked at his master. "I think the gladiator is finished. I'm ready for your critique," he said.

The sculptor did not answer for a moment but continued to gaze at the statue. "Come here, Davian. It's time we had a talk."

They sat at a nearby table, and Myronius poured two cups of mead. He looked soberly at Davian and stroked his beard with his fingers. "You know of the agreement I made with your father when I took you in. You receive instruction and experience from me—as well as food and lodging—and in return you help me with chores, clean the studio, do little jobs and errands, and in time assist me with my own work. As you become able to take commissions of your own, the fees you earn are mine until the end of your apprenticeship."

Davian nodded in assent, his mead yet unsipped.

"As you know, I have sold many of your small pieces already in the nine years you have been with me—clay figurines, terra-cotta house pieces, bronze castings, wood carvings, and even a few of your soapstone practice pieces. Everything you create sells quickly, and it brings twice the price of anything similar in the marketplace. This gladiator will be no exception; it will bring a fine price. A merchant from the city saw it a week ago while you were polishing it and offered me three times what I expected to get."

"Three times the price?" Davian was stunned. "Perhaps the statue isn't as bad as I feared."

"And just what did you fear? That it might come alive and slay you?"

"No, but I thought you would notice the hands being too large and the place in the back of the head where I chipped away too much hair, or the—"

"Davian, no piece of art is ever perfect. You will never be completely pleased with anything you do. And that's good, up to a point. But you must reach that point and let go. I assure you, the gladiator is a fine piece of work. There isn't an artist in the city who can approach it."

"I know of one who can surpass it," Davian said, grinning.

"I'm not sure that will hold true for long," the sculptor replied. "You will take the art far past where I ever could, which brings me to the point of this discussion." He took another sip from his cup and wiped his mouth with the back of his wrist.

"It's becoming apparent that with you here, this studio will start turning a handsome profit. Though the fees from your work are legally mine, I cannot in good conscience take them all. Not only do your sculptures draw good prices, they draw more business. Since the ecclesium doors are shut to me, my clients were few before you came. But in spite of the bishops, people will naturally turn toward good art when they're exposed to it. You can fool the elite with bad art, because they can be induced to buy for reasons other than quality. They find security in comparing their possessions with their peers, and like a herd following a wandering cow, they will go wherever current fashion leads them. They will buy whatever others consider fashionable. But you can't so easily fool the common people. They will not part with their money for foolery. Because your work is prospering my studio, I will start paying you a wage—not a great one, but enough that you can put away money for the future. In addition, I will give you a third of all commissions you take for yourself. And furthermore, I want to make you heir to this studio. You share my vision for reviving the art of Hrombulous's classic period, and you will advance idealism far beyond where I leave it. What do you say, son?"

Davian was stunned. Suddenly he saw great doors opening onto a future bathed in sunlight. He would never again taste the poverty that had plagued his childhood. In fact, he could soon lift his family out of poverty. He would be able to dedicate his life to his art. His mind whirled, and he could hardly speak. "I—I thank you sir. I never thought—I mean, I came here a beggar, with nothing. You have done more than take me in and give me food and shelter, even more than giving me a trade. You have been a second father to me. And I'm deeply grateful. It's more than I deserve or could ever earn."

Myronius grinned, his big teeth gleaming within his silver beard. "Every good that comes our way is more than we deserve or could ever earn. It's called grace, my boy. The Master delights in giving us joy as a lover delights in the pleasure of the beloved, and I am sharing his delight by passing on to you what he has given to me."

Davian was stricken with the enormity of the gift and could find no more words to express his feelings. Fumbling, he got up from the table. "It's time for dinner. I will see what I can find in the scullery."

"No, no, my boy!" Myronius boomed, slapping the table to punctuate his words. "It's a night not for bread and cheese but for veal and mutton. We have much to celebrate—the certain sale of your gladiator, your becoming my heir, and one other thing I have yet to tell you. Come, let's get down to Papialona's before dark."

Half an hour later they sat at a table on the veranda of Papialona's public house, breathing the spring air and sipping red wine. The sun had just set, and lanterns mounted on poles around the perimeter of the veranda bathed the diners in soft light, aided by candles on each table. Davian loved this place, though it had been many months since he had been here. It was neither new nor elegant, but it was lively. He tapped his foot to the rhythms of the small band of mandolin, flute, and timbrel playing lustily from the corner. His eyes followed the frenzy of brilliant color in the skirts and scarves of the women dancing with their men on the broad floor. Many patrons who were not dancing clapped their hands to the music, while others sang or bobbed their heads. The riverlike sound of human conversation filled the air, often accented with eddies of laughter.

A cascade of bright feminine laughter sounded to Davian's left, and he turned to see a serving girl setting a steaming bowl before a grinning patron, who ignored the food and took the girl by the wrist. The man stood and swept her into the dance as Davian watched, fascinated by the lively grace of her movement. After the dance she returned to her tables, filling glasses from her pitcher and laughing with the bantering men.

Soon she came to Myronius and Davian. "It's a fine evening to be out, no?" she said, smiling broadly, her white, even teeth flashing in the torchlight. "My name is Emeralda. What can I bring you fine-looking men tonight?"

Davian found her even more beautiful than he had first thought. Her wide eyes were the color of amber and rimmed with long, black lashes. Her hair, dark and lustrous, flowed about her head, soft and billowing as clouds, and rested lightly on her shoulders. Her smooth, olive skin was flawless, and a delicate flush of rose tinted her cheeks. Myronius ordered sausage stew, and Davian echoed his choice without thinking, gazing at the girl like a dog at a beefsteak.

"A fine choice." Emeralda smiled. "Papialona's sausage is the best in Hrombulous. You will have it shortly." She turned with a swish of her skirt and smiled over her shoulder as she walked away.

Myronius watched his young companion, his eyes twinkling. "You're gawking like you've never seen a woman before."

"She is beautiful," Davian said.

"You're a strange one, Davian. I've had the most beauti-

204

ful women in Hrombulous pose in my studio all the years you've been with me, and you study them as coldly as a judge on a bench. But I bring you out for the first time in months, and you stare in a trance at the first girl who flutters her lashes at you."

"But she is beautiful."

"You said that already. Ah, well, I suppose it's natural that you would see women a little differently now that your voice has dropped an octave and your chin is sprouting fuzz. But if I can get your attention for a moment, we need to talk about what I came here to tell you."

"Very well. I'm listening. I'll not give Emeralda another look." Davian faced his master with determined attention.

"Last week I got a new and lucrative commission. Since I'm already working on the figure for the magistrate's fountain, I want you to take this new assignment as your own."

"My first commission?" It was a heady night for Davian. "Do you really think I am ready?"

"Yes, I do, especially since I will be in the shop with you. You needed me very little on the gladiator, and its quality justifies its price. I have no doubt you can undertake this project."

"Tell me what it is."

"You know of the trader Melanius."

"Of course. Everyone in Hrombulous knows of him. He has caravans and ships all over the continent and the Southern Sea," Davian replied.

"That's the man. His daughter is soon to be wed, and he has built her a villa just outside Florienta. He wants a life-size garden statue of a dancing maiden as a wedding present."

"Why did Melanius come to you for the sculpture?"

205

"He shares my view of art. He wants the dancing maiden to express the beauty and joy of wedded love. No other studio in Hrombulous knows the meaning of these words. So if you want the commission, it is yours."

"I am greatly honored, Myronius. I can hardly believe you would trust me with such an assignment. Yet I will take it because I trust you. If you think I can do it, I must believe I can."

Myronius lifted his cup in a toast to the young man's success, not only with the carving of the dancing maiden, but in following his brightened path into the future. As they downed their drink, Emeralda arrived with their stew. She smiled and glanced often at Davian as she set their bowls and spoons before them, and her amber eyes and even teeth dazzled him yet again.

"Can I bring you anything else?" she asked, and Davian thought her voice had the quality of dark honey.

She turned away to serve other diners but not before flashing another smile toward the young artist. He watched her walk away, her skirt swishing from side to side with the entrancing rhythm of her swaying hips.

"Your stew is getting cold," Myronius said, his voice reflecting the twinkle in his eye.

"I think I've already found my model for the dancing maiden," Davian said as Emeralda disappeared through the door.

22

Davian walked onto the terrace at Papialona's and found a table near the door to the kitchen where he would be sure to see Emeralda when she emerged. He heard her silver laughter before he saw her. He looked toward the sound to see her dancing in the arms of a slightly drunken sailor, her dark tresses flying about her shoulders as he nuzzled his stubbled chin against her neck. A surge of jealousy reddened Davian's face. Why would she dance with such a man? When the dance ended, the sailor lunged clumsily, trying to clasp her in his arms. But laughing again, Emeralda whirled away, leaving him clutching the air and staggering into a table.

"Emeralda," Davian called. She turned, and a broad smile lit her face.

"My Davian, you have come again," she said as she approached his table. "We must have fed you well, no? Where is your father?"

"My father? Oh, you mean Myronius. He's not my father; he's my master. He didn't come tonight."

"Your master? You don't have the look of a slave."

"Oh, no. I'm not a slave; I'm a sculptor. That is, Myronius is a sculptor, and I'm his assistant—er—apprentice."

Davian felt his mind spinning like a leaf in the wind at the closeness of the girl and the liquid depth of her eyes, and his tongue could deliver no coherent thoughts. He was young and still growing, but working with stone had given him broad shoulders and powerful muscles. That, along with the height he had already achieved, gave him the look of a young man somewhat older than his sixteen years. Yet she suspected his youth by the naïveté of his open face and his obvious lack of experience with women.

"Oh," she said, her lips rounding into a beautiful rose. "Working with all those heavy stones must give you a big appetite, no? What can I bring you tonight?"

"Well, I will have . . . uh . . . what do you recommend?"

"Papialona makes a spicy sausage stew."

Davian ordered the stew, not caring that he had eaten the same fare before. As Emeralda returned to the kitchen, Davian sipped his ale, little hearing the laughter and banter that filled the place. He thought only of how Emeralda's exquisite face and undulating form would look in white marble. She returned minutes later and set the stew before him.

"That will be three denira," she said, holding out her hand.

Davian fumbled at his belt for his money pouch, and the girl's eyes widened at the glitter in the mouth of the bulging purse. He drew out five denira and placed them in her hand, thrilling to the touch of her fingers.

"Oh, thank you, Davian. Your patron is quite generous, no?"

"I just got a large advance on a commission," he replied. "And that's why I came here tonight. I need a model for the statue, and you're perfect for it. Would you pose for me? I will pay you well."

"Me? I'm only a tavern maid. Surely you don't think I have beauty."

As Davian opened his mouth to reply, a sharp, masculine voice called Emeralda's name, and she turned away. Near the door stood a stocky man of about thirty-five, dressed in a black velvet cloak hung with gold chains, and with black silk stockings sheathing his legs.

Emeralda turned back to Davian and said, "Eat your stew. We'll talk later." She went to the man, and they began to dance.

Again a surge of jealousy heated Davian's face. He ate his stew without tasting it and watched Emeralda's every move as she whirled and laughed in the merchant's arms. Soon the man drew her out of the dance and led her through a door beside the kitchen. Davian did not see them until a quarter hour later, when the merchant reappeared alone and strode swiftly out of the restaurant, straightening his collar and smoothing his coat. Three minutes afterward Emeralda emerged from the same door, placing a few coins in the purse on her belt.

Davian hoped she would come straight to his table. He wanted to get back to the studio. He had left his sketching board piled with paper and charcoal sticks. Myronius insisted on a clean workplace, and Davian would not sleep until the shop was straight. But Emeralda made the rounds of the tables, filling ale glasses and bantering with the men before she came to Davian.

"Ah, you are finished already. The stew was good tonight, no?"

"It was excellent," he replied. "Now, what is your answer? Will you pose for me?"

Instead of replying, she took his hand and tugged. "Come dance with me and I will tell you."

"But I can't dance. I've never done it. Besides, I must get back to—"

"Oh, you don't need to leave so early. I will teach you to dance." She pulled at Davian's arm until he stood and followed her to the floor. The band struck up a lively gallotte, and Emeralda took his hands and swung him into the circles of the dance. She laughed at his tripping feet, but soon he found the rhythm and managed to step in time to the music. "You're not bad for your first time," she said with a smile. When the dance ended, she pressed herself against his arm and spoke low in his ear. "It's terribly noisy in here. Come with me to the quiet of my room, where we can talk about your sculpture."

Davian was utterly oblivious to the nature of her invitation, but he refused it politely, saying he must go and he would visit her room another time.

"What do you pay posing models?" she asked.

"Fifteen denira for each day from noon until eventide. I think we can finish all the sketching in four days. I will pay you each day. We can start tomorrow."

"I will come," she replied.

After giving her directions to the studio, Davian left the inn and walked home in the darkness, unaware of everything around him as the wine of Emeralda's beauty flooded his senses.

"Now, come toward me once again, slowly this time." Davian looked intently at Emeralda as she began to dance, the soft folds of the white gown flowing from her supple limbs like willow fronds in a May breeze. His charcoal moved rapidly across the paper tacked to the board before

210

him. For three days she had danced across the open floor of the studio several times as he watched for the perfect point of graceful motion to capture in stone. He had chosen the moment when her front foot rested solidly on the floor while the toes of the other were about to lift from the surface and sweep into the next step. It was a moving pose that no model could hold, and she had to step through the dance over and over, allowing him to sketch a little more of it each time. With quick, sweeping strokes, his sure hand captured all the grace and energy of her motion.

"There, that does it for the frontal sketches," he said. He stood and poured a cup of water from the ewer on his board as she collapsed on a nearby bench, breathing hard. "After you catch your breath I will start sketching from your right side," he said as he handed her the cup. "Then we will be finished."

Emeralda drank deeply before she replied. "Why must you draw me from so many angles?"

"Because sculpture is not like painting. A statue will be seen from all sides, and it must appear perfect from each."

Again she danced, this time moving laterally across the plane of Davian's vision. He watched with single-minded focus, his hand feeling all the passion of the girl's fluid movement and guiding the charcoal across the paper to the rhythm of it. Three, five, six times she danced, and after the seventh he stopped her and stood back to look at what he had drawn.

"We are finished," he said.

He poured her another cup of water as she came to where he stood. She sipped slowly as she gazed at the drawing, standing so close to him that he could feel her hair brushing his shoulder like a caress.

"Am I really so beautiful?" she asked, leaning back against his chest.

"Yes, at least that beautiful," he replied, his voice husky from his deepening breath as he gazed enrapt at the velvet curve of her shoulder and arm.

Emeralda slipped into her cloak as Davian went to his corner and drew from his wallet six coins, which he placed in her hand. "That is for today."

"This much?" she replied. "This is more than you promised and more than you paid me the first two days. It's more than I earn in three nights at Papialona's."

"It's my first major commission," Davian replied. "And my patron is quite wealthy. What he pays me is like crumbs falling from his table."

She looked at him with a new gleam of interest, then turned toward the door. "Oh, look at the sun! I didn't know it was so late. I . . . I feel a bit uneasy about walking in the streets now." She took his arm and pressed her cheek against it as she looked up into his face. "You will walk me to Papialona's, no?"

Davian could think of nothing he would rather do. He explained his departure to Myronius, slipped into his cloak, and escorted the girl into the street.

Again he was oblivious to all around him as he and Emeralda walked. Her flowing hair and the movement of her arms and feet delighted his eyes. His ears heard nothing but the bright music of her laughter. Often she took his hand or flung her arm about his waist, her touch sending him into raptures to rival the angels. They arrived at Papialona's long before he was ready for the walk to end. She urged him to stay and dance.

"One dance only," he insisted. "I must get back; I left the studio in a mess."

But after the first he stayed for another and yet an-

212

other until he found himself hungry and thirsty. Emeralda brought a bottle of wine and a bowl of stew. He had finished his stew and just poured a cup of wine when she brought to his table a young man and a girl about her own age.

"Davian, greet my friends Torvio and Sofinia."

Though Davian had already grown taller than most men, Torvio towered over him by some six inches and boasted the torso of a young bull. A mandolin hung at his back.

"How be you, boy?" Torvio bellowed as he slapped Davian on the shoulder with his huge hand.

Davian staggered but bowed courteously. He took Sofinia's hand and kissed it as Myronius had taught him to do in the presence of noble couples who came to his studio. The girl giggled, and Emeralda laughed outright.

"Davian, look around you; this is a tavern, not a palace," Torvio boomed, pushing him back into his seat. "Here's how we greet girls in Papialona's."

He took Sofinia by the shoulders and kissed her full on the mouth. He laughed heavily as he dropped the girl into her seat, laid his mandolin behind the table, sat down, grabbed Davian's wine bottle, and poured himself a mug. He drained it in one draught, then banged it heavily on the table and belched loudly. He poured his mug full again and filled Sofinia's as well.

Lifting the cup toward Davian, he said, "Drink up, Davi. The night is short, and the kegs are full. We mustn't waste a moment or a drop." He drained his mug again and set it hard on the table. Turning to Sofinia, he said, "Come, Sofi, let's show our new friend how we dance in Hrombulous." He pulled the girl to the dance floor, where he twirled and pitched her about like a stuffed doll.

"Come, Davian, let's join them." Emeralda stood and offered her hands.

This time he actually began to enjoy the movement of his body as the music and the wine surged through him. After a few spirited dances, the music softened and the tempo slackened, and Emeralda held herself close to him, putting her head on his shoulder as they moved slowly about the floor. They danced three more rounds before she yielded to the men clamoring for more wine and stew. Davian returned to his table, where Torvio and Sofinia now sat. Torvio held his mandolin to his ear and plucked a string as he adjusted its tension.

"Do you sing, Davi?" he said.

"I don't know any songs."

"You don't know any songs? Ha! I've got the remedy for that." Torvio grinned as he strummed the instrument and began to sing:

> "I loved a girl from Evenshire
> With eyes like diamonds, hair like fire.
> I loved so much I would not wait
> But took her to the magistrate,
> Who told me I should give some thought
> Before I tied this Gordian knot:
> 'A girl who now seems fair and true
> Will soon become a nagging shrew.
> The love light shining in her eyes
> Will turn to glares you will despise.
> Her words so tender, soft, and dear
> Will turn to shouts that rend your ear.
> Her form so soft and sleek and swaying
> Will soon be drooping, sagging, splaying.
> Considering all that I have said,
> Are you still sure you want to wed?'
> 'Yes,' said I, and looked around;
> The girl was nowhere to be found.
> I overtook her miles away
> And asked her why she did not stay.

She said to me with perfect candor,
'What fits the goose must fit the gander.'"

Davian laughed long and loud. Torvio's voice was rough and heavy, but it had an earthiness that suited the humor of the ditty. Davian refilled the big man's mug and asked him to sing another song. Torvio emptied the cup in one draught, wiped his grinning mouth on his sleeve, and sang again. The patrons of the tavern began to gather around him. The bawdy lyrics would have made Davian blush only days ago, but now, in the presence of the beautiful Emeralda, his veins tingling with wine, surrounded by singing men and women, he merely laughed and tapped his foot to the raucous rhythm. By the third chorus he got the tune down and bellowed the song lustily to the rafters.

Davian did not even try to count the bottles Emeralda brought to the table, or how many of the singing patrons filled their cups from them. But in spite of his growing euphoria, uneasiness kept prodding his mind. He had work to do at the studio. He must go. He started to stand, but Emeralda, smiling softly, pressed him down again and eased onto his lap as Torvio began another song. After this one he would leave. But the warmth of Emeralda made his temples pound like drums, and it was three songs and two cups later when he forced himself to set her aside and struggled to his feet.

"I mus' go," he said, standing unsteadily.

"Very well." She smiled. "You had six dances, a bowl of stew, and five bottles of wine. Your total tonight is eighteen denira."

Davian was shocked at the amount, but he said nothing. He dropped the coins into her hand. Grinning, he turned to the patrons clustered about his table and waved expansively, the sweep of his arm causing him to stagger for balance. Emeralda and Sofinia both kissed his cheeks

215

and urged him to return tomorrow night. He left the tavern in the dark of the morning and made his way back to the studio, weaving and shuffling along the cobblestones as he bellowed Torvio's songs.

He let himself into the studio as quietly as he could, hoping not to disturb Myronius. He didn't even think of cleaning his table but fell into bed without undressing.

23

Davian's head felt as heavy as a block of Penoan marble. He slowly opened his eyes but instantly closed them. The sunbeams streaming from the window stabbed his brain like needles. He turned toward the wall, grimacing at the throbbing of his head. Moments later the rhythmic clang of Myronius's hammer and chisel rang through the shop, and Davian moaned, covering his head with his blanket. Soon the clanging ceased, and he lay in a stupor of misery.

Suddenly he felt the blanket jerked away and the shock of cold water dashed over his face and shoulders. He sat up screaming. Squinting through rapidly blinking eyes, he saw Myronius standing over him, a dripping bucket in his hand. Davian groaned and lay back on his sodden sheet, but the sculptor gripped him by the leg and dragged him to the floor. "Get up. Change your clothes and come to the table." Myronius threw the bucket aside, and it bounced across the floor with a clatter like a cracked bell. The boy pressed his palms to his ears and moaned.

Several minutes later Davian, holding his head, stumbled to the table where Myronius sat.

"Sit down and drink this," Myronius said, shoving a

cup of steaming brew toward him. "Where were you last night?"

"Papialona's," Davian mumbled.

"Do you know it was little more than three hours before dawn when you stumbled in last night? And you left your board looking like a rat's nest."

"I'm sorry," Davian muttered.

"Davian, you know I don't mind you having time for yourself. I've even urged you to get out more. But this girl Emeralda isn't good for you. I fear she's not a woman of the Master, and she could lure you into a deep pit. We've never talked much about women. Perhaps since your father is now gone, may his soul rest in peace, I should have told you a few things. You grew up fast, and I didn't see the need coming. You want to meet a girl? Let me find one for you. I know a few people of good reputation who specialize in making matches with women of character."

"It's all right, Myronius," Davian said. "I will stay away from Papialona's. I will see Emeralda only in this studio when she poses. I'm sorry about last night."

Myronius stood, and after putting his big hand on the boy's shoulder, returned to his work. Davian sat a half hour longer, his eyes closed against the light, sipping the pungent brew until the noise of the hammer and the light from the window became bearable. After cleaning his workplace he felt somewhat better, though his head felt dense and his hands trembled slightly. He began to make his armature—the skeleton for the clay model he would mold as a half-size preliminary to the final sculpture. Using tongs and a hammer, he twisted together several strands of heavy wire to follow the pose in the charcoal sketches of Emeralda.

The tendency of every novice artist was to hurry through the tedious preparatory stages to get his chisel into the

218

stone. But Myronius had taught Davian to spend much care on his preliminaries, especially in the shaping of the armature. The position, angles, balance, and proportion of the wire limbs had to be exact, because the clay could not correct mistakes in the armature. An accurate armature ensured an accurate preliminary, and an accurate preliminary ensured an accurate marble.

As Davian shaped the wires, his head began to clear. By noon he no longer felt nauseous, and a little of his appetite returned. After a meal of bread and cheese, his hands no longer shook. As he bent and twisted the metal, images of Emeralda drifted into his mind like airborne seeds through an open window. He remembered her musical laughter and her hair brushing his cheek when they danced. Torvio blustered into his mind as well, his rustic voice lifting ribald songs to the rafters. Absently Davian began to hum the melodies.

"The right arm is lifted too high."

Davian started at the sound and stopped humming. Myronius stood over him, staring intently at the armature. "Remember, the slant of the shoulders is always opposite to the slant of the hips. And I think the left thigh is an inch too long. Recheck your proportions."

"Yes, sir, I will," Davian said as Myronius walked away.

The apprentice checked the right arm of the armature against his sketch. His mentor was right; it was too high. He bent the wire downward, and the new position revealed a flaw in the angle of the elbow. Myronius never missed a thing. What if he was right about Emeralda as well? Was it possible she had no heart for the Master? He did not understand. How could anything so beautiful be anything but good? Did the Master of the Universe play tricks in creation, making beings with beautiful exteriors that were evil inside? If the Master was the God of truth, how could he allow such a paradox? Yet, apparently, Myronius thought it possible. He must remember to ask him to explain it.

He tried to thrust away all thoughts of the night before and think only of his work. For a while the armature kept him focused. He checked the measurements of each part by the golden mean Myronius had taught him. When Emeralda's laughter intruded again, he pushed her out by thinking on his future in the studio—how would he find patrons and clients? But soon he was humming Torvio's songs again, and his mind became a stage for the dancing Emeralda. He caught himself and forced his attention back to the armature. *What is wrong with me?* he thought. *Why can't I control my own thoughts?* Why were his duties in the studio becoming such dry, cold things compared with the splendor of Emeralda and the joy of song and dance? Once the thought hit him, he could see no comparison. Beauty won the tournament without breaking a lance. Duty might be necessary for survival, but it could never capture the heart. Only beauty made living worth the effort.

The sun streamed almost horizontally through the west windows when Davian called Myronius to inspect his armature. The sculptor turned it all about, comparing it to the sketches. Finally he stood back and said, "I see nothing wrong. It's ready for the clay. Come, you've worked enough today. Our dinner is ready."

The newly hired housekeeper, Helenia, served them baked fish with garlic bread and wine. Myronius was jovial and talkative, remembering his own experiences as a young apprentice building his first armatures. He never mentioned the night before, and Davian was grateful. When the meal was over, Helenia cleaned the table and washed the pots, then left for her home. Myronius returned to his room. Davian cleaned up the bits of broken wire he had cut during the day and put away his tools. Then he undressed and dropped into his bed.

For a while he thought no more of the night at Papialona's. Merely being in Myronius's presence seemed to have turned his mind in other directions. But soon Torvio's songs and Emeralda's dance crept in. He tried to drive them out with thoughts of armatures, clay images, and Myronius's tales, but they would not leave. He thought of his friends at the tavern laughing and singing as he lay twisting about in his lonely bed. He longed to be with them, but he had promised Myronius he would not. He tried to sleep, but sleep would not come. Why couldn't he just slip out and spend two hours at Papialona's? Even an hour? He thrust the thought away several times before he finally fell into a fitful sleep.

He thought he sat on a hard bench, twisting the wires to an armature. But as he worked he began to realize that the things in his hands were not wires but the bones of a human skeleton, though black and hard as iron. The studio was so dark he could hardly see his work. *I won't get the shoulders and hips slanted right*, he thought. His hands became heavy, and he looked down to find his wrists shackled. He felt rather than saw Myronius, tall and bulky as Goliath, looming over him, the man's silent presence forcing him to his work. A sudden light pierced the darkness, and he looked up to see a door open. Emeralda stood in the doorway bathed in bright sunlight and smiling her heavenly smile. She began a sinuous dance, then stopped and beckoned him to come. He got up and walked a few steps before the chain on his wrist jerked him back to the black skeleton. She repeated the provocative dance and beckoning gesture several times, each time moving farther away from the door. Behind her stood Torvio and his companions, singing, drinking, and laughing. Each

221

time she beckoned, Davian tried to go to her, only to have Myronius jerk the chain, forcing him back to his bench. Soon she danced away and joined her friends, who turned their backs and walked into the distance as the door closed, leaving him in darkness. He turned to Myronius in anger, ready to tell him that duty was too hard a taskmaster. But to his horror, his master had become the black skeleton, gripping the chain in its bony hand and towering over him like a spectral giant.

He awoke in the morning dull headed and sluggish, but he ate his breakfast and returned to the armature. He mixed a pot of clay and began applying it to the wires. As he worked he warmed to his task. This was Emeralda taking form under his hands. His work on the model and his attraction to the girl blended into a single passion, and his stupor lifted like morning fog. He worked rapidly, and by dinnertime the contours of the form were roughly established. From this point on it would be a matter of detailing and refining. After dinner he cleaned his workplace, undressed, and fell into bed.

Again Emeralda danced in his mind, but tonight the Emeralda of the tavern blended with the Emeralda of clay, and his euphoria over the progress of his model tethered him to his commitment. He needed rest to continue his work. Soon he fell asleep.

In five days the model was complete, though Davian was not pleased with the face and Myronius said that one of the hands was too large. "It's a persistent trait you've got to watch, boy."

Davian corrected the oversized hand, and his mentor approved the model. On the following day the young artist rigged a block and tackle to one of the horses, and with Myronius's help, hoisted the stone he had selected for the dancing maiden onto the wooden platform where it would be carved. He spent the day measuring his clay model and enlarging the proportions with geometric calculations, then marked his measurements on the block with pins, thin metal pegs driven into the marble to indicate the positions of major forms, such as hands, knees, shoulders, hips, and head. He also plotted the outline of the figure on the flat surface of the block.

An hour before dinner he called Myronius to check his work. He dared not let his chisel bite the marble until he was sure his proportions were perfect, for marble was unforgiving. Once too much stone had been chipped away, correction was impossible. Myronius examined the block for almost an hour, often checking measurements with his rule. But in the end he told his protégé to begin sculpting.

Standing on platforms of various heights, Davian began chipping away large masses of marble as he worked his way into the block toward the form of the dancing maiden that slept inside waiting to be freed from her rocky entrapment. At first he rested often, as the heavy hammers took their toll on the muscles of his arms. In a few days he would establish a rhythm enabling him to work steadily. But for three nights he went straight from dinner to his bed and fell into it sore and exhausted. Dreams of Emeralda came, but sleep soon closed the curtain on them.

By the third day Davian got his rhythm—three steady blows of the hammer and a pause, followed by three more blows and another pause. His arm felt strong, and his breathing settled into an easy cadence. As the stone began to suggest the rough promise of the form inside, the young man's spirits rose. Delighting in his strength and feeling the euphoria of creation, he began to hum Torvio's songs to the beat of his hammer.

An hour before noon on the following day, a visitor came into the studio. After greeting the man, Myronius sat him at the table, and Helenia served them wine. The two talked for over an hour. After the visitor left, Myronius came to his apprentice.

"Davian, that was a messenger from Galverus, mayor of Meloran. The mayor is planning a family tomb, and he needs three statues to adorn it. He has asked me to come and view the setting, and I have agreed. I will leave immediately. His messenger is also his coachman, and he will take me to Meloran."

"Congratulations on the commission," Davian replied. "When will you return?"

"In three days, perhaps a little longer. Helenia is preparing dinner, but I won't wait. She will come in daily to prepare your meals while I'm gone."

Myronius packed his bag, and a half hour later the coachman returned to pick him up. The sculptor gave the man his bag, then came over to where Davian worked. He walked slowly around the dancing maiden, eyeing it critically, sometimes bending down or kneeling to get a different angle. Davian kept pounding his chisel, uncomfortable at his mentor's scrutiny. Finally Myronius stood and placed his hand on the boy's shoulder.

"The maiden is looking very good," he said. "The proportions are accurate, and you have captured her movement perfectly. But watch those hands. From the way you are roughing the block around them, it appears that you may be making them too large. I will leave now."

"May your journey be safe and successful," Davian said.

"May the Master be with you," Myronius replied.

When Myronius had boarded the wagon, Davian expelled a breath, as if a weight had been lifted from him. Somehow he felt freer, and he wondered at it. He had never before felt such relief at Myronius's occasional absences; why did he feel it now? He knew the reason: Myronius did not approve of Emeralda, and his promise to stay out of Papialona's was chafing his soul. But Myronius did not understand. For all his talk of beauty being a gift from the Master of the Universe, he wanted Davian to stay away from the most beautiful creature the Master had yet made. If Myronius had looked deep into Emeralda's soft eyes as he had, he would find reason for trust. If she had smiled at his master as she smiled at him, if Myronius had thrilled to her laughter and the warmth of her voice speaking low in his ear, he would know that this woman hid no guile and was utterly dedicated to Davian's happiness.

Three beats and a pause, three beats and a pause; with each stroke of the hammer Davian's chisel bit deeper, ever closer to the entrancing contours of his Emeralda waiting to be revealed in the stone. He had left webs of stone between the figure's calves and ankles and between the side of the torso and the extended arm. They would remain until he had finished all the detail of the legs, arms, hands, and fingers. The stone web would support the fragile extensions so they would not crack from the stress of his driven chisel. Already he was using a smaller hammer and chisels without teeth but with smooth edges designed to plane along surfaces. Later he would use chisels honed so finely they could shave away layers of stone thin as a coat of paint.

After Myronius left, Davian began humming Torvio's tunes, then singing them outright to the rhythm of his hammer. Helenia had to call him twice before he heard her over the din. He ate quickly and got back to his work while she cleaned the kitchen and left for the night. As the sunlight faded, he laid his tools aside, stripped off his dust-whitened clothing, and went out to the water tank to bathe.

When he returned to the studio, he lay uncovered on

225

his bed, where he stretched luxuriously, sighing deeply as the warm spring air drifting through the open window caressed his flesh. Tonight he felt alive and restless, and the beauty of Emeralda and the songs of Torvio called to him like the voices of sirens. More than once he thought of slipping out into the night and joining his friends. For a while his promise to Myronius held him to his bed. But sleep continued to elude him, and the songs in his head became more persistent until finally he arose, donned his best clothes, and headed for Papialona's.

Guilt at breaking his promise dogged each step through the darkened streets. But when he walked through the door of the familiar tavern, it was all forgotten.

"Davian!" Emeralda cried. She ran to him as many of the men and women raised their glasses and greeted him cheerily. "You have come back to us, no? We have missed you."

She took his arm and led him to a table, where Sofinia pulled out a chair and offered it with an elaborate parody of a courtly curtsy. Immediately his friends gathered around. He ordered a bottle of wine, and everyone at the table filled their mugs from it.

Torvio soon appeared with his mandolin. "Davi, boy!" he boomed. "So our singer has returned." Grinning widely, he slapped Davian on the back, causing him to cough and spew wine over the table.

The songs began, and Davian joined in with relish. He loved the feel of melody rising from his throat. Though he took care to drink little, the first bottle was soon emptied and Emeralda brought another. She took Davian's hand and led him into the dance. After five dances he returned to the table to find that yet another bottle had been opened and his new friends had all filled their mugs. Torvio sang and Davian joined in, and soon the entire tavern rang with their melodies. The bottles kept coming.

After four hours he stood. "I must go. I have much work to do tomorrow." But Emeralda pulled him down and begged him to stay. Though her pleading eyes and the warmth of her closeness tempted him sorely, he insisted that he must leave.

"Very well," she pouted. "If you'd rather go to that cold cavern you call a studio than sing and dance with us, then go. Your bill tonight for six dances and five bottles is twenty-eight denira."

Again Davian was shocked. The charge was even higher than before, and he had drunk very little. He hesitated as he took the coins from his pouch. "I must admit that these charges surprise me somewhat," he said. "It seems I'm paying for the wine of half the customers here."

"And they are most grateful," Emeralda replied, her eyes wide with admiration.

"I don't mind treating them occasionally but not every night I'm here."

Emeralda reached across the table and laid her hand on Davian's arm. "I understand," she said. "But life has dropped these people into a pit. They have no land, no work, no livelihood. Those who have families can't support them because they can't find work. So they come here to forget their sorrows and find a little happiness by flocking with people as miserable as themselves. Their world is different from yours, Davian. You would like to help them, no?"

Davian was quiet for a moment. He could not risk being excluded from this world of companionship and high spirits. He had money, and more would come after the people of Hrombulous saw his dancing maiden. He must not be selfish.

"Thank you for telling me this. I had no idea they were so poverty stricken. Just keep giving me the bill."

She leaned across the table, took his cheeks between her hands, and kissed him deeply on the lips. "You are so good."

With his lips tingling from Emeralda's kiss, he left the tavern and returned to the studio.

His next three days followed the same pattern. He slept until midmorning, worked the marble until dinner, took a half-hour nap, worked again until sundown, then bathed and walked to Papialona's. At the tavern he continued to temper his drinking, indulging in just enough wine to lift his spirits.

In the daytime he thought of nothing but Emeralda. She was his life, the air he breathed, the songs he sang, the inspiration of his heart, the strength of his arm as he formed her image in stone. He could not bear to be apart from her, and he knew that when Myronius returned, he could not keep his nightly trips to Papialona's secret. He would simply tell the man that he would spend many of his evenings there. His mentor could do nothing about it. Davian was an apprentice, not a slave. Yet a stab of pain pierced his belly at the thought of telling him. He did not know how the sculptor would react. He had never been at odds with his master, and this rejection of the man's counsel disturbed the peace of his soul. No matter, it would have to be done, and the sooner the better.

Myronius returned an hour before dinnertime on the fourth day after his departure. Davian stood on a platform, grooving out the furrows in the dancing maiden's flowing hair. The master greeted his apprentice heartily and paused to look at the sculpture. After a nod of approval and a wink, he went about unpacking from his journey. At dinner he told Davian of the new commission. It comprised three major statues and five smaller ones, and he would need the young man's help on the peripheral pieces.

"You're not talking much, boy," Myronius said. "And you don't look quite yourself—a bit pale, I would say—and what are those circles under your eyes? Don't you feel well?"

"Oh yes, quite well," Davian replied. "I've been working hard on the sculpture."

"Have you been getting enough rest?"

"Uh, well, most of the time. Though I have, uh, been going to Papialona's in the evenings. In fact, I want to talk to you about that." Davian's mouth went dry, and he paused to gulp a swallow of wine. "I love Emeralda, and I want to spend time with her. I will soon ask her to wed me."

Myronius looked hard at his apprentice. "Davian," he said, "my arrangement with you is strictly one of business. I have no right to dictate what you do with your free time as long as you produce quality work for my shop. However, you know that I've come to feel toward you as a son. So while I cannot—and would not—force you to do anything against your will, I will tell you that I have grave misgivings about the course you are taking. Papialona's is a fine place to dine and sing a song now and then. But it's not a home for your heart. And as I've told you before, Emeralda is hardly a—"

"You don't know Emeralda," Davian said hotly.

"No, I don't know her. But I watched her when she was here posing. She has aroused emotions in you that she does not share. She will hurt you, Davian. I know it as surely as I know the contours of my four-pound hammer. She will do you no good."

"I won't believe this of her. She does have my good

at heart. Soon she will love me, if she doesn't already. I know it."

"Very well." Myronius sighed. "You must do as you will. As long as your work is good and you meet the terms of your commissions, I will say nothing of your personal activities. I pray that the Master of the Universe will have mercy on you."

24

For the next month, Davian left for Papialona's shortly after dinner three to four evenings of every week. Emeralda always greeted him warmly, and Torvio's songs filled the air. Davian sang heartily, and though he drank little, he kept wine flowing at his table. One evening as he sat with Emeralda, a tipsy farmer took her to the floor and danced two rounds. Davian stopped singing and glared at them, rage darkening his face. When she returned to the table, he told her to dance with no one else but him.

"But, Davi, I must dance. I don't have a great talent like you. I do what I must to earn a living, no?"

"I will buy your dances for the rest of the night," he said, taking from his pouch a fistful of coins and dropping them into her hands.

She went about her business filling glasses and serving food, but that night she danced with no one else. As often as possible, she sat snuggled up to Davian, singing and laughing with her arm draped about his shoulder. A few times when she made her serving rounds, a patron asked to be entertained in her room. Each time, she sent the man out separately, promising to join him within minutes. When she

231

was sure Davian was deep into a song, she slipped out and returned a quarter hour later. Davian innocently suspected nothing of the nature of her brief disappearances.

Emeralda continued to present him the bill for all the wine consumed at his table. In addition, she began to hint that her clothing was wearing thin and that Papialona had told her she must dress better if she expected to work for him. Davian gave her the money she needed. Several small pieces of jewelry followed, as well as a new pair of shoes. His purse began to empty rapidly. He redoubled his efforts to complete the dancing maiden in order to collect the balance of the fee. And he cut his trips to the tavern to no more than two per week.

On the evenings when he visited Papialona's, it was long after midnight when he returned to the studio. Usually he sprawled onto his bed fully clothed and fell asleep instantly. When the rising sun invaded his corner, he pulled the blanket over his head, turned to the wall, and slept till midmorning. He stumbled to the kitchen, avoiding Myronius, and prepared his own cup of the hot brew that had cleared his head weeks before. It was usually an hour before noon before he felt steady enough to take up his hammer and begin carving.

Myronius said little to him about his nights at the tavern. Yet Davian knew that his master was disappointed in him, and guilt gnawed at the young man's heart. He kept his hammer moving—three beats and a pause, three beats and a pause—often humming Torvio's songs to the rhythm of it.

Three months later the statue was completed. Myronius was amazed at the young man's speed as well as the quality of the piece. He had wondered whether the boy would be able to instill into the stone the genius he had seen in the sketches, especially with his distraction at Papialona's and his lack of rest. But the finished piece dispelled all doubts. The statue rivaled the perfection of the work in the ancient ruins of Hrombulous. He pointed out a few small places where the polish could be higher, and when Davian had corrected these defects, his master pronounced the sculpture ready for the patron.

The merchant Melanius was overjoyed with the piece. He happily paid Myronius the balance of the fee and added ten percent as a bonus for the young sculptor.

When Myronius paid Davian his fee and the bonus, the young man wasted no time getting to Papialona's. He beamed like a beacon as he walked in the door. "Drinks for everyone!" he cried, sweeping his arm about the room.

"What's the big occasion?" Torvio asked.

"I have finished my statue of Emeralda. I have collected my fee along with a generous bonus. I want to share my good fortune."

The tavern patrons cheered and applauded, and many gathered around the boy and clapped him on the back.

When Emeralda entered the room, he grabbed her and kissed her before she realized what he was doing. More cheers resounded through the house, and soon the serving maids scurried to the tables, their trays laden with wine bottles and mugs. Emeralda smiled, but it was a wan smile, and Davian could see the glistening of a tear in her eye.

"What is wrong, Emeralda?" he asked.

"Oh, you don't want to hear sad stories now. This is your night, and nothing should make you unhappy."

"No, I can't be happy when you are not. Tell me what is wrong." He took her arm and led her to his table.

She dabbed her eyes with her table rag. "It's my mother.

She's been ill for many months, and now she's slipping beyond recovery."

"I am very sorry, Emeralda." Davian took her hand in his. "Why have you not told me before now?

"At first it didn't seem serious, but now the physician says she may not live another fortnight."

"Can nothing be done?"

"Nothing within reach. All I can do is make her last days peaceful."

"What do you mean, 'nothing within reach'?"

"The doctor says there's a medicine that could help her—one mixed from rare herbs and animal secretions. The herbs are frightfully costly. Not even the doctor can afford them."

"How costly?" Davian asked.

She told him, and he blanched inwardly but kept his composure. The figure was two thirds of what he had just been paid.

"I will pay for the herbs," he said, reaching for his money pouch.

"No! I can't let you do that." She shook her head and pushed his hand away.

"Emeralda, don't you know that your sorrows bring pain to me? You will take the money." He filled her hands with gold coins and closed her fingers over them.

Tears flowed from her eyes, and her body convulsed with sobs. Davian held her hands tightly, keeping them clutched around the money. Finally she dropped the coins into her pouch and looked tenderly at him. Without a word she leaned across the table, took his face in her hands, and kissed him deeply on the mouth. Davian almost swooned in ecstasy.

When the kiss ended, he moved to her side of the table.

He took her hand and looked into her eyes. "Emeralda, I want to marry you. Say you will be my wife."

"Of course I will, Davi." She smiled softly as she embraced him yet again.

"You will? You really will marry me?"

"To be sure. I've hoped for months that you would ask. I think I've loved you from the day your master first brought you here." She stroked his cheek and kissed him again. "We can have the wedding soon, no?"

"I was thinking about next month," Davian said.

"How about tomorrow night?" she murmured between the kisses she lavished on his cheek.

"Tomorrow night? So soon?" Davian's heart pounded.

"If we wait, you will change your mind. You're a great artist, and I'm just a simple tavern maid. Soon you will wake up and wonder what you ever saw in me, no?"

"You are the most marvelous creature the Master ever formed," he said. "I could never do anything but love you."

"Then we should wed tomorrow night. The magistrate comes to Papialona's every Thursday, so he will be here to perform the ceremony. Papialona can give me away, Torvio can sing, Sofinia can be my maid, and our friends in the tavern can be the wedding party."

"It sounds perfect," Davian replied, his mind a whirlwind. "We will wed tomorrow night." After embracing her once again, he stood and shouted, "Listen everyone. Emeralda has agreed to become my wife. We will wed tomorrow night—right here. All of you are invited. Another round of drinks for everyone!"

Cheers and congratulations rang throughout the room, and Torvio took his mandolin and struck up a song—a bawdy ballad about a bridal night that brought a blush to Davian's face. But he laughed and sang along, pouring wine into every mug and dancing often with his bride-to-be. Goodwill and congratulations abounded, and Davian did not leave until two hours before dawn.

He awoke near noon the next day, and his heart leapt when he remembered that this was his wedding day. Where would he and Emeralda live? Strangely, he had not even thought of such things last night. Perhaps they could enclose the corner of the studio where he had his bed. But his bed was too small for two. Perhaps they could live in Emeralda's room at Papialona's until he made other arrangements. It didn't matter. Love would find a way.

He arose and dressed, then went to Myronius, who was at work on the Meloran commission. "You were wrong about Emeralda," he said.

Myronius stopped hammering. "What do you mean?"

"She is not the false woman you thought her to be. She has agreed to marry me."

"She has what?" Myronius boomed, his face darkening as he stepped down from his platform.

"You heard me right. We will be wed tonight."

"Tonight! What are you thinking, boy? You are hardly seventeen years old. You don't know your own heart yet. And what is she thinking? She must be twenty or more. And tonight! Davian, you've lost your senses. You must give yourself some time to think about this."

"I've thought of nothing else for six months. There is no point in delaying what we both know we want. We will be wed tonight. And I want you to come. It would mean much to me."

"I—I will come." Myronius ran his hand through his thick gray hair and sat heavily on the platform. "Of course I will come. But, boy, I urge you to give this some time. It's much too sudden, and you need to get your feet on the ground. Just wait until—"

236

"Myronius, we will wed tonight. And I want your blessing."

Myronius shook his head. "I don't know about my blessing, but I promise you my support. I have grave misgivings about this, but since you are dead set on it, I will do all I can to help you make it work. I will come with you tonight."

Davian was elated. He worked all afternoon with energy and passion buoyed by dreams of Emeralda, which never for a moment left his mind. Helenia prepared dinner early, and the two men ate quickly. Davian bathed first, followed by Myronius, and after donning their finest clothes—suits they reserved for visits from noble patrons—they left the studio and walked to Papialona's. They arrived minutes before the seventh hour, the time set for the wedding.

Davian walked in, grinning broadly, with Myronius close behind. The raucous cheer he had expected did not greet him. Men and women looked up at him briefly, then quickly looked away. He wondered at their strange behavior. *But of course!* he thought. *This is my wedding night. It will be a solemn occasion, and the customers sense it.* He looked around the room. No one was dressed for a wedding, but then he thought of what Emeralda had told him. All of them were poor and could afford nothing else. Where was Emeralda? Probably still in her room getting ready. In fact, he likely would not see her until the ceremony. He suddenly realized that the ceremony was another thing they had failed to plan. But no doubt Emeralda had worked it all out during the day.

But something was not right. As Davian looked around the room in bewilderment, some of the patrons began to grin and even snicker. For a moment he was mystified at their behavior, but again he thought he understood. It was a wedding, and these were earthy men and women who always saw the ribald side of things. No doubt jokes

237

about nervous husbands and blushing brides had already circulated among them, and his presence merely brought home the reality of it. He looked about for the magistrate, but the official was nowhere to be seen.

Soon Davian realized that everyone was staring at him, and the snickering increased. Papialona walked in from the kitchen, and when he saw the look of bewilderment on the young groom's face, he laughed and came to him. "Well, Davi, it looks like our Emeralda got the best of you, she did."

"Got the best of me? What do you mean?" Davian replied.

"I mean she's gone. Took your money and left."

"You mean she left to take the money to her mother."

"Ha! Her mother!" Papialona said. "That slut's mother has been dead for years. Has no family. She took you, Davi. Took you good." Papialona began to laugh again, as did many of the patrons.

Davian's mind reeled with what he was hearing. "No! She would not do this. There is some mistake. She will come back. I know she will."

"Look around, Davi. You see Torvio anywhere?"

Davian looked all about the room. "Where is he?" he asked, though a heavy dread in his heart told him he could guess the answer.

"Torvio and Emeralda left together. Early this morning. Wouldn't say where they were going. Said they could live six months on the money you gave them. Been a pair for years, they have, moving from one town to another. Yes, sir, got you good, they did." Again Papialona burst into laughter, and all the patrons joined in.

Davian slowly turned all around, gaping in disbelief at all the faces laughing at him. Sofinia, grinning from ear to ear, came to him, placed her arm on his shoulder, and batted her lashes in mock flirtation. "What do you need with silly old Emeralda, anyway? Won't I do for you, stonecutter?"

The laughter in the room redoubled, and in hot despair Davian wrenched her arm away and slung her back to her seat, where she would have fallen had not two men at her table caught her.

"Davian, no!" Myronius said, putting a restraining hand on the boy's shoulder.

But the deed was done, and immediately six angry men jumped from their seats and charged at Davian. He leveled the first with a fist to the jaw and the second with a knee to the stomach. Several more charged, and he began swinging and punching with fierce abandon, laying groaning bodies on the floor all about him. Soon the entire tavern roiled with angry men, all converging on Davian. They overwhelmed him and rode him to the floor, where they began punching and kicking his writhing body.

With a roar Myronius plunged into the fray, swinging his great arms right and left until he cleared a circle about the prostrate form of his protégé. Everyone stood aside, panting, as Myronius glared at them. No one moved as the big sculptor stooped and picked up Davian and laid him across his shoulder. Without a word he strode from the tavern.

25

For a week Davian did no work. The bruises on his arms and body and the two broken ribs were enough to keep him from lifting his hammer, but Emeralda's betrayal was the worse pain. It had crushed his spirit. He ate little and spoke little. He no longer slept till noon but awoke with Myronius as he had in the days before he had met the girl. Once awake he could not stay in bed, where unwelcome thoughts tortured his brain like the fires of hell. Every morning he hobbled up the road to the top of a rise where he sat and stared unseeing at the cottages below. Myronius said little to him, knowing he was grieving and would need several days, at least, to come to terms with his loss.

On the eighth day following the brawl, the two men finished their evening meal and sat at the table, sipping their wine as Helenia cleaned. Davian idly dipped a piece of straw into a puddle of spilled wine and watched the red liquid drip from the end of it. Without looking up, he said, "How did you know Emeralda was evil?"

"She had open windows that exposed her soul," Myronius replied. "She knew you were inexperienced with women, and she baited you with her beauty. If you think back, she showed little interest until she knew you had money. Had you been less enamored, you would have been more wary."

"I just don't understand," Davian said. "How could such a beautiful form contain such an evil soul? It's as if her appearance is a lie about her true nature. Why would the Master of the Universe create such a lie?"

"It's not the Master's doing," Myronius replied, tracing his thoughts in the air with his hand. "He designed our faces and bodies to express our invisible spirits. Therefore, in the beginning the appearance of every person accurately reflected his or her heart. You could look at a face and know the person behind it, because all features presented a true portrait of the inner self. When I had you drawing practice faces, you remember how some looked strong and stern, others hard and cold, some playful, some humorous, some warm and loving, some wise, some serene, and others open and accessible? The Master intended the face to be a book by which you could read the truth about the person inside."

"If that was his intent, what went wrong?" Davian asked, tracing idle lines on the table with his wine-dipped straw.

"The Master gave the first man and woman perfect beauty to reflect their perfect souls. But an enemy deceived them into believing they could refashion their souls to patterns of their own choosing. However, they lacked the power to remake themselves, and the attempt left them with souls no longer beautiful, but grotesque and distorted. To cover the shame of their inner ugliness, they emulated their enemy and became deceivers themselves, using their physical beauty as a mask to hide the deformity inside."

"But I don't understand. Few people have real beauty to serve as such a mask. In fact, some are dragonwart ugly."

"The Master's original intent was for every face to be beautiful, because every soul was beautiful. But nature suffered great damage when the first man and woman fell from created perfection. A contamination crept into their physical heritage, corrupting the physical beauty the Master meant for all of us. This contamination damaged some more than others. It has caused some to be, as you say, 'dragonwart ugly.' Even those who escape the worst of the contamination and retain beauty are far from matching the perfection of the first couple. In today's world no face is quite symmetrical, no proportion ideal, no form without some distortion, no skin without blemish." Myronius poured himself another mug of wine and took a sip. "Even Emeralda missed ideal beauty in many ways you didn't see, blinded as you were by your infatuation."

Davian's mind recoiled at the name Emeralda as from the reek of a rotting carcass. He wanted to banish every thought of the evil wench.

"The hearts of women are more corrupt than the hearts of men," he muttered.

"It may seem so because men are so vulnerable to female beauty. Like you, they want to believe the adorable face reflects an adorable inner self. Therefore, evil women can easily hide their intent behind their beauty. But you must take into account the disadvantages women endure because of the burdens nature has placed on them—physical vulnerability, the lunar cycle of pain, the use of their bodies to bear and nourish children. Men often take advantage of these limitations. Women are abused, used, violated, and dominated, and then they are often neglected or discarded when their beauty fades."

"It's no less than they deserve," Davian growled, still drawing on the table with his wine-dipped straw. "The

Master must have known what he was doing to put such burdens on women. Had he not muzzled them, they would have lured all men to perdition."

"Not all men are as vulnerable to the lure of beauty as we artists. Beauty is our stock in trade. It is to us as the sea is to a sailor. We map it and sail upon it in our quest for truth, all the while knowing it could overwhelm and sink us." His hands painted rolling waves in the air. "We want to find truth reflected in the beauty of a woman just as we find it in the beauty of a mountain. We forget that, unlike the mountain, the woman has free will and can use her exquisite face and form to hide a dragonwart-ugly soul."

"I will never trust another woman," Davian said. "The pain is too great to warrant the risk." He flicked the straw aside and arose from his chair. "Good night, Myronius. I'm going to bed."

Myronius knew he had said all the suffering boy could hear at the moment. He could not expect to improve his view of women now. As Davian walked away, his mentor came around the table to see what the young man had drawn. It was a woman hanging from a gallows, a puddle of red wine beneath her like a pool of blood. The sculptor sighed and shook his head as he wiped the table clean.

In the following days Davian threw himself into his work with renewed intensity. Myronius assigned to him the carving of three infant, winged putti that would adorn the tomb of the mayor of Meloran. Often the young man was awake before his master, sketching or transferring his drawings to blocks of Penoan marble. Though he finished the pieces in less than three months, the figures were exquisite. Their rounded, babyish contours invited motherly caresses, and the wings were wrought so delicately that they belied their stony substance and appeared to be feather light. Myronius's only fear was that the pieces would overshadow the primary figures in the group. His concern had nothing to do with jealousy—he gloried in the rise of his pupil. But he feared that the client would not appreciate the incidental putti drawing attention from the central figure.

The solution, he decided, was to let the young man help him with the main figures as well. Davian agreed but adamantly refused to work on the female statue.

"Why won't you sculpt the female?" Myronius asked.

Davian shook his head and mumbled, "I don't ever want anything to do with women again, flesh or stone."

Indeed, in the following days as the two men worked at the sculptures, Myronius noticed that Davian hardly even glanced at the female figure or the models that posed for them. He began to be concerned.

"Davian, you can't carry a grudge against all women because of what one did to you," Myronius told him after dinner one evening. When the boy did not reply, he continued. "Women are no more evil than men. In fact, history shows that it is men who have committed the most terrible deeds. They do the massacring, they rape and plunder, they wage wars—"

"Yes, all the nations about the Southern Sea warred for ten years—over what? A woman!"

"But was it Helen's fault the men chose to fight over her?"

"Perhaps it seems that men commit the greatest evils," Davian replied, "but it's because their evil is usually open and unhidden. The evil of woman is insidious. Like the adder, she strikes from secret places without warning. She is steeped in guile, wearing the face of innocence and dangling the promise of joy. But it's all a façade. The innocence is a mockery and the joy a sham."

Myronius pursued the subject no further, but now and then he would probe the boy's thoughts to see whether his hatred of women was abating. It was not.

One evening several weeks later, the two artists were riding to the Penoan quarry to cut a block of stone for the pedestal of the Meloran monument when they passed the Cathedral of Alborani. Myronius waved toward the church and said, "I forgot to tell you, Bishop Lanianti of that cathedral is thinking of giving us a commission."

"A commission from the ecclesium? How can that be? They hate our art."

"Not Bishop Lanianti. He understands that beauty is a blessing from the Master. He is often at odds with the hierarchy of his church, but he is so popular among the people that the leaders dare not call him to account."

"What does he want us to do?"

"Two figures: an Adam and an Eve. Do you see the stone walls going up just to the right of the nave?" Myronius pointed toward the cathedral. "Lanianti is building an abbey. It will have a courtyard in the center, where he will plant a lavish garden designed to evoke an image of unspoiled Eden. He wants his monks and acolytes to be sensitive to beauty and through beauty to feel a longing for the Master. He wants two life-size figures to adorn the garden: an Adam and an Eve showing their original beauty and innocence."

"I will not do an Eve," Davian said.

"He wants two figures, Davian. You and I are two sculptors. I will do the Eve; you can do the Adam. See how easily things work out when you apply proper mathematics? Besides, it will take almost two years to complete the abbey. Lanianti won't need the sculptures until then. By that time you may think women are the crown of the Master's creation."

245

"That will never happen. But I will do the Adam," Davian said.

"Incidentally," Myronius went on, "Bishop Lanianti invited me to dinner last week, and he told me of a father who is seeking a good match for his daughter, a young woman about your age. The girl is beautiful and decorous, loves the Master, and is of good reputation. I will meet with him soon to discuss the commission. I could arrange for you to meet the girl—"

"If you arrange such a meeting, I won't attend. If you bring the girl to the studio, I won't speak to her. Forget such things, Myronius. I've told you that I will have nothing to do with women. I am wedded to my work."

"Ah, indeed you are, indeed you are." Myronius sighed. "I worry about you, Davian. You do nothing but work. You need diversion."

The two men finished the Galverus commission four months ahead of the time allotted. Rumors of the extraordinary nature of the pieces reached the mayor, and he himself came with his porters to pick them up. He was openly delighted with what he saw. He paid the balance of his fee willingly, and Myronius gave Davian his share.

26

In the next year Davian took on several commissions of his own and completed them with quality far exceeding expectation and with uncanny speed. His fame grew not only in Hrombulous but throughout central Appienne. It began to be said of him that he could make stone breathe.

He worked from dawn to dusk every day. Except for trips to the Penoan quarry and weekly attendance at the nearby ecclesium, he never left the studio. Myronius often urged—even begged—the young man to get out more. "Go to the wine festival in Penoa, or see a comedy in the amphitheater. Come with me on Sundays to the Cathedral of Alborani. You would like Bishop Lanianti's sermons. Do anything! Just get away from these clanging hammers. This marble dust will clog your soul as well as your lungs." But Davian insisted that his work was his life, and he gave attention to nothing else.

On a Tuesday afternoon in early April, Bishop Lanianti came to the studio accompanied by a young acolyte. Both wore dark brown robes with hemp rope sashes tied loosely about their waists and cowls pushed back from their heads. Davian had heard that the bishop had little sense of his own importance, and his appearance confirmed the rumor. Nothing in his dress distinguished him from his acolyte. Myronius sat them at his table and called for Davian to join them. Helenia served them wine, and the bishop described his commission.

"The abbey is mostly complete," he said, his manner easy and unaffected. His eyes held a light and his mouth the promise of a smile that Davian had never seen in the face of an ecclesiate. "The remaining chambers will be finished in six months. The garden has been laid with paths and terraces. The ground is prepared, the trees and shrubs are in place, and the flowers and ferns are planted." He drew from his robe a scroll, which he spread on the table. On it was a detailed plot drawing of the garden. "As you can see, all these winding paths lead to the center of the garden, where the ground is tiered upward by low stone walls toward the central fountain. Here are the steps leading to the fountain's pool." His elegant fingers traced the forms on the drawing.

"As I have told Myronius, I want to train my monks and priests somewhat differently from those of other orders. We will focus not on the Master's wrath but on his love. We will teach that the essence of all creation is good. Of course, the fall gave men and women an evil nature and placed them in need of redemption. It also damaged the earth, bringing on death, rust, rot, famine, and disasters. Yet we teach that the good the Master instilled into creation remains intact beneath the canker of the fall, just as silver remains intact beneath its tarnish. We will draw men and women toward the Master by showing them the goodness he intended for all his creatures, which he wants to restore to them. We will draw them to the Master not through fear of punishment but by desire for him. I want this garden to reflect that viewpoint. I want to show all the beauty the Master infused into creation. I want to show the promise he holds out to us—that in spite of our griefs and burdens, with him our lives can be bathed in delight and love, just as a peak finds sunlight above the clouds in spite of the shadows that fall on it below."

Davian was mildly shocked at the bishop's words. He had never heard an ecclesiate say such things. He began to think he might accompany Myronius to the Cathedral of Alborani.

"The Adam and Eve figures will go here, above the fountain," the bishop continued, placing his finger on the center of the drawing. "They must be life-size, though taller than average and ideal in proportion. I want my Adam and Eve to be the most perfect and beautiful specimens of humanity ever carved in stone. I came to you because yours is the only studio in Appienne—and probably in the world—committed to the creation ideals of the Master."

Bishop Lanianti and Myronius went on to discuss the timetable for delivering the finished figures and the fee for producing them. When they had agreed on what Davian thought a quite generous sum, the young acolyte, Ignatio by name, wrote a simple contract, which the bishop and the sculptor signed. Then at the bishop's nod, Ignatio drew from a bag within his robe half the fee and placed it on the table as an advance payment. The four men shook hands all around, and after invoking the Master's blessing, the bishop and his assistant departed for Alborani.

Myronius could not begin the Eve figure until he completed a previous commission, which would take him another two months, but Davian began immediately to make sketches for the Adam. He spent eight days experimenting with poses and gestures, occasionally seeking advice from his mentor. In another week he had the pose he wanted, which he drew in fair detail from four sides. With the pose established, he went into Hrombulous to search for models. For six days he roamed the streets and fields about the city, looking for ideal specimens of physical manhood among stonemasons, smiths, vinedressers, wheelwrights, porters, carpenters, ploughmen, herders, and even merchants.

Of the hundreds of men he scrutinized, he sent only seven to the studio for further study. When each disrobed he sketched a likeness. Though all were superbly formed, none of them had the perfection he wanted. One had the musculature but not the height. Another was a touch too stocky, another a little too slender. One was nearly perfect from the waist up, but his legs were slightly overdeveloped. Another would have been perfect but for a very slight bulge about the waist and hips that his clothing had hidden. He paid them all for their time and sent them home.

On the evening after the last model had been sent away, Davian put up his tools, and Myronius accompanied him to the water tank to bathe. Afterward, as they stood on the bank drying themselves with towels, the older sculptor paused and looked at his protégé. "Forget your model. Go out and purchase a couple of mirrors."

"Mirrors? Whatever for?" Davian replied.

"You are exactly the model you are looking for. You will never find better. Go to the metal shop of Vangelan and buy two plated bronze mirrors at least your height and strike the pose yourself."

Davian was skeptical. In spite of his height and striking appearance, he had little vanity and rarely glanced into the tiny mirror Myronius had nailed to the wall of the studio even to comb his hair or shave his face. Yet he took his master's suggestion seriously. On the next morning he went out to the shop of Vangelan the smith.

When he arrived five smiths were pounding at their anvils. Rather than interrupt their work, Davian found their mirrors stacked against a wall and looked at his reflection in one of the golden surfaces. He turned first to the right, then to the left. He struck the pose he had chosen for his sculpture. Then he turned and struck it again from the other side. He tried the pose from several angles before he began to realize that Myronius might be right; he could pose for the Adam.

So intent was he on his mission that he did not at first notice that all hammering in the shop had ceased. Becoming aware of the silence, he turned to see the five smiths staring at him.

"Oh, I was just thinking of buying a mirror." He grinned sheepishly.

The smiths glanced at each other, and one of them laid aside his hammer, wiped his blackened hands on his leather apron, and walked to where Davian stood, watching the young man warily the whole time. "I'm Vangelan, owner of this shop. I'm sure your wife would love the mirror you're standing before now," he said.

"I have no wife," Davian said.

"Then it will make a fine wedding gift for your bride-to-be."

"I'm not about to get married, now or ever," Davian replied.

"That's no surprise," the man muttered under his breath.

"What's your price on this one?" Davian asked. "I will need two of them."

"Two?" the smith said. "Whatever for?"

"I need to see myself from the back," Davian replied. The smith glanced furtively at his co-workers.

When the haggling was done, Davian counted out the coins and instructed the man to deliver the mirrors to the studio of Myronius on the road to Alborani.

On the next morning Davian set up the mirrors, disrobed,

and drew himself from his own reflection. In three days he completed his drawings and began his clay model. In two more weeks the model was complete, and he selected his stone from the quarry at Penoa Mountain. He began working the stone just under six weeks after accepting the commission.

Davian was up every morning a half hour before Myronius, driving a stone-breaking chisel with his largest hammer. Three strikes and a pause, three strikes and a pause; he worked tirelessly until the noontime break, when he rested for a quarter hour and gulped down a half loaf of bread, a wedge of cheese, and a glass of wine. Then he returned to the stone and established his rhythm again and did not let up until Myronius insisted that he stop for dinner. He would have lit candles and worked into the evening hours, but Myronius urged him not to do it.

"You are working too hard," he said. "You must find some diversion to keep yourself in balance. It will help your art."

Davian would not listen, but in the days that followed, Myronius persisted.

Finally Davian relented for no other reason than to put a stop to his mentor's badgering. He packed a small bag, saddled a horse, and left without saying where he was going. On his return that evening, Myronius asked him where he had been. Davian took from his bag several sketches of ruined sculptures and columns in Hrombulous.

Myronius shook his head and threw up his hands. "I give up," he said. "Your work has become your life. You are truly wedded to the marble. But you will find that stone makes a cold bride."

Three weeks later Myronius completed his commission, an enormous, majestic, thick-maned lion crouched in regal repose. On the following day the patron came with his cart to load the piece. Myronius and the patron's five assistants rigged heavy ropes on rafter pulleys and prepared the lion to be lifted. The cart waited at the door of the studio, with the horses rigged and a driver on the board ready to back the wagon beneath the sculpture after it was hoisted.

"We're ready," Myronius called, and the men gathered at the two ropes—Davian and two assistants on one and Myronius with two assistants on the other. At Myronius's command they pulled, and the lion rose into the air. "Steady, now," he said. "You, on the front rope, bring your end a little higher."

When the sculpture hung level in the air, he barked the command to back the cart beneath it as the men at the ropes held it steady. When the cart was beneath the statue, he called, "Now let it down—easy."

The pulleys groaned as the men eased the lion downward. When it hovered little more than two feet above the cart, Myronius saw that the beams laid in the wagon bed were not aligned beneath it.

"Hold!" he shouted, and the six men held the ropes steady, stopping the lion's descent. "Can you hold the rope without me for a moment?"

The assistants assured him they could, and he released his hold and crawled into the cart beneath the lion to re-align the beams. At that moment, the sweat-dampened rope slipped from the grip of one of the assistants, and one end of the sculpture came down heavily on Myronius's upper back. He bellowed with pain as the men tried desperately to pull the stone upward again.

Davian roared in rage and gripped the rope with the straining men, and with three mighty heaves they lifted the lion from the back of its maker. The patron pulled Myronius from the cart, and the lion dropped heavily to its bed.

Davian kneeled over his master, who grimaced in pain as

blood trickled from his mouth. "Quick, go get Antionne the physician," Davian cried. "Take the horse in the stable."

In minutes one of the men galloped away as those remaining lifted Myronius to his bed, where he lay gasping for breath. Davian gave him wine and bathed the sweat from his brow with cool, wet cloths. When Antionne arrived, the patron and his assistants waited in the studio as Davian and the physician stayed in the room. Myronius groaned as Antionne probed his torso to determine the location and intensity of his pain. Finally the physician stood and took Davian's arm to draw him outside the room.

"No," Myronius rasped between his labored breaths. "Stay in here . . . I will hear . . . what needs to be said."

"Very well," Antionne said. "Several ribs are broken, and you are bleeding inside. I'm sorry to tell you that I have never known of such bleeding to heal. You will not survive this. I am very sorry."

"I understand," Myronius said. "How long . . . will it be?"

"You will not see the sun set tonight," Antionne said.

Davian was thunderstruck. He could not believe what he was hearing. "Surely you can do something. He's alive now. There must be a way to keep him breathing."

"I'm very sorry, Davian." The physician shook his head. "I can do nothing but ease his pain." He drew from his bag a small earthen vial little larger than his thumb. "Mix this powder in a cup of wine and give it to him. His pain will cease. Truthfully, I don't think he will last an hour."

Trembling, Davian took the jar and ushered Antionne to the door, then returned to his mentor and knelt by his bed. Myronius tried to talk, but a fit of coughing overcame him, and he groaned with the pain of the convulsions. Davian ran to get a bottle of wine and poured a cup for his master, mixing the powder into it as the physician had instructed. "Here, drink this," he said, holding the cup to Myronius's lips.

"No, I won't . . . die in a stupor." Myronius turned his head away. "Must keep a clear head . . . have something . . . to say to you. Must . . . say it right." Again a spasm of coughing racked him, and he grimaced as Davian dabbed the sweat from his brow.

"Just rest," Davian coaxed, his eyes blurring with tears. "You need not say anything more."

"I won't sleep . . . until I say it. Listen well, my son. You have been . . . a good student and a good worker. You . . . have learned all I can teach you . . . and more. The Master has . . . given you a wondrous talent. But . . . but watching you work . . . has given me a fear."

A frightful spasm of coughing convulsed the big man as Davian knelt helplessly beside him. But he regained his voice and continued, pausing often to grimace and breathe rapidly. "I fear that . . . your art is becoming your master. When art becomes a master . . . it becomes a tyrant, making demands like . . . like a god . . . Must not let art . . . become your god. It will demand . . . total adoration. Those who fall . . . under its spell will sacrifice their all to it . . . Must be . . . master of your art, not vice versa . . . Art is a means to an end . . . not an end itself . . . a means of communicating truth about the Master of the Universe . . . not to display human genius . . . or the spirit within man. Don't . . . don't let your art become your god, Davian . . . Keep your focus on . . . on the Master of the Universe."

Another spasm of coughing overtook him, and after it passed he fell back on his pillow, breathing hard and sweating profusely. Davian dabbed a cloth at his mentor's face, his own eyes swimming in a sea of tears.

"Davian . . . I . . . I have loved you. I have always tried—"

A fit of coughing gripped him again, this time deep and long. Davian held him as the convulsions racked his body. When the coughing was done, Myronius eased into the pillow, and a long sigh escaped his lips. He did not breathe again.

Davian fell on his mentor's beard and wept.

27

"I do not want my fee returned." Bishop Lanianti was adamant as he looked at Davian across the plain oaken table in his abbey chambers. "I know that Myronius signed the contract, but my agreement was not merely with him; it was with the studio. I knew at the outset that you would do much of the work, and that pleased me. I have seen your sculptures, and I agree with your late master; your skill is equal to his. I want you to finish the Adam and Eve."

Davian looked down at his hands. He could not tell the good bishop of his dilemma. He loathed the idea of sculpting the Eve. Even if he did agree to it, he wondered whether he could create the beauty his patron desired. Would not the touch of his hands infect the stone with his hatred of women? Yet a contract was a contract, and he must honor it unless the bishop agreed to cancel.

"I have heard that the archbishop of Hrombulous has died," Davian said. "You have my condolences."

Lanianti smiled ruefully. "I may need more than mere condolences. The archbishop and I were old friends. We studied together at the university. In time we developed quite different views of the Master's ways with men, but

257

he was always tolerant of my variance from orthodoxy. We must pray that the new archbishop adopts the same policy."

"Is that unlikely?" Davian asked.

"It depends on who is appointed. Two or three of the candidates would simply turn their heads and allow me to continue my teaching. One, however, certainly would not. Bishop Corilano of Salini has complained of me ever since I announced the building of this abbey. He is active in the councils and highly ambitious. If he becomes archbishop, he could make trouble for me."

"Perhaps you will be the next archbishop."

Lanianti laughed gently. "They would sooner make a drunkard the keeper of the wine cellar. They think I would destroy all the ecclesium has stood for these many centuries. Some in the hierarchy tolerate me, but none of them would place me in a position of wider influence. Even many of those who tolerate what I do rue the day of my appointment as bishop. No, I will not be the archbishop."

"Well, I thank you for your time—as well as for your kind words when . . . when you buried Myronius, may he rest in peace. I will call on you when the sculptures are finished." Davian took his leave and returned to the studio.

His work habits did not change after the death of his master. He arose at daylight and ate the hearty breakfast Helenia cooked, and as soon as the light grew bright enough, he began work. On cloudy mornings he hung lanterns until he could see to carve the stone without them. Often after dinner he lit lanterns and continued hammering until they went out. After two months of such intensity, he was using his lightest hammer and finest chisels as he shaved thin layers of stone from the surface of the nearly completed Adam.

After another week of tooling, followed by three weeks

of pumice polishing, he arose one morning and looked at the Adam. He realized there was nothing more he could do to it. Rather than feeling his usual elation at completing a work, he felt a sense of dread, and he knew the reason. He now had no choice but to begin the Eve.

Reluctantly he took charcoal and paper and began sketching. After a few experimental lines, the heat of anger rose in his heart, and his hand seemed to take on a life of its own, sweeping the charcoal across the surface ever more rapidly until his movements accelerated into a frenzy. Lunchtime passed and he forgot to eat. His hand moved as if possessed, pushing, slashing, and jabbing the charcoal against the paper like a swordsman at a mortal enemy. Helenia called him to dinner, but he could not stop. A half hour later he suddenly stood up. Gripping the paper in both fists, he growled, "There's your woman, Bishop Lanianti!" He flung the paper across the room and stalked toward the table to a cold dinner. As he ate, his agitation fell away, and he grew calm again. He was drinking his wine when Helenia's sudden cry startled him. She stood near the door with her cloak on and her bag in her hand, staring in wide-eyed dismay at the drawing where it had fallen to the floor.

"What demon possesses you?" she said, her voice quavering as she glared at him in reproach. "Master Myronius, may he rest in peace, would be groaning in his grave to see what you have done here. You should be ashamed to foul his studio with such a horror." The poor woman walked wide around the drawing, opened the door, and slammed it behind her.

Davian walked over to the sketch and looked at it. The hair of the figure coiled and writhed like the deadly locks of Medusa. Her eyes, opened impossibly wide, glared out in fiendish hunger with knotted brows frowning above them. Her long, haglike nose bulged, a huge wart on the bridge.

259

Her cavernous mouth gaped like a grinning snake about to swallow its prey. The teeth were long and pointed like those of a shark. The arms, stretching forward, were wiry and thin, ending with grasping fingers, knotty and claw-like, weaponed with nails like talons. Her breasts hung to her waist like bags filled with lumpy curdles, and her belly protruded as if gorged with the souls of men. The wide hips were bloated with lumps of fat, the knees were knobby, and the shanks were scrawny and covered with hair. Mottled blemishes, warts, and pockmarks covered the skin.

"Here I have truly captured the inner soul of woman," he said, "but I cannot do this to Bishop Lanianti. I must find a way to fulfill his vision." He ripped the drawing to shreds and threw the pieces into the fire in the hearth. Then he disrobed and went to bed exhausted.

When he awoke the next morning, the words of the bishop seemed to lay on the surface of his mind like parchment on a table. *I want to show all the beauty the Master infused into creation. . . . I want my Adam and Eve to be the most perfect and beautiful specimens of humanity ever carved in stone.* It struck Davian that it would be no violation of his honor to fulfill the bishop's vision. Instead of creating a figure that revealed the truth about woman as she is, he could create a woman as the Master of the Universe intended woman to be. Her beauty would so overwhelm viewers that they could not imagine her inner self to be anything less than perfect. The outward form would reflect the ideal of perfect womanhood, thus showing the truth about the women of today by making them look insipid and vulgar by comparison.

He jumped out of bed and pulled on his clothes. Helenia set his breakfast before him without a word, casting her disapproving eyes at him as he began to eat and sketch on the paper beside his plate. He sketched all week, drawing on his training in anatomy and his memory of the female models Myronius had brought into the shop. By the end of the week he had settled on a pose, and three days later he had firmed it up and drawn it from three angles. The next step was to redraw the sketch and perfect every part, using a live model for accuracy. He would go into Hrombulous the next day and begin looking for a woman as nearly physically perfect as possible.

But the next morning as he brushed his hair and sat down to breakfast, he remembered his futile efforts to find a model for Adam. Each male he considered had been a superb specimen, but none had reached the ideal of absolute perfection. How could he expect to find a female to serve as the ideal model of the feminine? The answer hit him suddenly. He would not try to find absolute perfection in one single model; he would search for perfect individual features in many models. He would take the eyes of one, the neck of another, the hands of another, the torso of another and combine them to create a summation of feminine perfection.

His quest for models took more time than he expected. For the next month he roamed the streets, shops, and alleys of Hrombulous, looking for archetypal feminine forms and features. Slowly he began to find them. The most perfect facial structure he had ever seen he encountered at a clothier's shop. When he walked in the girl was looking down, wrapping a bolt of wool. She glanced up, and he drew in a sharp breath. He had never seen such beautifully formed cheekbones, forehead, and chin. The face was beautiful, and would have been stunningly so had her eyes not been set a touch too close together and her nose a fraction of an inch too short.

"Do you need a suit, sir?" she asked.

"No. I haven't come to buy anything. I'm an artist—a

261

sculptor—with a commission to carve a statue of our mother Eve for Bishop Lanianti. I'm looking for models. You have just the face I need. Will you pose for me?"

"Pose for a statue? Why I . . . I've never . . . I cannot pose for you. I cannot leave my father's shop."

"I will pay you fifteen denira. It will take only four hours, plus your travel from your shop to my studio."

"Fifteen denira! That's more than I earn in a week. But why should I believe you? How do I know you are not setting a trap for unsuspecting young girls?"

Davian choked down his disgust at such typical female suspicion. "I will pay you five denira in advance—right now—and the rest after you have posed. You need not be concerned about my intentions. My housekeeper will be present, and you may bring with you anyone you wish."

After thinking briefly the girl accepted the offer. Davian paid her the five denira and set the appointment for mid-morning the next day, then left the shop to continue his search. As the days passed he began to find the other ideal features he needed. He found the perfect hands on a flower seller near the market. He made a bargain with her similar to the one he had made with the shopgirl. Over the next five weeks, he found all the features he was looking for—neck, shoulders, eyes, nose, bosom, torso, hips, arms, legs, and feet. He persuaded each young woman to pose, offering the same terms he had offered to the shopgirl except that he paid those he required to disrobe five denira more. Thus his drawing moved toward completion. Though he had taken great pains to find the most ideal forms and features possible, he often embellished them from his growing inner vision to achieve an even higher perfection of form and proportion than he could find in reality.

After nine weeks of searching and drawing, Davian was satisfied—indeed he was elated—with his detailed drawing of Eve. She was as perfect as he thought it possible for the feminine form to be. Immediately he built his armature and made his preliminary clay figure. As the clay dried he spent two days searching the quarry of Penoa for a block of marble with the whiteness, purity, and granular fineness he wanted. On the day following its delivery, he began work on the actual statue.

Davian soon found himself consumed with the Eve project. He worked from sunup to sundown, often failing to take lunch or merely eating bread and cheese as he worked. On some evenings he was loath to stop working; he set up lamps and continued deep into the morning hours.

As the Eve emerged from the stone, even her rough-cut shape was arresting. Each contour, each form, each proportion promised to have the appearance of inevitability—to be exactly what the eye desired to see, as if the human mind held within it a template for perfect feminine beauty that reality had never been able to match. As he began to use smaller hammers and clean-edged chisels, the result was astonishing even to Davian. The image began to consume him, and he could think of nothing else day or night. Often he awoke in the mornings, his heart pounding with the anticipation of a lover in his eagerness to get to his Eve.

Over the next few weeks he smoothed all the surfaces to their ultimate shape, giving complete attention to each subtle nuance of form and feature. With a pointed chisel no larger than a nail, driven by delicate tappings of his smallest hammer, he shaped the lids and irises of the eyes, the nostrils, and the undulating curve of the full lips.

A morning came in mid-March when Davian arose and looked at his Eve for any flaws or incomplete areas. He could find none. The perfect, ideal feminine radiated like the glow of the moon from every part. As he gazed his heart beat faster and his breath came deeper. He looked into the

Eve's eyes and forgot they were of stone. He saw in them the very soul of ideal woman—receptive, loving, nurturing, responsive, accepting. Every feature of the creation before him, from the delicate toes to the thick waves of cascading hair, spoke with the same voice. This was the Master's perfect complement to man—his crowning glory, his completion. As he gazed enraptured, Davian understood the impelling desire of every man to both lose himself and find himself in a woman. He knew he could love a creature like this—one whose outward form was an eloquent expression of a glory inside. *Indeed, I believe I do love her,* he thought. He had told Myronius he was wedded to the stone he worked with. Now he saw a deeper meaning within that declaration. He was in love with beauty and perfection as personified in the exquisite form before him. Through the process of creating, he had tapped the source of all creativity in the Master himself and had fallen in love with the Creator's masterpiece—ideal woman. He was wedded to his Eve. She had become his bride of stone.

28

Though the Eve statue was complete, it still needed the pumice stone to achieve the sheen of warm skin. As Davian stood on his platform, gently polishing her cheeks with the stone, his mind began to darken at the thought of delivering her to Bishop Lanianti. She had become part of him, and to give her up would bring to his heart a grief as for a death. He wondered if he could do it. He thought of returning the bishop's money and keeping the statue. But such a course would destroy his honor. He was obligated to fulfill the contract. Perhaps he would become a monk in Lanianti's abbey. He could visit the garden often and adore his beloved.

As such thoughts troubled his mind, the door opened and in walked a man Davian had not seen since early in his apprenticeship—the sculptor Hadrianni of the most successful shop in Hrombulous. The man's rounded bulk and fine dress proclaimed his prosperity. He wore a rich, red velvet surcoat and matching leggings with the sheen of silk. His long, dark hair was oiled and combed and his beard carefully trimmed.

"The best of the morning to you, Davian," Hadrianni said, wheezing from the walk from his carriage.

"And to you, Hadrianni," Davian replied, stepping down from the platform. "What brings you here?"

Hadrianni did not speak, but in spite of himself gaped thunderstruck at the stone figure of Eve elevated on her platform in the center of the studio. After a long moment he forced his eyes to look away and saw the Adam figure standing several feet away. He said nothing as he walked around the two figures, scrutinizing them from all sides. He returned to where Davian stood and said, "These figures must be the commission from Bishop Lanianti the whole city is talking about."

"They are the bishop's commission. May I ask what brings you to my studio?"

"We had heard rumors that the bishop had commissioned statues that would defy the will of the ecclesium, and I wanted to see for myself. I thought I should bring you a warning." As he spoke he glanced often at the exquisite figure of the woman.

"A warning? What do you mean?" Davian asked.

"Few know it, for the appointment has not yet been announced. But reliable sources assure me that Corilano of Salini has just been appointed archbishop of Hrombulous. Not only is your commission in danger of being aborted, but you may be in danger of excommunication, or worse. It would surprise no one if the new archbishop declares Bishop Lanianti a heretic and has him imprisoned."

"Surely, he would not do such a thing," Davian said. "The bishop is dearly loved by all in his diocese."

"The people are fickle. They love Bishop Lanianti today; they will love his successor tomorrow. Some think Corilano will make an example of Lanianti to display his power and establish the tone of his rule. He sees the bishop as a threat to the purity of the ecclesium." Hadrianni lowered his bulk into a chair.

"Why are you telling me this?" Davian asked.

"I have been concerned about you since the death of your master and especially since the appointment of the new archbishop. You are in peril if you continue to follow the philosophy of Myronius with his slavish adherence to nature."

"Myronius didn't copy nature. He used the language of nature to express deeper realities. He taught me to go beyond nature and show the Master's original creation ideal."

"Whether one copies nature as it is or as he perceives it in the mind of the Master, still he copies. He doesn't express his own creativity. Davian, I have seen your work around the city, and you do have skill. You know how to shape the stone. I am prepared to offer you a position in my studio. I have ten sculptors working for me now. I no longer do work myself but manage the time and commissions of my artists. Join me, and I will teach you an artistic language not dependent on nature. I will teach you to draw forms from your own inner vision. You will no longer be a slave to physical reality. You will soar on your own imagination and break the shackles that bind you to nature."

"Thank you, Hadrianni. But I believe Myronius was right when he said that an artist who abandons nature abandons the mind of the Master, which leaves one adrift in a sea of meaninglessness."

Hadrianni frowned and shook his head. "You have much to learn, young man. Still, the offer stands. If you ever change your mind, come to me—that is, if you're not rotting away deep in the archbishop's prison." He heaved himself up from the chair, and with a final long look at the Eve, he bid Davian farewell.

267

Two weeks after Hadrianni's call, Davian was applying the pumice to the calves and ankles of the Eve when the door suddenly burst open. He looked up to see a robed and hooded figure enter quickly and close the door behind him. The man stood with his back to the door and looked all about the studio, then pushed his cowl back from his head. Davian recognized the young acolyte who had accompanied Bishop Lanianti at the signing of the contract.

"Ignatio," Davian said. "What brings you here—and in such haste?"

"Davian," the acolyte said, continuing to look all about him. "Is anyone else here?"

"No one at all," Davian replied.

"Not even your housekeeper?"

"She won't come today. She sees her daughter in Alborani on Saturdays."

"We must talk. Evil is afoot, and you must—" He stopped speaking and drew in a sharp breath as he saw the Eve standing behind Davian.

"What evil?" Davian asked. "What are you speaking of?" But Ignatio, staring openmouthed at the statue, did not hear him.

"That is the most beautiful thing I have ever seen in my life," the acolyte said, still staring. "It's as if I'm seeing a true woman for the first time."

"But the evil that's coming. What do you need to tell me?"

Reluctantly Ignatio tore his eyes away from the Eve and looked at Davian. "I thought you might have heard. Corilano has been appointed archbishop of Hrombulous."

Davian's heart sank. Hadrianni had been right. He ushered the acolyte to the table and poured him a glass of wine. "Tell me what has happened."

"Archbishop Corilano's first act was to issue a writ to Bishop Lanianti demanding that he desist from teaching his theology of love and desire for the Master and return to the orthodox doctrine of fear and wrath. He demanded that the bishop rescind his edict allowing his priests to marry. He also demanded that the bishop abandon his plans for the Edenic garden and turn it into a plain lawn. And he demanded that the bishop cancel his contract for the statues of Adam and Eve and send men to your studio to destroy them."

"What? Destroy my statues?" Davian cried. "How did the archbishop learn about them?"

"Apparently, he was informed by one of your fellow artists. Do you know of a sculptor by the name of Hadrianni?"

"Yes. He was here two weeks ago." Anger heated Davian's face. "He came with a pretense of friendship and concern. The liar!" He banged his fist on the table and stood suddenly, toppling his chair. He paced about the floor, running his hand through his hair in agitation. "And what will Bishop Lanianti do?"

"He has seven days to reply to the writ. If he agrees to comply, the archbishop will do nothing, and Bishop Lanianti will have been tamed. But if the bishop defies the writ, he will be arrested and tried for heresy, which carries a sentence of long imprisonment."

"He has seven days," Davian said. "He could flee."

"No, the archbishop posted armed guards around the cathedral and abbey. Bishop Lanianti is already a prisoner. I had to take extreme care to be sure I wasn't followed here."

"Will Bishop Lanianti accede to these demands?"

"No. He is prepared to suffer the consequences. But he is concerned about the sculptures. He won't be able to accept them now, of course. Even if he chose to do so, the guards would intercept and destroy them. And he fears that after the seven days have expired, the archbishop's men will come to your studio and destroy the images here."

"No!" Davian shouted. "It must not happen."

"Bishop Lanianti said exactly the same thing," the acolyte replied. "He wants me to help you save them."

"How? What must we do?"

"We must hide them, and the bishop has told me of a way to do it. Far beneath Hrombulous is a network of caves where the ancients buried their dead. A thousand years ago when Hrombulan emperors outlawed those who followed the Master, the fugitive believers hid in these caverns. They have long since been abandoned and the entrances sealed. However, Bishop Lanianti knows of an entrance. He befriended the owner of a certain inn at a time of need. That inn was constructed adjacent to a bluff. While building the inn, the owner dug into the bluff and found a network of the caves. As his business grew, he finished off some of these caverns to make additional guest rooms. They are popular in the summers because of their coolness. He sealed off the rest of the caves but installed a door giving him access to them. The bishop has contacted the innkeeper—whose name is Lexian—and he has agreed to hide your Adam and Eve in his caves."

"But can he be trusted?" Davian replied.

"I would trust my life to him, as indeed the bishop has. You needn't doubt. He is a just and true man who loves the Master of the Universe."

"What shall I do?"

"You won't do it alone; I will help. We will build crates for the statues. We will pack them with wool and load them onto your cart. I will guide you to Lexian's Inn, where he will have men to carry the crates into the caves."

"I'm very grateful," Davian said.

"I'm happy to help you, Davian. The bishop wanted to help you partly to preserve the beauty you have created and partly because he cannot pay the balance of your fee. The archbishop has confiscated all cathedral and abbey funds. Bishop Lanianti releases you from your contract and so states in this document." Ignatio drew from his robe a parchment scroll, which he handed to Davian. "These papers revert ownership of the Adam and Eve to you. You are free to sell them to another patron. He sends his deepest apologies."

Ignatio shed his robe and donned a tunic and leggings, and the two men began working. They finished the crates in two days, and using ropes and pulleys, they eased the figures into their temporary coffins. When they had packed the statues with cushioning wool, sealed the lids with nails, and secured them with ropes, they brought in the cart and loaded the crates onto it. On the following morning they rose early and drove to Lexian's Inn. By early afternoon the crates were safely hidden in a dark, stony corridor deep in the cliff behind the inn.

After unloading the crates, Davian and Ignatio mounted the wagon. "I thank you for your help," Davian said. "I will drive you to the abbey."

"No! You don't understand. I escaped from the abbey, and if I return I'll be not only punished but also questioned. And they have effective measures to get the answers they want. Bishop Lanianti forbade me to return."

"Where can I take you, then?"

Ignatio grinned at Davian. "Take me to your studio. I am your guest until things settle."

Darkness had fallen by the time they reached the studio. After putting away the horse and wagon, they entered the door and Davian lit a lamp. When the flame steadied, he

271

looked up and started. Facing them across the table was a man, robed in black with his face hidden in the shadows of a cowl.

"Who are you? What are you doing here?" Davian demanded.

The dark figure slowly pushed the cowl back from his head, revealing a craggy, heavy-jowled face with eyes glaring from under thick, black brows. "I am Lucian, the accorder for Archbishop Corilano. Are you the sculptor Davian?"

"I am. But you have no right to—"

"And is your companion the acolyte Ignatio of Alborani Abbey?"

"I am," Ignatio answered.

"It is my duty to arrest both of you in the name of the ecclesium. Davian the sculptor for heresy and Ignatio the acolyte for violating the quarantine of Alborani Abbey."

"But this arrest is illegal," Ignatio said. "The archbishop's edict gave Bishop Lanianti seven days to comply to his demands. You are violating the terms of the edict."

"Besides, the statues have already been destroyed," Davian said. "Look around you. You don't see them, do you?"

"I have already noted their absence. But I am not fool enough to believe you have destroyed them. Where are they?"

"I will answer none of your questions. And I will not submit to this illegal arrest," Davian said.

At that moment he gasped as he felt his arms clutched firmly from behind. He tried to wrench free, but it was futile. He realized that two men were gripping him, each holding one of his arms with both their hands. He glanced at Ignatio and saw that he had been captured in the same manner. As the two captives struggled, three additional faces came into the circle of the lamplight, all large men with brutal expressions and tattered tunics. Obviously, the accorder had hired them from alleys and taverns.

Davian and Ignatio quit struggling, and the accorder grinned, his face flickering ghoulishly in the light of the lamps on the table. "As you can see, it is futile to resist." He drew from his robe a heavy leather purse, which he laid on the table. "Do you recognize this, sculptor? It is your life savings, is it not? You should take more care to hide such valuables. I have counted the contents, and co-incidentally, I find that the sum exactly covers your fine for creating art unauthorized by the ecclesium. Of course, this does not eliminate the need for strong discipline to purge you of the sinful desire to create such work." Again he grinned, and Davian thought the devil himself could not have looked more evil.

"Now, I ask you again," Lucian said, "where have you taken the statues?"

Davian glared at the accorder, saying nothing. Lucian nodded toward the hulk of a man standing next to him. The man stepped forward, drew back his hand, and hit Davian full on the side of his face.

"Where are the statues?" the accorder demanded.

Davian remained silent, and a bruising blow hit his jaw.

"Where are the statues?" Lucian asked again.

Another blow left blood flowing from Davian's mouth.

"Where are the statues?"

The next blow almost closed Davian's right eye.

"Where are the statues?"

The brute of a man drew back to strike again when Ignatio cried out, "Stop! I will tell you where we hid the statues."

"No, Ignatio!" Davian bellowed. "You must not tell."

"I will tell. Else they will kill you. They are only stone, and you are a living person. It's not worth it. We took them to—"

Davian's shout drowned his words. He kept yelling until the accorder's brute clamped a heavy hand across his mouth.

"We buried them on the far side of the hill of the Zeus temple," Ignatio cried. "I can take you to the place."

Davian twisted his head violently, causing the rough hand pressing his mouth to slip to one side. A finger pushed into his mouth, and he bit hard. With a bellow of pain the man jerked his hand away, peeling skin from his finger. In that moment of confusion Davian pushed backward with all his strength, driving the men clasping his arms into the bench behind them. As they tumbled to the floor Davian wrenched free of his captors and rolled away. He scrambled to his feet and ran toward his box of chisels. But a hand caught his ankle, and he crashed into the table, overturning it. The lamp clattered to the floor, spilling its oil across the planks. The oil burst into flame, and the room glowed red in the spreading fire.

The oil spattered the leggings of the man gripping Ignatio's right arm. He howled with pain and began beating at his burning clothing with both hands. At that moment Davian slammed into the man holding Ignatio's left arm and brought him to the floor along with Ignatio. Ignatio wrenched free as Davian began to pummel the man's face.

"Run, Ignatio!" Davian yelled.

But Ignatio did not run. As one of the men jumped onto Davian's back, Ignatio picked up a chair and hammered the attacker's head, crumpling him to the floor. Davian got to his feet and stood with the acolyte. They began backing

274

toward the door as fire spread rapidly across the planked floor and began to lick at the walls.

"Stop them now—before they reach the door!" Lucian shouted. The three men charged forward.

Davian ducked a wild blow and kicked hard with his boot, feeling it go deep into the soft belly of his attacker. Air exploded from the man's mouth as he doubled over in pain. Ignatio reached the door, but the second attacker caught his tunic and tugged him back. Davian grabbed the man and pushed him hard into a support beam. The acolyte's tunic ripped from his back, and he reached the door and pushed the bar away. The door swung open, and the two young men ran out into the darkness.

"Go after them, you idiots!" Lucian shouted.

The night was moonless but clear. Davian knew the road, and the stars overhead gave just enough light for him to see. Ignatio followed closely. Soon they heard their pursuers some thirty feet behind.

"We must leave the road," Davian said. "I know a path. Follow me."

Moments later he turned to his right and disappeared into the brush. Ignatio plunged after him, and soon they were descending a steep, rocky bank covered with trees and brush. Twice Ignatio fell. Davian helped him to his feet, and they continued their descent. Soon the ground leveled, and they could see the gray of the river to their right. They reached a cluster of cypress trees at the edge of the water and stopped there to catch their breath.

The two young men looked back and saw no sign of pursuit, but atop the bank they had descended, the glow of flames and the shadow of black smoke billowed into the heavens.

"We've seen the last of Myronius's studio," Davian said.

"That's not the worst of your problems," Ignatio replied. "The accorder's dogs are still coming."

They both listened, and the sound of approaching footfalls and heavy breathing was unmistakable.

"Do you swim?" Davian asked.

"Yes," the acolyte answered, "and our friends here don't look as if they would stay afloat."

Without another word both men slipped into the river and stroked toward the far shore. When they reached the bank, they pulled themselves from the water and looked back across the river. Though they could not see their pursuers, their bellowed curses rang across the water.

The two friends sat on a stone to catch their breath. "We're in a pretty fix," Davian said. "No money, no home, no work, and outlawed by the ecclesium. You don't even have a shirt. And we cannot show our faces in Hrombulous or the towns near it. We must leave this city, even this country."

"Perhaps," Ignatio replied. "But we need not be hasty. We must deliberate on what we should do next. For now we can go to Lexian's Inn. He will hide and feed us until the Master of the Universe shows us our path."

29

The innkeeper Lexian gladly made a place for Davian and Ignatio deep in the caverns behind his inn. He provided cots and blankets as well as a change of clothing for each of them. Davian placed his cot next to the two crates containing his statues, which were set upright at the end of a long, hewn stone corridor. He thought of little but the Eve hidden inside. Ignatio placed his cot a few feet away from Davian's. They slept during the days and at night did work for Lexian, sweeping out the restaurant, repairing furniture, cleaning stables, hauling away refuse, or performing any task needed. They began to let their beards grow to prevent recognition by any ecclesiates who might come to the inn.

In their idle hours they talked mostly of their future. Ignatio thought they should act on Davian's original suggestion to leave the country, traveling by night and sleeping in the days. But in the relative safety of Lexian's Inn, Davian turned reluctant, pointing out that they were penniless and could not purchase food and lodging on the road. Ignatio answered that they could beg or find menial jobs along the way. The Master would take care of them. But Davian held

277

back. The root of his reluctance was his refusal to leave the statues, especially the Eve. He insisted that they should bide their time and wait for the right solution.

Unlike most owners of inns, Lexian closed his restaurant an hour before midnight, and he did not allow raucous behavior or obnoxious drunkenness. Davian and Ignatio usually began their tasks an hour before the doors closed. Most of the time they worked in the kitchen or behind the inn where patrons could not see them. When it was necessary to venture among the patrons, they took care to keep their faces turned away from searching eyes.

They had been at Lexian's eight days when the innkeeper came into their cave with news that Bishop Lanianti had been arrested and brought immediately to trial. The trial had lasted less than a day, and the bishop had been found guilty and condemned to death.

"Condemned to death?" Ignatio was incredulous. "Surely the report is mistaken. Punishment for bishops who vary from the ecclesium's teachings is imprisonment, not death."

"Archbishop Corilano charged Lanianti not with variance but with high heresy," Lexian replied. "As you know, the penalty for high heresy is death. Since the jury was of the archbishop's own picking, he got his conviction."

"When is the execution?" Ignatio asked, heartsick at the news.

"It has already occurred," Lexian answered, placing his hand on the acolyte's shoulder. "He was beheaded last night."

Both young men were stunned at the news, but Ignatio grieved deeply. Davian, knowing the pain his friend was feeling, offered to assume his duties while the acolyte spent time in fasting and prayer. He would work longer into the daylight hours of the morning to complete them.

On the second night after the terrible news, a ray of hope beamed into the young men's lives. Davian had just finished emptying the refuse barrel. He set the empty container back in place and went to the washpot to scrub pots and pans. The chief cook, Manzoni by name, came to him with a tray containing two plates of vinegared lamb.

"Davian," Manzoni said, "Marita tore her dress and has gone to mend it. I need you to take these plates to the table by the east window."

He took the tray into the dining room. At the table sat a dark-haired man of about forty-five years—likely a merchant, Davian judged by his dress—and a younger man with long blond hair. As Davian approached, he was surprised to hear them speaking the Anglais language, which he had not heard spoken since his mother died.

"The old relics are now so picked over that one can hardly find anything more than an occasional hand or part of a head," the dark-haired man said. "And the new art—bah! The king of the Seven Kingdoms is right. It doesn't deserve the name. Crude renditions of the body, distorted, ugly shapes that would make a vulture vomit." Davian set the plates before the men as the merchant continued. "And it's all the fault of the ecclesium. They won't let artists produce beauty here. The Master must turn his head in disgust rather than look upon the wretched forms that come out of the studios of Hrombulous."

"Renalleo, keep your voice down," the blond man said, looking furtively around the room. "The ecclesium just executed one of its own bishops for defying the very art you are ranting about."

"That is why I'm speaking in your tongue. No one around here can understand a word we say. If only we could find the sculptor that unfortunate bishop commissioned to do his pieces, we might get back into Perivale's good graces."

"If you had not spent all your time combing the ruins of Hrombulous for relics and spent a little time in villages around the city, you might have heard of this artist," the blond man said.

Davian turned away and began to clean the table next to the two men so he could listen as the merchant continued.

"I know, I know. You don't have to tell me again. But what am I to do now? I have lost my best patron—a king with more money than he can spend who has a voracious appetite for art. And I have run out of pieces to bring to him. He won't see me again until I bring more work in the ancient tradition, not to mention a sculptor for his monument." The merchant shook his head and threw up his hands in despair.

Davian finished cleaning the table and returned to the kitchen, his heart pounding at what he had heard. He remembered that his mother had mentioned something about seven kingdoms. Wasn't the country where she was born somehow connected with seven kingdoms? Rhondilar! That was the name of her birthplace. And he was sure she had said it was one of seven kingdoms on a large island in the Northern Sea.

And this merchant had a patron—a king in the Seven Kingdoms who wanted art—more art, new art. He thought of his Adam, entombed deep in the burial cave. Perhaps the merchant would buy the Adam. He could sell it for more than enough money to buy Ignatio and himself passage to some other country and ship the Eve with them.

When Marita returned, Davian went back to his pots. As he scrubbed, the idea of offering the Adam to the merchant boiled in his mind like an egg in a pan. He could see no flaw in the thought, and soon it took on the status of a decision made. He looked out the kitchen door to see if the merchant was still in the restaurant. He was at his table, and Marita was pouring more wine for him.

When the serving girl came into the kitchen, Davian asked her to let him know when the customers at the table by the east window began to leave. Marita was elated at his request. Since she had first laid eyes on this tall young man with dark hair and curling lashes, she had mooned over him. But he had never even glanced in her direction. Tonight was the first time he had ever requested anything of her, and her heart pounded in her breast as he spoke. She would gladly comply.

Ten minutes later she came scurrying into the kitchen. "Davian, the merchant and his friend are leaving now," she said.

"Thank you, Marita." Davian dried his hands and slipped out the back door, and the girl almost swooned to hear her name on his lips.

He circled around to the front of the inn and found the merchant and his companion about to step into their carriage.

"Renalleo, may I have a word with you?" Davian said as he approached.

"Who are you? How do you know my name?" the startled merchant replied.

"My name is Davian. I work in Lexian's Inn. I overheard you talking tonight, and I would have a word with you."

"You overheard us talking? Impossible. We were speaking in another language."

"I understood every word," Davian replied in Anglais, and the two men blanched in the darkness. "I mean you no harm," he continued. "Indeed, I believe I can do you good."

281

"What in the Master's name do you mean?"

"I am a sculptor, a fugitive from the ecclesium, daring to venture out only at nights. I am a student of the late Myronius of Hrombulous, may he rest in peace, who taught me the sculpting techniques of the ancients. Indeed, I am the sculptor Bishop Lanianti commissioned to do his garden pieces. I have one of those pieces in my possession that I would like to show you."

As Renalleo stared at the young man, his companion said, "Renalleo, let's go. This could be a trap. He may be an ecclesiate himself."

"How can you prove yourself?" Renalleo asked.

"I have a sculpture that will surely impress your patron in the Seven Kingdoms."

"Indeed you heard much tonight," Renalleo replied. "Where is this sculpture?"

"Not more than five minutes from where you stand. I also take a great risk in showing it to you. Before I will lead you to it, you must swear to forget where you saw it."

"Renalleo," his companion said, "the more we hear, the more this has the sound of treachery. Let us go now."

Renalleo made no move but continued to look hard at Davian, whose face he could barely make out in the dim light from Lexian's windows. "No, Kolar, if I don't explore this mystery, I will surely regret it later. Davian, we will see your statue. Lead the way."

Davian turned and walked toward the back parts of the inn. When he reached the kitchen door, the two men followed him inside. He turned to them and said, "Give me a moment to take leave of my duties."

In a moment he returned and led the men out of the kitchen and into the hallway leading to the rooms that had been carved into the caves. The merchants followed. After passing the guest rooms, he took a torch from the wall. Then using a key on his belt, he unlocked a door that opened into a damp, stony, unfinished hallway.

Kolar stopped and put a restraining hand on his companion's shoulder. "No, Renalleo. We'd be fools to go in there. Who knows what this man may do to us in that dark cavern where no one could hear our shouts."

Without a word Davian turned back and walked past them, leaving them at the entrance to the caves as he retraced his steps and disappeared into a side door. Seconds later he emerged carrying a short sword in his hand. The eyes of the two men went wide, and Kolar backed against the wall, gasping in terror. As Davian approached he turned the hilt of the sword toward Kolar.

"Take this. As you can see, I am unarmed. I will walk ahead of you and you can keep the point at my back." Without awaiting a response, he entered the stony corridor, lighting the way with his torch. The merchants followed.

After making several turns, the young sculptor approached the cot where Ignatio sat reading a borrowed book by the light of a candle. His eyes grew wide as he saw the men approach, one with a sword pointed at his friend.

"Ignatio," Davian called. "Don't be afraid. Things are not as they appear. Will you now lower your sword, Kolar?"

The man sheepishly complied.

"Ignatio, this is Renalleo, a merchant dealing in art, and his companion Kolar. I have brought them to see my Adam. Should Renalleo choose to purchase it, you and I will have the means to flee Appienne and escape the ecclesium."

Ignatio arose from his cot and greeted the visitors. Then he held the torch as Davian untied the ropes about the crate containing the Adam. He removed the lid and began to pull out the rolls of wool stuffed around the marble. When all of the packing was removed, he called the men

283

closer and took the torch, illuminating the white marble standing inside the crate.

Renalleo drew a sharp breath and stared, his mouth gaping open. After a moment he spoke softly. "I have never in my life seen anything to match this. It is truly magnificent." Slowly, almost reverently, he stepped closer to the image, never taking his eyes from it. He put his head inside the crate, looking first at one side then the other as he ran his fingers lightly over the velvet surface. "This is as perfect as any work I have ever seen. Name your price."

Davian gave him a price equivalent to the unpaid balance on both figures of Bishop Lanianti's commission.

"I have never paid that much for a sculpture before, but I will pay it for this. I know my patron will be delighted with it. Do you have other pieces?"

"Nothing I can sell," Davian replied.

"Then what is in the second crate?" Renalleo demanded.

"It is another sculpture. But I won't sell it."

"What is the nature of it that you won't sell it?"

"It is the complement to the piece you are buying," Davian said. "He is Adam; in the other crate stands the matching Eve."

"Open the crate. I must see it."

Since coming to the caves, Davian had longed to see the Eve himself. So he willingly opened the second crate, pulled away the woolen packing, and held the torch for the two men to see.

Renalleo stared as if he had turned to stone. He could not speak. He could not look away. He thought he had never understood the meaning of feminine beauty until this moment. His eye told him that every line, every curvature, every subtle undulation of surface was exactly what the Master had intended when he created woman.

His mind told him that every feature and every nuance of form displayed the deeper reality of the ideal feminine. His heart told him that from this moment on, every time he looked at a woman he would see in her something of this Eve.

Renalleo finally found his voice. "Davian, surely you don't want to separate these two magnificent creations. You must sell them both to me."

"As I told you, she is not for sale."

"I will pay you double the price of the Adam."

"She is not for sale."

"I will pay you triple the price of the Adam."

"You waste your breath, Renalleo. I won't sell her at any price—not to anyone. I will keep her."

"Then you must work for me. I can sell everything you create. I will keep you busy for years. I will offer you a contract even tonight."

"You forget that I'm a fugitive. I cannot set up shop here. When you pay me for the Adam, I must flee this country."

"Come with me to the isle of the Seven Kingdoms," Renalleo said. "A project awaits you there that is beyond the ability of any artist I know. My patron, the high king of the island, has asked me to find a sculptor to create his own monument. You are certainly the man. We can leave immediately."

After a moment of thought, Davian said, "Let me take you back to the entrance of these caves. You may wait for me there while Ignatio and I consider your proposal."

When the two young men were alone, Ignatio looked at Davian and grinned broadly. "The Master has heard me. My petitions these last two days have been not merely for the followers of Bishop Lanianti but for you as well, Davian. It seems that the Master has spoken."

"Then you think we should accept Renalleo's offer?"

"I think we must," Ignatio replied. "The path seems clear to me."

"I agree. Let's go back and tell Renalleo that we will journey with him to the Seven Kingdoms."

Part 3

The Monument

30

Renalleo stood outside the oaken doors of Morningstone's great hall, awaiting his name to be announced to the king. He could not stand still. He rubbed his hands, stroked his beard, adjusted the folds of his robe, and checked again the white sheet that veiled the sculpture. The statue was set on a low planked platform equipped with four wooden wheels. His assistant, Kolar, stood silent, his eyes heavy lidded, and stifled a yawn.

"What is taking the king so long? Is he sleeping?" Renalleo said.

The guards at the door stared ahead impassively.

Finally the doors swung open. King Perivale sat on his throne elevated on the three-tiered dais at the far end of the hall. Renalleo nodded to Kolar, who began to push the platform across the polished stone floor. At the rumble of the wheels, everyone in the hall looked up and watched in curiosity until the cart rolled to a stop at the foot of the dais.

"Renalleo," Perivale said, "I have warned you not to show your face in this hall with more of your tired and broken artifacts. I hope you have given heed."

Renalleo smiled and bowed to the king. "Indeed I have, O great King Perivale. You will be immensely pleased with what I show you today. I have here a masterpiece like nothing yet seen in the known world. In fact, it is the very "

"No more words, Renalleo. Show me what you have," Perivale said.

Renalleo signaled to his assistant, who whisked the sheet away with a dramatic flourish. Perivale slowly stood from his throne, his lips parted and his eyes wide with wonder at the dazzling image of the nude man, perfect in every detail, muscular and heroic in size and proportion.

"I have never seen anything like this," the king said. He stepped down from the dais and walked slowly around the image, staring in awe. "It does not have a single flaw. The skin looks as if it would yield to the touch. He looks as if he could step down and walk. Where did you find such a marvelous wonder—and so well preserved?"

"Preservation has nothing to do with the perfection of this sculpture," Renalleo replied. "This was carved from marble not more than one year ago by a young genius who is alive now."

"But this looks nothing like other carvings by artists of today," Perivale said. "Everything you have shown has been flat and misshapen, a parody of humanity. This is at least as magnificent as work done by the masters of the ancient world."

"That is quite true." Renalleo beamed with pleasure. "A generation ago a master sculptor in the city of Hrombulous revived the art of the ancients. This piece is the work of his protégé, a brilliantly talented boy of less than twenty years. It bears the title *Adam*. He has a matching female image of equal perfection named *Eve*. I tried to purchase it as well, offering thrice what I paid for this piece, but he refused to sell."

"Quadruple the price. I will pay ten times the amount," Perivale said.

"He will not sell for any price," Renalleo said. "But what he will do is sculpt your monument."

Slowly a smile lit the king's face. "Renalleo, you are a wonder. You have accomplished what you said to be impossible. You shall be knighted for this. Return immediately to your country and bring the artist to Corenham."

"The king honors me more than I deserve." The merchant bowed low, relief draining away the tension that had plagued him since his last encounter with the king. "The artist is here, and he is ready to begin."

On the following day Renalleo took Davian to Morningstone Castle to meet King Perivale. They dismounted at the gatehouse, and stablers took their horses. The merchant led the artist across the bailey and along a cobbled walkway lined with trees and shaped hedges on both sides. A fifteen-foot stone wall stood just beyond the trees on the left. Dense vines covered the wall at irregular intervals, and Davian could see spreading above the stones the leafy branches of several shade trees growing inside the wall.

Suddenly he heard the plucking of a mandolin followed by the clear tones of an exquisite feminine voice weighted with unspeakable tragedy and pathos. She sang a melody so mournful that it brought an ache to Davian's heart. He clutched Renalleo's arm and stopped to listen.

"What a beautiful voice!" he said. "And such a plaintive melody. Who is singing?"

"I don't know," the merchant replied, walking forward again. "But we have no time to dally. We must see the king now."

Davian was reluctant to leave the bailey before the song

was finished, but his escort urged him on, and the sound faded behind them. The voice and the elegy continued to haunt him like an echo from the crags of a desert until the two were ushered into Perivale's presence.

The king was eager to begin the project, and Davian found him quite willing to accede to all of his requests. Perivale gave him a studio with an attached room near Cheaping Square, a team of five master stonecutters as assistants, and carpenters to erect and change the scaffolding as needed. In addition, four temporary wooden towers would be built, each three stories high and one hundred paces from the monument in the four compass directions. They would serve as surveying points for checking proportions.

Perivale explained what he wanted in the sculpture. "It must fill the entire height of the marble stone, and it must be designed in the heroic Hrombulan style—noble, nude, and idealized. The face must be an accurate portrait of my features."

They agreed that as the four towers were being built, Davian would study the shape of the stone and make drawings of possible configurations for the image. The king would select from these, and then he would pose three days of every week for sketches, which Davian would use to make the preliminary clay model. When the terms were set, the king called a scribe to write the contract. After Davian and the king signed it, the scribe advanced half the fee—an amount three times the young sculptor's most ambitious dreams—and gave Renalleo the largest commission he had ever received.

Davian and Renalleo spent the next two days making all the arrangements stipulated in the agreement. The merchant hired carpenters for the towers and scaffolding and stonemasons to help Davian cut away massive sections of the stone. He ordered the beams and planks needed for the carpentry and put Davian in touch with a blacksmith to have his tools made.

Davian invited Ignatio to live in the studio with him, but the young man declined. He could not secure employment without knowing the language, and he would not idle away each day while Davian worked. He chose rather to seek admission to the abbey of Corenham, where he could learn Anglais and resume his studies in theology. Renalleo, now high in Perivale's graces, spoke with the king about Ignatio's desires, and Perivale sent a message to Archbishop Norvan of the kirk, as the ecclesium was called in the Seven Kingdoms. After a lengthy interview with Ignatio, with Davian serving as interpreter, the archbishop deemed the young student solidly educated to his claimed level and accepted him as an acolyte.

Davian spent the next several days studying the great stone that would become the monument. First he examined its base, finding the direction of the grain, studying the faint veins of varied color that ran through every kind of rock, and looking for fissures and cracks. He walked all about it, scrutinizing and sketching it from all angles. He viewed it from across Cheaping Square, walked the streets around it, sketched it from vantage points between cottages, and got permission from shopkeepers to view the stone from the upper stories of their buildings.

When he had accumulated over thirty drawings, he tacked them to his studio wall and sat in a chair to study them, looking for the image that resided within the stone. He made several sketches of ways a body could fit its shape, but he knew that for the monument to be authentic, the pose would need to be Perivale's own.

On the next morning he mounted his horse and rode to Morningstone Castle. He requested an audience with the

293

king, and it was granted immediately. He asked permission to follow the king for several days, watching his manner of movement, the way he held his body, his use of his hands, the angle at which he held his head. Perivale understood the request and granted it for three hours of every afternoon. Davian bowed, thanked him, and left the hall.

As he walked down the cobbled pathway from the keep to the stable, he heard the haunting song again. He stopped to listen. He had never heard a woman's voice more beautiful, but the melody was almost unbearably sad. He listened to the plaintive strains, sung in round, resonant tones to the minor chords of the mandolin, and his eyes brimmed with tears. He hardly breathed until the song ended. He sat on a nearby bench, waiting to see if another would begin. But it did not, and the young man took a deep breath, wiped his eyes, and left the castle.

Davian visited Morningstone Castle at midday for the next several days. Perivale took his lunch with several knights and lords in the little hall, and Davian was given a seat where he could watch the king. Afterward he followed the king wherever he went, sometimes to the falcon fields, sometimes to the arena where knights were trained, and sometimes to practice archery or inspect a new horse or hunting dog.

Twice on these daily trips, Davian again heard the heart-wrenching song from beyond the wall, and both times he stopped, spellbound and on the verge of tears. Once he asked a guard at the gate who the singer was, but the man would not answer.

In the evenings when he returned to his cottage, Davian sketched the king in the poses he had observed during the day. As a result, he built up a considerable pictorial documentation of Perivale's bodily mannerisms. But he did not yet see a position that would convey to all eternity the nobility of the hero of the Seven Kingdoms.

The Kirk of Meridan did not restrict their acolytes as did the Hrombulan ecclesium, and Ignatio often dined with Davian at the Red Falcon Inn. He was determined to speak nothing but his new language in the presence of his friend.

"I learn the Anglais good, do you think not?" the acolyte said as they sat at a table.

"Quite well indeed. No doubt you will soon be teaching it," Davian said with a laugh.

A winsome young maiden arrived to take their order, glancing often with obvious admiration at the young sculptor. She walked to the kitchen with a swing of her hips intended to attract Davian's eye, but he did not even glance in her direction.

Ignatio was perplexed. "Female person look to invite at you. But you not at her looking even. You not liking . . . uh, what is word . . . female persons?"

"Girl, woman, maiden," Davian said. "Those are our words for young female humans. No, I do not like women. I will have nothing to do with them."

"I not to undersit. You—"

"What do you mean, 'undersit'?" Davian asked.

"Undersit. You know, to know of meaning—to have mind see."

"Oh, you mean understand," Davian said, laughing again.

"Yes, yes. I not to understand. You make most fairest girl woman maiden ever in marble rock stone. But you looking not at fair real girl woman maiden."

"It's a long story, Ignatio, but you may as well hear it." Davian told his friend the entire tale of his infatuation with the barmaid Emeralda and her cruel betrayal. "So you see, women have fallen too far from the Master's ideal. I will have nothing to do with them."

"But not all girl woman maidens being bad. Maybe some have real loving."

"Perhaps somewhere a woman exists whose heart is true. If so, she is a rarity. I saw too many at Papialona's, and they were all alike. I will not risk it again. I will stay away from women and be as celibate as the monks in your abbey."

"What you meaning? Meridan kirk monks allow to wedding girl woman maidens. Same as Bishop Lanianti let us too. It one thing got him dead."

The two young men spent the rest of the evening talking of their new life in Meridan, Davian correcting Ignatio's Anglais and Ignatio correcting Davian's misunderstandings about the kirk. At two hours before midnight, Davian left coins on the table and the two friends parted.

31

On the following afternoon Davian went as usual to Morningstone Castle to observe the king in his daily routines.
As Perivale left the hall and strode into the bailey toward
the kennels, Davian followed. The artist watched as the
king strolled beneath the great oaks standing like leafy
sentinels along the flagstone path. Perivale stopped and
looked to his right, and Davian moved forward to see the
cause. A fair young woman richly dressed in noble finery
was pointing up into the branches of a tree and saying
something to the king. The king smiled, walked toward
her, and looked to where she pointed. Davian could see a
small, white cat clinging to a branch a few feet above her
head. Perivale reached up with his right hand, extending
his arm to its full length, and gently grasped the animal
and handed it to the woman. She cuddled the kitten in her
arms, then stood on her tiptoes and kissed the king on the
cheek. He quickly pushed her away and looked all around
them. When he saw Davian, he glared momentarily but said
nothing and walked on as the woman remained beneath
the tree, cooing and stroking her pet.

But the king need not have been concerned about what

Davian saw. For the moment, the artist in him rose above the moralist. He had seen nothing but the grace and power of the man as he reached upward to retrieve the cat. Here was the pose he had been searching for. He dropped to a stone bench, took the paper and charcoal from his cloak, and began sketching. Within minutes he had captured the essence of the pose—a man reaching toward the heavens, his hand open as if to grasp the promise of eternity. The entire form exuded grace, power, nobility, aspiration, and hope. And Davian knew it would fit the stone perfectly. He stuffed the sketch into his cloak and hurried to his studio.

He spent the rest of that day and the next refining the pose to show Perivale. On the following morning he got an early audience with the king and presented the drawing. Perivale saw in the work exactly what Davian intended and approved the pose immediately. And for the next nine afternoons, the king posed in his chambers as the artist rendered four drawings in high detail, one from the front, one from the back, and one from each side. With the sketches complete, Davian began to render the preliminary clay model, which he chose to do life-size to ensure accuracy of the proportions.

With his goal established and his course set, he arose each day at dawn, ate a quick breakfast, and lit lamps to give him light until the sun shone fully through his windows. He made his armature and applied the clay to it, building up the forms rapidly and molding them into the shape of the reaching Perivale. When the evening light faded, he lit his lamps again and often worked an hour or two past midnight.

As he molded the clay, he felt the eyes of his Eve watching, admiring, and approving his work. Each evening before he blew out his lamps, he sank into his chair and gazed at her, communicating silently with the perfect mind and heart he knew such a woman would possess. Then he undressed and slipped into bed, where she came alive in his dreams.

For the next three weeks he shaped, smoothed, and refined the clay model of Perivale, seldom leaving his studio except to meet Ignatio at the Red Falcon for their Thursday evening dinners. It was an hour before midnight after one of these dinners when Davian parted with his friend and walked down the street toward his cottage. Rain had fallen earlier, and light from the oil streetlamps and shopkeepers' windows gave the cobblestones the shimmer of golden nuggets. Several pedestrians milled about. A coach rolled down the street, the clop of the horse's hooves accenting the musical laughter of the couple inside. Davian strolled past the doors of several alehouses still alive with laughter and song. At one of these a fair young woman who saw him pass came out and caught his arm, urging him to come inside and buy her a mug of ale. Davian jerked his arm away and continued walking, paying no heed as the girl spat at his heels and cursed him.

He reached his studio and entered. As he lit a lamp and sat in his one chair, he gazed at his white Eve, standing in all her glory against the opposite wall. He had come to know the heart that should beat in such a woman. He could hear her voice whispering words of endearment in his ears. He could see the glow of adoration in her eyes. He could see her smile of delight beamed on him as he rested before her after a day of hammering. He could feel her arms around his neck and her delicious warmth against his body as she kissed him with a passion pure and eternal. Were she alive, he knew that her perfect female face and form would be the temple of a perfect feminine soul.

A sudden clamor at the window startled him. He turned

to see a black shadow fly across the room and alight on the head of his Eve. His blood ran cold as he stared wide-eyed at the largest blackbird he had ever seen. The creature sat unmoving and eyed him balefully. Anger quickly displaced his momentary fear, surging in him like volcanic spume. How dare such an evil thing perch atop the pristine beauty of his Eve?

"Get off of her, you foul harpy," he cried. He picked up his measuring stick and swung it at the black intruder. But the creature was undaunted and merely flew to a rafter just above the statue. Davian lifted his stick to strike the bird, but he froze and shuddered as he looked into the evil intelligence of its pale eyes. The two stared at each other for the space of five breaths before the bird lifted its black wings and flew across the room and out the window.

When Davian's heartbeat returned to normal, he went into his room and slipped out of his clothing and into his bed. But each time he closed his eyes he felt the presence of the evil creature perched on his bedstead, waiting for him to sleep so it could peck out his eyes. He lit a candle and checked his room, but the bird was not there, and the windows were latched. When he did drift into sleep, he felt a coldness move over his body and sensed it to be the shadow of the giant bird, rendering him as immobile as a block of ice. Throughout the night the black creature flew in and out of his dreams, often perching on the rafters above, where it watched him sleep with its baleful yellow eyes.

When the blackbird left Davian's window, it flew up toward the pale moon and made its way northeastward toward the forest of Maldor. The wings of the great fowl beat all through that night and well into the next before the spires and turrets of the abandoned Maldor Castle jutted on the horizon. The bird flew over the castle and the plain beyond until it reached the River Rynde and the cliffs of Dornagan Mountain that formed the northern bank of the waterway. The dark fowl swooped down and glided over the treetops that lined the bluff, then turned inward and disappeared into the foliage, which concealed the entrance to a cave. It flew deep within the winding caverns until it came to a rough-hewn room dimly illuminated by an oily torch on the wall. The bird flew through the door and alighted on the floor.

In moments a smoky fog engulfed the black creature, and when the air cleared, in the place of the bird stood a tall woman robed from head to foot in black. Shelves, cases, and tables lined the walls of the room, cluttered with ancient books, bones, skulls, candles, lamps, embalmed animals, a large hourglass, rows of earthen jars in many sizes, a few bowls, an astrolabe, and several brass instruments of indeterminate purpose. A mirror hung on one wall, mounted within a frame of writhing serpentine creatures with demonic faces. The skeleton of a serpent thick as a man's arm coiled in a webby corner. An empty suit of rusted plate armor stood in another corner, and a brass gong hung in yet another.

The tall woman struck the gong with a mallet, and in moments a misshapen, dwarflike creature—bald, hunchbacked, mottled, and covered with warts—appeared at the door.

"I will take my dinner now," Morgultha said. With piglike grunts, the creature nodded and hobbled out of the room.

The woman took from a shelf a thick, leather-bound book a cubit high and over a foot wide. She placed it on the table, sat before it, and began to turn through the stained and wrinkled pages, which crackled with each movement.

They were filled with runes, diagrams, spells, incantations, and drawings of various roots, herbs, and body parts. Occasionally she stopped to read a passage, tracing the words with the bony index finger of her left hand. Each time, she shook her head and continued turning the pages. Her meal arrived, and she placed it to the side of the book and ate as she read. When she reached the last page, she muttered a curse and replaced the volume on a shelf, then drew down another and continued her search.

For three days she did nothing else, neither resting nor sleeping, turning page after page in book after book, taking her meals as she searched. After she turned the final page of the last book, she cursed emphatically, rose, and struck the gong with needless force. Immediately the dwarf thing appeared at the door.

"I am not to be disturbed for six hours," she said. "Close the door, and if you allow anyone to knock or call for me, you will rue the day of your creation."

With many grunts and squeals, the creature bobbed its head, backed out of the door, and quickly closed it behind him.

Morgultha took a piece of white limestone and drew on the floor two circles, each four feet in diameter, three inches apart. In one circle she drew a star, its five points touching the outline of the circle, and in the spaces between the points she drew five necromantic runes. She filled a brazier with oil, lit it, and set it on a tripod eighteen inches high just to the left of the empty circle. She laid a wooden wand about fourteen inches long in the brazier, letting the end protrude over the edge. Then she stepped inside the empty circle and sat with legs folded, facing the circle containing the star and the runes. She took care that no part of her body or even her robes extended beyond the circle. She pulled the cowl of her robe over her head and sat immobile for one hour, breathing ever more slowly and clearing from her mind all thought until she felt nothing but a black void both within and without. Then with a movement almost mechanical and involuntary, her left hand reached out and took the wand, its tip now aflame, and touched it to the star on the floor in front of her.

Immediately the star, the circle, and the runes began to glow yellow-green, faintly at first but with increasing intensity until every line she had drawn burned with cold flame. Morgultha stared unblinking at the circle of fire. Soon the walls and ceiling of the room disappeared, and she neither saw nor felt the floor but seemed to float in a vast black void extending endlessly in all directions. Her mouth opened, and from it issued a low moan like a cold wind from a dark cavern. Slowly the moan became words uttered in a tongue unknown since before language was fragmented at Babel. The words were dark and hideous, their very sound exactly expressing the horrors they named. The darkness stirred under the unholy incantation, and indefinite forms even darker than darkness—forms more felt than seen—writhed and billowed before her like ink roiling in water.

Morgultha's voice ceased abruptly. A deep, vibrating rumble began to sound, almost imperceptibly at first but building until it shook the darkness, causing the starred circle to jerk erratically. As the roar increased, the black forms in the darkness writhed torturously until they coalesced into an unthinkably huge, stygian shape just beyond the starred circle. The thundering roar became a voice, black, deep, and terrible, reverberating into the far reaches of space with unbearable force.

"Who is this who dares to call me forth?" The voice shook the woman's entire body, so that she felt the words as much as heard them.

"I am your servant Morgultha. I desire the secret of animating human figures carved from stone and metal."

"What need have you for such knowledge?" the voice thundered, and the darkness seemed to expand and loom toward her.

"With it I can regain the Crown of Eden and conquer the Seven Kingdoms, which will be my stepping-stone toward greater conquests."

"No!" the dark voice boomed, and the reverberations of the word overlapped themselves like the twisting coils of a serpent, their dying echo seeming to reach the orbit of the moon. "Years ago we gave you the secret of animating dead flesh, which you desired to create an army to conquer the Seven Kingdoms. But you failed. We will not waste more time with you." The voice began to diminish.

"Do not try your games with me," Morgultha answered. "You need me, and you know it. You and all your race have been disembodied since the great flood, and without a body you can effect nothing of your vengeance against the Master. Of all the sons of Adam and daughters of Eve, only I have plundered the great store of knowledge your kind buried deep beneath the Seven Kingdoms. Only I know the doom you have set for this island. Only I can be your body on earth and unleash that doom when the time is fulfilled. In return, I desire the secret of animating stone and metal."

"You do not know what you ask," the voice groaned. "We gave you the secret to animating dead flesh because it was more readily done. All flesh, even in death, bears latent receptivity to life, which cold stone does not."

"Yet it can be done," Morgultha replied. "Your ancient tablets speak of it."

"We have no ability to grant true life," the voice replied, "though we can devise a semblance of it. We can cause a figure made of stone or metal to become soft and pliable so that limbs and organs move like living ones. We assign our own spirits to manipulate the limbs and organs from the outside, much as puppeteers control a marionette. The more lifelike the figure, the more efficiently we can make it move. If it is realistic enough, we can duplicate human movement and speech perfectly."

"And will the illusion of life be only in the movement and speech of the image, or will it also appear living to the human eye?" Morgultha asked.

"The image not only will appear real and alive, taking on the color and texture of human skin, but will be lifelike to the touch. We can even extend the illusion of reality to hidden shapes the sculptor does not form, such as the tongue, the teeth, the flesh inside the mouth, and the eyelids. Even the hair will appear complete down to each strand."

"Give me the incantation," Morgultha said.

"We will give it to you, but we will impose conditions," the voice said. "You have failed us once, and we have no cause to trust you. Therefore, we will give you a spell to animate one image only."

"But one image only will be worthless to me. I must have an army," Morgultha said.

"Hear me out, woman." The weight of a threat reverberated in the words. "We will give you the power to animate one image only. That image will be the key from which you can animate others. But that key image must belong not to you but to another."

"But I cannot—"

"Silence!" the voice boomed, and the echo resounded in the vastness of space. "After animating that one key image, you may pass on the semblance of life to as many images as you wish. And each image thus animated can also pass the animation forward as a candle passes its flame. The key image will be animated by a form of the power that resides in lightning, accompanied by a spell that can be recited but once. We will give you the incantation and the formula for harnessing the power. This original animation can be passed on to an inert image by a touch from the animated image and the reciting of another incantation.

"Now hear me well. All animated figures but the key image will be slaves to your will. Any one of these can be destroyed individually, and its destruction will have no effect on the rest. But the key image, which you may not own and is not subject to your will, holds the power of animation over all the others. If that image is destroyed, the animation of all the rest will cease immediately, and they will revert to immobile stone or metal."

"How can the images be destroyed?" the woman asked.

"We maintain the illusion of life right up to the point of death. Therefore, they can be destroyed just as a living human can be killed—by decapitation, a sword or arrow thrust into the location of a vital organ, a fall from a ledge, or the trampling of a horse."

"All you describe is acceptable but for one thing," Morgultha said. "I do not like your terms. I want the key image in my control."

"The terms are not negotiable," the voice thundered. "When we give you control over the manipulated images, we lose control of them ourselves. We do not trust you with so much power. At this moment your aims coincide with ours. But were you to turn against us, we would have no way to stop you. By placing the key image in the hands of one who knows nothing of us, we can hold you hostage to our wishes. Once you step out of our will, we can withdraw animation from that key image, and all the images under your control will revert to stone or metal."

Morgultha continued to protest, but in the end she accepted the unholy bargain, and the dark voice gave her the formula and incantation. She completed the rituals to send the terrible darkness away and trembled at its hideous moans and tortured wails as it was drawn downward into the bottomless pit of darkness.

32

Six nights after the encounter with the strange bird, Davian was nearing completion of the Perivale model. Midnight was approaching as he did a final smoothing of the shoulders and then stepped back and looked hard for any flaw, any nuance of form needing adjustment. He could find none. He would show it to the king, and then he would plot its proportions to the massive stone. Elated, he poured himself a mug of ale and settled into his chair for his evening reverie with Eve.

When he had emptied the mug, he got up and took one last look at the Perivale model before he disrobed for bed. Suddenly he gasped in dismay. The hands! They were too large. His old persistent tendency had struck again. He examined the hands closely, wondering if he could simply pare them down. If not, he would have to break them away and rework the armature. His heart sank at the thought. At that moment a knock sounded at his door.

"Who could that be at this hour?" He went to the door and opened it. A tall woman stood before him, robed from head to foot in black. Her face shone thin and pallid in the light from his lamp, and her eyes chilled him to the bone.

They were pale and yellow like those of the blackbird he had encountered a week ago.

"Who are you?" he asked. "And what do you want?"

"I am one who loves great art," she replied in a voice cold as frost and almost as heavy as a man's. "I wish to purchase a sculpture from you."

"I have nothing to sell. And I have a commission that will dominate my time for at least three years."

"Nevertheless, I believe we can come to an agreement that will please you. Pray let me come in," she replied.

Davian stood aside, and the woman entered, keeping her right arm hidden in the folds of her robe. She went directly to the model of Perivale and walked all around it. After scrutinizing every detail, she turned to Davian, and again her eyes made his blood run cold.

"I will purchase the male nude," she said.

"It is not for sale," Davian replied. "It's a clay model for a larger work. I will use it to cast my proportions. Besides, it would be a bad bargain for you. The clay would soon crack and crumble."

"Nevertheless, I will have it," she replied. "And you will sell it to me willingly."

"No, as I said, it is not—"

"I know your deepest desire," she said, stepping toward him and speaking almost in a whisper. "And I can give it to you if you will give me that statue."

"You know nothing about me. How can you say you know my deepest desire?"

Morgultha walked to the stone Eve. "Here stands the most beautiful woman created since our mother Eve, more beautiful than any woman of legend or history—more beautiful than Helen of Troy, Rachel, Esther, or Venus. The tragedy is that she is mere stone, a fantasy created from your longings. No such woman exists." Morgultha

309

turned to Davian and locked her pale eyes on his. "But what if she were to become a living being and step down from her pedestal into your arms?"

"You speak nonsense. I don't know who you are or why you came here. But it's midnight and—"

"I can make her live," the woman said.

"That is preposterous," Davian said, laughing. "She is stone, and stone she will always be. You are moonstruck, woman. I must ask you to leave."

"I know the secret to bringing your dream alive. To show you that I speak the truth, look behind you."

Morgultha reached toward the Perivale model and spread her long fingers, muttering under her breath words unintelligible to Davian. He hardly dared to take his eyes off her, but he slowly turned to look behind him. He gasped and staggered back at what he saw. The model no longer had the color of clay but of living flesh. And the arm, which he had sculpted reaching high above the head, now hung naturally at the figure's side. Davian could see each strand of hair on the head and even the rise and fall of the chest as the figure breathed. What he saw was merely an illusion and not the demonic animation promised Morgultha by the dark voice. She lacked the power to hold the illusion long, and as the young man gaped, dumbfounded, the figure again raised its arm to the original position, and in moments its color changed from that of flesh to the grayness of clay. Davian went to the statue and felt its contours. It was indeed clay, with every detail exactly as he had modeled it. He turned to the woman.

"How did you do that?"

"That was a sampling of what I can do for your Eve. I can give life to her—the kind of life you have dreamed of. And not merely for a moment but for as long as you live. My only price is that you give me this clay figure."

310

"What do you want with him?"

"I am a lover of art. I will cast it in bronze for my manor."

Davian was still shaken from the phenomena he had just witnessed, and the prospect of his Eve actually coming to life terrified him almost as much. Yet he found the offer irresistible. As much as he hated the thought of creating the clay model again, it would solve the problem of the oversized hands. He looked at the Eve and imagined her body changing to living flesh and descending from her pedestal. He found that he could think of nothing else.

"I agree to your bargain."

"I knew you would," she replied. "Now, you must leave me alone with the image while I work. Go outside and do not return until I call you."

Davian hesitated but did as he was told. He took a blanket and went out into the night. He walked to the shed where his horse was stabled and sat huddled in his blanket as he watched the studio. He watched and waited, but he saw no change in the light from the window and heard no sound from within. After a while he lost all sense of time and had no idea whether he had waited a half hour or several hours. He struggled to keep his eyes open, and when he nodded and almost fell from the bench, he got up and walked around the stable to rouse himself. He sat again until the urge to sleep became irresistible, then arose and walked again—a pattern that repeated itself several times before he looked up and saw that the black sky was beginning to turn gray in the east.

Surely she is done by now, he thought. He almost convinced himself to get up and knock on the door, but he decided he should wait a little longer. He heard the cart of the milk seller creaking down the street, its cans and kegs clattering in the morning silence. Somewhere a rooster crowed, and he decided he had waited long enough. He went to the door and knocked hesitantly. He heard no sound. He slowly opened the door and peered inside. All was dark. The lamps had burned out, and the dawn light did not yet penetrate the curtained windows.

"Woman, are you done?" he called. No answer came.

He stepped inside and fumbled for a lamp and a canister of oil. He filled the lamp and lit it with his flint. As light filled the room, he could see that the woman was not there, and neither was the clay model of Perivale. He looked toward the Eve. She stood on her pedestal exactly as he had sculpted her. His heart sank. He had been duped. But as he moved toward the Eve, he thought he detected something different in her color, and his heart began to pound. As he approached, it became clear that her body was no longer white, but a tint of rosy ivory. Now he could see her eyes. They glistened blue and liquid in the lamplight, and her hair fell silky and golden about her shoulders. She was alive! In awe he reached out and touched her arm. Her flesh felt soft and warm, and a thrill ran through him like an ocean tide. He held her hand, and her fingers gently closed on his. He looked into her face, and she smiled warmly and tenderly, her even teeth flashing like pearls in the lamplight. She gazed at him with utter adoration. His knees began to tremble. As stone she had been more perfect in face and form than any woman he had ever seen. As living flesh her beauty was overwhelming, almost too rich a feast for mortal eyes. He did not know if he could endure it. He stood undone but entranced, as if the window of heaven had opened.

No word had yet been uttered, and he wondered if she could speak. What about her knowledge and understanding? Would he have to teach her everything as if she were an infant? Could she even walk? As if in answer to his unspoken questions, she stepped down from her pedestal, each movement the essence of perfect grace, and wrapped her arms about him in a loving embrace.

"My Davian," she said in a voice like warm velvet. "My dear, dear Davian."

33

As soon as the shops opened, Davian ran to Cheaping Square to buy clothing for his Eve. He bought three dresses: a light shift to wear within the studio, a skirt and bodice for shopping in the market, and a rich, elegant gown for balls. He hurried back to the studio as if he thought she were an apparition that might disappear. When he entered the cottage Eve rose from her chair and came to him, entrancing him with her loving smile.

"These are your clothes," he said. "I will show you how they should be worn."

But without a word, Eve took the shift and slipped it over her head. It fell gracefully over her, and she turned in a full circle, causing the hem to flare outward. Then she looked at him, smiling all the while as the fabric settled to the contours of her body.

"Does it please you?" she asked.

Davian had never seen her clothed before, but he found the effect of the simple adornment breathtaking.

"It pleases me very much," he answered.

"Then I am pleased as well," she said.

Davian sat down and simply gazed at his Eve, his heart

soaring. She sat quietly beside him. He took her hand in his and stroked it. He half expected to feel some telltale hint of the stone he had sculpted, but he found none. The hand was in every way that of a living woman. The skin was soft and velvety, the nails precisely shaped and hard. He could feel the bones of her hand beneath the warm flesh. He was so ecstatic at his good fortune that the question of how the mysterious woman in black had given life to cold marble faded into unimportance. Eve was alive and real, and nothing else mattered.

"You must be hungry," he said. "I will cook some break-fast."

"Oh no, allow me to do it," she replied. "You need never cook again. I will do it all for you."

"But do you know how to cook?" he asked.

"Not yet, but if you show me once, I will know."

He took her into the yard behind the studio, where he gathered eggs from the nests of his hens. He showed her how to draw water from the well, then led her back into the house. He showed her the pantry, where they found flour and honey for honey cakes. He made the honey cakes and put them in the oven to bake while he fried the eggs. When the cakes were cooked, he put them on two plates, along with the eggs, and set them on the table. He sat at his plate and motioned for her to sit at hers. He began to eat, but she merely watched him, her face glowing with admiration

"Aren't you going to eat?" he asked.

"I'm not hungry," she replied.

"It seems improper for me to eat when you do not."

"Oh, no, you mustn't feel that way. It pleases me to watch you enjoy your food."

Davian finished his meal and began to clean the dishes. Eve came and took them out of his hands. "I will do this," she said. She kissed him on the cheek, and he went to his bed to spread the blankets over the mattress. But she followed and pulled him away from the task. "I will make the bed," she said. "You need never do any of these chores again. I will clean your studio, wash your clothes, make your bed, cook your meals, mend your clothes, feed your hens, gather your eggs, go to the market, and do anything else you wish. You need only show me once, and from then on I will know how to do it."

"I don't want you as my slave; you are my companion. You can spend your days reading, knitting, singing, or merely daydreaming if you wish."

"I want one thing only," she replied, "and that is your happiness. Nothing else matters to me; nothing else ever will. I will do only what makes you happy."

The rest of that day Davian showed Eve how to do the various chores about the studio. As they worked, he could not keep his eyes off of the exquisite creature. He delighted in her every move. Her look of love made him feel like a king on a high throne. When she touched his hand or kissed his cheek, his heart bounded like a deer in a meadow. The next morning when he arose, he found that she had the oven fired, honey cakes in it, and eggs frying. She was as good as her word. He never had to show her any task but once, and after that she performed it with perfect efficiency.

As he ate she made the bed and swept out the studio and his room. When he finished his meal she washed the pans and plates and placed them on the shelves. After completing her chores she came to him and clasped him in a long embrace. He felt her heart beat against his and her warm breath on his neck, and he thought his life was complete.

"I must go across the city to buy clay from the brick maker," he said, holding her away so he could revel in

316

her sparkling blue eyes. "There's no need for you to sit here alone. Get into your skirt and bodice and come with me."

"I will do as you wish. If you wish me to remain here, I will remain. If you wish me to go with you, I will go."

"But you wouldn't be happy sitting here alone all day."

"If it pleases you to have me stay, staying will make me happy. If it pleases you to have me go, going will make me happy. I will be happy doing what pleases you."

"Then come with me. You are so beautiful I can hardly bear to let you out of my sight."

She glowed at the compliment and again kissed him on the cheek.

Arm in arm they walked toward the carter's where he would rent a wagon to haul the clay. He noticed that many of the people on the street turned their heads to stare at them. He understood why: Eve's beauty was irresistible. He felt a stab of uneasiness that she drew such inordinate attention, but he was pleased that she looked straight ahead and acknowledged none of it.

He became uneasy again when he thought of a thing he had not considered. What if he met Ignatio? Or the merchant Renalleo? How would he explain this living Eve to them? Without thinking, he picked up his pace. He wanted to get out of the public eye as quickly as possible. Eve did not complain, stumble, or fall behind but seemed just as content to walk swiftly as she had been to amble. He sensed that had he decided to run, she would have accepted the pace without question.

After renting the cart, he drove to the brick maker's yard and purchased eight blocks of clay wrapped in wet burlap. When they returned to the studio, Eve moved to help him unload the heavy blocks, but he absolutely refused to allow it and sent her into the cottage to rest. When he had stacked the clay and wet it down, he walked into the cottage to find dinner waiting for him.

"You must be the most perfect woman since your namesake Eve," Davian said.

She smiled as she took his hand and led him to the table. Again she did not eat but sat watching as if the mere sight of him was the only nourishment she needed.

That evening Davian felt like singing. He remembered some of Torvio's tamer songs, and as he and Eve sat side by side before the glowing hearth, he began to sing them. After hearing a song once, Eve could sing it perfectly, and they sang many together. He told her stories and jests he remembered from Papialano's, and she laughed with glee at each and begged for more. They sang and laughed and chattered happily until deep into the night.

The next morning Davian again awoke to find Eve already cooking breakfast. She greeted him with a smile that put the sun to shame and embraced him as he came to the table. She did not eat but sat and chatted brightly as he ate. After breakfast he went into his studio and began making an armature for the new model of Perivale. When evening came he was so absorbed in his work that he forgot dinner until his stomach began to rumble. He hated to break into his work to eat. Shortly he would get himself a mug of ale and a little cheese and bread and eat while he worked.

"I brought you this." The wonderful feminine voice spoke from behind him. He turned to see her smiling broadly and carrying a tray containing a mug of ale, a block of cheese, and a half loaf of bread. She set the tray on the table beside him, kissed him on the mouth, and returned to the room that was their living quarters. He did not quit working until two hours after midnight. He expected her to be in bed asleep, but he found her still up waiting for him.

318

He was too tired for conversation. She was not bothered at all by his silence or neglect but smiled contentedly as she tucked the covers about his shoulders and kissed him warmly before laying quietly beside him.

Davian finished the new armature in two days and began to apply the clay. He often worked through the noon hour, and without being asked Eve brought food he could eat with his fingers as he worked. Whether he stopped work early to be with her or worked deep into the night hours did not matter. She was always solicitous to his every need, seeming to live only to make him happy. She matched his every mood perfectly. When he was jovial so was she. When he was solemn, thinking on some nuance of form that was not quite right in his model, she remained quiet yet content merely to be in his presence. Whether he was playful, gleeful, pensive, reflective, or loving, so was she in equal measure.

She soon anticipated his every want, and he often found that he had no sooner wished for something than she brought it to him. Over the next few days, she learned exactly what foods he liked best and prepared them for his meals. She learned where he wanted household things kept and saw to it that they were always in their place. When he explained to her his philosophy of art or spoke of theological matters he had learned from Ignatio, she affirmed his every belief, agreed with his every opinion, and adopted his views of the world as her own. Often she watched him work, wearing an expression of rapt awe at his genius, expressing wonder at the lifelikeness of the form that took shape under his creative hands.

She offered to go to the market in Cheaping Square to purchase their food. Although he felt that she should get out of the cottage occasionally, he found himself reluctant to let her out in public. She accepted his decision without complaint and seemed perfectly happy to remain confined to the cottage.

When Thursday night approached, Davian sent word to Ignatio that he would not be able to make their weekly dinner. He did not want his friend to know about his Eve, nor did he want to take her out in public again.

On the following Thursday he wrestled with his dilemma as he smoothed the clay of Perivale's new model. He could not in good conscience keep Eve imprisoned within his cottage while he enjoyed an evening with his friend. Yet to explain her to the acolyte was unthinkable. He tossed the problem back and forth in his mind as he shaved a layer of clay from the model's abdomen.

He felt a gentle touch on his arm and turned to see Eve standing behind him, the window in the studio roof lighting her like a goddess from heaven. She smiled and said, "Davian, you have been working much too hard. Go and dine with your friend tonight. I will wait for you here."

"But how can you be happy sitting here alone while I enjoy the companionship of another?"

"My dear Davian." She took his hands in her own. "Your happiness is the river that gives me life. I can be happy in no other way than to see you as happy as you can be. Please go. It will bring me great joy to know that you are enjoying your friend."

Davian went to the Red Falcon and dined with Ignatio. He returned near midnight, feeling guilty in spite of Eve's assurances. But she met him at the door and threw her arms about him and kissed him as if he had been gone six months. She asked him many questions about the evening and listened with rapt attention as he recounted the details. Slowly it became clear to him that she meant what she said: his happiness was the sole source of her joy.

He could hardly believe his good fortune. He had as his

bride a woman like no other who had existed since the fall of Adam's Eve. She was perfect in every way, the ideal complement to him. Her inner being had conformed itself to her outer appearance. He had created a woman as the Master of the Universe intended woman to be.

34

The hulking man slouched on the board of the wagon and peered ahead into the darkness beyond the bobbing heads of the two horses. He could barely make out the road. Beside him sat his master Oggrum, swaying sleepily to the lurch and sway of the creaking cart. Sideboards four feet high hid the bed of the wagon, and inside lay six men, all drugged and manacled, a single chain running through their shackles and binding them together like a stringer of fish.

Oggrum had earned his sleep. He had completed a successful raid on the prison in Sunderlon, just over Meridan's northern border, in the kingdom of Rhondilar. The raid had not been difficult, for he'd had the help of Sunderlon's sheriff, which he had secured with the bribe Morgultha had provided. The bribe was not sizable, but the sheriff was in need because of gambling debts. Now Oggrum was taking the prisoners back to Morgultha's stronghold inside Dornagan Mountain. The mountain bordered the Sunderlon River near its fork into the Rynde and was the western anchor for a stone dam that held the Sunderlon back from the Plain of Maldor. The dam had been built by the ancient invaders of the island centuries before the yellow-haired seamen from the east conquered them. It was said that before the dam was built, the Plain of Maldor had been a huge, foul swamp that had bled from the southern side of the river like a leak in an irrigation trench. The dam had dried up the swamp, exposing many miles of fertile earth that drew the settlers who built the town of Maldor, later the site of Maldor Castle.

At the drying of the swamp, the water had receded from the base of Dornagan Mountain's southern face, exposing a crevasse that hid a maze of natural caves. Morgultha had discovered these caverns long before her war with Perivale, and after her escape from him she had made them her headquarters.

The driver peered ahead into the darkness as he slowed the horses. He would soon be crossing the top of the dam, which was only three feet wider than the wheel span of his wagon. A mistake in the darkness could plunge him off either side. If to the right, his wagon would fall into the Sunderlon; if to the left, it would be dashed to pieces on the boulders fifty feet below. The man hated crossing the dam for other reasons as well. It was no longer stable. Water seeped through cracks in the ancient mortar, forming moss-covered rivulets down the landward side. Twice he had crossed the dam during thunderstorms and felt it shudder at the pounding of the wind-whipped waves. But when he reported the fact to Oggram, the man had dismissed his fears with a wave of his hand, muttering something about the dam having lasted for more centuries than Maldor Castle. At the edge of the dam he pulled the team to a halt and shook Oggrum awake.

"Oggrum, we be at the dam," he said. "I'll be gettin' out and leadin' the horses across. You hold the reins."

They crossed safely. The driver expelled an oath in relief

and mounted the board again. He drove the cart down along the base of the mountain and into the crevasse that hid the caverns.

A quarter hour later Oggrum stood before Morgultha's thick, oaken door and knocked twice before he entered. She sat at a planked table, writing with an eagle talon quill on a sheet of parchment. Stacks of books, rolled parchments, an hourglass, a mirror, several vials of liquid, three or four bones that appeared to be vertebrae, and an elaborate chalice littered the table.

"How many men did you bring?" she asked without looking up.

"We brung in six, m'lady."

"What? Only six?" Morgultha glared at the man. "I must have twice that many at least. You must do better, Oggrum."

"Six be all the sheriff had in his jail, m'lady."

"You know I must have more. You will find a way to get them."

"Yes, m'lady." Oggrum's voice quavered.

"I want a report on our horses. How many do we have now?"

"We got three more five days back. Stole 'em from a merchant headin' for Sunderlon. Brings us up to forty-two."

"Only forty-two? What have you been doing, you sloth? Picking up two here and three there will not do. You know I must have a hundred—and not next year!"

"Yes, m'lady. It will be done."

"And what about our armor and weapons?"

"M'lady, you know how hard it be to find—"

"I will not hear excuses, Oggrum. Either you get what I need or you know the consequence. You've been in the snake pit before, I believe."

"But, m'lady, where does we get armor? We done cleaned

out Maldor Castle. We stripped three knights on a road up in Rhondilar. Found some beat up breastplates in Braegan Wood close by where you fought Perivale."

"Have you no ingenuity at all? Have you thought of making a night raid on the smith's shop in Corenham where Perivale's knights get their armor repaired? Have you thought of raiding the graves of knights who were buried in their armor? Have you thought of digging on Judgment Mound, where thirty Oranthian warriors were buried in a mass grave right where they fell in battle?"

"But that be a sacred place, m'lady. They say the ghosts of dead warriors—"

"Nonsense! You dig that mound and get that armor and those weapons."

"We—we will do it, m'lady."

At that moment another knock sounded at the door. At Morgultha's word, the door opened, revealing a mountain of a man with his head shaved bald.

"It be ready for you to see, m'lady," he said in deep, guttural tones.

Morgultha dismissed Oggrum with a parting threat as she arose and followed the bald giant. He led her through a stony passage dimly lit with oily torches. The passage opened into a cavernous, high-ceilinged room filled with vats, ingots of metal, wooden platforms, and stacks of black coal. An orange fire burning in an open hearth lit the room. A cluster of five men standing near the hearth parted as she approached, revealing a bronze image that was an exact duplicate of the clay model of Perivale, which stood beside it.

"The mold came off clean, m'lady," one of the men said.

Morgultha did not reply but looked hard at the casting as she walked slowly around it, stroking her chin.

"I told you I didn't want to see a single mold seam,"

she said, glaring at the men. "Look at this! Here is one line running from his shoulder to his elbow and another running down the length of his thigh. You must file these ridges down and polish the surface until no hint of them is visible. I want each bronze to be flawless. Flawless! Do you hear me, Malbritt?"

"We hear and we obey," the big man growled. "I will put two men to filin' and polishin' while the others reset the mold for a new cast."

"You do that," she replied. "Remember, I will have a hundred bronzes before the year is out—all of them flawless."

"But m'lady, we'll be needin' more casts and leastwise six more men to do the castin'."

"Oggrum brought in six prisoners tonight. Put them to work."

Morgultha turned and strode from the room. When Oggrum was certain she was out of earshot, he muttered to Malbritt in tones too low for the other men to hear, "Sometimes I be thinkin' I'd have been better off standin' trial for stealin' that cow. Leastwise my sentence would've had an end to it."

35

It was midmorning when Davian walked through the gates of Morningstone Castle to answer the king's summons. He now came so often that the guards no longer questioned him. But when he presented himself at Perivale's hall, he was told that the king could not see him yet. He should wait in the bailey until he was called.

Davian left the keep and strolled aimlessly down the shaded flagstone walkway bordered by gardens of flowers, thick elms and oaks, and cropped lawns. Just beyond the trees to his left stood the high garden wall from where he had heard the voice of the mysterious singer. He sat on a garden bench to watch the birds and squirrels flitting about the shaded lawn. As he basked in the still warmth of the morning, his eyes grew heavy and he began to nod. Suddenly he sat up. The song had begun. He kept still and listened. As before, the melody was mournful beyond bearing and sung with a passion that brought tears to his eyes. Finally the song died away as if the singer were borne down with the weight of her grief.

But the haunting melody stirred Davian deeply. He arose from his bench and approached the wall, circling around a high, dense hedge that hid the base of it from the walking paths. He looked among the vines for some window or door in the wall. At first he found nothing, but he followed the wall to a corner where it turned away from the bailey gardens into a dense growth of hedges. He made his way behind the hedges, and his search was rewarded. He found a narrow gardener's window, little wider than his own head, used by caretakers to pass through tools and bags of seed. Thick vines covered the window, and he cleared enough of them away to barely see into it. But it did him little good, for the wall was three feet thick—uncommon for an interior wall—and vines also covered the opening on the other side.

"My lady," he called through the opening. "My lady, can you hear me? Will you approach the wall? I would speak with you." He waited for a response, but none came. "My lady," he called a little louder. "I have heard your songs, and they are beautiful beyond expressing. But they wound my soul and break my heart. I would know who sings such songs." Again he waited, but no answer came. After a few minutes he sighed and returned to the vestibule of the great hall to see if Perivale would see him yet.

"The king will be unavailable the rest of the day," the guard told him. "Be here tomorrow morning, and he will see you then."

Davian left the castle and returned to his studio.

The next morning he went again to Morningstone, and again the guards turned him away but told him to stay within the castle to await the king's summons. As on the day before, he passed the time in the bailey garden, and again the haunting song came over the wall. He listened in rapt attention, then ran behind the hedge and worked his way to the little window, where he called to the singer.

He called three times, and after waiting several minutes for an answer, he turned back toward his bench.

"Who are you?" A wonderfully rich woman's voice came from the window. Quickly he returned to it, spread the vines apart, and peered inside. He could see nothing but the vines covering the other side.

"I am Davian, the sculptor for the king's monument. I have listened to your songs many times, and I have never heard anything more heartrending."

"If my songs tear your heart, why do you listen?"

"I cannot help myself. I have never heard anything more beautiful." A long pause followed, and Davian began to think the woman had left the window.

"Of course. You are an artist. It is natural that you would love beauty," she said.

Davian wondered at the sadness in her voice. "Who are you, my lady?" he asked.

"One who must forever abandon all hope of happiness," the voice replied.

"But why?" Davian asked. "Why must you give up all hope of—"

"I will go now," the voice said.

"No! Please! Forgive me. I had no right to ask the question." He waited for a response, but none came. "Lady, please come back." After a long silence he called, "Will you speak with me again?"

He waited for an answer, but none came. He called into the window a few more times, but no sound came from it, and finally he returned to the bench. He stayed in the gardens for another hour before approaching Perivale's guards again. The king would not see him today. He should return tomorrow.

As Davian rode back to his studio, his mind would not let go of the sad woman behind the wall. Who was she?

What was the mystery of her mournful songs? What terrible doom had driven all hope from her heart? Davian felt as if his own heart could break because of her profound sadness. No one should feel such despair alone. He arrived at his studio to the loving arms and adoring eyes of his Eve, and all thoughts of the mysterious singer left him.

On the next morning Davian was ushered immediately into the presence of Perivale. He bowed low and said, "What is your wish, Your Majesty?"

"I thought we would have seen stone being chipped away by now," the king replied.

When Davian explained the proportion error he had discovered and the need to remake the clay model, the king flared into a rage. But he calmed quickly and urged the sculptor to move forward with the utmost speed. Davian left the audience little bothered by the king's impatience. He knew he worked unusually fast, and any time lost in remaking the model he would regain when working the stone. In fact, it was time to erect the scaffolding around the stone. Before he returned to his studio, he would call on the carpenter Renalleo had secured and order him to begin construction.

He strode through the bailey, intent on his mission, when the song of the woman arrested his step. He stopped and listened until it was complete, then he rushed to the hidden window.

"My lady," he called. "Please forgive me for my forwardness yesterday. I had no right to probe your wounds. But I sense that your sorrow is beyond bearing, and my heart can hardly stand for anyone to be in such pain. It would ease my heart if I could help you bear your grief."

"My grief is mine alone . . . ," the voice from the window said, and Davian's heart leapt at the sound, "and I must bear it alone. Yet I thank you for your compassion. No one has ever offered such kindness before."

"Lady, if I cannot help you bear your grief, at least I can divert you from it a little."

"How would you divert me?"

"I would teach you new songs—happy songs, songs sure to bring laughter to your heart. I haven't the voice of an angel as you have, but I can sing a little. Listen to this.

"Steven the thievin' stevedore,
Stealin' away from Ensovandor,
  Wanderin' off to the shore of Farenglen.

"Finds a fair female from Sorendale,
Woos her, pursues her to no avail,
  Bags her and drags her away to Magorman's Inn.

"Now Steven's receivin' a grievous surprise;
Steven's not b'lievin' his bulgin' eyes.
  His maiden's a mermaid; she's flippin' a tail and fin.

"He's tradin' his mermaid, so I hear tell,
For a fat flounder and mackerel,
  And now Steven's got him a whale of a tale to spin."

When Davian finished the song, he waited for the woman's response. He heard no sound for several seconds, and he feared that the silly rhyme had driven her away. He was about to call to her when she spoke.

"You do not do yourself credit. Your voice is deep and rich and fine. I'm sure that being an artist, you endow all you touch with beauty."

"Thank you, my lady. But did you like the song? I will sing it again, and you can sing with me."

"No, I cannot sing such a song. My spirit will not rise high enough to give it wings. Yet I thank you for it. While your song is beyond the reach of my grief, I value the kindness of your heart that wished my happiness."

Davian found the woman's gratitude unaccountably thrilling. The fact that his kindness had such an effect on her encouraged him to do more.

"Lady, you say that no one has ever offered to lighten your grief. Surely you have friends or companions who care for you."

"I have a serving woman my own age who is like a sister to me. Without her I would go mad or die. There is no other."

"If my songs will not lighten your heart, then let me be your companion. Allow me to meet you. We can sit in the garden and stroll among the trees."

"No, we can never meet. Indeed, I have spoken with you more than I should already. I will go now."

"No! Wait, my lady. I would speak with you again. Allow me to come tomorrow at this time."

A long pause followed, and Davian feared that she had already fled. Then she spoke again.

"Very well. I will speak with you tomorrow at this time. Good day, sir. And I thank you for the kindness of your heart."

"Good day, my lady."

Davian left Morningstone elated over his success in reaching the mysterious woman. He rode directly from the castle to the carpenter's shop, where he spent the rest of the day describing and sketching the configuration of the scaffolding. The first scaffolds would give him access to the upper half of the stone. After shaping the upper half, the scaffolds would be dismantled and reassembled around the lower half. The carpenter agreed to begin work immediately, assuring the young sculptor that the structure would be ready for use within a fortnight.

As the day drew to a close, Davian turned his horse toward his studio. He had not eaten since morning, and as he approached home, he began to feel hungry. He decided he would ask Eve to run out to the market and buy a thick cut of beef. His mouth watered at the thought. When he opened the door to his cottage, Eve was waiting for him at the threshold. She threw her arms about his neck and kissed him deeply, then beaming her Edenic smile, she led him to the table, where a plate loaded with a steaming slice of beef an inch thick awaited. He wondered, as he had often wondered before, just how she always knew exactly when he would be home and exactly what he wanted to eat. *But why question perfection?* he thought. He plunged into his meal as Eve watched, pleasure lighting her face like a harvest moon.

Avalessa walked away from the window where the sculptor's voice had penetrated her isolation. She hardly knew what she thought of his visits. At first she had ignored his plea to speak with him. Why entertain this fleeting diversion to her grief and loneliness? It held no future. She could not reveal her sorrow to him; indeed, she could never meet him face-to-face. She must not allow her hunger for companionship to bring about even more sorrow. He would finish his monument and move on to other things, leaving her even more bereft for the loss of his company. But his solicitude for her grief had touched her heart and broken her resolve to shun outside contact. No doubt many strollers in the bailey gardens had heard her songs, yet none but this artist with a soul sensitive as a leaf to a breeze had been so affected by them. No one else had found the compassion to seek her out and express concern. It may have been pity that drew him, but it was the first touch of kindness she had experienced from anyone other than Lady Elowynn since her mother's death.

She crossed her garden and climbed the steps to her chambers. Elowynn stood at the door.

"I thought I heard a man's voice singing a tavern song," the lady-in-waiting said. "I was coming out to find the meaning of it."

"You heard right, Elowynn. A man did sing such a song through the gardener's window. He wanted to teach it to me."

"What? How did this come about?"

Avalessa explained how the man had heard her songs in the bailey and had tried for three days to speak with her. "When I finally decided to answer him, he thought he could lift my sorrow by teaching me a song full of life and humor."

"Good for him!" Elowynn cried. "And did you learn it?"

"No. I cannot. My heart won't soar high enough to express such happiness. Yet I loved the man for trying. No one but you has shown me such kindness since . . ." Avalessa could not finish the thought. "He is the artist who will carve the monument to the king. I promised to speak with him again tomorrow, but I think I erred. I will keep my promise, but I won't speak with him further after tomorrow."

"You did not err," Elowynn replied. "You are a prisoner in this castle. You are never allowed out of your chambers or your garden except to attend the highest state dinners, and even then you are veiled, and the king keeps you in his sight and has you escorted back to your chambers the moment the dinner is over. Except to exchange meaningless pleasantries with visiting kings and ambassadors, you have spoken to no one but me for seven months. Avalessa, let him teach you his song."

"But I can't. I—"

"You let him teach you his song. You think you can't sing it because you haven't the spirit for it. But the singing of it may give you the spirit for it. Besides, I'm tired of your dirges and laments. Let him teach you his song!"

Davian had no business to attend at Morningstone, but he took advantage of his freedom to enter the castle without question and kept his promise to the woman behind the wall. She met him at the window as she had promised, and they spoke to each other for more than a quarter of an hour before she told him she would return to her chambers. Davian asked if he could meet her again in two days, and though her answer was long in coming, she consented.

He spent the following morning with the carpenter, reviewing the drawings for the scaffolding. After making a few adjustments, he went to his studio and worked on the Perivale model the rest of the day.

On the next morning the invisible singer extended the length of Davian's visit to a half hour, and he began to ask more about her. But she would reveal little. He did not learn her name, what she was doing in Morningstone, or where she had come from. Once he asked her to part the vines on her side of the window and show her face. But she refused emphatically and warned him not to ask again. Yet he did find that she was not yet twenty years old, she was unmarried, she was not ill, and she loved birds. "I love them because they sing and they fly," she said. "They aren't confined by walls." She would speak no more of herself. Any time Davian veered toward the cause of her grief, she grew silent, and he feared she would terminate the visit. The more he learned of her, the deeper the mystery became. When she ended the visit, he asked if he could meet her again on the following Monday. To his surprise, she agreed, and he left the castle feeling strangely elated.

When he returned on Monday, she was waiting for him at the window. After an exchange of greetings, Davian said, "I have something to give you. Come to the window, and I will hand it through."

"A gift? For me?" Her voice lifted a little, conveying surprise and wonder that Davian had not heard before. "I don't know whether I should take it."

"You must take it. I made it expressly for you."

He had in his hand a wooden box about six inches square, which he extended deep into the window. He heard the rustle of parting vines on the other side and felt a thrill at the brush of her fingers on his as she took the box.

After a moment he heard her voice, tremulous and little more than a whisper. "It's beautiful." After a long pause she said, "I cannot believe you really made this. Though it is of stone, this bird looks as if it could fly. The wings . . . they are so delicate. And the eyes . . . so soft and alive. Thank you, Davian. I can see that you have a heart for beauty."

Davian was ecstatic at her response—not because of her admiration of his talent but because he could hear in her voice inflections of emotion not tainted by grief. For the moment she had forgotten her sorrow. He thought the time was right. He began to sing Torvio's song. To his delight, her voice joined his on the second stanza, timidly and haltingly at first but soon with energy and confidence. When the song ended, she laughed. He had never heard her laughter before, and he thought it was more musical than the song itself.

Immediately he began another song. He sang it through once, then asked her to join in as he repeated the first verse. She sang with him, and when the song ended she laughed again, and Davian laughed with her for the sheer joy of hearing her laughter. They talked of the song for a few minutes, and then she told him that she would leave now.

"But, Davian, I thank you so much for your gift today."

"Please, think nothing of it. It was easy to carve, and I—"

"I was not speaking of the bird, though I thank you deeply for that as well. Good day, Davian."

As Davian left Morningstone, he could not remember ever being filled with such joy. He could not understand why the unknown woman's newfound brush with happiness thrilled him so deeply.

"Elowynn," Avalessa called after walking away from the window. Her lady-in-waiting appeared at the chamber door, and the princess went to her, holding the stone lark cupped in her hands, her face aglow with wonder.

"What is it?" Elowynn called. "What's wrong?"

"I laughed," Avalessa said.

"You laughed?" the lady repeated, not understanding.

"Yes, the artist made me laugh. And we sang. For the moment I forgot all else, and I was happy. And it lingers with me yet. My grief is within me somewhere, but I don't feel it at the moment. And he gave me this." She extended the bird toward the young lady. "Isn't it beautiful?" Her voice was light and animated as Elowynn had not heard it since the girl's tragedies.

Elowynn took the stone lark and marveled at its delicacy. "It's beautiful indeed but not as beautiful as you are at this moment. Praise to the Master of the Universe! This artist has performed a miracle."

Elowynn turned and ran quickly inside the princess's chamber and returned with the mandolin. She handed the instrument to Avalessa and said, "Sing the song for me."

Avalessa took the mandolin and began to sing. She sang both of Davian's songs before she laid the instrument aside and smiled at her lady.

"Forgive me, Elowynn, for inflicting my dirges and laments on you. I'm sure I will continue to sing them, but surely I can sing these as well. Perhaps you will find your life with me a little easier to bear."

"You are never a burden to me, my princess."

Avalessa continued to meet the sculptor at the gardener's window twice each week. She thought the relationship was perfect for one in her condition. She would never need to show her ruined face, and she knew that he was enchanted by the mystery that she was to him. Perhaps somewhere in her mind she knew the meetings must end someday, but she refused to allow the thought to surface. She came to depend on his visits as a bird depends on air. Over the next several weeks he taught her many songs, and she taught him some of the finer points of music, including how to harmonize and add counterpoint as they shaped some of the songs into duets.

In a fortnight Davian finished the new clay model of Perivale, and the carpenter completed the scaffolding at the marble stone. Avalessa could see the stone in the distance as she overlooked Corenham from her second-story window. She often watched as Davian climbed the steps to the uppermost scaffold, and each day she prayed fervently for his safety.

36

With the scaffolding in place on the jutting stone at Cheaping Square, Davian took his four final position drawings of Perivale—one from the front, one from the back, and one from each side—and drew a series of grids over them, each square of the grid measuring one inch. Then he created a wooden frame exactly the size of the drawings and drove tacks one inch apart along each side and along the top and bottom. Next he stretched strong lengths of twine across the frame both horizontally and vertically, creating one-inch grids that matched those on the drawings exactly.

Taking his grid and four identically gridded sheets of blank paper the exact size of his preliminary drawings, Davian climbed the first of the four towers built as surveying posts. He set the framed grid on a stand so that he could view the entire stone through the frame. Then he placed the gridded paper on a board in his lap and carefully drew the stone, observing the position of each contour and feature through the string grid and matching it to the corresponding square in the grid on his paper. He drew the scaffolding as well.

In the afternoon he moved to the second tower and repeated the process. On the following day he drew the stone from the third and fourth towers. Matching his gridded drawings of the stone to the identically gridded drawings of the figure, he plotted the position of each feature of the statue onto the stone. He marked each position clearly and assigned to his stonecutters the task of climbing the scaffolds and driving spikes into the stone to identify the position of each major feature of the statue. By the end of the week, the stone was marked with twenty-seven spikes on each of its four sides.

The following week Davian and his stonecutters began to remove large slabs of stone from the block, using the spikes as guides. Their methods for cutting the stone varied depending on the contours and the amount of mass to be removed. The limitations of the scaffolding kept them from removing larger portions than the framework would bear. Commonly, they would identify a portion of the stone to be removed and drive a series of metal wedges around it, angling them inward toward each other. Beneath the section to be excised, they positioned an angled wooden ramp that would slide the waste over the edge of the scaffolding to the ground below.

In the first week they made surprising progress, clearing away much of the stone from around the extension that would become Perivale's upstretched arm. By the third week the mass from which the head would emerge became visible, though the workers left it webbed to the upreaching arm. And in the two weeks following, the vague suggestion of a shoulder emerged.

Davian settled into a regular routine. Each day, except for Tuesdays and Fridays, he worked from sunup to sundown on the stone. On these mornings he went first to Morningstone Castle and spent an hour at the wall with the unknown woman. Though it was clear to him that the woman found his visits to be a light in her darkened world, he sensed that any misstep could cause her to draw back or even put a stop to the visits.

Why should it matter to me if she did stop the visits? he asked himself. He had begun them for her sake, not his. He had felt pity for the woman and had attempted to draw her out of her sorrow. He had succeeded more than he had thought possible. He had not heard one of her mournful songs in several weeks. The heaviness was gone from her voice, and now she sometimes laughed with him and sang the songs of joy and happiness he had taught her. His task was finished. He had done his duty. Let her stop the visits if she wished.

Yet he did not want them to stop. Something about this woman drew him. Perhaps at first it had been the heavenly beauty of her voice. But now he thought it was her *otherness*, as he called it—her thoughts, expressions, viewpoints, and emotions that sometimes differed delightfully from his own. Her mind and personality were not merely mirrors to his, parroting his own thoughts and reflecting back to him his own desires. Her otherness gave him continual surprise, unexpected enlightenment, and new insights, refreshing his mind like a cool breeze on a summer day.

He realized that all of her attributes combined—voice, expressions, and emotions—had led him to form a visual image of her. She could not be other than beautiful. He longed to see her face. He had not asked since the first days he had spoken to her, because she had told him never to ask again. But he knew he would not wait long before his desire to see her overcame the prohibition.

On a Friday in late spring he stood at the window in the wall. The two of them had just sung a ballad together, and she had told him that his harmony was marvelous. The pleasure in her voice was unmistakable.

"I want to see your face," he said suddenly. "Push back the vines so I can see you." He held his breath, half expecting her to turn away.

"Why do you want to see my face?" she answered.

"I want to know if the image of you I hold in my mind is close to the truth."

"And just what is this image you hold in your mind?"

"Well, I believe your hair is long, perhaps falling almost to your waist. It is the color of sunlight, with soft waves cascading over each other like a mountain waterfall. Your eyes are wide, clear, bright, and blue. Your face is a perfect oval, smooth as velvet, and the color of ivory tinted with rose. Your lashes are long and dark. Your eyebrows are delicate and arched like longbows. Your lips are full and red as cherries."

Avalessa caught her breath. He had given an exact description of her before her scarring. "And just what makes you think this description might fit me?"

"It matches what I know of you. It seems an apt outward expression of your inner self."

"So you think one's appearance always displays one's inner being?"

"Not always. Not anymore. It was the Master's original ideal that the face and form should tell the truth about the heart and mind. But since the fall that ideal no longer holds. People can use their beauty to mask an evil and deceitful heart." A touch of bitterness crept into his voice.

"And is it not possible that a heart filled with purity and love could reside behind a face without beauty?"

"Yes, that also is possible."

"So how do you know I don't have the face of a warthog?"

"I suppose I cannot really know. But it's impossible to imagine that you are anything but beautiful."

Avalessa paused long before answering. Davian could not know that her eyes were filling with bitter tears. "Tell me, Davian, what first caused you to speak to me through the wall?"

"It was the beauty of your voice." Davian chose not to tell the whole truth: that it was also his pity for the weight of sorrow in her songs. "I could not help but stop and listen. And the more I heard, the more I wanted to discover the fountain of such angelic sounds. And now I want to see the face from where that fountain flows. Push back the vines. Let me see you."

"Your dream of me is rich enough to sustain you. Be content with it."

"I beg of you. Come to the balcony on the top of your wall. I must see your face."

"You may not see my face."

"Why? Is your beauty so great it would blind men or turn them to stone? Would it drive them mad? Would the magnificence of your face cause all other women to lose their luster?"

"I will leave you to guess which of your surmisings hits the mark. But for now I must leave. Good morning, Davian."

"Good morning, Helen."

"Helen? Why do you call me Helen?"

"You have refused to give me another name. Until you do I will think of you as Helen of Troy, the woman whose beauty incited a great war and brought about the death of gods."

As Davian rode toward the stone monument, he felt more than elation; he felt something akin to exultation. And he did not understand it. This woman—Helen he would call her—was undermining all his conceptions of what women were like. She was nothing like Emeralda. Emeralda had

343

been false from the moment he met her, harboring a heart filled with deceit while showing the face of love. On the other hand, this Helen clearly held some terrible secret in her heart, but she did not erect a façade to deceive him into believing that all was well with her. She was candid about what she would not reveal. And she made no attempt to hide her differences with him but expressed them freely and without guile. As a result, he knew he could trust what she said to be true. She was honest in her refusal to reveal everything, and she would not lie to conceal what she thought he might find disagreeable.

Neither was Helen like his Eve. Eve never refused the least of his desires. She would never have refused to show her face when he wished to see it. Indeed, she would never do anything that did not exactly reflect his wishes, even to the smallest detail. She lived only for him.

If indeed she lived at all.

A sharp pang pierced his belly as he allowed the thought to surface. The nature of Eve's existence raised questions he could not answer and did not want to explore. But he had begun to realize that her complete dedication to him, even to the submerging of her own personhood, was not satisfying. She had no independent being. There was no real interplay between them, no innervating interchange of thought or emotion. She offered no sense of otherness except in her gender, which, as Davian was coming to realize, was not enough to satisfy his hunger to become one with another being. Before a person could become one with another, there must be an other to become one with. And in Eve he found no otherness.

Yet the idea of being without her was unthinkable. How could he turn his back on a creature so perfect in every way—beautiful, dedicated, loyal, adoring, loving, and compliant? Was she not exactly what men dreamed of? Yet he had begun to feel dissatisfaction with himself for his dependence on the life she offered. He shook his head; it made no sense. How could he be attracted to an unidentified woman hidden behind a wall and yet not be happy with the most beautiful and perfect woman who had walked the earth since Adam's Eve?

When Davian left the window, Avalessa turned and strolled slowly along the flagstone path of her garden, unaware of the birds that twittered in the trees or the merry gurgle of the fountain. Her heart was torn between two emotions. She had found Davian's vision of her beauty strangely exhilarating. It had been long since a man had told her she was beautiful. Though she knew his image of her was a fantasy, she had found bittersweet enjoyment in the game.

On the other hand, she found much of what he had said today profoundly dismaying. It was clear that Davian was enamored with beauty. It was the beauty of her voice that drew him to her. In his imagination this artist had painted her portrait, endowing her with the ideal beauty he worshiped. How could she expect him to do otherwise? He was an artist, after all, and beauty was his life. But beauty was a commodity she could not offer him. If he knew the truth about her face, he would surely cease his visits and never give her another thought, except as a monster haunting his nightmares.

Of course, she had known all along that their companionship could never progress beyond its present level. She was royalty; he was a commoner. He was free; she was a prisoner. If these barriers were not enough, now there was this: beauty was his life, and she had no beauty. She should never speak to him again, but she was not certain she could survive without him. He had saved her life. He had lifted her from a pit from which she could never have climbed alone. He had reached down into her darkness and lifted her into the light. Without him she feared she would sink back into the blackness so deeply that she would never find her way out again.

Slowly she began to realize that what she felt for this man Davian went beyond mere gratitude. She had come to love him. And the realization filled her not with joy but with bitterness, for it was a love that held no hope. It was doomed to die, for love must grow or die, and her stunted life had no room for such growth. She sat on a stone bench near the fountain, and the old melancholy began to spread its black wings over her again.

37

Davian walked past the guards at the gate of Morningstone Castle and crossed the bailey toward the garden wall. As he approached he was dismayed at what he heard. The minor strains of a sorrowful lament filled the air. He had not heard Helen sing a lament in many weeks. He did not wait for the song to end but hurried to the window and called to her.

"Helen, stop your song. Come to the window."

The song ceased, and a moment later he heard her voice through the window. It chilled him to the bone.

"I am here, Davian," she said in listless tones so heavy he wondered that they did not drop to the ground before they reached his ear.

"What is wrong? It has been long since you sang such a song. And your voice—you don't sound well."

"I am well, Davian. Indeed, it is you who staunched my wound and saved my life. But though the wound is staunched, it is not healed."

"What do you mean? I know you bear some terrible sorrow, but surely it no longer rules your life."

"My dear, dear friend, you have opened a window to my closed heart and shown me the sky. In these past happy weeks I began to dream that I could soar into the heavens and outpace my sorrows. But the truth is, I am chained and cannot fly. I am sinking again into the pit of my despair, which will be much deeper and blacker for having been tantalized by the window you opened. At this moment I feel that it would have been better if I had never met you."

"Don't say that!" Davian replied. "If you would confide in me, I would move heaven and earth to get you out of your prison. But you won't tell me who confines you or why."

"No, there is no escape. I carry my prison with me as a tortoise carries its shell."

"How can I understand such veiled talk? Why won't you tell me in plain words what has befallen you?"

"Davian, you must leave me. You must not come back. Our . . . friendship has no future. I will tell you this much: I am imprisoned by my own father, who forbids all contact with anyone he does not specifically approve, and he approves no one. You would be in great jeopardy if he knew of your visits. I will undoubtedly be confined by these walls until I die."

"Your father? Who is he? Why does he do this? Explain to me, Helen. Let me help you."

"I have not told you all. If I could, you would know that I am beyond help. Now leave me. Leave with my thanks for brightening my life for a little while. I will always cherish your . . . your kindness. But we must never speak again. Good-bye, Davian." He could hear the heartbreak in her voice.

"Helen, no! No one is beyond help. We will find a way." He pressed against the wall and tore at the vines. "Helen, speak to me!" he called louder. "Helen!" He heard nothing more but the rustle of her dress as she walked away.

"I will not abandon you," he called. "I will come to you every Tuesday whether or not you will speak to me. And I will find a way to free you."

Davian and the stonecutters usually worked until darkness made treading the scaffolding dangerous. But on Thursday he stopped work an hour before sundown so he could get home and clean up for his weekly dinner with Ignatio.

"I see you almost finish top half of statue," Ignatio said through a mouthful of stew as he looked across the table at Davian.

"Yes, and I see that your Anglais is much better," Davian replied.

"Yes, thank you." His friend beamed at the compliment. "I make excellent progress. I speak every day better than day before. Since you begin statue, you no longer visit Morningstone and see King Perivale?"

"I have no more need to see the king, but I go to Morningstone once each week."

"Why go if model finished?"

"I have encountered the strangest thing there. On my first visits I heard a woman's voice, rich and beautiful, coming over a garden wall in the bailey. But her songs were so mournful, they brought me to tears. Later, I found the source of the voice and began to speak to the woman through a gardener's window. Though she won't show her face or reveal her name, I have learned that she suffers from some terrible calamity. Her father keeps her shut behind the wall. But my visits seem to cheer her. So I have kept a regimen of one visit each week."

"You do not know name of woman's father?"

"No. She won't even tell me her own name."

"I will tell you. Some abbey monks minister at Morning-stone. They know of voice. I hear them tell. She is King Perivale's daughter, Princess Avalessa."

Davian was stunned. "The Princess Avalessa? Are you sure? Can it be that the high princess of the Seven Kingdoms bears such sadness?"

"Yes. I hear she lost young man who love her. Not man of king's choosing. King Perivale imprisoned young man and ordered to unman him, but he hang himself in prison. Very sad. Now king is not trusting Princess Avalessa. Keeping her isolated. Will not allow men to look on her face. Doesn't want wrong man to stumble in love with her. So he makes her—"

"Stumble in love? What do you mean?"

"You know, silly Anglais idiom: 'stumble in love.' What a man does when he finds woman and can't help feelings. He stumbles in love."

"Oh, you mean *fall* in love." Davian laughed.

"Yes, fall in love. Thank you to correct me. King Perivale does not want wrong man to fall in love with beautiful daughter. Makes her wear veil. Some say she is so beautiful that if man looks on her he will go mad with love. She wears veil to keep men sane."

Davian was stunned. So he had encountered the high princess of the Seven Kingdoms.

"You have look of sickness," Ignatio said. "Do you feel well?"

"I am well," Davian replied. "But your story—how do you know if it's true? Parts of it have the flavor of legend."

"I cannot say to be certain. I tell you what I hear in abbey. But monks often know. Say, I think you may be in love with beautiful princess."

"Oh, no, of course not," Davian replied. "I do pity her though."

"It was good of you to help her. The Master will reward you."

The conversation drifted to other subjects, and the two friends finished their meal and parted. Davian mounted his horse and pointed it toward his cottage studio.

So the mysterious woman was the Princess Avalessa. Her royalty dismayed him, as did the rumor that she mourned a lover, which, he was surprised to find, made him strangely jealous.

He wondered why any of this should matter to him. He did not love this woman; he merely pitied her. Indeed, it was madness even to think of another woman. His Eve was the most beautiful, loving, loyal, dedicated, and compliant woman on the face of the earth.

But was she really a woman? Again the burrowing thought surfaced. He had observed signs that she might not be real, but he had refused to examine them. Though her mouth was warm and moist, complete with teeth and tongue, she never ate. He knew she never eliminated either. Her nails and hair grew no longer, though she never trimmed them. Although she was the perfect complement to his every wish, his every need, his every word and thought, she had never expressed an original idea. Everything she did, every word she said either reflected his thoughts or responded to them. He wondered how she seemed to anticipate his every wish even before he articulated it. Did his thoughts somehow flow into her, providing her only motives for action?

Of course she was real! How could he think otherwise? Her flesh was warm and soft. He could feel the bones of her arms and hands beneath the supple skin and finely toned muscle. He had felt her heart beating against his own and felt her breath on his face. Perhaps her life was of a different mode than a woman born of the seed of Adam, but it was life nonetheless. Yet the questions persisted until he arrived at his studio, stabled his horse, and entered the door to her tender welcome. Then all questions evaporated in the warmth of her embrace.

38

Davian continued his Tuesday visits to the gardener's window in Morningstone Castle. Each time he called to the princess, but she did not answer. He was sure she would not be pleased that he knew her true name, so he continued to address her as Helen. Though she did not respond to his calls, occasionally he heard her mournful songs as he approached the window. But the song always ceased when he called out to her, leaving nothing but silence in its wake.

As the weeks passed into months, Davian began to despair of ever speaking with Avalessa again, yet he sat by her window a half hour every Tuesday morning. At first he clung to the hope that she would relent and speak with him, but as time wore on, his visits became a mere ritual performed in obedience to his promise.

He was pleased with the progress of the Perivale monument. The upper part from the fingers of the extended arm to the hips was almost finished, giving the figure the look of a man emerging from raw stone like Adam from the clay of the earth. Davian and his assistants were now using rasplike instruments to smooth the surface textures. In no more than three weeks he would instruct the carpenters to dismantle the scaffolding on the upper body and erect it around the lower half.

Davian continued his Thursday dinners with Ignatio. His friend made excellent progress in speaking the language, and Davian told him that were it not for his accent, the only way anyone would know he was not a native of Meridan was that he spoke Anglais too well. Ignatio always asked about Avalessa, and Davian's reply became perfunctory: she would not speak with him. His friend could not help but notice the melancholy in the young artist's voice as he answered.

"You miss her," he said.

"Yes," Davian admitted. "We had become friends, and I enjoyed her company."

"Are you sure it was nothing more than friendship?"

"Of course. How could I love the woman? I've never even seen her."

Davian did not tell Ignatio why he could not allow himself to love Avalessa. He already possessed a bride. He had never told his friend of the transformation of Eve into a living woman. As they continued to meet, he often felt a strong need to unburden his heart and tell the story, but he could not bring himself to do it.

Ignatio might never have learned of the transformation had not Davian failed to show up for one of their Thursday dinners. Ignatio waited for half an hour, then rode to Davian's studio to see if his friend was ill.

"If he isn't ill now, he's about to be," he muttered as he dismounted at Davian's door and knocked. When the door opened, Ignatio's jaw dropped at the sight that met his eyes. Before him stood a woman of incredible beauty, endowed with the exact features of the statue of Eve.

"I . . . I have come to see Davian. I didn't know . . . I mean, how did you . . . Who are you?"

"I am Davian's Eve," she replied, her voice warm as honey and her diction flawless. "Davian is not yet home. He is at the statue now but will come soon. You may wait for him if you wish."

"No, I will not wait." Ignatio sensed the presence of an insidious evil, and he did not want to spend even an instant in the proximity of this beautiful horror. He wanted only to be away from it. He bounded from the door and ran the few yards to the Perivale monument.

He saw the light of a lantern high on the scaffold, and the faint scraping sound of metal on stone reached his ears. "Davian," he called. "Davian, come down. Come down now! I must speak with you."

He saw the lantern move and descend by a series of ladders. In moments Davian reached the ground where his friend waited.

"I'm very sorry, Ignatio. I was smoothing out the king's shoulder when the sun went down. I thought I could finish quickly, so I—"

"Davian, who is that woman in your cottage?"

Davian blanched, then sighed. "It's a long story, but I will tell you all. Indeed, I have long wanted you to know. Let's go to the inn."

He untethered his horse, and the two men rode to the Red Falcon and took seats in a corner far from other diners. When the serving maid brought their stew, Davian told Ignatio the entire story, starting with the visit of the woman in black and finishing with a description of Eve's uncanny attention to his every wish.

"I don't suppose you can believe a word of this," he said when he had finished.

"I believe every word," Ignatio replied. "I saw the evidence at your door with my own eyes. And I have heard of such things. We learn of magic in the abbey—spells, witchcraft, and necromancy. We must know how to counter these evils. And I assure you, Davian, that thing in your cottage is evil."

"If you knew her, you would not say such a thing," Davian replied. "She is good beyond my most extravagant dreams."

"Davian, you once told me that a woman's beauty could be a mask for terrible evil. With your Eve that is true far beyond what you can imagine."

"She is not evil," Davian protested. "She is the perfect woman—the first since Adam's Eve whose physical beauty is an accurate picture of the soul within. She is exactly what she appears to be. She lives and breathes only goodness and love."

"That thing—I cannot call it a woman—doesn't live at all, Davian. It is dead—as dead as this table." He rapped his spoon on the wooden surface.

"But you saw her. It's quite obvious that she's alive."

"No. Its life is an illusion. Let me explain. At the abbey we have been studying the origins of witchcraft for several weeks. I have learned that before the great flood, creatures called Nephilim roamed the earth—monstrous giants begat by angels upon beautiful human women. These rebel angels passed on to the Nephilim enormous intelligence as well as many of the deep secrets of creation. They understood the inner properties of all substances. And they learned how to manipulate stone and metals, changing their textures, their suppleness, and even their color.

"The great flood destroyed the Nephilim. But their spirits still roam the unseen world. Over the centuries a few magicians found the key to contacting them. And they have often given of their knowledge to create chaos in our world to avenge themselves against the Master of the Universe, who exiled them forever in the underworld region of Tartarus."

"I see where your trail is leading," Davian said, "but you don't know any of this to be true. The Master of the Universe himself may have endowed my Eve with life."

"No, Davian; it's against all nature. He ordained that having once created humans, they should populate the earth by bearing young after their own kind. Even when he needed a perfect man to take the guilt incurred by the fall, he didn't create a new man from dust. He placed himself in the womb of a woman to be born according to nature."

"But not only does my Eve appear lifelike, she moves about and speaks. She even breathes and has a beating heart. Manipulating the inner substance of stone cannot explain all that."

"The explanation for that thing's movement, voice, and volition is more horrible than what I have already told you. Every word and every action is manipulated by spirits. If you could see the invisible powers that move the limbs and organs of its body, you would see scores of these demons attached to every part of it, mimicking human movement and sound with uncanny accuracy. This thing you call a woman is an unspeakable demonic horror."

"How can that possibly be true? There is nothing demonic in anything she does. Not once has she ever said an evil word or committed an evil deed."

"Can you tell me whether she has ever said any word or committed any deed that was not a response to your own desire?"

For a moment Davian was silent. "No, everything she does is in response to my desires."

"You see, Davian, this Eve thing has no mind, no self-awareness. It is a dead puppet manipulated for your entertainment and pleasure. Your own thoughts dictate how it should move, and demonic spirits work the strings. This brings up the question of why this thing has been given to you. I can't answer that right now, though I will explore it. But be assured, Davian, this Eve thing is nothing more than a pleasure machine, and she has been given to you for some malignant purpose."

"Surely it isn't true," Davian said, his head in his hands.

"I think you know it is. You told me you never take it out among people. Why?"

"Because of her beauty. Men stare at her. They want her."

"You have been with this thing for more than a year," Ignatio continued, "and all this time I have been your closest friend, yet you never told me of her. Why?"

"I . . . I thought you wouldn't understand. I didn't know how to tell you. I couldn't find a way to . . . I don't know why."

"I think I do," Ignatio answered. "It was not jealousy; it was not its beauty; it was not because I wouldn't understand. It was shame. You hide this thing you call your bride because in your heart you know the truth. You are ashamed of this 'marriage' because you know it is no true marriage. It cannot be a marriage, because only one person is involved—yourself."

"But even if what you say is true, how can she harm me? Why shouldn't I look on her as an innocent pleasure?"

"There is no innocent substitute for woman. That thing is a pit in which you wallow in self-indulgence. The Master gave woman to man for completeness—to find himself by loving another person as himself. This thing you call Eve isn't a person; it satisfies your desires with no love involved. Pleasure without love becomes self-centered and uncontrollable. It eventually closes a man in on himself, shutting out all but the need to scratch the itch. You must destroy this inhuman creature, Davian, or it will consume your humanity."

Davian sat for a moment with his face in his hands. "Ignatio, I sense that what you say may be true. But, may the Master of the Universe forgive me, I'm not sure I can give her up. You don't know how it is to have such a thing in your grasp. When I think of my future without her, it looks bleak as a dry riverbed. I fear I would never cease to long for her."

"It only appears so from this side of the decision. Release your grip on this paltry thing, and your hand will be open to receive the true blessing the Master intends for you, which will be to your Eve thing as the sea is to a puddle. You must destroy it, Davian."

"I will think hard on it," Davian promised.

As he left the inn, his mind reeled with all he had heard. He let his horse walk the distance to his cottage. He knew Ignatio had spoken the truth. It had been half-buried in his own mind before his friend forced it into the light, where it showed itself in all its horror. Yet in spite of the horror, Davian could not make the hard decision that would remove this beautiful creature from his life forever. And he loathed himself for his lack of will. He would do it, but he could not do it suddenly. He would work himself up to the decision, taking time to steel himself against the bleakness of life without her. A few more nights with her could do no harm.

39

Davian would have pronounced the upper half of the Perivale statue finished, but something about the face bothered him. He spent a half day at each of his four tower stations, surveying his work. Overall, he knew it was good. The face was an exact portrait of the king. The reaching arm was taut with tension, its sinews clearly defined to express the strength and passion of the monarch's upward reach. The torso was strong, exuding masculine power and grace. He decided the only inaccuracy was in the jawline, which was too wide by perhaps less than two inches—an inaccuracy so insignificant at such a scale that no one but him would ever notice. But the flaw bothered Davian, and he could not leave it uncorrected. He would not remove the upper scaffolding until he met with Perivale to measure the king's jaw.

As he descended the western tower, he saw a rider on horseback making his way toward him as fast as the busy street would allow. Soon he could see that it was his friend Ignatio. Davian reached the ground as the young kirkman reined his horse to a stop, dismounted, and hurried toward the sculptor.

"What's wrong, Ignatio?"

"Davian, have you destroyed the Eve thing?"

Davian looked down in shame. "No. I couldn't do it yet. But I will—very soon."

"You must do it now," Ignatio said, his voice tense with urgency.

"I will do it very soon. I must adjust to the idea. When I—"

"No, Davian. Now!" Ignatio gripped his friend by the shoulders as he spoke. "I have learned that she may hold even more evil than I knew. She may be a danger to the entire Seven Kingdoms."

"Ignatio, you have lost your wits. What on earth are you raving about?"

"I'm not raving. I must tell you what I've just learned. Quickly, get your horse. Let's go to the inn."

When they were seated at the isolated corner table, Ignatio leaned toward Davian. "Tell me, the woman in black who brought your Eve to life, did you see her right hand?"

"No. As I think on it, she kept it hidden in her robes the entire time she was with me."

"Just as I thought! Do you know who that woman was, Davian? She was Morgultha, the witch Perivale defeated to become king of this island."

"Morgultha? How can you know that?"

"From your description of her. Morgultha's right hand is missing. That's why she kept her right arm hidden in her robes. To show it would have revealed her identity."

"How strange that she would want the model of Perivale," Davian said.

"We can be sure she didn't want to worship it. Perivale is her mortal enemy. No, she needed it for some devious scheme she has plotted."

361

"How could a clay statue possibly help her?" Davian asked.

"I may have just learned the answer to that. All this week we have heard a visiting lecturer in the abbey—Granthon, a monk from Sorendale who was once a sorcerer. Now he uses his knowledge of the darkness to fight against it. At the end of today's lecture, I asked him how the ancient Nephilim gave the illusion of life to an image. He didn't know the secret, but he knew it involved harnessing the power in lightning and infusing it into the image. This somehow alters the elemental substance of stone or metal. This power can be passed from one image to another by a mere touch. As the images touch, an incantation must be recited to enslave invisible spirits to manipulate the movement of the image."

"So the Nephilim need only convert one statue to life, and then that life can be passed on to other statues," Davian said.

"Precisely," Ignatio said. "Now, as I remember, you had only two statues in your studio when Morgultha came to you: the marble Eve and the clay model of Perivale. She put you out of the cottage as she performed the transformation, and when you returned, the Eve was apparently alive and the Perivale was gone."

"That is correct. And I have always wondered how she moved the model of Perivale out of the studio. Its weight was three times that of a man. Now it's clear."

"Yes, he simply walked out. She animated one of the two images in your studio, led it to where the other stood, and had the 'living' one touch the other, passing on the substance-altering power."

"I suppose it looked a bit strange that she had a naked man accompanying her through the streets of Corenham." Davian grinned.

"It was in the wee hours of the morning, and it's not likely that anyone saw them. But it is a shame that you didn't witness the transformation. It would help to know which she animated first—the Perivale or the Eve."

"Why does that matter?" Davian asked.

"Because Granthon told us that the first form animated was the key to the animation of the rest. When that key image is destroyed, all the rest revert to hard stone or metal. We have no idea why she wanted the statue of Perivale or why she took the risk of uttering the perilous spells necessary to contact the disembodied Nephilim. But we can be sure that her purpose is deadly. She plots some scheme against the Seven Kingdoms. If your Eve was animated first, it is the key image and you hold the power to stop whatever evil she is planning by destroying your statue."

"But Morgultha wouldn't be so stupid as to place such power in my hands," Davian said. "She would certainly animate the Perivale image first."

"No, she wouldn't willingly animate the Eve first and leave in your hands the key to all other animations. But she might have been forced to do it. Our lecturer had heard of such a thing occurring hundreds of years ago. A certain wizard had come to the Nephilim requesting the spells for animation to create a small army, but they didn't fully trust him. To protect their interests, they didn't allow him to own or control the image that was the key to the animation of the other images. If that wizard were to deceive the Nephilim or try to use his images to thwart their purposes, they could "kill" the key image, and the images in the wizard's control would revert to lifelessness. Thus the Nephilim kept the wizard at their mercy."

"Very clever. Very devious," Davian said. "But that happened hundreds of years ago. We have no reason to think it is happening again now."

"Don't we?" Ignatio said. "Why would the Nephilim trust Morgultha again? She failed them once, at least. Assuming they didn't trust her and insisted that she couldn't possess the key image, she has found a way to protect herself quite well."

"What do you mean?"

"She is convinced you will never destroy the Eve statue. You are too enamored with the thing. She thinks you will protect it. Therefore, if she, like that ancient necromancer, is planning to create an army by duplicating the statue, she would believe her own images of Perivale animated from your Eve, the key image, are perfectly safe."

"Ignatio, this is all an elaborate conjecture. You don't know that any of it is true."

"But we cannot take the chance. You must destroy the Eve and put a stop to whatever evil Morgultha is spawning. You must do it now, Davian."

"Yes, I will do it soon."

"Davian, you should have done it already for your own sake. Now you must do it for the sake of this island. You must do it now."

"You' are right. I will destroy her."

With Davian's promise secured, Ignatio returned to the abbey. Davian mounted and rode to his studio, his palms sweating and his heart racing at the thought of what he must do.

He went into the studio and took up his ten-pound hammer. He opened the door to his room. Eve stood at the door, never more perfect in her beauty, with the soft firelight rimming her golden hair. She waited for him as usual, her eyes filled with adoration. She opened her arms and reached for him, but he mustered up the will to push her away, a thing he had never done before. For the first time her flawless face took on an expression of confusion and hurt. He lifted his hammer and approached her as she backed away, her eyes wide and her lips parted and quivering.

"Wait, Davian," she said. "I know what you are doing, and I understand why. But I beg you not do it. I want to live. I want only to love you and make you happy. If you destroy me you will regret it, for you will never find another who adores you as I do."

She gazed at him with pleading eyes, and Davian hesitated. Could he stand to be without her? Should such beauty ever be destroyed? His hands trembled, and sweat beaded on his brow as he lifted the hammer.

"Please, Davian," she pleaded as she reached toward him, love and longing glowing in her eyes.

Davian sighed and lowered the hammer as Eve stroked his face.

"You will not regret this," she promised. "I have loved you much, but now I will show you a greater love than any man has ever known."

Davian dropped the hammer to the floor and took her in his arms, loathing himself as he pressed her to his bosom.

That night he could not sleep. He tossed and turned, abhorring his lack of will. As the night wore on, he came to a decision. He would store Eve away in the crate to see if he could live without her. If he found that he could, he would simply open the crate and destroy her. If he could not . . . He would face that decision later.

When morning came he led her into the studio and to the crate. He hoped she would not speak or look at him, and he was pleased that she did neither. She did not protest but meekly stepped into the crate as he instructed, and he nailed down the lid and walked away.

For the first three days, he commended himself that he did quite well without his Eve. He prepared his own meals as he had done before. He planned to go to Cheaping Square and hire a maid to clean the cottage and wash his clothes.

On Tuesday morning he made his habitual visit to the garden wall in Morningstone Castle, where he sat for half an hour in silence. As usual, he heard nothing from behind the wall. Before leaving the castle he went to the seneschal and made an appointment for a sitting with Perivale to measure his jaw. The man found a morning early in the next month when the king would be available.

Davian went to the scaffold, where he and the stone-cutters sliced off a few more layers from the lower parts of the stone. The day was dreary, with a soupy, overcast sky that held no promise of rain. And its grayness seeped into his soul. When darkness fell he wandered through Cheaping Square rather than returning to the empty cottage. After a meal of sausage and bread, he walked about the streets until they emptied and the watchman began to scowl at him. Then he returned to his cottage and went to bed. But it was some time before he got to sleep. Images of Eve's gentle voice and warm embrace haunted his mind.

He repeated the same pattern the following night. After tossing and turning in his bed until long after midnight, he arose, lit a candle, and made his way to the crate in his studio. He pried off the lid and set it aside, then took Eve by the hand and led her from the crate like a living corpse from a coffin.

When she looked at him, her eyes radiated love and adoration and held no hint of reproach for her imprisonment. She wrapped him in her arms and kissed him deeply.

"Davian," she said, "I know I have no life of my own. I know I am merely a reflection of your desires. And I know that what I offer you is only a substitute for real love. But where will you find a living woman who will give you exactly everything you want as I do? You know how real women are. They are full of lies and deceit. Isn't what I offer better than all the difficulties, misunderstandings, compromises, sacrifices, and pain of coming to terms with a real woman?"

Davian said nothing but took her hand and led her through the door to his room, despising his lack of will with every step.

Part 4

The Minstrels

40

King Perivale sat at the polished table with his arms folded. A frown creased his forehead, and he glowered as he spoke to his three closest advisors, Lord Reddgaard, Sir Danward, and the newcomer Senevel. "This ape who calls himself a king has been a pebble in my boot ever since I came to the throne. Why does he think Rhondilar should not be subject to the same taxation and policy as the other six kingdoms?"

"Taxation and policy are not the primary issues, sire," Reddgaard said. "He has rattled his sword ever since you dismissed his claim to the town of Sunderlon. When the Sunderlon River changed course and put the town on Rhondilar's bank instead of Meridan's, he claimed that the people of the city sought protection and trade from him rather than from Meridan. Therefore, he says Sunderlon should be ceded to Rhondilar. His recent complaints are steam boiling out of that pot."

"The accident of a river changing course gives him no excuse to steal a town," Perivale retorted.

"The people of Sunderlon cannot trade with Meridan because the ford over the new river channel is often too deep for wagons," Reddgaard replied. "You might consider asking reasonable compensation for the town—say three years' taxes—and deed it to him for the sake of peace."

"On the other hand, if Agrilon makes good his threat to withdraw from the Seven Kingdoms, we can go to war and depose him," Perivale replied. "Then not only is the town ours, we can place our own man on Rhondilar's throne and be rid of this gnat who thinks he's a hornet."

"I am certain that Agrilon does not want war," Reddgaard said. "He is not strong enough to defeat you, and he knows it. In spite of his bluster, I do not think he really wants to leave the federation. He is clanging his sword on his shield to get some sort of concession for having to deal with the people of Sunderlon."

"He will get nothing from me!" Perivale slammed his fist on the table, causing the cups to jump. "Unless it's the point of my sword. And I will say that to his pig of an ambassador when he comes strutting in."

"Sire, I suggest that you listen to what the ambassador has to say."

The words, spoken in a voice smooth and low, came from the new man in Perivale's inner circle. Senevel was gaunt and pale and had not a hair on his entire body, not even eyelashes. Where he had come from no one knew. He had come to Perivale's attention when he bought a large estate in southern Meridan and thus secured invitations to many of the king's balls and banquets. He quickly gained the ear of the king and became one of his closest advisors.

"Whatever offer Agrilon makes," Senevel continued, "whether a demand or a conciliation, we would do well to examine its strengths and weaknesses before the king gives a reply."

No one could gainsay such advice. Perivale ended the

meeting and took his position on the throne as his advisors took their seats at the side of the dais.

When the herald announced the name of Dunthor, the ambassador from Rhondilar strutted down the great hall toward the throne. His black eyes glared straight ahead, and his rust-colored cape billowed behind him. When he reached the dais, he bowed, but not low, and after the king's restrained welcome, Dunthor spoke.

"I greet you, King Perivale, in the name of King Agrilon of Rhondilar. Today I will not waste words; too many have passed already between your kingdom and mine. My master, King Agrilon, has no wish to cause division among the kingdoms or to disrupt the unity of this island. He is prepared to announce that the great kingdom of Rhondilar will remain in the Seven Kingdoms federation, giving this island unassailable strength and solidarity."

"I am pleased to hear it," Perivale said.

"But my king desires one compensation, which he feels confident that you will grant, Your Majesty. For it is more than a condition. Indeed, it is a token of King Agrilon's desire for the closest and most permanent bond of unity between our great kingdoms. He believes that Your Majesty will—"

"What is your king's condition, Dunthor? If it is ceding the town of Sunderlon, do not waste my time with more words."

"King Agrilon will put the matter of Sunderlon aside, Your Majesty, if you will grant to him one thing only. He desires that you bestow upon him the hand of your fair daughter, the Princess Avalessa, in marriage."

Perivale looked long at the ambassador. He did not let his face reflect his glee at Agrilon's request. Let this pompous rooster sweat for a while for all the trouble he had caused.

373

"We will consider your king's offer," he said. "Stay the night and return this time tomorrow to hear our answer."

Dunthor made his shallow bow, formally thanked the king, and strode from the room. Perivale remained on the throne until late morning, when he dismissed all waiting supplicants and withdrew to his council chambers with his advisors. He fell into his seat, grinning like a boy who has caught a fat trout.

"We could not have hoped for anything better," he said. "That boor of a king has drooled over my daughter since he first laid eyes on her. I should have bartered her to him two years ago and bottled up this buzzing fly forever."

"Surely you will not force the princess into this marriage," Reddgaard said.

"Why should I not?"

"You know he is not the sort of man to make a woman happy."

"Can any man make a woman happy? It's a thing that can't be done. They find unhappiness in the best of circumstances. She will be as happy in Rhondilar as she is here."

"I expect that is true." Reddgaard sighed. "She can hardly be happy here, held as a prisoner in her own father's castle. I don't know why you keep her isolated. She can hardly be happy."

Perivale glared at the venerable lord. "You speak beyond your rights, Reddgaard. You know nothing of this matter, and you had best refrain from speaking of it."

"I have refrained too long, sire. I would know why you give no consideration to her happiness."

"Very well, I will tell you. She is a rebellious, wanton girl. She refuses to obey her father, and if I were to free her, she would play the harlot with any swain who parades beneath her balcony. I keep her isolated and veiled to protect her

374

chastity. So, as you can see, this marriage to King Agrilon solves more than one of my problems."

"Sire, I know your daughter—at least I knew her before she was isolated—and I must tell you plainly that you are mistaken. She is not a wanton. Far from it, she has always been upright, chaste, and obedient. You are hiding something from us, and I fear you are using your daughter for your own purposes and utterly disregarding her happiness. Not only do I urge you not to sell her to this king, I urge you to examine your heart and uncover the true reason you are willing to inflict such unhappiness on her."

Perivale's face grew livid, and his eyes glared at the aged man. He stood suddenly, overturning his chair, and pointed a shaking finger at his venerable advisor. "Get out of my sight, old man. Never show your face in these halls again. I will not allow such disrespect to my crown. Get out! Now!"

Reddgaard stood slowly and hobbled toward the door. When he reached it he turned to the king. "I will leave you, Your Majesty. I have seen too many years to fear your anger. My only fear is that you will soon bring ruin upon yourself and this kingdom. May the Master of the Universe have mercy on you."

Reddgaard opened the door and left the council. Perivale stood glaring after him for a moment before he picked up his chair and sat facing his two remaining advisors.

"I have another reason for the marriage of Agrilon to my daughter, one that Reddgaard wouldn't understand at all. The Princess Avalessa is no longer beautiful. Her face has been severely scarred in an unfortunate accident. Besides myself, only her lady-in-waiting knows of it, and now the two of you. That is why I keep her isolated and veiled. I have had to keep her scarring secret until I could get her wed. Now that opportunity has come. And not only do I rid myself of damaged goods at a top price, I get vengeance on a man who has been a thorn in my side since my coronation. Can you imagine Agrilon's consternation when he awakens to her ruined face the morning after his wedding night?" Perivale laughed as Senevel grinned broadly.

But Danward was appalled. "You cannot do this, sire," he said. "Not only will it undo any possibility of peace between Meridan and Rhondilar, it will likely provoke a war."

"We need not worry on that score," Senevel said. "The agreement between the two countries will be signed before the wedding, and Agrilon will be legally bound by it."

"But he will claim the agreement nullified because of the deception," Danward said.

"Surely you don't think he has a case," Senevel said. "Nothing in the agreement will guarantee the beauty of the princess. We will have violated no provision in the document."

"Besides, I welcome a war with Agrilon," Perivale said. "Let him try us. We will crush him as if he were a dung beetle."

"It is deceptive nonetheless," Danward insisted. "And it is a terrible thing to do, both to the princess and to the king. We must not go through with it."

Perivale reddened at Danward's protest, but he kept his temper. "I am sorry you don't agree, but it will be done. We have nothing more to discuss. Senevel will draw up the agreement between Meridan and Rhondilar and present it to me tonight. I will sign it and give it to Dunthor in the morning. You may leave, Sir Danward. Senevel, you stay with me awhile yet. We will discuss the terms of the agreement."

After Danward left the chamber, Senevel turned to Perivale and spoke in his low, silky voice. "You told the man more than he should know, Your Majesty. His overly sensitive sense of honor could lead him to reveal what he knows to Dunthor. Give the word, and I will follow him. Tonight he must sleep not in his bed but in his grave."

"Yes, it must be done," the king said.

"It will be done, sire." Senevel rose, bowed low to the king, and left the chamber to follow Danward.

41

From her tower window Avalessa looked out toward the monument to her father. The shape of the upper half of the figure was clearly discernible in spite of the scaffolding around it. Though she hated the man the statue portrayed, she could not deny that it was beautiful—a magnificent expression of ideal manhood aspiring to touch the hand from the heavens. She had trouble thinking of the figure as her father. The perfection of the form belied the darkness of the man's heart.

She marveled at the enormous talent of the monument's creator. Every day she observed Davian on the scaffolding, working the stone with his hammers, chisels, and rasping tools. Though she could not discern his features at such a distance, she had often watched him as he left the statue and rode toward Morningstone, and she could see that he was tall and well formed.

She also marveled at his unwavering honor. True to his promise, he had never missed a Tuesday coming to her garden window, though she had not spoken a word in response since the day she had told him not to return. On some days she knew he sat alone in the rain; on others the

378

cold must have bit into his fingers and toes. She often wept as she fought down her longing to run to the window and pour out her love for him. She knew he had developed a strong attachment to her that could easily cross the border into love. She could not let him cross that border. She could not give him cause to hope for an impossible future simply to fill the void of her loneliness.

When messages came to Avalessa, or when servants entered to clean her chambers or bring meals, the guard outside her door always knocked before opening it. But on a rainy day in the middle of spring, she heard the key turn in the lock without a knock to precede it. She dropped her veil over her face as the door opened and Perivale entered. Avalessa paled and stepped back involuntarily. The king took a seat near the door and motioned for Avalessa to sit opposite him.

"I have good news for you, my daughter," he said, smiling as if the past did not exist. She remained silent, looking at him warily through her veil. "You will be happy to hear that you are to become a bride, and quite soon," he continued.

Avalessa did not respond.

"Aren't you even curious to know who your husband will be?"

"It hardly matters, does it?" she replied. "You will sell me to the highest bidder."

"Listen, daughter," he growled. "With your face, you are fortunate to be wed at all. Your groom is to be King Agrilon of Rhondilar."

"I guessed as much. I'm not surprised that you would wed me to a man old enough to be my father. I'm not surprised that you would dump me off to a man who treats women as drudges and playthings. But I am surprised that he would wed me now. How did you persuade him to take such ruined merchandise as I am?"

379

"He knows nothing of the ruination." Perivale chuckled. "You will be veiled for the wedding. He won't discover the truth until the following morning."

Avalessa was appalled. "How can you deceive the man this way? Have you no thought of his rage when he sees my face? I will not be a party to it. I will not say the vows, and you cannot force me to do it."

"You will do it," the king said, glaring sternly. "I will see to it."

Without another word he arose and left her chambers.

Shortly after the king departed, a knock sounded at Avalessa's door and Lady Elowynn entered, distress showing in her face.

"Elowynn, what is wrong? You're pale as a winter moon."

"Terrible things have happened in the night, Your Highness. Lord Reddgaard died in his sleep, and Sir Danward was murdered. Guards found him this morning near the chambers of the ambassador from Rhondilar. He had been stabbed in the back."

"Lord Reddgaard and Sir Danward? Both in the same night? Oh, Elowynn, this is terrible. They were the last two voices of reason in the king's council. Why were they killed? And who is the murderer?"

"No one knows whether Lord Reddgaard was murdered. He was an old man, and his health was failing. As to Danward's murderer, we may never know who or why."

"These are terrible times, Elowynn. Troubles pile upon us like stones crumbling from a wall. And another stone has just fallen. Unless we can avert it, more carnage will follow."

"What do you mean?" Elowynn was alarmed.

Avalessa told Elowynn of her impending wedding to Agrilon and explained the deception Perivale intended.

"Who knows what Agrilon will do when he sees my face. He isn't the sort of man to let such an affront go unavenged. I'm sure bloodshed will follow—even war."

"This is terrible. We must do something, but what? Your two most likely sources of help are now dead." The lady shook her head sadly. Suddenly she looked up and said, "Ah, but there is another."

"What other?"

"Your artist friend, Davian. He still comes to the wall every Tuesday. Didn't he vow to help you escape? I will tell him what is afoot, and he will surely help us. He is a man who keeps a promise."

"No. There is too much risk. We must not pull him into this. It's none of his affair."

"My dear princess, have you considered that Agrilon's rage could strike first at you? He will certainly think you conspired with your father."

"It doesn't matter. I will not risk Davian to save myself."

"Do you think he would want to be spared with your life at stake? I will speak to him."

"No, Elowynn. I forbid it."

"Avalessa, you know I love you like a sister. In all my years with you, not once have I failed to make your wish my command. But I must disobey you in this matter. I am sorry, but I must do for you what you will not do for yourself."

Elowynn knocked at the chamber door. When it did not open, she knocked again and called to the guard. "It's Lady Elowynn. I am ready to leave. Open the door."

"I'm sorry, m'lady," the guard called. "The king has ordered that you remain in these chambers until after the wedding. All your needs will be met, but you may neither send nor receive messages except those approved by the king himself."

The two women looked at each other in despair. Now the chamber held two prisoners.

On the morning of the wedding, Senevel handed a vial of clear liquid to the chief cook of Morningstone Castle and instructed him to add its contents to the princess's morning mead. The cook complied, and the drink was delivered with Avalessa's breakfast.

An hour after Avalessa drank the mead, she felt as if she were dissolving. Everything around her became distant and dreamlike. She could hear the voices of others, but she could only vaguely comprehend the meaning of their words. She could move her limbs but only with concentrated effort. She found it impossible to exercise any will of her own, though she could perform simple movements in compliance to commands. She could not speak at all, but she could nod her head or shake it in dissent. She was utterly dependent on the direction of others.

Avalessa sensed an undefined terror, a dark and malignant presence that seemed to loom somewhere within the fog that engulfed her. At brief moments she faintly saw in her mind the skull-like dome of a head, devoid of hair and holding her in the beam of its piercing stare. She wanted to scream, but she could not find her voice or even move a single muscle to signal that she was trapped in hell.

Shortly after midmorning, pages brought water for her bath, and a tailor with three female assistants arrived with a massive bundle of beige cloth that Avalessa dimly realized was a wedding dress. The tailor said something to the three women, and they moved toward her. As in a dream, Avalessa saw Elowynn step between her and the women, and she heard her lady say something about no one undressing the princess but herself. Elowynn seemed to dismiss everyone from the room. The tailor said something about the king's orders, and all began speaking at once, though Avalessa could understand nothing they said. Soon the tailor and the women left, looking angry and offended.

When the guard closed the door, Elowynn turned to the princess and said, "That peacock of a tailor and his three clucking hens came to bathe and dress you. I would not allow it, but in the end I had to promise the guard that I would do it myself, or he would not have allowed them to leave. Forgive me, Your Highness. I intended that neither of us would obey a single order to prepare for the wedding, but now I see no hope of avoiding the inevitable. They have drugged you into a stupor, and we are at their mercy. Now we must dress you for your wedding. I am very sorry, my princess."

Avalessa found that she could neither respond nor make any protest as Elowynn undressed her, bathed her, combed out her hair, and fitted the gown to her. She could do nothing but follow every direction as her lady put the veil in place, tucking it inside the high collar of the gown and pinning it so it could not be lifted, as Perivale had ordered.

When evening fell servants came and led Avalessa into the corridors of the castle. She followed and found herself in a procession filled with vague shadows of people both ahead of her and behind her, all moving silently toward the great hall. As she entered the hall, she was dimly aware of misty, faceless figures on each side as she glided like a ghost toward the dais, where two dark figures loomed. She stepped up the dais, and the hard, stony face of Agrilon loomed before her like a craggy mountain bluff. Behind him stood a cleric in black robes.

She heard the drone of words but found no meaning in

them until someone asked her to nod her head. She complied. After a few more meaningless words, she felt herself being led away from the dais, again down long corridors, and into a candlelit chamber in which she could see nothing but an enormous bed stretching before her like a vast desert. She heard the door close behind her, followed by the clank of the bolt, and then the hulking shadow of Agrilon loomed over her, blocking the candlelight that had been her only solace. Though she felt terror pulsing through every vein, she could not find the volition to move even a finger as she felt his fumbling hands unpinning the veil and then lifting it from her face.

Agrilon's bellow of rage resounded through the corridors of Morningstone. Sleepers came awake in rooms all over the keep as Agrilon's chamber door crashed open and he banged the hilt of his sword on his captain's door, shouting at the top of his lungs. Soon half the castle was awake as Agrilon and the fourteen knights who had accompanied him stormed through the corridors toward Perivale's chambers, raging and cursing as they went. Castle guards met them in the hallway with swords drawn.

"I demand to see that false cur who is your king," Agrilon shouted.

"The king has retired. You may see him in the morning," the captain of the guard said.

"I will see him now!" the wronged monarch bellowed. "If you will not awaken him, your dying screams will."

"Hold your sword. I will ask if the king will see you."

The guard signaled to another behind him, who rapped on the door to Perivale's chamber. The door opened, and Perivale stepped out.

"What is the meaning of this?" he demanded.

"You know the meaning!" Agrilon cried. "You have

deceived me. You didn't tell me your daughter had been marred."

"You didn't ask. Her condition wasn't a part of our bargain. I violated nothing in the agreement."

"There is no agreement. It is now null and void."

"It's too late for that, my dear Agrilon," Perivale replied with a hint of mockery. "You have deflowered my daughter, and the terms have been sealed. You cannot back out of it now."

"I certainly can, and I will. The marriage has not been consummated, and I will not take damaged goods as the price for my remaining in the Seven Kingdoms. Rhondilar withdraws from the federation. I will not serve a false king."

"If you break our agreement, Agrilon, be sure that you will bring disaster down upon your head."

"We will see just whose head the doom descends upon," Agrilon said. He turned and commanded his men to prepare for immediate departure. They awakened their women, gathered their gear, and went out into the night to ready their horses and load their wagons.

Perivale ordered the castle gates opened, and he listened with a gleeful smile to the clop of hooves and the roar of wagon wheels at the gate as the entourage from Rhondilar stormed out of his castle and into the darkness.

42

The sun hovered low on the western horizon when King Agrilon first saw the trees lining the Sunderlon River, a mile distant. "It's not wide enough by half to divide me from Meridan's dog of a king," he growled to his aide. He was two days out of Corenham after his aborted marriage to the Princess Avalessa, and the hot embers of anger still smoldered in his belly. Impatience to reach his castle in Stenholm prodded him like a restless demon, for there he would call together his Hall of Knights and determine how to avenge Perivale's insult to his kingdom. But he could not move at the pace he wished because of the twelve ladies traveling with him, wives of lords and knights who had journeyed to Corenham in ponderous carriages for their king's wedding.

"Someone stands in the road near the river, sire," his aide said.

"Ride ahead and see who it is," the king commanded.

Several minutes later the rider returned and reported what he had learned. "The rider is a lady, sire, mounted on a horse like a man. She would not reveal her identity, but she desires an audience with you. She says she can benefit you greatly."

"A lady? Very well. No harm can come from speaking with a mere woman."

Agrilon took two of his knights and galloped ahead of the procession. The three men drew rein a few feet from the woman, who sat astride a black horse and wore a black robe that covered her from head to foot. The king could now see her face. It was pale and thin, though well formed, but he blanched when he looked into her eyes. They were almost colorless and cold as frost, and their gaze pierced his brain like an arrow.

"King Agrilon," she said in a voice deep and steady. "It is good of you to speak with me. You will not regret it."

"Who are you?" the king demanded.

"I will reveal myself but to you alone. Have your men back up ten paces. I will not harm you. As you can see, I am weaponless."

Agrilon ordered his men back.

"Now speak your piece, my lady," he said.

"I am Morgultha. I have heard the tale of how King Perivale has deceived you. Like you, I have reason to hate the man." She drew from her robe the stump of her right wrist. "I have a plan by which we can both avenge ourselves, and soon. Will you hear me?"

The superstitious Agrilon would have found it unthinkable to entertain alliance with this infamous witch had not the desire for vengeance burned hotter than his reason. "I will hear you, lady. Speak on."

"I will outline my plan in its simplicity," Morgultha said, "then we can smooth out the details tonight in the comfort of an inn. The essence of it is this: the disputed town of Sunderlon can be yours tomorrow. You can easily take it even with the few knights who accompany you, and likely with no bloodshed. As you know, the town is not walled, it has little military presence, and many of its citizens are already sympathetic to you. All you need to do is ride in, take the hall, proclaim the town to be under your rule, and it is done."

"Nay, my lady. I am angry, but I'm no fool. I have but fourteen warriors with me, and I am yet two days from my capital, Stenholm. Perivale would get word of my invasion in a day, and Meridan's knights would swarm on me like a nest of hornets before I could get help to come."

"To be sure, King Perivale will attack you. Indeed, he strains at the bit to come against you. That is part of my plan for vengeance. You see, I have a hundred mounted knights of my own. They rest outside the city just over the river even now. They will join you when Perivale attacks, which I predict will be immediate because of his lust for the battle. He won't be able to muster over fifty men on such short notice. Nevertheless, he will come, because he knows you have only fourteen knights with you. He won't know of my hundred men and will ride into my trap. His defeat is inevitable. Meanwhile, you can send immediately for reinforcements to come to your aid should the war be prolonged."

"Ah, but I see a flaw in your plan," Agrilon said. "Riders sympathetic to Perivale will ride out of Sunderlon the moment I invade to warn Perivale of your army, and he won't dare come against me without amassing all his knights."

"I have already thought of that," Morgultha replied. "My men have been watching the city to see that no rider from the town crosses the river. I have my own paid messenger standing ready to ride out from Sunderlon at the appropriate time. He will deliver to Perivale a message of my own devising, and I assure you, it does not include a report of my hundred warriors."

Agrilon rubbed his chin and thought on the woman's words.

"In fact," she continued, "you will likely take Sunderlon with no bloodshed at all. The very presence of my army around the city will induce its leaders to turn over the government to you, especially since most of them have little love for Perivale."

"I would see your army, lady," the king said.

"Very well. Follow me."

She turned her horse and loped toward the river, a hundred yards distant. She halted just above the descent to the ford and swept her arm toward a clearing across the river and to their right. Agrilon saw the gleam of the evening sun on the armor of a mass of mounted men, all on chargers and armed with shields and swords. The king sat quiet for several minutes as he counted the number. The total was one hundred and two.

"Who are these men?" he asked.

"That I will not reveal. But I can tell you they will fight like the devil himself."

"I like your plan, Lady Morgultha. Let us ride into Sunderlon and complete the details."

Perivale sat straight and rigid in his chambers, his head pressed against the back of the wooden chair. At Davian's request he had removed his crown and placed it on the cask beside his bed. Davian stood over the monarch, his calipers opened with one point touching the top of the king's head and the other the underside of his chin. The artist removed the instrument and jotted down the measurements.

Perivale glanced toward the crown. He could hardly bear to take it off, even to sleep, and the need to remove it now filled him with apprehension, though it was easily within arm's reach.

"Are you not yet finished?" he asked.

"I still need to measure the width of your jaw," Davian replied.

"Be quick about it. I cannot remain here all day while you do things you should have done months ago."

At that moment a knock sounded at the door, and at the king's bidding a page entered. "Your Majesty, you are needed immediately in the council chamber. A most important matter has arisen that requires your attention."

Perivale grabbed up his crown, placed it on his head, and strode from the room.

When Perivale arrived at the council chamber, Sir Gorlac and Senevel were seated at the table. They rose and bowed as the king entered and sat down.

"Your Majesty," Senevel said. "Sir Gorlac brings startling news."

"King Agrilon has taken Sunderlon," Gorlac said.

"Ha! The fool!" Perivale said. "He couldn't wait, could he? Let's see, he's been gone from here three days, and with his women and wagons, it would take him two days to reach Sunderlon. Then it would take the messenger bearing the news one day to reach us." He counted on his fingers. "That means he took the town on his way home from here."

"You are correct, sire."

"But in the heat of his anger the fool didn't think ahead." Perivale grinned. "He had only fourteen knights with him. By now he must realize I will ride against him the moment I get the news. No doubt he is already quaking in his boots, sending desperate messages to his knights scattered all over Rhondilar."

"Sire, you should know that King Agrilon took the town with over a hundred men," Gorlac said.

"Over a hundred? How is that possible?" Perivale said.

"We intercepted a messenger from Sunderlon who first told us that Agrilon had taken the town with his fourteen knights. But we discovered a quantity of gold in his purse that belied his claims of quick escape. We applied certain measures to extract the truth and found that he was in the pay of Morgultha, who has assembled for Agrilon an army of a hundred."

"Why that two-faced devil!" Perivale slammed his fist on the table. "This means that even before he came here for the wedding he intended to invade Sunderlon. He and that black witch had already assembled an army and had them marching toward the town. And he accuses me of duplicity! That hulking ox will pay for this treachery with his life. Call together my knights. We will ride out at dawn tomorrow."

"But, sire, most of your knights are not in Corenham. Many are at their own estates, and some are away on quests," Gorlac said.

"How many are available?" Perivale asked.

"We would do well to muster fifty."

"No matter. Call them together. We will ride in the morning."

"Only fifty knights, sire? When he has an army of a hundred?" Gorlac said.

"You know that Agrilon doesn't have a hundred knights," Senevel said in his oozing voice. "His entire Hall is made up of little more than thirty. And we know that most of those are on the seacoast in northern Rhondilar, clearing port towns of pirates. If Morgultha has assembled a hundred men for him, she has gathered them from the farmers and herders about the country. They cannot be trained fighters but mere rabble armed with hoes and hay rakes."

"Exactly," Perivale boomed. "Fifty of Meridan's finest knights can defeat this band of ruffians while picking their teeth. We will show this island the difference between a man from Meridan and a cur from Rhondilar. Agrilon has seen his last days on this earth."

"But, sire, wouldn't it be prudent to wait and take a hundred knights to match his numbers?" Gorlac persisted. "We know nothing about who these hundred men are. Morgultha may have hired trained mercenaries. Or she may have assembled monsters from the parts of dead men and animals as she did before."

"From where would she hire mercenaries?" Senevel said. "All the men of the Seven Kingdoms love you, sire, and they are loyal to you. They will not lift a hand against their high king. And as to Morgultha creating her own army, Agrilon would never fight beside such monsters. You know him, sire. He is among the most superstitious of men and fears any hint of the supernatural. He wears an amulet about his neck to ward off spirits and keeps a priest with him on all his journeys to exorcise ghosts from the chambers of inns and castles where he lodges."

"Senevel is right, Gorlac," Perivale said. "You worry too much. Think of the songs and legends that will be sung of us—how fifty routed a hundred. The battle will live on the tongues of bards for generations to come."

"You are right, my king," Senevel purred. "You incur no real risk with your fifty Meridan knights, and this battle against such apparent odds will add to your already considerable glory. You cannot lose, sire."

"Agrilon is as good as dead!" Perivale cried, his eyes bright with anticipation. "Gorlac, call the knights to battle."

Davian sat quietly on the stone he had rolled up to the gardener's window. He had arrived twenty minutes earlier, after being dismissed from the king's presence, and had called to Avalessa as he usually did. He was about to leave when he heard voices from the other side of the hedge that hid him. He sat quietly and listened as the voices drew closer, obviously belonging to two men who had left the path and walked among the hedges seeking privacy. He kept quiet and listened.

"So you got word to Morgultha in time for her to meet Agrilon at Sunderlon?" a thin, precise voice asked.

"Yes, she met him there," a low, smooth voice replied. "Gorlac's report confirmed it. The trap is set, and King Perivale has taken the bait. In the morning he leads little more than fifty knights against King Agrilon in Sunderlon. Perivale realizes that he will meet an army of over a hundred men. The fool Gorlac told him, and for a moment I thought Perivale would wait to assemble his entire Hall and our plan would be ruined. But the king's battle lust made it easy for me to convince him that Morgultha's hundred soldiers could only be untrained farmers and tradesmen. He wants the glory of defeating them with an army of half their number."

"But if fifty knights are to ride with Perivale, surely I will be among those called," the first voice said. "And I must remain here if our plan is to work."

"You need not worry, Lord Fenimar," the smooth voice replied. "I told the king that you were away and that Lord Kramad Yesenhad was ill. And I convinced him that we needed Lord Ashbough here to maintain the defense of Corenham in his absence."

"Well done, Senevel," said the first voice, which Davian

393

now knew belonged to Fenimar. "This means that after Perivale leaves, we can—"

"We must not move until the second night after Perivale has gone," Senevel said. "To move before Perivale has been declared dead would appear as rebellion. You would lose the goodwill of the people. But after the report of his death, you won't be challenged, for you are the legitimate successor to King Landorm. Two days from tomorrow we can claim to have news from the battle that Perivale has been slain. I will see that the castle is poorly guarded. And with most of Meridan's knights away, you will get little resistance as you move on Morningstone, eliminate the succession, and seize the crown."

"What makes you think the Crown of Eden will be in Morningstone?" Fenimar asked. "Perivale is never seen without it."

"He is never seen without it except when he journeys. He fears for the safety of it when he is on the road. He leaves it somewhere within the castle."

"Very well," Fenimar replied. "Your plan appears to be sound. Lord Ashbough, Lord Kramad Yesenhad, and I will assassinate Prince Rhondale and Princess Avalessa, thus eliminating all competing claims to the throne. We will find the Crown of Eden in the castle and turn it over to Morgultha. She will claim sovereignty over the Seven Kingdoms and give me the throne of Meridan."

Davian's heart went cold. He hardly dared to breathe.

"But, Lord Fenimar," Senevel said smoothly, "why give the crown to Morgultha?"

"It was our agreement. She would provide the hundred warriors to defeat Perivale, and we would eliminate the succession and give her the Crown of Eden."

"But you will have the crown in your possession. And you will have the throne itself. And you will have command of all the knights who weren't available to ride out with Perivale. You could keep the crown and rule the Seven Kingdoms yourself."

Davian heard a low chuckle, followed by the voice of Fenimar saying, "We made the right move when we brought you to Meridan, Senevel. Your future is bright if our plan succeeds."

"It will succeed, my lord. King Perivale will not return to Morningstone. In three days you will be the sole ruler of the Seven Kingdoms."

Davian's every muscle tensed as he leaned forward on his stone seat, eager to hear every word of the conspiracy. Suddenly his stone tipped slightly, and his arm brushed the leaves of the hedge. His heart came into his throat.

"What was that?" Fenimar said.

The two men were quiet for what seemed to Davian an eternity.

"No doubt just a squirrel," Senevel at last replied. "But we've said enough. Let us leave here separately. We will meet again two days from tomorrow when Perivale is sure to lie dead in Sunderlon. Then we will move on Morning-stone."

Davian had no thought but to climb the wall immediately and warn the princess of the threat on her life, but he dared not move a muscle as he heard one set of footsteps walk away. Another minute passed before he heard the second set follow. He forced himself to count another five minutes before he began to scale the wall, clutching at the vines in wild desperation. Clumps of ivy ripped away in his hands and tore from beneath his feet. The climb took longer than he expected, but he reached the top of the wall, swung his feet over, and looked down into the garden. A young woman he assumed to be the princess sat on a stone bench facing a flowing fountain. She wore no veil, but her back was to him, and he could determine nothing of her appearance except for the golden hair that billowed about her shoulders. She had neither seen nor heard him, and he dared not call out. He ran along the top of the wall until he reached her balcony. He leapt down to the balcony and scrambled down the steps and into the trees and paths of her garden. He ran among the trees and hedges toward the fountain where he had seen the princess.

Suddenly the door to Avalessa's chambers burst open, and seven guards with drawn swords clamored into the garden and made straight for Davian. Avalessa screamed and dropped the veil over her face. In an instant the guards surrounded the unarmed artist and took him, pinning his arms behind his back. As they fought to hold him, the face of Senevel, dark and threatening, appeared before him.

Davian cried out, "Princess Avalessa, you must get—"

Senevel's sword hilt came hard against his head, and the world went gray before his eyes. He collapsed to the ground. Avalessa ran to where he lay and knew immediately by his coat, his dark hair, and the brief shout of his voice that the fallen man was Davian. She was terrified that he might be dead.

"We must call the physician," she said.

"Take him to the prison," Senevel said to the guards. Turning to the princess, he bowed low and smiled reassuringly. "Your Highness, any cur who invades your garden and threatens your honor does not deserve a physician. I am glad we got here in time. It was fortunate that I heard the vile creature creeping beneath your wall just moments ago. Immediately I called the guards, and it seems that we arrived just in time."

"What will you do with him?" she asked.

"I will put him in the dungeon and inform your father.

He will punish this man as he always punishes those who attempt to defile his daughter.

"Do you know who this man is? He is Davian, the king's sculptor. Harm him and the king's monument is in jeopardy."

"Oh, you need not worry about that. No harm will come to his hands." With a cold smile and a deep bow, Senevel left Avalessa's chambers, and the guards dragged Davian to Morningstone's dungeon.

Senevel did not tell Perivale he had caught the sculptor in Princess Avalessa's garden. He knew the king's rage at the young man would be tempered by his desire to have his monument completed. He suspected that Davian had overheard much of his conversation with Fenimar, and he could not risk the king questioning the prisoner and learning what he might know. He also knew that the king punished such offenses not with death but with emasculation. He must see that this man was executed. He would wait for news of Perivale's death, and then he would behead his new prisoner.

43

Lady Elowynn sat at the table, her hand pressed to her forehead as Avalessa paced the floor of her chamber. It was an hour till midnight, and the two women had not gone to bed. Every thought was turned toward finding a way to get Davian out of prison.

"If only I were free!" Elowynn said for perhaps the twentieth time.

"If only we knew someone we could send to bribe the barber," Avalessa added.

"Let's look again at what we have already considered," Elowynn said. "Davian has told you that he has a friend in the abbey named Ignatio. If we could get a message to him, he could go to Davian, though how he could help I don't know."

"And even if he could help, how would we get a message to him? The guards screen every message we send."

"We could call for a confessor and send a message to Ignatio through him," Elowynn said.

"But the confessor has come to my door every fortnight since my captivity, and I have always refused to speak to him. Wouldn't the guard find it strange that I asked for a confessor just now?" Avalessa replied.

"If that were the only obstacle, we could overcome it. But the guard is sure to listen as you confess, just to prevent your giving such a message."

"If we can get a priest to come, perhaps I could word a confession that hides within it a message to Ignatio that the guard would not suspect," Avalessa said.

Elowynn raised doubts that a message vague enough to get by the guard could carry enough information to spur Ignatio to action. But she could not think of a better plan, and after the two women had examined it thoroughly and worked out the details, she called to the guard and requested a confessor priest to come to the princess as soon as possible. Though it was in the black of the night, the guard complied and sent the message to Corenham Abbey. The two women went to bed, and Avalessa slept fitfully until Elowynn awakened her shortly after dawn the next morning. A priest was at the door to hear her confession.

Avalessa dressed hurriedly, dropped the veil over her face, and met the priest as he entered. The guard followed the kirkman into the princess's chambers.

"Bless you, Your Highness," the priest said, bowing to the princess. "I am here to assist you in confessing your sins, not to me, but to the Master of the Universe, who is quick to forgive and eager to love. Please speak what is on your heart."

"Thank you, father," Avalessa said quietly. She got to her knees before the holy man, who took both of her hands in his own. The guard stood impassively behind the priest. "Father, I have sinned," she said. "My unholy desire for the artist Davian has lured the young man to a terrible fate. Lonely in my confinement, I enticed him with wanton promises until he could not contain his desire and scaled the wall of my garden. I repent of my selfish lack of concern for his fate. I know I cannot save the man, for many die of the wound he is to endure, but I would not send him to perdition without the prayers of holy men. I would sleep well if I knew that you would convene the priests and acolytes of the abbey to petition the Master for his soul—even this morning. Pray for him, that he may endure and survive his grievous wounding and that the Master will forgive him for succumbing to my wanton enticement."

"Is that all, my child?" the priest said.

"There is one thing more," Avalessa said. "It would give me peace if you would send a priest to the young man immediately following your prayer in the abbey. I would not have him walk the valley of death unconfessed."

"Bless you, my child, for your confession and your concern for this poor man. All you ask will be done. And be assured, the Master forgives you and loves you dearly. Please rest in peace tonight."

The priest rose, made the sign of the three trees, and left the chamber accompanied by the guard.

"You did all you could and did it quite well," Elowynn said after the guard's key had turned in the lock. "It is futile to worry now. When the priests gather to pray as you requested, Ignatio will surely be among them. When he hears that Davian is in prison, he will certainly go to him. And you know he will do everything in his power to save his friend."

"I know he will," Avalessa replied. "We must pray continually for his success."

Davian groaned and with a trembling hand gingerly touched his head, which throbbed as if hammers were driving chisels into his skull. He lay flat on his back in rancid straw on a stone floor damp with moss and mildew. He tried to move, and pains shot through his back like arrows. Wherever he was, he knew he must have been lying there for hours. He opened his eyes and looked across the floor. At first he thought he was in complete darkness, but it was hard to know, because blurs of dim, grayish color pulsed and flowed at random within his field of vision. He tried to focus his eyes, but it was several minutes before he could make out vertical bars of black iron that told him he was in a prison cell.

The princess! She is in danger! He suddenly remembered the conspiracy he had overheard. He recalled scaling Avalessa's wall, the entrance of the guards and the bald man, then nothing. He must get out of this cell. Avalessa's life was at stake.

He forced himself to sit up, grimacing and groaning at the protest of his limbs and the sensation that his head was cracking open. He crawled to the wall and sat with his back against it, breathing hard and fighting down nausea. With great effort he pulled himself to his feet, moaning softly at the pain of every movement. His vision improved a little, but gray clouds continued to writhe and pulsate before his eyes.

"Guard!" he called, his voice rasping in his throat.

He coughed and spat, then called again more loudly. But the word merely echoed in the corridor. He called a third time. A weak voice from somewhere down the passageway replied, "It be no use hollerin'. No guard will hear ye. They's too far away and behind a locked door. They canna abide the stench of us."

Davian fought off his weakness and dizziness and went all around his cell, feeling high and low for any stones that might move. None did. He pushed and tugged at each bar, checking for any that might be loose. None were. He rattled the lock, but it held firmly. Now sweating and breathing hard from pain and exertion, he slumped to the floor. He must find a way out. Avalessa's life depended on it. But sleep soon overtook him.

A scraping sound awakened him. He opened his eyes, and for a moment he could see nothing but the gray clouds that marred his vision. He could barely make out a dark, huddled figure pushing two bowls into his cell. The shadow moved on down the corridor, and Davian crawled to the bowls. One contained a thin soup, and the other water. On the floor beside one of the bowls lay a hard crust of black bread. He drank the soup and ate the bread slowly in deference to his unsettled stomach, then sipped a little of the water, leaving the rest for later. He did not know how often he would be fed. The food revived him a little, and his mind began to function with better clarity, though his eyes did not. A surge of panic swept through him. How was he to get out and warn the princess? He forced his mind to be calm. He could do nothing at the moment. He must rest, conserve his strength, and think.

As he sat brooding, all his thoughts were of Avalessa. He longed for her with an intensity he could almost taste, and he wondered why. Waiting for him in his studio was a woman of unparalleled beauty and perfect complicity. Yet here he sat, longing for a woman he had never seen and knew only by voice.

Ignatio was right. The imitation woman could not satisfy his longing for oneness with another. Counterfeits satisfied only for a moment before their imitation proved a thin substitute for the many dimensions of true reality. He had clung to his Eve in spite of his friend's warnings partly because he thought Avalessa to be unattainable. But this new turn of events might change that. If he could get out of this prison, he could help her escape Morningstone and the Seven Kingdoms. In exile, she would no longer be a princess, and their future together would be a possibility.

Such thoughts brightened Davian's mind until doubts began creeping in like burrowing moles. Though he delighted in Avalessa's otherness, otherness had a drawback. It could lead to conflict. Her desires and needs would not always mesh with his own. Furthermore, should her appearance not matter to him? She was rumored to be a ravishing beauty, but what if the rumors were false? What if her veil hid a dragon's face, or a witch's? He knew Ignatio was right: his inward-turned union with the artificial woman was self-serving and destructive. But in Eve he knew what he had—beauty and harmony—whereas in Avalessa he would be taking a huge risk. Did it make sense to give up known perfection for uncertainty?

When Davian could no longer endure the continuous cycle of questions without answers, he moved about the cell, feeling again for loose stones. But the search was futile, and he dropped to the floor and brooded over his vacillation between Avalessa and Eve. Panic often interrupted his endless questions. He had no more than two days to escape this prison and save Avalessa. And escape seemed impossible.

44

Shortly after dawn the thunder of hooves in the high street of Corenham startled many sleepers awake. They jumped from their beds and peeked through the shutters to see the cause of the commotion—fifty-one knights, armored and armed, mounted on their warhorses and galloping eastward. At the head of the band, silhouetted against the graying sky, streamed the banner of Perivale. It was a sight no one in Corenham had seen since early in Perivale's reign, and wonder at the meaning of it kept many from returning to their beds.

Perivale rode straight and tall at the head of his warrior knights. His golden-hued armor gleamed in the rising sun, and his burgundy cape billowed behind him like wings. He kept the pace of his men brisk, meaning to camp just south of the Sunderlon River by nightfall. The distance from Morningstone to Sunderlon was reckoned as a day and a half by horseback, more than two days with wagons. Perivale was determined to ride the distance in one long day.

In addition to his fifty-one warriors, he had brought with him the historian Archelous and the bard Lysantos.

He had charged Archelous to witness the battle and record it in the annals of Meridan. He had hired Lysantos to sing to his men when they camped and commissioned him to compose a ballad of the event to be sung in the halls of the Seven Kingdoms.

Already those songs of valor and victory rang in Perivale's head. Already he could read the lines in the book of the wars of Perivale, telling how the great golden king had routed a hundred invaders of one of his cities with only fifty staunch Meridan knights. As he rode and dreamed, his face began to mirror his thoughts, taking on the noble and heroic aspect of his likeness in the stone monument.

The warriors rode all day, stopping only briefly to rest their horses and eat from their packed provisions. They reached the town of Surrifax as the rim of the sun touched the western horizon. Sir Waldrone urged the king to stop and lodge his men in the inns, but Perivale would not hear of it. He halted briefly before entering the town and ordered all banners up, all capes in place, and all helms donned. When he was pleased with the look of his army, they rode in splendor through the high street as the people of the town came to their doors and windows to gape at the passing procession.

When they reached the thickly wooded banks of the Sunderlon, the only light was an orange glow in the western sky. Perivale brought his men to a halt in a grove of oaks fifty yards from the river and ordered fires by which to pitch the tents and tend the horses. Though Perivale seemed alert and vigorous, his men were exhausted. After taking their meal they wanted nothing more than to get under their blankets. But Perivale insisted that Lysantos entertain them with war ballads before he let them sleep. When the chords of the last song faded, the king told his weary men that they would ford the Sunderlon River and ride into the town of Sunderlon at sunrise.

Midnight was an hour away, and Morgultha sat alone in her tent. It was pitched in the woods at the edge of a cleared field just east of the town of Sunderlon, some five hundred paces north of the river. She had not seen the fires of Perivale's camp because of the thick woods between her and the river. But she smelled smoke and knew the meaning of it. Perivale had arrived.

"My lady, may I enter?" came a guttural voice at her tent door.

"Enter," she replied. The tent flap opened, and she could see outlined against the star-filled sky the knobby silhouette of the dwarf thing Gruebek. She did not rise or light a candle. "Did you get the information I required?" she asked.

"That I did, m'lady. I have learned all ye need to know. First, ye'll be pleased to hear that Perivale is only fifty-one strong."

"Exactly as we had hoped. The man is a fool," Morgultha muttered. "Did you learn anything of his plans?"

"Yes. He'll attack Sunderlon at sunrise tomorrow."

"And what of Perivale himself? Was he wearing his golden armor with his burgundy cape?"

"That he was—all polished and clean as a beggar's cupboard."

"Good. You may go, Gruebek. Send King Agrilon to me immediately." Gruebek bowed low and backed away.

All was going exactly as Morgultha had hoped. She was pleased that the king was wearing his so-called golden armor and burgundy cape. His battle apparel alone would ensure his defeat. Only she knew the secret that was certain to bring down the high king of the Seven Kingdoms. She had carefully kept her hundred warriors separate from Agrilon's men, not even allowing Agrilon or his captain to approach them. Now her army hid deep in the woods, half on each side of the wide clearing flanking the road that ran from the river to the town.

The tread of heavy boots announced Agrilon's approach. Morgultha's tent flap opened, revealing his bulky silhouette.

"Come in, Agrilon," she said, her low voice almost a whisper. The king stepped inside, his eyes straining to make out her features in the darkness. She bade him sit on a stool and told him of Gruebek's report.

"Only fifty-one men?" Agrilon was incredulous. "It's just as you predicted."

"Yes. Apparently, Perivale knows nothing of my army here. I will give you our battle strategy. Your knights are few, and most of your best warriors are absent. I suggest you spare your men and let my knights engage Perivale's warriors. Group your knights at the gate of the town to draw Perivale to it. As he approaches, my warriors will emerge from the woods on both sides of the road and attack them before they can reach you. Your men need not draw a sword. You will get your town from Perivale at no cost, and I will get my vengeance against him."

Agrilon readily accepted the witch's offer. He left Morgultha's tent and, in the darkness of the night, positioned his fourteen men at the gate of Sunderlon.

Perivale roused his men shortly before dawn. They ate their breakfast, donned their armor, and mounted their steeds. As the first shafts of sunlight shot through the trees, Perivale gave the order and his fifty-one knights galloped toward the ford. Their horses splashed through the river and up the northern bank. When they reached the top of the rise, they could see the sunlight glimmering on the armor of Agrilon and his knights, who waited in two lines in front of the gate of Sunderlon.

Perivale drew his sword and bellowed with a feral roar as he spurred his charger to an even faster pace. With a collective shout, his men drew their weapons and followed. They had closed half the distance to the gate when Sir Waldrone cried above the thunder of hooves, "Men look to your flanks!"

Perivale's knights reined their horses and turned both right and left to face the two lateral charges of Morgultha's horsemen. They blanched at what they saw. Each charging warrior wore armor of burnished gold and a burgundy cape exactly like that of their king. As the attackers drew near, the Meridan knights gaped in horror. The face of each attacking rider was exactly that of Perivale.

The Meridan army fell into confusion. Five knights turned in panic and fled for the river, but Morgultha's warriors rode them down and slew them. The rest tried to back away from the ambush, but they collided with their own men retreating from the onslaught on the other side. The knights were unwilling to strike the likeness of their king, and in their consternation they did little but ward off their attackers' heavy blows. Four more of Perivale's men fell in the turmoil.

"Stand and fight!" The voice of Perivale roused the men from their shock, and they began to rally and wield their weapons in earnest.

Sir Everedd was the first to slay one of Morgultha's warriors. He caught the blow of a spiked mace on his shield, but the force of the iron ball shattered his arm. As his attacker raised the mace again, Everedd plunged his sword

408

deep into its side. He stared horrified at what happened next. The moment his sword entered, the attacker froze instantly in midmovement, its body and limbs rigid as a block of ice. The exposed skin took on the color and texture of bronze, and the body fell from its horse and clattered to the earth, stiff and immobile. As Everedd looked on stunned, an enemy spear entered his back and emerged from his chest.

Several of Perivale's warriors soon made the same discovery and were slain in that unguarded moment of dumbfounded horror. Eight more turned and fled in panic after slaying their first enemy and witnessing the unearthly transformation. Others overcame their shock and wielded their weapons with a determination born of hopelessness. They knew they were battling supernatural powers and chose to go down with honor.

The decimated Meridan warriors began to stand their ground, but the rally came too late. Their first losses were too severe to withstand their enemy's greater numbers. One by one Perivale's men fell, and the earth became strewn with bodies, both human and bronze.

All the while Perivale lived up to his great reputation. He fought like a cornered lion, raining blows on the multiple images of himself in a frenzy of desperation. When he saw more of the images coming at him than he could handle at once, he turned to beat a brief retreat, intending to circle about and come in on his attackers from the side. But as he circled he saw that he was the last man of his army left standing. Thirty or more of the enemy were still mounted, all now charging toward him.

Perivale had never in his life failed in battle or suffered defeat in any duel or joust. He looked down on the bodies of his fallen men, sprawled among the stiff, metallic figures lying ruined about them. He looked up at the thirty images of himself now pressing toward him, and for the first time in his life, fear gripped his heart. Instead of standing firm and ending his life nobly, he sat frozen in his saddle; his eyes widened and his body began to tremble like a beaten hound. With a wail, he dropped his sword, turned his horse toward the eastern woods, and savagely spurred it forward. The thirty warriors followed.

Morgultha, looking on from the woods, watched in satisfaction as her warriors pursued the disgraced king among the trees. She was confident they would soon overtake him and end his life. She turned back into the woods and walked a little way until she reached a clearing. In the center of the clearing stood one more warrior, the original clay image of Perivale, armored identically to the king and mounted on a charger the size and color of the king's own. Before she reached the image, she stopped and stood perfectly still, and in moments the outlines of her form began to blur and grow smoky, with gray billows curling about her until she could no longer be seen. Out of the cloud of smoke flew the huge blackbird with eyes of pale yellow. When the smoke cleared, the place where Morgultha had stood was empty. The giant bird spread its wings and circled the clearing once, then settled on the shoulder of the lifelike image of Perivale. Instantly the charger leapt forward and galloped out of the woods. It crossed the ford of the Sunderlon and turned southwest toward Corenham.

The true Perivale rode hard through the woods, spurred on by the beat of his pursuers' hoofbeats behind him. He reached the bank of the Sunderlon and rode eastward along it until he found a fording place. He splashed across the river and into the woods on the south side. After riding another quarter hour, he no longer heard sounds of pursuit, but he did not slow his pace. He rode hard, weaving among the trees until his charger began to stumble and its great sides heaved like a blacksmith's bellows. He came to a thick copse near a stream and reined the horse to a stop. He dismounted quickly, drank from the stream, and allowed his steed to lap water for several minutes. Perivale had no thought of resting, but even in his panic he knew his horse could not continue the pace he had been keeping.

For the rest of the day he alternated between riding and walking. He heard no sound of the pursuing warriors and thought he must have eluded them. As darkness closed in, he stopped in a grassy clearing to let his horse graze while he paced, unable to rest. He would have moved on, but in the blackness of the nighttime woods he found it impossible to see a path. He let his horse sleep, but he remained awake, starting at the sounds of the forest and listening for the hoofbeats of his enemies.

At the first light of dawn, he remounted and rode toward the rising sun. He came out of the woods at midmorning. He paused and looked across the Rynde River to the wide Plain of Maldor. In the distance he could see the towers and spires of his old castle, beckoning him as a sanctuary, perhaps three or four miles away. He urged his horse along the riverbank until he reached the stone bridge on the road to Maldor. He crossed the bridge and had ridden a quarter mile onto the plain when he heard a distant drumming behind him. He turned, and his heart raced like a fleeing hare when he saw a cloud of dust at the edge of the plain. His enemies had found him. He gouged his heels into his horse and galloped full pace toward Maldor Castle.

Moments later he looked back and saw that his pursuers had gained on him. He judged that their numbers had diminished to about twenty. Apparently, some had been lost in the woods. He bellowed at his horse and kicked its sides unmercifully. Looking back again, he saw that his enemies had cut the distance by almost half, and his exhausted mount was losing speed. He took his coiled whip and began to beat the struggling animal's sides and neck.

He was now only minutes from the castle. He reached the western wall, rounded it, and rode hard toward the gate. To his relief, it was open. He rode through the gate and toward the door of the keep when his horse stumbled and collapsed to the ground, dead from exhaustion. He picked himself up and scurried to his saddle pouch, where he fumbled frantically until he retrieved a cloth-wrapped package. Clutching the parcel, he ran to the keep, flung open the door, and ran down the echoing corridor to the great hall.

He entered the hall and ran the length of it, passing the dais and coming to the door of a small room behind the throne. Inside the room he found the royal robe he had left behind, as Rianna had given him a new one trimmed with golden threads on the day of the move to Morningstone. He slipped the robe over his shoulders, not noticing the caked dust that dulled its color. He took up his old scepter and stepped regally up the dais to his throne. He sat upon it with great pomp, then opened the parcel he had taken from his horse and took from it the Crown of Eden. With both hands he solemnly set the crown on his head just as the twenty remaining images of him entered the hall, swords in hand, and advanced toward the throne.

"Stop!" Perivale shouted, and his voice echoed in the hall. But the images kept advancing. "Stop, I said!" Perivale repeated. "I am your king. I forbid you to bear arms in my court. You have no right here. Now begone!"

The images continued to advance, the closest now only

a few paces from the dais. Perivale's eyes rounded, and he trembled violently as they reached the dais and stepped up toward him.

At that moment the hall door opened and a tall, robed figure entered. The advancing images stopped in their tracks. Perivale could not make out the features of the man, silhouetted as he was against the light from the open door. But as he strode forward the king recognized him as the white-haired man who had appeared to him at Morningstone. All the images stood still, as if awaiting the newcomer's command, while he marched forward until he reached the foot of the dais.

Father Futuras turned to the standing figures, raised his arms, and spoke in a ringing voice that no living being would dare defy. "Place the images in the seats of the hall, then leave them forever and return to your pit."

Immediately the twenty images turned and sat themselves in the first twenty of the chairs that had once been the seats of the knights of Meridan. The moment they sat down, a moaning sound arose, hideous and dissonant as the wails of a thousand demons. Perivale clapped his hands to his ears as the unbearable noise swelled to the rafters and then faded toward the door at the far end of the hall. When the sound ceased, the twenty images sat immobile, facing each other across the width of the hall, their eyes staring ahead but seeing nothing.

Futuras turned toward Perivale, who had regained his regal composure and now sat impassive on his old throne. "Hear me, Perivale. Your pride has brought you to ruin, but you can be saved yet. Renounce the Crown of Eden, beg forgiveness from your daughter Avalessa and others you have wronged, plead for the grace of the Master, and be redeemed."

"I have wronged no one," Perivale replied. "I merely

disciplined my daughter as any father would. I cannot relinquish my crown; it is the talisman of my duty to my subjects." With an indolent air he swept his hand toward the immobile images seated in the hall chairs. "My people need me, and I cannot leave them helpless as sheep without a shepherd."

"You now rule nothing but a miserable little kingdom you have created within yourself. You will not face the terrible reality of your own sins, choosing rather to escape into madness. I would lead you back to sanity, but the journey requires that you face the evil within you so it can be killed. Since you refuse your only hope of redemption, I can do nothing for you. You have brought doom upon yourself."

The ancient man turned and walked out of the hall between the two rows of staring images. Perivale remained upright and impassive, the Crown of Eden on his head and his scepter in his hand, as the sound of the closing door echoed in the cavernous hall.

45

Ignatio crept down the stairway toward Perivale's dungeon and made his way along the damp corridors lit only by feeble torches thirty feet apart. He had passed his first test, convincing the guard at the gate that he was sent from the abbey to hear confessions from the prisoners. The corridor was long and turned several times before he could see ahead the glimmer of torchlight on the iron gate to the prison cells. A single guard sat before the gate, his head bowed, snoring lightly. He looked up as Ignatio approached, and he immediately stood at attention.

"What is your business, kirkman?"

"I have come to hear the confessions of the prisoners," Ignatio replied.

"You are not the priest assigned, and you are one day early. Father Nallar always comes on Fridays."

"That is true. But tomorrow is the holy day of the three trees, and all in the abbey will be in worship. So the prior chose to send a confessor today. Nallar could not come because of a confinement, and I was chosen."

"I cannot let you in. Your name is not on Senevel's list of approved visitors. So begone."

"We didn't have time to change the list. But as you know, a new prisoner was brought in two days back who hasn't been given the opportunity to confess. It would be a tragedy were he to meet his fate without the comfort of the Master. I beg you to allow me entrance."

"I will do no such thing," the guard replied. "Flouting Senevel's orders would land me in prison. You could carry a weapon or a tool for escape for all I know."

"You may search my robes. I assure you that I am un-armed—oh, except for this." Ignatio drew from his robe a small earthen bottle, stoppered at the neck.

"What is that?" the guard asked.

"A jug of Rhondilar wine. I had forgotten I had it. Jarvan the wineseller gave it to me after I heard his confession this morning. I should give it to the prior on my return, but I would give it to you if—"

"I cannot drink on duty," the guard said, but Ignatio noticed that the man could not take his eyes off the bottle.

"I understand," he replied. "I will go now. But to show that I harbor no ill will for barring me from your prison, I will leave the bottle for your enjoyment after your watch." He set the bottle on the table and began walking away.

"Wait," the guard called. Ignatio turned to see him pulling the stopper from the bottle with his teeth. He put the bottle to his lips and drank deeply, then grinned at the acolyte. "Go on in, kirkman. I can't see you doing any harm. But you will say nothing of this, do you hear?"

"I assure you that I will say nothing." Ignatio watched the guard drink deeply once again and then slowly slump to the floor as the bottle shattered beside him, spattering wine over the flagstones.

The acolyte bent over the guard and took the key ring from his belt. He found the key to the gate, opened it, and walked along the dark passageway, looking into each cell

416

as he went. He could not see into the darkness beyond the bars, so he called Davian's name as he went.

"I'm here," a voice replied from a cell just ahead.

Ignatio hurried to the cell and found his friend standing with his hands clutching the bars. "How did you—" Davian asked, but Ignatio put his finger to his lips and shook his head.

He tried several keys before he found the one that turned the lock, and in moments the artist was walking back toward the entrance with him. They passed through the gate and stepped over the still-sleeping guard.

"What did you do to him?" Davian said.

"Sometimes it pays to give attention to Granthon's lectures on the evils of magic, especially the ones on how witches and wizards mix their potions," Ignatio replied with a grin. "No serious harm will come to him. He will sleep a few hours and awaken with a headache. He won't even remember my visit."

Ignatio dropped the keys beside the guard, and the two friends made their way up through the tunnels that led to the gate of the castle. Roiling gray masses still hampered Davian's sight. He could see well enough under the glare of the torches they passed, but he struggled in the darkness between them. As they walked he told Ignatio all he had overheard of the plot to trap King Perivale and kill Prince Rhondale and Princess Avalessa.

"I must go immediately to her chambers and warn her," he said.

"You forget that you are now a fugitive," Ignatio replied. "You dare not show your face inside this castle. But Father Nallar told me Morningstone is webbed with hidden passages. Among these are little-used underground tunnels beneath the castle that Perivale designed for secret escape. Nallar drew me a map showing one of these passages from the dungeon to the postern gate. I will put you in that passage and—"

"I won't leave without warning the princess and the prince," Davian insisted.

"I will warn them myself," Ignatio said. "I know where the prince's chambers are, as I once accompanied Father Nallar on his rounds. Prince Rhondale can direct me to the chambers of the princess. I will warn them to leave not by the main gate but through the passages to the postern gate. You can wait for them just outside that gate and take them to your studio. I will exit openly through the front gate to keep from arousing the guards' suspicions. I will meet you at your studio. We can work out what to do next when we meet."

Reluctantly Davian agreed to the plan, and Ignatio put him in the passage to the postern gate. Following Nallar's map and holding a torch to aid his foggy vision, he had little trouble making his way through the maze of turns until he reached a door that opened onto the bailey. The postern gate was twenty paces away, just around the corner of a tower. Davian peered around the corner, then quickly drew back. An armed guard stood at the postern gate. He turned back to the door he had just exited, opened it again, and slammed it loudly; then immediately he crouched behind the hedge next to it. As the guard rushed around the corner toward the sound, Davian charged at him, knocking the breath from the man's lungs. The sculptor sat on top of the downed man, grasped his head in his hands, and banged it against the flagstone pavement until he fell limp. He went out the gate and descended several feet down the steep path. The orange sun hovered just above the distant hills as he settled beneath a spreading oak to await the coming of Rhondale and Avalessa.

Ignatio walked swiftly across the bailey to the keep and bounded up the stairway to Rhondale's chambers. He rapped on the door several times before it opened a mere crack. A manservant glared at him.

"I must see the prince, and quickly," Ignatio said.

"The prince is at his dinner, kirkman, and he does not wish to confess yet. Come again in the morning. He will have need of it then."

The man began to close the door, but Ignatio thrust it back on him.

"No! I must speak with the prince now! His life is in danger."

"Wait here." The servant crossed the room and entered the door to Rhondale's bedchamber. Ignatio did not wait but followed the man inside. Rhondale sat at a small table, his dinner spread before him and a fair young woman sitting at his side.

"Prince Rhondale," Ignatio said, "I have urgent news that I must deliver to you alone."

"What sort of trick is this?" Rhondale said. "Why should I believe—"

"You may believe what you wish later when you have the luxury. But you must hear me now. Your life is in immediate danger."

Rhondale stared long at the acolyte and decided that his face conveyed sincerity. He sent the girl away and told his servant to wait outside.

"I have learned of a plot against your life," Ignatio said. "Senevel and Lord Fenimar have led your father into an ambush at Sunderlon that they are sure will bring him his death. Senevel has reduced the guard at the castle so that Fenimar and his men can come here tonight and assassinate both you and Princess Avalessa. You must leave now."

"How did you learn of this?" the prince asked.

"I will tell you all at another time. But I have it on good authority that Senevel and Fenimar will strike tonight. You must make your way through the hidden passages and leave now by the postern gate."

Rhondale stared long at the kirkman before answering. "Very well. I will choose to believe you. But if I find that you have lied to me—"

"I do not lie, Your Highness. You must not waste more time. Please leave now!"

The prince called his servant and commanded him to gather essential items in a bag for his quick departure.

"Your Highness, if you will direct me to your sister's quarters, I will go to warn her," Ignatio said.

"You need not worry about the princess. I will warn her myself and help her escape with me. You may go now, kirkman. I thank you for your warning. If you tell the truth, you will be greatly rewarded. If you are lying, you will regret it."

Ignatio bowed to the prince and left his chambers. A few minutes later Rhondale's servant handed the prince the pack of clothing and money he had prepared. After sending the man away, Rhondale took a torch from the wall and pressed the stone that levered open the door to his hidden passage.

Far from being dismayed, Rhondale was elated at the news of the plot against his father's life. He fervently hoped it succeeded. He had no intention of informing his sister of it. Being a year older than he, she could make a claim to the crown herself. Though the people had little taste for the rule of a woman, he knew she was loved, while he was not. All that was needed for the crown to come to him uncontested was to get out of the castle, go into temporary hiding, let the plot take its course, then show himself alive before the Hall of Knights and claim the throne by right of direct succession. Rhondale slipped into the darkness of the passage and made his way toward the postern gate.

In the gathering shadows below the postern gate, Davian waited for Rhondale and Avalessa to emerge from the castle. His heart raced like a galloping horse, not only from the danger, but also from the prospect of seeing the princess for the first time. While brooding in the darkness of his prison cell, he had already formed a plan to help the prince and princess escape. He had told Ignatio a little of it as they walked through the dungeon corridors. He would wait until the darkness was complete and then take the royal siblings to the site of the monument and hide them in one of the wagons his assistants used to haul away the rubble that fell from the carved stone. He would hitch his own horse to the wagon and take them through Braegan Wood and into Vensaur. By morning they would be far from Corenham.

As Davian watched, the gate opened and the single shadowy figure of a man emerged from it. The man locked the gate, looked about him in all directions, and began to descend the hill. Though Davian could not identify the man because of his diminished vision, he assumed him to be Rhondale, and he watched for Avalessa to follow. But she did not appear. When Rhondale reached the tree, Davian stepped out of the shadows and took the prince's arm. Rhondale screamed in fright and tried to run, but Davian clamped a firm hand over his mouth and pressed the undersized prince against the tree.

"Quiet!" he whispered. "I mean you no harm. I know of the plot against your life, and I am working with the kirkman to help you escape. But we must wait for the princess, who has also been warned."

421

"She isn't coming," Rhondale said.

"Not coming? In heaven's name why not? The kirkman Ignatio was to warn her."

"I sent the kirkman away and warned her myself, but she would not believe me. She refused to come."

"You should have dragged her out. I must go get her. Give me the key to the postern gate and wait for us to return. I will take both of you out of Meridan tonight."

"I will not give you the key," Rhondale said. "I don't know you. You may be part of the plot yourself for all I know."

"Give me that key, or I will take it from you," Davian said.

In answer Rhondale drew his sword and came toward the sculptor. But he swung the weapon so clumsily that Davian had no trouble dodging and wrenching the hilt from his hand. Davian turned the weapon toward the prince.

"Give me that key—now!"

Rhondale took the key from his tunic and handed it to Davian. With the prince's sword in hand, Davian ran up the path to the postern gate as Rhondale disappeared into the shadows at the bottom of the hill.

Ignatio had no reason to doubt Rhondale's assurance that he would warn his sister of the plot. Thus as he left Rhondale's chambers, he considered his mission completed and retraced his steps down the castle stairway and out of the keep. As he made his way across the cobblestone path through the bailey lawn, he stepped aside to allow four men to stride past him, all walking swiftly and with determined faces. He could not help but shudder at the visage of the thin man with the bald head. He had never seen such cold eyes.

When Ignatio reached the gate, he was surprised to find it closed. It was not yet sundown, and he wondered why it had been shut early. He would have to leave by the postern gate. He descended again into the corridors of Perivale's dungeon and found the doorway to the passage leading to the postern gate. He took a torch from the wall and entered through the door, hoping he could find his way without Nallar's map.

46

As Ignatio was leaving Rhondale's chambers, Lord Fenimar rode through the gate of Morningstone Castle with Lord Kramad Yesenhad and Lord Ashbough following close behind. Senevel met them as they passed the gatehouse. As the riders dismounted, he ordered the gatekeeper to close the gates and let no one enter or leave for the rest of the night.

"But, my lord, it be yet an hour to sundown," the guard protested.

"You will do as I say," Senevel demanded. "The king has left me in charge of his castle, and if you disobey me, you will answer to him."

The guard hesitated for a moment under Senevel's glare, then barked the order to close the gates. The four conspirators turned and marched up the flagstone path toward Morningstone's keep.

"There will be no guard at the keep or at the door of the hall," Senevel said as they walked. "One guard is still posted at the chamber door of Lady Bloeudewedd and another at the door of Princess Avalessa." He paused as a cowled kirkman passed, and then he continued. "The Crown of Eden will likely be hidden in King Perivale's chambers, which usually have two guards posted at the door. But tonight they will have none. The castle guards now answer to me as the voice of Perivale, and I gave them both leave for the evening. First we must eliminate the two heirs who can claim succession to the throne. And then we must get the crown from Perivale's chambers."

"How do we know the crown is in the castle?" Ashbough asked.

"We cannot know with certainty," Senevel answered. "But he never wears it when he journeys from Morning-stone, so it's likely that he leaves it in his chambers under the double guard. We know that in the past he has left it in his chambers; Lady Bloeudewedd told us as much."

"I say we must get the crown first," Fenimar said. "We can deal with the prince and princess at any time. Rhon-dale is a weakling who can give us no resistance. Princess Avalessa is imprisoned in her chambers with no way of escape. The crown has uncanny powers, and the people fear it. Having it in our possession will strengthen our position and possibly even give us some kind of power. We must get the crown first. We cannot risk that part of our plan going awry."

Senevel sighed and assented with a shrug. The four men strode quickly through the corridors until they reached Perivale's door. Senevel unlocked it, and they entered.

"He keeps the crown in this cask," Senevel said as he picked up the oaken casket reinforced with bands of iron. To his surprise, it was unlocked. He opened it and turned to his companions. "It's empty. I know he wasn't wearing the crown when he rode out three days ago. He was determined to look every inch the warrior and wore his helm."

"Men, tear this room apart until you find that crown,"

Fenimar said as he pulled the blankets from the bed and began ripping the mattress with his sword. Kramad Yesenhad and Ashbough joined in, pulling coats and robes from the wardrobe, slashing the curtains, and sweeping the contents from every shelf. Soon the room had the look of a battlefield.

"It's not here," Kramad Yesenhad said. "We must question Lady Bloeudewedd. She knows the king's habits better than anyone."

The five men descended the stairway to Bloeudewedd's chambers. The guard stood aside to let Senevel knock. Bloeudewedd's lady-in-waiting answered, and her eyes widened with fright as the four men brushed her aside and stormed into the room. Bloeudewedd screamed as they entered, jumping up from her chair and holding her hands before her as if to ward off a blow.

"Answer us truthfully and we will not harm you," Senevel said. "Where is Perivale's crown?"

"I have told you before. He—he keeps it in an oaken cask beside his bed, th—though sometimes he leaves it on the table so he can touch it in the night," the lady said, her voice quavering.

"It is not in his room," Fenimar said. "Where does he store it when he leaves the castle?"

"I don't know," Bloeudewedd replied.

"Search this room," Fenimar ordered.

The men began ripping, flinging, and slashing as they had done in Perivale's chambers. Bloeudewedd and her lady screamed in horror at the destruction, huddling in a corner, where they trembled like pups in a thunderstorm.

"Let's take these women to the dungeon," Fenimar said. "They have seen too much."

"There is no need," Senevel replied. "We can imprison them right here and get on with our business. I will have the guard lock them inside their chambers until we have you settled on the throne."

The men left the room, ignoring the two terrified women, and Senevel locked the door behind them. He ordered the guard to keep the ladies imprisoned.

"The crown is likely locked inside the castle vaults," Senevel said. "Unfortunately, the king trusts no one with that key, not even me. He keeps it with him always. We have little choice but to forget the crown for the moment. Tomorrow we can bring in stonemasons to break the walls of the vault. Let's get on with our next task."

He led the conspirators to Rhondale's chambers. Kramad Yesenhad rapped on the door with the hilt of his sword. When no answer came, he rapped again much more loudly. Senevel drew a key from his robes and opened the door, and the men entered. The rooms were empty.

Senevel uttered a vile curse. "This is most baffling. The prince took dinner in his chambers tonight with a wench from the city, and I was sure neither would leave until morning. But it matters little. I will post a watch for his return. If he's still in the castle, we can easily deal with this weakling when we find him."

Senevel began to walk toward the stairway leading to Avalessa's chambers. But Fenimar did not follow.

"Where are you going, Senevel?" he said.

"To the chambers of the princess," he replied. "Since we cannot find the crown, she's next on our agenda."

"No. We can deal with the princess anytime. Besides, I have been thinking: I have better plans for her. What would better solidify my claim to the throne than for her to become my queen?"

"She would hardly agree to wed you," Ashbough said. "You are known to be her father's enemy."

"That will be no obstacle," Senevel said. "We have ways

427

of forcing compliance. Besides, the princess has no love for her father. She may be more receptive to the idea than you think."

"Let's get to the great hall and take the reins of the kingdom," Fenimar said. "Though we don't yet have the crown, we can robe me in the king's clothing and locate all the other trappings of kingship. Then tomorrow when we open the gates and announce Perivale's death, we can also announce my legitimate assumption of the throne. We must draft the edict and get all the details in place tonight."

"But what about the knights of Meridan? What will happen when they return?" Ashbough said.

"Ashbough, more than half of Perivale's knights are with him." Senevel spoke as if explaining a simple lesson to a dull schoolboy. "Most, if not all, are likely to be slaughtered. The only survivors will be cowards who fled, and we have nothing to fear from such as them. Of the remaining forty-two knights of Meridan, three of you are right here. Of the other thirty-nine, at least twenty are disaffected with Perivale and will support Fenimar's succession. Six or more hardly care who rules Meridan and will go along with any king the Hall endorses. The castle guards are mine. What else do we have to fear?"

"Morgultha," Ashbough said. "Morgultha wants the crown, and we promised to get it for her."

"Oh, hang Morgultha!" Senevel said. "We tried to find her precious crown. We will break into the vault tomorrow. What more can she expect of us?"

"But when she finds that we don't have the crown she covets—"

"Ashbough, Morgultha's power is vastly overrated. We had no intention of giving her the crown if we did find it. What can she do to us? Now, let's get our edict written and have Fenimar on the throne ready to rule at sunrise."

Without another word the hairless man turned and strode toward the great hall. Fenimar and the two other knights followed.

Morgultha, maintaining her guise as a blackbird, entered Corenham at sundown, riding on the shoulder of the animated clay image of Perivale. In spite of her agreement with Fenimar and Senevel, she knew it was unlikely that they would relinquish the Crown of Eden even if they found it. She also knew the crown might be difficult to find. Perivale would undoubtedly have it well hidden and carefully guarded.

A few pedestrians still moved about the streets of Corenham, all carrying bobbing lanterns as they returned from shops and fields to their cottage homes. When they heard the clop of approaching hooves, they looked toward the sound and saw the shadow of the mounted rider on the huge warhorse looming in the darkness. All gave wide berth as the shadow rode into the light of a streetlamp, revealing the image of Perivale with the huge blackbird perched on his shoulder. They stopped and stared, mute with dread wonder at the strange sight of their king returning alone at night three days after riding out at the head of his best knights. After he passed from the circle of the light, a few onlookers clustered and spoke in hushed tones.

"What's that black monster of a bird doin' on the king's shoulder?"

"It ain't King Perivale, it's 'is ghost, I tell ye," one grizzled farmer said, his eyes wide as moonflowers.

"It's an evil omen, I say. Some doom has befallen the king."

"Did ye see 'is face?" a fishwife said. "Grim as the angel of death and starin' ahead like he wasn't seein' nothin'."

429

"He had the look of defeat about him," a merchant said. "I say he's lost the battle and all his knights. He's returned home alone in disgrace."

The image left the workers gaping and trotted to Morningstone Hill and up the steep road to the castle. The gate was shut, and the image reined its mount to a halt beneath the gate towers. Controlled by the mind of the blackbird, the image shouted to the one guard on duty.

"Open the gate."

"I will not," the guard replied. "It is long after sundown. You must return tomorrow."

"Open the gate," the image bellowed. "I am your king, and I command you."

At once the guard recognized the voice of Perivale, and he thrust his head out the window to look down at the rider. By the lamp at the gate, he could see the muted gold of the king's armor and the burgundy cape flowing behind him. And he was sure the horse was Perivale's favorite. He gave the command, and the guards on the ground unbarred the gate and swung it open. They stood back and stared in wonder at the huge bird sitting on the king's shoulder. The image entered the castle without a word and rode directly to the door of the keep, where it dismounted and stepped inside.

In spite of her bargain with Fenimar and Senevel, Morgultha had no intention of giving them the throne of Meridan. She would have both the crown and the throne. She hoped she had reached the castle before the conspirators made their move. If she could find the crown before they did, her seizure of power would be much easier. She guided the image up the stairway to Perivale's chambers. It entered the open door of his rooms, and the bird squawked in rage at the disarray that met her. Obviously, Fenimar had been here. Either he had already found the crown or it had not

430

been in the room. She would next go to the chambers of Bloeudewedd. Perivale might have revealed to her where he kept the crown.

At the command of the image of Perivale, the guard opened Bloeudewedd's door. The image entered, roughly grabbed the lady-in-waiting by the arm and flung her screaming out into the corridor, and closed the door after her.

"Oh, Perivale, I am so happy to see you," Bloeudewedd said as the image came toward her. "That terrible Senevel just—oh! What is that awful creature on your shoulder?"

"What has happened here?" the image said as it looked about the ruined chamber.

"Lord Fenimar, Senevel, and two knights stormed in earlier. They were searching for your crown. I insisted I didn't have it, but they wouldn't believe me and tore up my room looking for it. They ruined my best ball gown," she wailed as she held up a shredded crimson dress.

The Perivale image took the dress in both hands, twisted it around Bloeudewedd's neck, and knotted it tightly. The woman's eyes bulged, and her face went purple as she struggled wildly, tugging at the garment and flailing her fists at the image's face. The image dropped her to the floor, where she writhed in panic, clawing at the knotted gown at her neck.

Morgultha marched the Perivale image toward the door of the great hall. Kramad Yesenhad and Ashbough stood before the door. When they saw their king approaching, their faces went white as limestone.

"Sire, we did not expect you . . . uh . . . so soon," Ashbough said.

Perivale's image did not speak but drew its sword and, with a single blow, struck the man's head from his shoulders. On the backstroke it thrust the sword deep into Kramad Yesenhad's belly. The image gripped the handles of the great door, swung it open, and marched into the hall gripping the bloodied sword in his hand. Fenimar sat on the throne with Senevel leaning over his shoulder, pointing to a parchment document in the usurper's lap.

"What is the meaning of this? You cannot come in—" Senevel stood speechless as he gaped at Perivale approaching the dais with the monstrous blackbird perched on his shoulder. Senevel bowed to the image, now only a few feet from the dais. "My dear King Perivale," he said, "How good it is that you have returned safely. We didn't expect you so soon. As you can see, Lord Fenimar and I are keeping your kingdom's business—"

"Where is my crown?" the image said.

"Your—your crown? How would we know, sire? I—uh—that is, we—"

At that moment Fenimar scrambled to his feet to run from the hall. But in his panic, he crashed into Senevel, knocking him to the floor at the feet of the image and falling hard on top of him. The false Perivale lifted its sword in both hands and drove the blade through the backs of both men. Their dying screams echoed from the rafters. Without changing expression, the image turned and stalked out of the hall, stepping over the bodies of the slain knights outside the door.

Morgultha was certain the conspirators had not found the crown. The eager Fenimar would have had it already on his head. She guided the Perivale image up the stairway toward Rhondale's rooms. She would now kill the prince and the princess to eliminate any possibility of succession. Then she would search the entire castle for the crown.

Morgultha found Rhondale's chambers empty. It mattered little. He was a weakling, and she could deal with him later. She turned the image toward Avalessa's chambers.

47

Davian, with Rhondale's sword in hand, rushed up the moonlit path to Morningstone's postern gate and entered the castle. Though he was acutely aware of the need for haste, he knew he must find a way to get past the guards posted at various doors inside the castle. He almost stumbled over the guard he had overcome in his escape and realized the man's uniform could be his key. Working feverishly in the near darkness, he undressed the guard, got out of his own clothing, and donned the uniform. Thus attired, he marched down the stone path toward the south side of the keep and the wall to Princess Avalessa's garden. He was surprised that he encountered no one but the few castle servants and pages still on duty.

He reached the garden wall and climbed the vines to the balcony. When he descended the steps inside the wall, all was dark and silent, and with the lingering haziness of his sight, he had to guess and feel his way toward the steps to the door of Avalessa's chambers. As he reached the steps and mounted them, he stopped and froze in his tracks. Standing at the door was an armed guard, dressed exactly like him. Davian knew he would be no match for the guard at swordplay, so he resorted to bravado.

"What are you doing here?" he demanded. "The king only posts a guard at the inner door to the princess's chambers."

"True, but tonight Senevel suspects foul play," the guard replied. "I should ask you the same question. What are you doing here?"

"I was told to watch the outside of the garden wall. I heard a noise from inside and scaled the wall to see the cause of it. Senevel didn't tell me you would be here." Davian moved slowly toward the guard, hoping to draw his sword before the man suspected anything.

At that moment the terrified scream of a woman sounded from beyond the wall. Instantly the guard bounded across the garden and up the steps to the balcony. Davian stumbled along behind, following the sound of the man's footsteps. Below the balcony they saw a young woman running down the cobblestone path toward the postern gate. She was attired in the gown of a lady and lifted her dress high to avoid tripping. "Oh, they have killed her! My lady is dead. Ashbough and Kramad Yesenhad too! And Senevel and Lord Fenimar. All dead! Blood everywhere! It's awful. Run for your lives, everyone! Run! They will kill us all!"

"It's Lady Bloeudewedd's servant," the guard said. "Seneval was right; foul play is afoot tonight."

"Quick, we must get inside the castle. We will be needed," Davian said. The guard scrambled down the steps and across the garden to Avalessa's door, with Davian following.

"Open it, quickly!" Davian demanded.

The guard took a key and turned the lock, and the two men entered the darkened chambers. The princess and her lady screamed from their beds.

"Be silent!" Davian said. "We will do you no harm. Death

stalks the castle tonight. Get up and dress immediately. You must leave the castle at once."

The two men groped their way to the door to the inner passageway and banged on it, yelling to the guard outside. "Open the door, quickly." When the door opened Davian and the guard stepped into the corridor.

"There is murder in the castle tonight," Davian said to the second guard. "We must find the prince and save him."

The three men ran down the hallway. As they rounded the first corner, Davian dropped back and returned to the princess's chambers. Lady Elowynn had lit a candle, and the two women were slipping into their dresses.

"Wait outside," Elowynn demanded. "We will be dressed in a moment."

Davian closed the door and stood outside, looking anxiously down the corridor in both directions. He was about to knock on the door to hurry the women when he heard Elowynn's voice bidding him enter. As he put his hand to the latch, a movement in the distant hallway caught his eye. At first he could make nothing of it because of the pulsating gray masses in his eyesight. But when the figure moved into the light of a torch, he froze. King Perivale himself, as Davian thought the image to be, walked toward him, his drawn sword glistening with fresh blood and a huge blackbird perched on his shoulder. Even with the dimness of his sight, Davian was sure it was the same creature that had flown into his studio. He had never seen another bird of such size. He knew a deadly danger was approaching.

He rushed into the chamber of the princess. Both women were dressed, and Avalessa was veiled.

"What is happening?" Elowynn said, her face a mask of terror.

Without stopping Davian took the women by their arms and forced them roughly out through the garden door. He

435

hurried them across the garden, explaining as they went. "Lord Ashbough, Lord Kramad Yesenhad, Senevel, Lord Fenimar, and Lady Bloeudewedd have been murdered. Even now King Perivale is coming toward your chambers wielding a naked sword covered with blood. And a monstrous evil accompanies him," he said. "We must go over the garden wall—and quickly."

He hurried the women up the steps to the balcony. "Now, we must climb down the vines into the bailey," he said. The two women looked at him but made no move. "Climb down, now!" he demanded.

But the women looked over the edge and drew back. "We can't do it. We don't know how," Elowynn said.

At that moment they heard the chamber door burst open, and all looked to see Perivale stepping down into the garden, light from the chamber glinting on his bloody sword and the huge bird a black shadow on his shoulder. Both women screamed. They grasped the vines at the top of the wall and swung themselves over the edge. Avalessa began to slip, and Davian seized her wrist. She clutched at a mass of tendrils and clawed her way to the ground below. Davian could hear Perivale's footsteps on the stairs behind him as he swung over the wall and half slid and half fell to the earth.

The three ran down the path along the eastern side of the keep and toward the postern gate. As they made the turn, Davian looked back to see the king drop to the ground beneath the wall and begin lumbering toward them.

"Hurry!" he urged the women as they ran toward the gate.

They went through the gate, and with much stumbling and sliding, descended the hill into the woods west of the castle. Davian led them through the edge of the forest, into the streets of Corenham, and toward his studio. They ran

436

until the women gasped for breath; then they walked until they could run again. Davian looked behind them often, but he saw no sign of Perivale, though he could be certain of nothing because of his mottled vision. He began to think they had lost him in the woods. But when they were only a hundred paces from his studio, he looked back to see the stalking shadow of the king moving relentlessly toward them no more than forty paces back.

"He's coming! Run!" Davian cried, and the exhausted women hitched up their dresses and ran with all their remaining strength.

Davian kept himself between the women and the advancing shadow of Perivale, who was rapidly gaining on them. As the three approached the base of the monument, Davian saw that they would not make it to the door of his studio before Perivale caught up with them.

"Get beneath the scaffolding," he cried to the women as he turned, drew Rhondale's sword, and faced Perivale.

Perivale raised his sword and swung it toward the artist. Davian met the stroke with his own blade, but the force of the blow drove the sword from his inexperienced hand and sent it spinning beneath the scaffolding. Perivale slashed at his head with a wide, arching stroke, but he ducked beneath the swing, falling to the ground and rolling among the vertical beams supporting the scaffolds. Perivale swung again, but the sword cut deep into a wooden beam and lodged there, causing lost time as the king worked the weapon back and forth to free it. In that moment Davian felt his hand close around the cold metal of a prying rod, one of several he and his assistants used to dislodge blocks of stone and topple them to the earth. The rod was eight feet long, an inch in diameter, and flattened to a wedge at one end. It was much too heavy to be an effective weapon, but Davian could not be selective. He scrambled from beneath the scaffold, took the bar in both hands, and ran toward Perivale.

At that moment Perivale freed the sword from the beam and swung it hard at Davian. He managed to get the heavy bar up to catch the blow, and the sword shattered against it. The king flung the hilt away and advanced toward the artist, holding his hands before him like giant claws.

Those hands! Davian thought. *They are much too large. This isn't Perivale! This is the clay image I sold to the woman in black.* He took the metal bar in his hands and again ran toward the image, bellowing in fury. But the image stepped aside, and Davian could not adjust the heavy tool in time to meet its dodge. A huge fist dealt him a savage blow to the side that sprawled him on the ground. The image turned away from Davian, reached down between the supports of the scaffolding, clutched the hiding Avalessa by the arm, and pulled her to her feet. She screamed, but the image clutched her throat and began to close its grip. Instantly Davian was on his feet, rushing at the image. He hit it solidly, knocking it back a few paces, causing it to let go of Avalessa. She fell back and caught a rung of the scaffolding ladder to keep from falling. Immediately she began to climb the ladder. The image began to follow and was three rungs up when Davian clutched at its leg and pulled it back to the earth, where it landed hard on top of him, knocking the breath from his lungs. As Davian doubled over and wheezed, the image stood and kicked him hard in the head, sprawling him across the ground. It turned and again started up the ladder Avalessa had ascended. Elowynn followed.

Davian lay stunned and felt himself slipping into blackness. *I cannot lose consciousness now*, he thought. He blinked hard and shook his head vigorously to clear away the darkness that engulfed him. He heard the sound of foot-

438

falls on the scaffolds above and the intermittent screams of the two women. He looked up, but he could see nothing. Though his head spun like a leaf in a whirlpool, he forced himself to stand and again tried to shake off the darkness, but nothing was visible at all. He had been blinded. He stumbled toward the ladder. He realized the futility of trying to help Avalessa in his blindness, but it didn't matter. He would die with her rather than do nothing.

But suddenly a thought hit him, and he knew what he must do. Guessing the direction of his studio, he ran stumbling toward it, falling twice on the way. He reached a wall and felt along it, searching for the door. He came instead to the corner. Panic welled up in him as he heard the women's screams and footfalls on the boards of the scaffold, and he quickly reversed his direction and felt along the wall until he reached the studio door. He opened it and stepped inside. Groping among the tools until he found his nine-pound hammer, he gripped it and called out, "Eve!" He heard the door of his quarters open and soft footsteps come toward him.

"Oh, my dear Davian," Eve said in her voice of warm velvet. "I am so glad you are home."

He felt her arms encircle his neck and her soft, warm lips upon his. Though he could see nothing, he knew the look on her face. Her eyes were shining with love and adoration. He mustered up the will to push her away and raised his hammer to strike the fatal blow.

"Wait, Davian." Her voice was sincere, intense, pleading, and utterly devoid of reproach or anger. "You don't want to destroy me, my love. You know how much I love you. You think I am only stone, but something wonderful has happened while you were away. I have been changed. I am no longer a mere manipulated image. My maker has given me new life—real life. I am indeed a woman. For your own sake as well as mine, I beg you not to destroy me. You will surely regret having my blood on your hands, and you will never find another who adores you as I do."

Davian lowered his hammer, wondering at her words. Was it possible she was speaking truthfully? No! It could not be. As Ignatio had said, such a thing was against nature. Using her voice as a guide to her position, again he raised his hammer.

"Please, Davian," she pleaded as she reached out and gently stroked his cheek. He hesitated, wondering if he could deliver the blow.

At that moment a shrill scream came through the open door, cut short by a choking sound. Davian knew that the terrible image of Perivale had caught Avalessa on the scaffolding. With a mighty effort he brought the hammer down hard on the Eve's head. He heard the stone shatter as fragments of marble scattered about the room. The sound reverberated like the crack of a thunderbolt over all of Meridan. A terrible moaning arose in the room like the wail of a thousand voices of the damned, reaching a crescendo and then dying in a rumbling echo.

Immediately the twenty images sitting immobile in the great hall of Maldor Castle reverted to bronze metal. The mere force of the sound caused the dam over the river Sunderlon to shudder, enlarging the crack and allowing water to trickle through. Moments later the crack spread farther, and in minutes the dam gave way, spilling a torrent of water over the Plain of Maldor. The raging flood rolled toward the walls of Maldor Castle and thundered against the gate, breaking it down and spreading across the bailey. The underground floors of the castle soon filled. The honeycombed soil became saturated, and the foundations of the structure began to crumble and collapse. The stone walls slowly tilted and split with explosive cracks that resounded across the plain as great fissures opened from the crenels to the foundations. The real Perivale, his scepter in his hand and the Crown of Eden on his head, sat rigid and motionless, staring impassively ahead as Maldor Castle slowly began to sink into the earth.

The instant Davian's hammer struck the Eve's head, the image of Perivale on the scaffold reverted to hard clay, its oversized hands deathlocked on Avalessa's throat. The blackbird flew from its perch into the nighttime sky, screeching in fury.

"Davian, where are you? Help me, please!" Elowynn called from the scaffold. Though he could see nothing, Davian heard her cry and fumbled for the door, his feet slipping on the shards of stone that littered his floor. He groped in the tool bin for a smaller hammer and reeled out the door and toward the sound of Elowynn's voice.

"Quickly, come break the thing's hands before the princess strangles to death," the lady pleaded.

"I am blinded and can see nothing," Davian called as he ran toward the sound of her voice. "Come down and guide me up to Avalessa." In seconds Elowynn met him on the ground and guided him to the ladder.

"Climb!" she said. "I will tell you when to step off." He scrambled up the ladder until she told him to stop. "She is to your right," she called, climbing the ladder just behind him.

Davian stepped onto the platform and felt his way to the image. He could hear the rustling of Avalessa's dress and the scuffling of her feet as she struggled in the image's grip. He reached the image and felt for its hands. Shielding Avalessa's head with his arm, he lifted his hammer and dealt two blows to the arm, and the clay fell away from the armature. He pulled the wires away from Avalessa's throat, and she sank to the platform, gasping for breath.

Elowynn stepped onto the platform and dropped to her knees beside her.

Davian pushed the clay image of Perivale over the edge of the scaffold and listened as it shattered on the earth below. Avalessa sat propped in Elowynn's arms, still gasping. After a few minutes she began to breathe normally and told her lady she felt steady enough to stand. Davian drew her to her feet and followed as Elowynn helped the shaken princess descend the ladder.

When they reached the ground, Davian said, "Lady Elowynn, will you guide me to where the image of Perivale fell?"

The young woman led him to the scattered pieces of clay, and with her direction he pounded at the lumps until they were unidentifiable clods and patches of gray powder. Then he twisted and pounded the armature until she assured him it retained no shape that could suggest its original purpose.

48

As Davian destroyed the remaining pieces of the clay image, Avalessa sat with her back against a beam of the scaffolding. She was still dazed from her near strangulation by what she had thought to be the king. She did not understand what had just happened, but the moment the image changed from the likeness of living flesh to the coldness of hard clay, she knew she no longer hated her father. He had once been good to her, but the weight of the crown had crushed his humanity. Now she could only pity him and pray for his soul.

Guided by the sound of her tremulous breathing and sporadic sobs, Davian went to the trembling princess. He knelt beside her and placed his arm around her shoulder. "Why did you not flee with Rhondale when he warned you of the plot against the two of you?"

"What do you mean?"

"My friend Ignatio warned Prince Rhondale of the plot against your lives, and Rhondale promised him he would warn you. I met the prince as he fled through the postern gate, and he told me he had warned you but you would not believe him."

"Rhondale warned me of nothing," Avalessa replied, anger hardening her voice. She realized that her brother had again dealt with her falsely, this time with deadly intent. "I have not even seen the prince in several weeks."

Davian's blood ran cold at the implications of Rhondale's actions. "Then we are still in danger. We must leave Meridan," he said, gently lifting Avalessa to her feet. "We are not safe here."

"Not safe?" Elowynn said as she placed Avalessa's veil over her face. "It seems to me that the crisis is over. The murderer is dead, as are most of Meridan's enemies."

"But not all of Meridan's enemies," Davian replied, still holding Avalessa on his arm. "It appears that a most deadly enemy is still at large. I don't know why Prince Rhondale escaped without warning the princess, but for her safety we must assume the worst. He could have hoped the plotters would murder her, leaving him an open path to the throne. With his enemies now dead, Princess Avalessa could be the only obstacle to his succession. He may search for her. She must flee and waste no time doing it."

"But how?" Elowynn said. "We are but two women, inexperienced in the ways of the road. And we have no transportation or provisions."

"I will flee with you and give what help I can, though I fear it will be of little value. At the moment I can see nothing. We must pray that my sight returns soon. For transportation we can take one of the wagons we used to haul stone from the monument. I have a horse that can pull it. As to provisions, we can stock a little from the larders in my studio. I also have money that will feed us along the way."

"But where will we go?"

"First to Vensaur. Its border is nearer to Corenham than that of any other kingdom. We can travel south through

Vensaur until we reach the Narrow Sea and then take a ship to the great continent and travel by land to a country of your choosing. If the princess wishes to follow some other plan, she may do so, of course. But for her safety, we must at least get her out of Meridan and into Vensaur tonight."

"I agree. We will do as you say," the lady replied.

"Good. Now, lead me to the stable. I am blinded, so you must help me rig the horse to the wagon." He turned to the princess. "Can you walk, Your Highness?"

"Yes, I feel much stronger now," Avalessa said. "I won't be treated as helpless royalty, letting the two of you do all the work. I will do my part." She took Davian's hand and led him toward the stable. Elowynn fell in step beside them.

As they walked, Avalessa said, "Many things puzzle me about all that has just happened, Davian. The first is, how did you learn my true identity? And how did you learn of the plot against my life?"

"My friend, Ignatio, the acolyte in the abbey, learned of your identity through the priests that minister to Morning-stone Castle. Then I learned of the plot against you accidentally. I was sitting by your garden wall and overheard Lord Fenimar and the advisor Senevel plotting just on the other side of the foliage that hid me. They thought they were hidden away from any possible listeners."

"Then it was your constancy to your vow to visit me that led to my rescue. I owe much to you and your acolyte friend," she replied.

As they approached the stable, Davian became aware of the sound of shouting and milling about the streets. The noise had been going on for some time, but his other preoccupations had diverted his attention from it. "Who is in the streets at this hour?" he asked.

"It's the people of the town. They heard the terrible

thunderclap and the unearthly voices and came out to find the cause of them. It was a most awful sound." Elowynn shuddered. "It could hardly have been thunder, for there's not a cloud in the sky. I hope all the people won't hamper our escape."

"They may actually help us," Davian said. "We won't look as conspicuous as we would traveling alone in empty streets."

When they reached the stable, Davian told the women where to find a lamp and a flint. With much fumbling and misdirection, he managed to get the heavy harness on the neck of the animal and guided Elowynn in slipping on the halter and reins. They began to lead the horse from the barn, when Avalessa stopped suddenly, gripping Davian's hand and pulling him back. "Someone is here—blocking the doorway!" she whispered.

"Who goes there?" Davian bellowed in a stentorian voice, glaring toward the door with sightless eyes as he slid Rhondale's sword from its sheath. He knew he would be helpless in a fight, but he hoped to bluff the intruder into turning away.

"What kind of welcome is this? Don't you know your old friend?" The voice was heavy with the accent of the Southern Sea.

"Ignatio!" Davian cried. "I've never been happier to see anyone. Where have you been?"

"I couldn't leave Morningstone by the front gate. It had been closed early. I went back to the tunnel that led from the dungeon to the postern gate, but without the map I got lost in the turns and forks of the passages. I finally reached the gate, but you had already gone, of course. I came here as quickly as I could. What has happened?"

"I've no time to explain it now. I'm helping Lady Elowynn and Princess Avalessa escape from Prince Rhondale, and I—"

"Prince Rhondale? But he said—"

"We've no time for explanations. The princess must assume her life is in danger and flee the country. And I have been blinded—"

"Blinded! What happened?"

"Explanations later, Ignatio! I need your help hitching the horse to one of the wagons near the monument. Then we must get food and provisions from the cottage."

"I will hitch the horse, and I will do better. I will flee with you."

"You will flee with us? But the prior will expel you from the abbey."

"Explanations later, Davian. You take the princess to your cottage and gather provisions. The lady and I will rig the horse to the wagon and bring it to your door momentarily."

Ignatio gathered the rigging and, with Elowynn at his side, led the horse toward the monument, where the wagons were parked. Avalessa took the lamp and led Davian to his studio. She entered first and stopped short.

"There's a statue of a woman lying on the floor, and its head has been shattered."

"Yes," Davian said, pushing Avalessa on across the room, "and you deserve an explanation, which will really be a confession. I will tell you the whole story as we travel."

They crossed the studio floor to his living quarters. He told her where to find blankets, his clothing, pots, cups, plates, rags, and foodstuffs such as meal, bread, dried beef, fruits, and clusters of carrots and turnips he had bought on Cheaping Square. He groped until he found several sackcloth bags, in which he stuffed the items as Avalessa set them on the table. When they were packed, he felt his way to a loose plank in the floor. He lifted the board and drew from beneath it a heavy bag of coins, which he strapped to his waist.

As he stood he felt a hand slip gently into his own.

"Davian," Avalessa said, her soft voice only inches from his face. "How can I ever thank you for what you have done for me? You have been a . . . a loyal friend; you brought me out of despair. Yet I shunned you as if you had the pox. And now you have saved my life. I have never seen a man fight as bravely as you did against the image of my father. Can you ever forgive me for my poor treatment of you?"

"I can forgive you easily. I knew you were only trying to protect my happiness. Besides, I have much to be forgiven for myself. As for saving you, that task is yet ahead of us."

He moved his hand up the side of her arm and reached about her, enfolding her and drawing her to his heart. She did not resist, and the warmth of the embrace was dear to both of them.

At that moment they heard the clattering of the wagon outside the door. The four fugitives quickly loaded the packed bags. The two women hid themselves beneath the blankets in the wagon's bed as Ignatio and Davian sat on the board. A few people still roamed the streets, but they paid no heed as Ignatio took the reins and drove the wagon across Cheaping Square toward Braegan Wood. Several minutes later they left the city and entered the wood, where darkness enfolded them. But the moon was bright, and soon Ignatio could make out the narrow road among the trees well enough. Davian advised the women to sleep all they could, but sound sleep was impossible. The rocking and bumping of the wagon on the rough path tossed them about like eggs scrambling in a pan.

All fell silent but for the creaking and bumping of the wagon and an occasional cry from a forest animal.

Ignatio turned to Davian and said, "Now you must explain to me why the princess is in danger. When I warned Prince Rhondale of the plot against his life, he promised to warn his sister and help her escape. What happened?"

"Instead of warning her, he escaped alone. I met him at the postern gate, took his sword from him, and came back into the castle to get the women. Either the prince is a dastardly coward or he wanted the princess dead to eliminate her possible claim to the throne."

"The prince's fears that the Hall could prefer her to him may be well founded," Ignatio said. "From what I hear through the abbey, the people love the princess but not the prince. All this means I am as much a fugitive as you or the princess. I warned Rhondale of the plot and know he left his sister to be murdered. He cannot let me live holding such knowledge. If I remain in Meridan, my head will roll. When we get to Vensaur, I will write a letter to the prior explaining all that has happened. He is a good man who serves the Master well. He will help me join another abbey in another kingdom."

"I regret that you lost your place in the abbey, but I'm thankful to have you with us. I don't know how I would protect the women without my sight."

Davian explained how he had destroyed the Eve statue and the blow that had cost him his eyesight. But conversation seemed an affront to the silence of the forest, and the two men spoke little more, choosing to save other explanations until they camped and the women could hear them as well.

Davian's head no longer throbbed, but he could see nothing at all. The thought entered his mind that he might never see again, but he quickly pushed it away. He would not carry that burden until it was placed upon him. His thoughts drifted to the image of Eve, now lying shattered on his studio floor. He had not found the courage to destroy her before tonight because he knew the act would be irrevocable, and he feared he would regret it. But strangely, he felt no regret. He felt only freedom, even elation. He had thought of her presence in his life as a great pleasure, but now he saw that it had been a great burden. The burden was the guilt he bore from knowing he had been bound to her only by his own selfish craving. Yet he realized that he might never have destroyed the Eve had he not been forced to make a hard choice. He had destroyed the Eve to save Avalessa, even though the Eve had been securely his and Avalessa was not. As he thought on it, he began to understand the reason for his decision. It was love. Sitting on that hard board bumping along blind in a dark, forbidden forest, he realized he loved the princess.

How was such a thing possible? Beauty had always been the passion of his life. He craved beauty as people crave food. He did not think he could live without it. Yet he had never seen Avalessa's face. Her beauty was merely a rumor, but what if the rumor was false? Would he still love her? He loved her now, didn't he? And he had never seen her face. What would it matter if she were not beautiful?

Yet, as an artist, he understood the power of imagination and of the intrigue of the hidden. As long as he could imagine her beautiful, it mattered little whether it was true. When truth was hidden, imagination filled the void. But once truth was revealed, imagination must yield to it. What if in truth she was plain, or even ugly?

What a shallow man I am! he chided himself in disgust. Either he loved Avalessa or he did not. If his love was conditional on her beauty, it was the beauty he loved and not the woman. To desire her solely to delight in her beauty

450

was to love himself rather than her. This had been the perversity of his passion for the Eve. Yet he wondered why the Master made beauty at all if not for delight. Was it wrong to desire what he intended that we should enjoy? No, it could not be wrong to enjoy beauty. Yet it occurred to him that beauty could be enjoyed without being possessed. One could delight in a sunset without owning the sun.

He had learned by bitter experience that beauty lacked the power to sustain love. He had come to hate Emeralda in spite of her beauty. The evil of her heart overwhelmed the beauty of her face, making it a thing he loathed to look upon. Might not the opposite be true? Could a less than beautiful face become glorious when lit by the glow of a beautiful heart, as gray clouds became glorious in the light of the rising sun? He knew that to dedicated lovers, beauty hardly mattered. He had seen couples with faces that would frighten trolls who utterly adored each other. And he had seen how love anchored in the heart of the beloved remained unaffected as youthful beauty faded into sags and wrinkles.

"Ignatio," he said softly, "can an acolyte hear a confession?"

"Anyone who follows the Master can hear a confession," Ignatio replied. "He need not be a kirkman at all. I learned in Meridan's abbey that priests cannot stand between individuals and the Master. We all stand before him directly. But if it will help you confess to him, I will hear anything you want to say."

"I have been a selfish fool," Davian said. "I have rejected the blessings of the Master while chasing my own poor artificial substitute for joy. Can he forgive me?"

"He already has, Davian, my dear friend. He already has."

451

49

Lord Greyhorne rapped the hilt of his sword on the oaken table in front of him. The table stood at the foot of the dais beneath King Perivale's empty throne. Greyhorne, a long-time friend of Lord Reddgaard, had retired from the Hall to nurse his failing health. But when several knights had come to him with news of the disaster at Sunderlon and the murders in Morningstone, he had yielded to their pleas to guide the Hall in rebuilding Meridan's government. Beside the venerable lord sat a scribe with parchment, quills, and an inkwell. The twenty-seven knights and lords standing about in clusters quit their hushed talk of the tragic events and took their seats.

"Lords and knights of Meridan," Greyhorne began, "this is a most unhappy day in the history of our kingdom. As you have already heard, two nights ago four of our number were murdered: Lord Fenimar, Lord Kramad Yesenhad, Lord Ashbough, and the king's counselor, Senevel. Worse still, riders from Sunderlon have reported that all fifty-one knights accompanying King Perivale on his quest to defend that town were lost. The king's body was not among the dead, but he has disappeared. Lady Bloeudewedd was also murdered in the night, and Princess Avalessa is missing, along with her lady-in-waiting. Prince Rhondale was spared, thanks to his being outside the castle at the time of the murders. He is now grieving in the chapel with Nallar the kirkman. You men now sitting in this hall were fortunate not to have been in Corenham when Perivale assembled his doomed army. We thank you for responding to our call. You, along with fifteen other knights who have not yet been reached, are all that is left of Meridan's Hall. Today it falls on you to restore the government and defense of Meridan."

Sir Gorlac stood and said, "Is the murderer known?"

"He is not. Strangely, five witnesses claim to have seen King Perivale in the castle the night of the murders. A guard at the gatehouse insists that the king rode to the gate alone and demanded entrance. Lady Bloeudewedd's lady-in-waiting also insists that Perivale entered her chambers demanding the Crown of Eden. Two women servants and a page thought they saw the king in the hallways. A horse resembling the king's was found near the door of the keep."

"It has the ring of witchcraft," Sir Baldorne said.

"It is most baffling," Greyhorne replied. "But we can draw no conclusions at this time. We must get about the business of bringing order to Meridan's government."

At that moment the door of the hall opened and a tall man robed in the colors of the forest stepped inside. Hair and a full beard white as lightning framed his face. He walked toward the dais, his carriage straight and noble as a mountain pine. He stopped before Greyhorne, and his eyes looked upon the elder statesman with the wisdom of eternity.

"Who are you, and what is your business here?" Greyhorne said.

"I have many names, but you may call me Father Lachrymas, for I bear tidings of sorrow, though tempered with promise."

"Say your piece, Father," Greyhorne said.

Father Lachrymas turned and addressed the remnant of the Hall. "Noblemen of Meridan, it falls to me to tell you that your king will not return. He has brought down upon his head the judgment of the Master of the Universe for offenses both against his own house and against heaven. The empire of the Seven Kingdoms will crumble, and Meridan will sink into its former obscurity. Yet I bid you heed the words of hope I am given to deliver to you."

The strange man raised his arms high and spoke the prophecy in the tones of a chant:

> "Beyond the fateful fall that followed pride,
> A hundred times shall ring the fount of light,
> When glow of golden prince and silver bride
> Are heaven born to 'lume the ebon night.
>
> "Then times shall ring the light a score and one
> Ere Eden's hues from darkness shall emerge
> To coronate the Perivalian son
> As golden star and silver bride converge.
>
> "Then shall the king his cherished princess wed
> As gold and silver blend in unison
> To glorify the throne inherited
> And bind his father's seven into one."

"Let him who has ears to hear the prophecy heed and understand." The man lowered his arms and without another word strode from the hall as the astounded lords and knights watched in wonder.

After the closing of the great doors echoed through the

hall, the deliberations turned to the words of the strange prophecy. The scribe had recorded the prophecy as the visitor spoke it, and though he read it to the Hall several times, the nobles could find little meaning in the obscure words. They soon gave up the attempt and turned to the more practical matter of Perivale's successor.

The debate was short, marking the Hall's haste to bring quick stability to the kingdom. No one could offer a reasonable alternative to Rhondale's ascension, and that very afternoon he was called into the hall and informed of his election. King Landorm's old crown was placed on his head with little ceremony. Before the sun went down, criers rode throughout Corenham announcing the coronation of Rhondale as king. On the next morning, Greyhorne sent messengers bearing the news to the other six kingdoms of the island.

The knights and lords of the Hall remained at Morningstone until the following morning, when they reassembled with King Rhondale presiding from the throne. The Hall offered several names to fill ministry posts left vacant by the slaughter at Sunderlon. Rhondale thanked them for their suggestions but filled all the posts with younger men—confidants he had met in the city's inns and taverns.

He stood and addressed the sparse assembly. "Knights and lords of the Hall, I join you in grief over our losses and in your prayers for all the newly made widows and orphans. I also grieve the loss of my own father, whose death leaves not only a vacancy on our throne but a vacancy in my heart as well.

"My anguish is compounded by the disappearance of my dear sister, Princess Avalessa. We have no knowledge of her whereabouts. She may have heard of the slaughter in the castle and fled for her life. She may be hiding in the darkness of some cellar, not knowing that the brother who loves her now sits on Meridan's throne. Or she may have been abducted as some strand of the plot that has taken so many lives. You can understand my deep concern for her. My first decree as king is to initiate a search for her not only in Meridan but throughout the Seven Kingdoms. I will not rest until I bring her back to the safety and comfort of Morningstone.

"Furthermore, I wish to bring to justice the black witch Morgultha. I think we all suspect that she was the insidious power behind the evils that have befallen us. I offer a reward of five hundred crowns to any man or woman who brings either my sister or Morgultha to me."

Rhondale dismissed the Hall of Knights, and that very afternoon several lords and knights conscripted bands of searchers, giving orders to spread throughout the kingdom, leaving no corner unswept, until the princess and the necromancer were found.

50

Beams of golden morning light broke through the trees to the left of the four fugitives weaving along the forest trail. Avalessa and Elowynn finally slept in spite of the lurching of the wagon. Davian and Ignatio sat on the board, Davian's head nodding and swaying.

"Wake up. It's morning," Ignatio called.

Davian looked up, momentarily forgetting his blindness. But he could see nothing at all. "Are we out of the woods?" he asked.

"No, but we should be coming to the edge soon. We forded the stream bordering Meridan and Vensaur some three hours back, as I judge it."

"We must stop soon," Davian said. "You need sleep, the horse needs rest, and we all need food."

After discussing their options, they decided against stopping until after they left Braegan Wood. The trees and brush grew too thick for the wagon to leave the narrow trail. They would ride farther into Vensaur until they found a thick copse of trees in which they could hide the wagon as they rested.

They emerged from the woods a half hour later. Ahead

Ignatio could see the rolling swells of Vensaur's fields and wilderness, accented with many groves of oak, elm, and conifers. The ridges of the Dragontooth Mountains some twenty miles distant formed the blue horizon ahead of them. After another three miles, he found the grove he wanted and turned the wagon into the trees. Though the women's backs and limbs were sore from the jarring ride, Elowynn and Avalessa wasted no time unloading blankets and foodstuffs as Ignatio unhitched the horse and led it to a patch of green grass.

Davian, unwilling to sit about while the others worked, tried to help lift some of the bags of food, but twice he collided with one of the women and hit his forehead painfully against the side of the wagon. Avalessa urged him to sit and wait, leading him by the hand to a grassy spot beneath a spreading tree. He sat in frustration as the women continued their work. Was this his future? Was he to be a helpless burden to others, unable even to meet his own needs? The thought darkened his mind and sank him into silence as the women chattered happily, relishing their new freedom. Moments later his three companions joined him beneath the tree, and the women divided the food among them.

"Where do we go from here, Davian?" Avalessa asked.

"The only safe course is to get you out of the Seven Kingdoms, Your Highness," he replied.

"Please, don't address me as royalty. Exiled from my kingdom, I am no longer a princess. I am simply Avalessa. How do we get out of the Seven Kingdoms?"

"We travel south through Vensaur to the Narrow Sea. Then we buy passage to the great continent," Davian said.

"And what then?" Elowynn asked.

"Well, my lady—"

"If Avalessa is no longer a princess, I am no longer a lady. Please address me simply as Elowynn."

"Very well, Elowynn. I hardly know what to suggest after we reach the great continent. We will be in the land of the Frankens. You could settle there if you know their language."

"I don't speak Franken at all. Can any of you speak it?" Avalessa asked.

"I can speak a little but not fluently," Davian said.

"I speak Franken," Ignatio said. "I spent much of my childhood there, as my grandparents were Frankish."

"Perhaps you could take us through the land of the Frankens to your homeland in Appienne," she replied.

"Neither Ignatio nor I can safely return there," Davian said. "We are both fugitives from the ecclesium, I for my art and he for aiding my escape."

"It seems that you keep repeating your crimes," Elowynn said with a laugh.

"What of passage across the Narrow Sea?" Avalessa asked.

"I think I have enough money to purchase passage for four," Davian replied, "but little more. It will take at least five days to reach the sea, maybe longer since we must cross the Dragontooth Mountains in this wagon. We must think of how we will live on our journey while conserving our money for sea passage."

"And we have another problem that requires money," Ignatio said. "You women are dressed in the clothing of nobility and royalty. Davian wears the uniform of a Morningstone guard. We must find plain garb for all of you. And you, Avalessa, should remove your veil. It marks you as the fugitive princess as surely as if you were branded."

Avalessa blanched at the kirkman's words and replied, "I—I cannot remove the veil."

"Why can't you?" Ignatio asked.

"She has good reasons that you need not know," Elowynn replied. "Don't ask again."

"I brought clothing from my cottage," Davian said. "I will change today."

"Still, the need for new clothing for the women means we will likely need more money than Davian has," Ignatio said.

"But how can we earn money without risking exposure?" Avalessa said.

"We must put our heads to the matter and figure out something," Ignatio replied.

As the little group discussed possibilities, Davian found his spirits lifted somewhat. In spite of his blindness, the others seemed to look to him for direction. *It is a fine blessing to be needed*, he thought. Yet he wondered how long such a need would last after the journey was complete. Their roles would reverse, and he would be helpless and dependent. He thrust the dark thought aside and put his mind to the dilemma at hand.

"I have an idea," Elowynn said. "It may sound strange at first, but hear me out. The princess—I mean, Avalessa—is an excellent musician, both vocally and on the mandolin. Davian is also a fine singer and knows scores of songs. I have heard the two singing duets through the wall of Avalessa's garden. They could entertain in the towns we go through on our journey to the sea. We would collect money in our hats to pay for our food and lodging."

"But there's the matter of the princess's veil," Davian said.

"Yes! And that will actually help us." Ignatio jumped up in excitement. "Since everyone in the Seven Kingdoms will be looking for the princess, we will make it our act to pretend that Avalessa is a princess in exile. We can make up a story similar to all the rumors about her—that she is veiled because her unearthly beauty would bring death to all who looked upon her. She has fled the castle because her evil father would force her into marriage with a brutal ogre. A blind minstrel has befriended her, and she has fallen in love with him because he is the only man in whose presence she can unveil her face. Together they are wandering about the world singing of their love. Elowynn and I can drum up crowds, and I can be the narrator who tells the story to introduce the two singers. Then you both can come onstage and sing ballads and love songs. What do you think?"

"Where is your mind, Ignatio?" Davian said. "You want to display Avalessa so blatantly before the very people who are looking for her? You may as well pin a sign on her reading, 'Here is the princess of Meridan.'"

"No, Davian, I begin to see what Ignatio is thinking," Elowynn said, excitement building in her voice. "Hiding the princess in a wagon is the real danger. That's exactly what Rhondale's searchers will expect. We're traveling too slowly and too conspicuously to escape them. But no one would expect the real princess to engage in an act depicting herself so obviously. It will be the best way she could hide. Ignatio, you are brilliant." She smiled broadly at the acolyte, who belied the compliment by grinning foolishly and flushing red as a holly berry.

"I think you may be right," Davian said after musing over the idea. "It's a bold and daring plan, but it likely exposes us to the least risk. I agree to it. What do you think, Avalessa?"

Avalessa had hardly breathed as Ignatio described his plan. Did he know how closely his made-up tale resembled the truth? Even the part about her being in love with the blind poet? The story opened a window in her heart, and the draft of fresh hope rushing in caught her breath. For the first time she realized that if Davian's blindness were permanent, he might love her, for he would never see her scarred face. Her heart beat faster at the thought, and she fought to keep her voice steady as she answered, "Yes, Ignatio, I agree to your plan."

Cheers and laughter and handclasps celebrated the decision.

"We can buy a mandolin in Ironwood," Davian said. "It's the next town, lying in the foothills of the Dragontooth Mountains. We can also get changes of clothing there."

"Don't we risk being caught if we go into town as we are?" Elowynn asked.

"Not yet," Avalessa answered. "It will take at least two days for Meridan's Hall of Knights to meet and confirm Rhondale as king—assuming he is their choice. At best he could not instigate a search until tomorrow. Even if riders left immediately to post my disappearance throughout the Seven Kingdoms, we would still be over a day ahead of them."

"But we do have need for caution," Ignatio said. "You women cannot show yourselves in the town. You must remain hidden in the wagon, for when searchers do follow us, we don't want townspeople reporting that two women, one wearing a veil, had been seen passing through. I will make the purchases alone."

The four fugitives rested and slept in the grove until sundown, when Ignatio once more hitched the horse to the wagon, with Elowynn helping him. Avalessa gathered the blankets and led Davian to the wagon, her breath coming deeper at the touch of his hand. With the horse rigged, Ignatio and Davian mounted the board, and the two women hid beneath the blankets and stores of the wagon bed.

"We should reach Ironwood by morning," Davian said as

Ignatio flipped the reins, and the wagon creaked eastward on the starlit road.

They arrived in Ironwood an hour after sunup, and already the town square teemed with vendors and buyers. Ignatio parked the wagon in an area reserved for such vehicles, and leaving Davian on the board and the women hidden in the bed, he went to the square. He made the purchases in little more than an hour and returned to the wagon accompanied by a porter carrying a bag of potatoes and a bundle of clothing. Ignatio carried only a mandolin and a small bag of spare strings for the instrument.

As he mounted the board, Davian said, "If you see the sign of a physician on a shop door, stop the wagon. I wish to speak with him about my eyes."

"A village this small is unlikely to have a physician other than a barber," Ignatio replied. "But I did see a barber's sign. It's on the north street bordering the square. I will take you there now."

Ignatio led Davian to the shop and rang the bell hanging on the door. In moments a keen-eyed man of about fifty appeared. Unlike many barbers, he was shaved and well groomed, and his planked floor was caulked and swept clean.

"Are you a barber only or also a physician?" Ignatio asked.

"I was trained in the medical arts at the abbey of Corenham," the barber replied. "How may I serve you?"

When Davian told him of the blows to his head and the blindness that had followed, the physician sat him down and examined his eyes, holding a candle so close to Davian's face that he could feel the heat of it.

"Can you see the flame of this candle?" the physician asked.

"Not at all," Davian replied.

Then with his fingers the man probed all over Davian's head, often asking whether he felt pain or soreness at the touch. He sat back in his chair and asked, "Though you cannot see images, do you see blackness, grayness, or moving spots?"

"After the first blow I saw pulsing clouds of gray. But after the second I have seen nothing at all, not even blackness. I have no sensation of sight whatsoever."

The man sighed deeply, shook his head, and glanced sadly at Ignatio, who sat watching the examination. "I have seen many types of blindness, but few are curable," he said. "Your eyes appear normal, but the blow to your head has damaged them inside or broken the cords to your brain. I have no skill to restore your sight and know of no procedure, herb, or medicine that can help you. I am very sorry."

"Is there a chance that my sight will return?" Davian asked.

"I wish I could offer such hope, but I cannot. If you saw colorful spots or grayness, I would have reason for encouragement. But I've never seen a case where sight returned to eyes that had no sensation of light at all. I am very sorry."

With his heart sinking in despair, Davian tried to pay the barber, but he refused the coin. Ignatio led the blinded artist back to the wagon in silence.

51

Woodlands increased and fields diminished as the wagon bearing the four fugitives climbed into the highlands of Vensaur. The road meandered upward toward the pass in the Dragontooth Mountains. The women no longer stayed hidden but, now wearing their plain skirts and bodices, sat in the bed of the wagon. Davian insisted that at least one of them face the rear and keep a sharp eye on the road. At the first sign of any approaching traveler, they must cover themselves again. Avalessa could wear her veil openly on stage, but it must not be seen on the road.

As the horse began to tire, Ignatio left the road and drove deep into a wood at the base of the mountains, where they made their camp for the day. A creek flowed nearby, and the steady sound of the rippling water, along with the greenness of the forest, lifted the spirits of all but Davian. The women gathered wood, and Ignatio built a fire to cook their eggs and sausage. They forgot their danger, laughing and bantering as they ate their breakfast. Davian tried to join the merriment, but his spirit would not rise above the weight of what the physician had told him. When the meal was over, the three cleaned as Davian walked toward the stream, using a long stick to probe the way before him. Avalessa watched his hesitant, stumbling steps and started toward him, intending to help him find his way. But Ignatio caught her arm and drew her back.

"What's wrong with him?" she asked. "He seems down-cast and distant."

"The barber in Ironwood gave him terrible news," Ignatio replied. "He will never see again. It was an awful thing to hear. We must give him time to grieve his loss."

"Oh, how dreadful!" Avalessa said. "And he an artist too. He loves beauty dearly, and he will never see it again."

Ignatio went to rub down the horse, and Elowynn helped him. Avalessa stood by the tree where the blankets were spread and looked toward the still figure of Davian sitting beside the stream. As they had traveled he had confessed to her his obsession with the stone woman and the shame that clung to him because of it. She had forgiven him easily and confessed her own hatred of her father. She yearned to go to him and comfort him in her arms, telling him he could cling to her and she would be his eyes. Would he welcome her love? Would he love her? Or had she been nothing more to him than some trapped animal he had pitied and freed? Perhaps now he expected her to bound away and let him brood his loss of the world of beauty. But the thought came to her again that his blindness could bring them together. No longer need she fear his revulsion at the sight of her face; he would never see it. She need not fear any comparison between her ruined face and the perfection of the ideal woman he had given up. His blind-ness removed the one remaining barrier between them.

Suddenly she checked herself. Was she actually pleased that he was permanently blind? The possibility horrified her. How could she be so selfish? Yet it was undeniable that their handicaps fit each other like a key to a lock. Was his blindness her key to love? Perhaps the Master of the Universe meant for them to . . . No! She must never be grateful for Davian's blindness. The thought was evil, and she banished it from her mind. Love should never wish anything but the best for the beloved, even if the cost was lifelong loneliness.

Yet he was blind, and she could help him. Avalessa walked slowly toward Davian. She sat down beside him on the grass, slipped her arm around his waist, and took his hand in her own. "Davian, I would gladly pluck out my own eye and give it to you if it would give you sight. But as such a thing is not possible, I will do the next best thing. My eyes will be your eyes. I will see what you want to see, take you where you want to go, read to you what you want read. I give my eyes to you, Davian—forever. I commit myself to be your sight just as you committed yourself to be my hope when I lived in despair at Morningstone."

"I don't want your pity, Avalessa."

"I give you something dearer than pity, Davian; I give you love. I have loved you since you first sang to me at the garden wall. I will always love you."

She turned his face toward hers, lifted her veil, and kissed him softly on each eye. Her lips slipped down over his hot tears until they met his lips, and her own tears blended with his like streams merging in a wilderness. When their lips parted, he clasped her to his breast as if pressing her love into his heart.

"I cannot yet speak of love, Avalessa," he said.

"I understand," she replied. "I didn't speak to compel a response."

Without another word, they stood and walked arm in arm back to the camp. She did understand—or at least, she thought she did. At the present he had a mountain to climb in coming to terms with his blindness. She could not expect him to make a lifetime commitment to her the day after he learned of his fate. She would be patient.

When Ignatio and Elowynn finished grooming the horse, they spread four blankets on the grass, and the fugitives slept until late afternoon. They arose refreshed and prepared another meal, roasting a plump hen Ignatio had bought in Ironwood. After all had eaten their fill, Avalessa tuned the mandolin, and she and Davian sang ballads, love songs, comic songs, and dancing tunes. Ignatio and Elowynn listened spellbound at their fine voices and blending tones, often clapping their hands to the rhythm. When the singers began a lively Lochlaundian jig, Elowynn stood and began to dance. Ignatio stared entranced at the fair young woman's grace and liveliness.

"Are you too much a kirkman to join me?" she asked, dazzling him with her smile.

"I would trample your toes like an ox on a threshing floor," he said with a laugh. But she pulled him up from the blanket, and the two stepped through that dance and several more without inflicting serious damage to her feet.

When the woods began to darken, they stopped and loaded the wagon. With the western sky still pink behind them, they got back on the road that would take them through the Dragontooth Mountains.

The travelers spent two nights on the road before reaching Lorganville, the first town west of the mountains. Each day when they stopped to eat and sleep, they spent several hours preparing and rehearsing their songs and stories. And as they approached Lorganville near dawn, they decided they were ready to perform. They stopped in a grove a mile outside the city and slept most of the day. When the sun hovered an hour above the horizon, they drove into the town and parked the wagon at the edge of the square.

Ignatio, now dressed in the garb of a crier, went about the square, calling people to the performance. Elowynn arranged the few who straggled toward the wagon into a semicircle around one side of it where she had set two borrowed stools. When about fifteen people had assembled, Ignatio stepped onto one of the stools and, in a voice that reached the far corners of the square, told the sad story of the exiled princess and her blind minstrel. Then at his signal, Elowynn opened the gate of the wagon. The two singers, who had been sitting in the bed, hidden by the high walls of the wagon, stepped out, and Avalessa led Davian, his eyes bound with a white cloth, to his stool. She strummed the mandolin, and they began to sing.

> "In days of old when warriors bold
>   sailed out across the foam,
> A horn-helmed knight sailed into sight
>   of this our island home.
> He stepped ashore, so says our lore,
>   for ventures he was questing,
> And came upon a vile dragon
>   upon its hoard a-resting.
> A maiden fair with flaxen hair
>   beneath its wing was captured.
> Such beauty in that loathsome den
>   the brave knight's heart enraptured.
> The dragon glared with long fangs bared
>   and turned on him in fury.
> The knight advanced and aimed his lance.
>   'This worm I soon will bury.'
> The maiden fair said, 'Sir, beware
>   of its fell weapon hidden,
> This worm's foul breath has burned to death
>   all who approached unbidden.'

As he went in the dragon's den,
   the worm blazed all the hotter,
But the knight had wound himself around
   with sheep's wool soaked in water.
With one great heave his lance did cleave
   the dragon's scales asunder;
Its belly burst, and the worm accursed
   fell down with sounds of thunder.
The maiden fair with flaxen hair
   looked on the knight with favor.
No other knight had dared to fight
   the dragon fiend to save her.
He clasped her hand, and to his land
   o'er waves of blue he took her.
The maiden fair with flaxen hair,
   he wed and ne'er forsook her."

As Davian and Avalessa sang, the crowd doubled, and when they finished the song, the listeners applauded vigorously, grinning and nodding and shouting enthusiastic approval. Song followed song, and the crowd grew steadily until most of the buyers and many of the vendors on the square stood spellbound around the wagon. As the light began to fade, Ignatio announced that the next song would be their last and placed four hats on the ground in front of the onlookers. The song, a plaintive tale of a lost love found, climaxed with Avalessa's clear soprano soaring on a high note that filled the air like liquid light. When the singers finished, they bowed deeply as the cheering crowd burst into vigorous applause accompanied by the welcome sound of coins clinking in the upturned hats.

The crowd dispersed, and Ignatio and Elowynn gathered the hats and poured the contents of each into one.

"Davian, feel this," Ignatio said happily as he thrust the loaded hat into his friend's hands.

470

The unexpected weight almost caused Davian to drop it. "We did well tonight," he said.

"We did well indeed!" Ignatio replied, clapping him on the back. "I think we needn't worry about earning our fare across the Narrow Sea."

After a hearty meal at a Lorganville inn, they traveled southward into the night. Two days later they performed at Dunnestan, and at the mayor's request repeated their performance a second night. Their purse swelled with each appearance. After each act they assessed their performance and made refinements based on the reactions of the crowds, dropping some songs, adding others, and adding two stories. Their spirits were high, and Davian began to find the burden of his blindness lightened. He was not utterly useless.

As they rode in darkness toward Levonwicke, all his thoughts were of Avalessa. He had refrained from telling her that he loved her. He felt that once he made such a declaration, he should take the next honorable step and wed her. But he could not burden her with his blindness. In time he would come to terms with it—everyone who bore a handicap did—and would be less a burden to her than now. He knew she loved him and had pledged herself to be his eyes. But as time wore on, enduring the daily weight of his dependence could cause her to regret such a commitment.

The elation of success remained with the four fugitives as they reached the square of Levonwicke and set up for their performance. But an ominous discovery sobered their high spirits. While waiting for Ignatio to herd listeners to the wagon, Elowynn began to read the notices posted on the board at the corner of the square. The most prominent of these was a parchment the size of a washboard. As she read it, her blood ran cold.

> Be it knownne to all that Avalessa, the hie princesse
> of the Sevene Kingdoms, is loste from Morningstone
> Castle. King Rhondale of Meridan, having in his heart the
> deepeste concern for his beloved sister, hereby offers a
> rewarde of five hundred crownnes to the bearer of tydings
> of her whereabouts. Suche information may be imparted
> to the sherriffe of your countye. By the order of His
> Majesty, Rhondale, King of Meridan.

Elowynn's hand went to her breast to calm her racing heart. She ran to tell Ignatio.

"We must perform," he said. "It's the best way to divert suspicion from ourselves. To pack up and leave now would mark us as fugitives."

They performed, and all went well. In fact, they got their heaviest hat yet. Word of their music had traveled ahead of them, and Ignatio found that he had to do little but announce their presence to raise a crowd. They left Levonwicke in relief and pointed their horse toward Ensovandor.

When morning came they topped a rise and saw Vensaur's capital city spread before them, the spires of the king's castle glowing in the rising sun.

"We are about two miles away," Ignatio said. "We will camp in those trees at the right of the road and enter the city in late afternoon."

"We could encounter more than mere notices in Ensovandor," Davian said. "It being the capital of Vensaur, Rhondale may have sent soldiers there to search for Avalessa. Or warriors seeking the reward could be waiting for her."

"But we must go through the city to reach the Narrow Sea," Ignatio replied. "Our performance is still our best disguise."

"Can we not circle the city?" Elowynn asked.

472

"No, I asked at Levonwicke. The only road runs through the town. We must take the risk."

As evening approached they drove into Ensovandor and stopped the wagon at the edge of the square. Shortly a crowd began to assemble. It was all Ignatio and Elowynn could do to keep them far enough from the stools to give the performers their needed space. Even before he began his introduction, Ignatio estimated a crowd of well over two hundred, with more coming every moment. Those in the back could see nothing, yet they stood waiting for the performance to begin.

He was relieved to see no knights, warriors, sheriffs, or other troublesome officials in the crowd. He stepped up on his low platform and told his introductory story, and to widespread applause the two singers came out to perform. Davian and Avalessa were in top form, and the audience responded with high enthusiasm. Ignatio began to relax and enjoy the songs.

The performance had just passed the halfway mark when he first saw the danger approach. A single knight, mounted on horseback and fully armored in chain mail but without a helm, eased his mount into the rear of the crowd to the performers' right. Ignatio tensed. He watched in dismay as a second knight approached from the left, also armored but unhelmed. And to his horror, a third knight eased his horse into the crowd near the center. As the three drew nearer, Ignatio could see the crest of Meridan blazoned on their shoulders. Rhondale's men had indeed arrived. He saw the first knight look at the two others and give a slight nod. They approached slowly, and soon Ignatio could see their faces, stern and glaring from beneath heavy brows.

When the song ended and applause erupted, he leaned over to Avalessa and whispered, "Whatever happens, just keep singing. It's still our best cover." Avalessa nodded and continued.

Throughout the rest of the performance the three knights remained silent and rigid, their only movement a slight edging forward toward the singers. When the last song was sung and the long applause died away, the crowd surged toward the singers to drop coins into the hats. The first knight signaled to the others, and they prodded their horses forward until they reached the line of hats on the ground. In unison the three knights reached to their sides, and the three sighted fugitives tensed and looked quickly about for somewhere to run. Avalessa took Davian's arm and began to tug him toward the wagon. At that moment the knights raised their arms and released handfuls of coins into the hats below, many missing their mark and scattering across the cobblestones. They grinned and waved at the performers before turning their horses and loping from the square.

Weak with relief, Avalessa clung to the still-oblivious Davian as he repeatedly asked her to tell him what was happening. Elowynn and Ignatio watched the knights ride away, then collapsed into each other's arms, laughing like children.

52

The crowd dispersed, and vendors on the square began closing their booths as Ignatio and Elowynn gathered the money from the hats and cobblestones. Ignatio poured the coins into a bag and hefted its weight.

"Tonight we must have doubled all we have taken in up to now," he said.

"And we had already recovered our investment and earned more than enough to pay our ship fares," Davian said. "We needn't perform again before we cross into Franken."

Elated with their greatest success yet, the four packed their wagon to leave Ensovandor. The wagon was almost loaded when the clopping of an approaching horse turned their elation into alarm. A rider in the uniform of a king's herald drew rein before them.

"I bear a message from His Majesty, Danthane, King of Vensaur. The king requests your presence to perform for his court at the royal castle tomorrow night. This letter will be your pass." The messenger handed Ignatio a small rolled parchment tied with a scarlet cord. He took the letter and bowed as the herald bid them farewell and trotted away.

"We cannot do this," Davian said. "Playing in town

squares is danger enough. In a king's hall we invite disaster. Guests will likely include nobles from Meridan, as well as Vensaur nobility who have been in Meridan's courts."

"Davian is right," Avalessa said. "We dare not risk the exposure."

"But how can we refuse?" Elowynn asked. "A king's invitation is a command."

"We must flee," Ignatio said.

"But how? We will be sought out and compelled. And our flight would raise suspicion about who we are," Avalessa said.

"We must leave the wagon and buy three more horses," Davian said. "We can ride tonight for Souport. Souport is more than a three-day journey by wagon, but we can make it in two days on horseback. They won't know we have fled until we fail to show at the castle tomorrow night. They could not begin a search until the following morning. Our wagon remaining here will prevent suspicion until then. They won't think we would abandon it. We can pack our blankets and as much food as we can carry."

All agreed to Davian's plan, and after working out the details, Ignatio shook his head ruefully. "We are victims of our own success. An invitation to a king's court could have secured our performing careers." He struck an exaggerated thespian pose and emoted dramatically, "Alas, the fell and capricious turns of cruel fate!"

Ignatio left the women to select what items to carry and crossed the square to the pens of poultry and livestock where he had seen horses traded earlier in the day. He found a trader from Newfrith in his tent nearby and bargained with him for three good mounts and four saddles.

"I heard yer songs and tales, my man," the trader said. "My missus right near swooned over some of yer music, mainly the duets with the blind one and the veiled one.

And I found yer own tales well to my likin'. Can't imagine why mummers like ye are needin' my good horses."

"We're thinking of adding an equestrian act," Ignatio said. "Should you hear anyone ask about us, we will be practicing in a field somewhere north of town all day tomorrow."

He returned to his companions, and they decided to take their dinner before riding out. It was not completely dark, and the square still held too many witnesses. Elowynn and Ignatio purchased two roasted hens, a loaf of bread, a wedge of cheese, and a jug of mead, and they ate at the wagon. After the square had darkened and people were few, the four fugitives mounted and rode the high street of Ensovandor to the north gate, where they made their exit. But outside the city they turned and circled southward and threaded their way through copses and underbrush on narrow animal paths. Ignatio and Elowynn rode in the lead, and Davian brought up the rear, following the sound of Avalessa's horse.

Though the night was moonless, the sky was free of clouds and the road shone clearly in the starlight. Just before dawn they passed through the small village of Tarnbury, where they encountered no living soul, not even a constable or town crier. After a day of rest near a wooded stream and another night of travel, they topped a rise in early morning and looked down on the city of Souport and, beyond it, the gray expanse of the Narrow Sea. The masts and spars of scores of ships rose like the pickets of a fence shielding the town from the sea. Gray smoke from cottage chimneys drifted like pennants in the light eastward breeze.

Patches of fields lined with green hedges surrounded the town on its three landward sides. A thick forest lay beyond the fields to the west, and as they descended toward the

477

city, Ignatio left the road and led his companions into the forest. They found a campsite to their liking, where a clear stream threaded its way through the leafy oaks. After a breakfast of honey cakes from their saddle pouches, they spread four blankets on the ground and slept until early afternoon.

"I will go into Souport to sell the horses and buy our passage," Ignatio said when his companions awoke. "The three of you can wait here and rest. I can't say when I will return. I won't sell these horses at a loss. And it may take time to find a ship leaving soon that will take us aboard. You have food for two days. I will sleep at an inn tonight, but if I haven't sold the horses and booked passage before tomorrow night, I will return here and report to you."

"I will go with you," Elowynn said. "You will need help managing four horses, and I can help you carry food back to our camp."

Ignatio seemed pleased with her offer. He saddled their steeds, and the two of them rode toward Souport, leading the other two horses behind them.

As the clops of the hooves faded into the forest, Davian said, "I wonder why Elowynn seemed so eager to accompany Ignatio?"

"You wouldn't wonder if you could see their faces when they look at each other," Avalessa replied.

"Ignatio and Elowynn?" Davian was incredulous. "But he's such a kirkman! I never thought a woman would turn his head."

"He may be a kirkman, but he's also a man, and Elowynn is a very fair woman. His isn't the first male head she has turned. But this time her head has been turned as well. She's quite smitten with your friend."

The fast-paced flight from Ensovandor had exhausted Avalessa. She excused herself and lay back on her blanket and slept again. Davian took the stick she had found for him and, following the sound of the brook, made his way to the bank some fifty paces behind the tree where she lay. He felt about until he found a flat stone, where he sat and let the music of the water soothe his mind.

Though he could not see the stream, he delighted in its soothing sound. All his life he had relied on his eyes as the sole gateway to beauty. Sight had always overwhelmed his other senses as the sun overwhelms candlelight, causing him to ignore delights clamoring for his attention in modes the eye could not see. The dazzling surface glamour of the Eve had overshadowed the exquisite beauty of Avalessa's soul. The glare of brass in the sunlight had blinded him to the gold in the shadows. Truth had shouted to his soul through the garden wall, but he had heard it only faintly because his eyes were enamored with a lie. He smiled ruefully to himself. He thought it ironic that he had to be blinded in order to see that beauty was a truth infinitely greater than the eye could fathom, and even more ironic that he, an artist devoted to the pursuit of beauty, could have destroyed the most beautiful creature he had ever beheld for the love of a woman he had never laid eyes on. His eyes had been at war with his heart, which was wiser than his eyes.

Myronius had told him that a time was coming when the intent of the Master of the Universe would be fulfilled and the appearance of every created thing would be a truthful expression of its inner reality. On that day the eye and the heart would no longer be at war. Both would see as one.

He decided to bathe while Avalessa slept. He returned to his blanket for a change of clothing. He listened until the regular sound of her breathing assured him she was asleep, and then he made his way back to the stream. He removed his clothes and slipped into the cool water. After bathing and scrubbing his clothing, he lay on the grass until the soft breeze dried his skin. He donned a clean tunic and leggings and sat on the rock, listening to the song of the stream.

"Won't you just look at this mess!" Avalessa's voice came from behind him. "Clothing scattered all over the grass as if a windstorm had swept through a laundry. Isn't that just like a man!"

He had pitched his wet clothes on the bank and forgotten them. She draped them across a low branch of the cypress tree that spread above them. Moments later he heard the rustling of her clothing as she undressed and stepped into the water.

"What are you doing?" he asked.

"I'm bathing," she replied.

"Oh, then I will leave until you are finished."

Embarrassed, he began to rise, when her laughter rang out. Suddenly realizing the silliness of his needless modesty, he laughed as well, and he sat again and talked with her as she splashed about and scrubbed her dress clean. She got out of the water and walked about until dry, then donned her singing princess costume—her only change of clothing—and sat beside him on the stone.

He put his arm about her waist and drew her to him. "Avalessa," he said, finding her hand and clasping it, "I'm sure you must know I love you—deeply and dearly. But I cannot wed you now. Please understand. I cannot be to you all a man should be for his wife. The Master meant for a man to cherish his woman and to be her protector. I cannot be that for you. I would be helpless were you under attack or in danger. Indeed, you are more my protector than I am yours. I'm dependent on you more than you are on me."

"That is not so," Avalessa replied. "You have protected me

in ways few women ever experience. It was in protecting me that you sacrificed your ability to protect. You defended me heroically and paid for it with your sight. And you lifted me out of a black hell and into the sunlight." She clung to his hand with both of hers, and the powerful arm encircling her waist was all the shield she needed against sorrow. "We must accept life as it is, not as we wish it to be."

"That is true," he replied. "I will come to terms with my blindness. Other blind men do. But I haven't done it yet."

"I will wait as long at it takes, my dear, dear Davian."

He knew by the feel of her breath on his cheek that she was not wearing her veil. He turned to her and kissed her lips, bringing his hand upward to stroke her face. But she took it and brought it down again to her lap, clasping it in both of her own.

Feeling the heat of desire rise in his veins, Davian drew away and said, "I'm getting a bit hungry. Shouldn't we see what we can find in our bags?"

Their shared adversity and growing love had given them both a heightened sense of the Master's presence, and though they were alone and in love, they would not mar their chastity. She took his arm, and they walked back to the camp and ate their evening meal.

Avalessa gathered enough wood to build a fire and feed it throughout the night. As dusk approached, she lit it to keep nighttime animals at bay. She and Davian sang and laughed until the woods darkened, then curled up in their separate blankets and talked softly as the crickets chirped, the fire crackled, and the brook sang its never-ending song.

Davian soon fell asleep, but Avalessa was much too happy to close her eyes. Davian loved her. She had known it, but to hear the words spoken swelled her heart like an ocean wave. For the first time since her father had doted on her in childhood, she felt the security and euphoria of being loved and cherished by a man. She loved this new life of hers. The road had been hard in many ways, with no place to call home, none of the comforts she had been brought up with, and no idea what the next bend would bring. But in the fine companionship of the four friends—and now the love of Davian—she felt the sunlight of the Master shining upon her. If only Davian were not blind and her face were still beautiful, the last impediment to their complete happiness would be removed.

When Davian had been still for half an hour, she arose, still dressed in her princess costume, and sat facing the low fire. She mouthed a silent prayer to the Master of the Universe. It was a simple prayer—merely that Davian would regain his sight and that her face would regain its beauty. She got up and added a few branches to the fire, then stood over the sleeping Davian, gazing at his fine face and manly form with a longing to fall down beside him and cling to him forever. But she stepped softly past him and returned to her own blanket, where she lay down and soon fell into a sound sleep.

Deep in the night she awoke suddenly. She had heard a voice. At first she thought it was Davian's, but she looked over at him and saw that he had not awakened. She lay down, and moments later the sound came again, unmistakably a voice calling her name, though little more than a whisper. For a moment she thought she was dreaming, but the crisp reality of the woods, the orange glow of the fire, the even breathing of Davian, and her own heightened senses convinced her that she was fully awake. Her heart began to pound, and she sat up and looked into the darkness all about her. She saw no one. Could Rhondale's searchers have caught up with them? Should she awaken Davian? As she sat, alert, wide-eyed, and not far from the edge of terror, the voice called her name again, and a tingling thrill ran up her spine. But it was not fear that caused the sensation so much as awe. This time she heard the voice quite clearly, and it called so softly and was so full of love and care that she felt her fear drop away like an opened shackle.

She rose and walked toward the sound of the voice, which now called from some distance in the forest. Later she would wonder why she had trusted this disembodied voice in the night, but as she heard its gentle, soothing tones she had no thought but to do as it bid her. She followed for a quarter hour until she saw a dim glow of light, cool and steady, in the distance ahead. The voice no longer called, but the light seemed to have replaced it and drew her forward. Soon she could see in a small clearing a rustic cottage built of rough-hewn stone. The light shone from its two windows and an open door. Feeling awe as if she were approaching a cathedral, she walked softly toward the door and entered.

Directly ahead stood a grand stairway with polished oaken balustrades and wine-red carpet covering the steps. Having seen the cottage from the outside, she knew it had no second story. Whether it was magic or miracle or vision, she knew she must ascend the stairway, for the light she had followed now shone from the top of it. Slowly she stepped upward like an angel ascending Jacob's ladder to the heavens.

On reaching the second floor, she stopped and drew a deep breath. Before her opened a room fit for an emperor's palace. Indeed, Morningstone had nothing to compare with it. The walls were of deep red velvet overlaid with patterns of gold filigree and inset with alcoves containing exquisite alabaster sculptures of men and women as beautiful as gods and goddesses. The ceiling was high and filled by a magnificent painting depicting angels and saints adoring a male figure of surpassing unearthly beauty who sat upon a massive throne. The floor was of marble polished to the sheen of a placid lake. Draped curtains of royal blue trimmed with gold hung at the four corners. The room had no furniture except for an altarlike table standing in the center. It was made entirely of black marble, smooth and clear as a mirror. The room was lit by an unseen source directly above the table. The light bathed the table's surface with a glow clear as sunlight yet soft as moonlight. On the table she could see two small, bright objects, though she could not identify them from where she stood. She took a step toward the table, then gasped and stopped. A figure stood facing her across the room, and it had taken a step toward her. In a moment she realized she was looking into a mirror mounted on the far wall. It was almost the height of the room and set in a gold frame carved with nude miniatures of male and female figures she knew to be Adam and Eve.

Avalessa walked slowly toward the table, and when she reached it she stopped and read the words etched into the surface: *The Stone of the One Choice*. She could now identify the two small objects, which were set on each side of the engraved words. They were identical casks, rectangular in shape and golden in color, elaborately carved with intertwining vines and floral patterns. On the lid of the cask to her right was engraved the word *Beauty*, and on the lid of the left, *Sight*.

Her heart leapt in wild elation. Here were the answers to her prayer! With her hand trembling like a leaf, she reached out for the cask labeled Beauty and picked it up. With her other hand she reached for the cask labeled Sight. She grasped it and tried to lift it, but it would not move. She gripped it tighter and tugged with all her might, but it was as if the cask were bolted to the table. She set down the cask of Beauty and used both hands to lift the other. To her surprise, she now lifted it easily. It was no heavier than the cask she had lifted. With the cask of Sight now in hand, she reached to take the cask of Beauty and found that now she could not lift it. She set them both on the table and tried to lift them simultaneously. Neither would budge. She tried in several ways to lift both of the casks but found she could pick up only one at a time. Neither would budge from the table while she held the other.

She pondered her dilemma, and her heart chilled as she sensed another presence in the room. She looked up to see the face of an ancient man standing across the table between her and the mirror.

"Who—who are you?" she gasped, her heart pounding.

"You may call me Father Resolaus," he said in a voice that was soft and soothing yet reverberated within the walls of the room, "though I have many names. It was I who called you here."

"Father Resolaus, tell me the meaning of these casks."

"Each contains an ointment of restoration. The ointment of Beauty will restore to your face its former splendor. The ointment of Sight will restore to Davian his vision. You may take either cask, but you may not take both."

She shook her head in anguish at the cruelty of the choice. If she chose beauty, she would be healed and Davian would remain blind and dependent on her. She could have both her beauty and his love. But if she chose to heal his blindness, she would have neither. She would remain scarred for life, and he would leave her, unable to endure the sight of her face. Or worse, he would stay with her because of his own honor or out of sheer pity. Why should she not choose beauty? He would never know. She reached for the cask of Beauty and held it in her hand. Father

485

Resolaus stepped aside, and she looked up to see herself in the mirror. She drew a sharp breath. The scarring was gone, and she was as beautiful as a goddess.

"I—I am beautiful . . . more beautiful even than before my wounding," she whispered, her heart beating with joy as her fingers caressed the velvet-smooth skin of her cheek.

"What you see is not what is," Father Resolaus said. "You are looking into the mirror of what can be."

She did not know how long she gazed at her image, reveling in the dream of her beauty restored. But she thought of Davian's blindness and slowly replaced the cask of Beauty on the table. Once again the mirror showed her scars.

"Why?" she cried, tears welling up in her eyes. "Why must it be one way or the other? Cannot the Master of the Universe grant healing to both of us?"

"He grants all prayers, though often we do not understand the answers. His reasons are eternal in their scope. I can tell you that to grant the kind of healing you want for both of you would bring a ruin upon your lives that would extend beyond the termination of time. The greatest of the Master's proclaimers had a persistent affliction that the Master would not remove, though the man pled with him three times. Had he removed it, the man's pride would have consumed him."

"Then tell me, Father, which choice should I make?"

"That I will not do. When the Master created you, he gave you the high compliment of freedom, allowing your hand to have a part in the shaping of eternity. He will not violate that enormous gift by making your decisions for you. The choice is freely yours and no one else's."

As she gazed in anguish at the two casks, she realized that to choose Beauty would prove that she had no love for Davian but clung to him only to meet her selfish needs. She knew that if she made such a choice, her conscience would torment her each time she looked into his sightless eyes. She loved Davian, and that love could not leave him blind when she had the power to restore his sight. With tears blurring her eyes, she reached with trembling hands and took the cask of Sight. She looked up to see whether Father Resolaus would signify his approval. But the man was no longer there.

She turned from the table and walked to the stairs, refusing to think on her choice lest she turn back and exchange the casks. She descended the steps and walked through the doorway and into the forest. She was not sure she could find her way back to the camp, but as she walked she began to sense a presence beside her and a guiding arm about her shoulder. Though she did not see him, she heard the voice of Father Resolaus low in her ear. "You have made the right choice, Avalessa. You need not fear that you will regret it."

Avalessa reached the camp and found Davian asleep as she had left him, the embers of the fire still glowing. Silently she knelt beside him. She opened the cask, dipped her fingers into the ointment, and smoothed it gently over his closed eyes. She gazed on his dear and wonderful face and breathed another prayer, then closed the cask and crept to her own blanket. With tears filling her eyes, she fell asleep and did not awaken until morning.

53

Avalessa awakened at the first sunlight breaking through the trees from the east. After a moment the strange events of the night flooded into her mind—the forest cottage with the impossible second floor, the stone table, Father Resolaus, and her wrenching choice. Quickly she arose and donned her veil before Davian woke up. She went to the brook to wash herself, and when she returned he was beginning to stir. Hardly daring to breathe, she watched him as he opened his eyes and felt around on the grass, fumbling for his boots and cloak. Her heart sank; he was still blind. What had gone wrong? Had it all been a dream? She crept back to her blanket and felt beneath it where she had hidden the cask. It was there; she had not dreamt it. She watched as Davian groped about his blanket.

"What are you trying to find?" she asked.

"Have you seen my walking stick?"

"It's just to your right, about two feet from your blanket."

She watched as he found the stick and then got up and picked his way into the woods. Bitterly she ripped away her veil and threw it to the ground. Nothing had changed.

As Davian began to walk back to the camp, he became aware of the sensation of rolling grayness. It startled him, and he stopped to determine what was happening. In moments the grayness began to pulsate with throbs of multiple colors. He dropped his stick and leaned against a nearby tree. As he stared ahead, the spots of color began to resolve into blurry, vibrating images. He began to tremble. In another minute the images sharpened into shapes he recognized—trees, grass, flowers, and beams of sunlight. In his elation, he almost shouted for joy, but he did not. Instead, he picked up his stick, and holding it to the ground before him as he had done for days, he returned to the camp.

He came around the bole of the huge oak that sheltered their blankets, and suddenly he stopped short. No more than twenty paces before him sat Avalessa, taking two honey cakes from a food wallet. Her left side was turned toward him, and he drew in a deep breath. The rumors were true; she was beautiful—even more beautiful than he had imagined. The flow of her dress revealed a form that could have been his model for Eve—full and womanly, lithe and graceful. Her face in profile had the look of a goddess. His heart bounded at the sight of her. Then she turned toward him and said, "Good morning, sleepyhead. Are you ready for a bit of breakfast?"

Then he saw the scars. Instantly anger welled up within him. Who could have done such a thing to this woman he loved so dearly? His stomach knotted, feeling the pain she must always bear at the awareness of her disfigurement, and his heart reached out to her with a desire to enfold her and love her so much she would never think of it again. He wanted to be her shield from stares and jokes and insults. Only after these surges of overwhelming emotion washed over him did he think to be surprised that he was neither

489

shocked nor repelled by her face. He did not care about the scars. Whether he saw her from the left side or the right did not matter. She was simply who she was, and the scars changed nothing. He had loved her before he could see her at all, and nothing he saw of her now could change that. Her scars were of no more consequence to him than the shape of her hand or the color of her hair. The beauty of her that he had seen so clearly in his blindness shone through the scars like sunlight through mist.

Avalessa looked at him, wondering why he stood silent without responding to her question. A wasp began to fly about Davian's face, and he swatted it away.

"Oh!" Avalessa cried. "You can see!"

Immediately she turned her face away and ran to her blanket. She reached it and grasped her veil, but Davian was there before she could put it on. He pulled it from her fist and crumpled it to the ground.

"No!" she cried in anguish. "Let me have it! I must have it!" She fell to her knees sobbing and covered her face with her hands.

Davian knelt beside her and enfolded her convulsing body in his arms. Gently he drew her hands from her face and kissed both of her tear-streaked cheeks, then clasped her to him. "There will be no more veils or walls between us," he said softly. She felt as much as heard the richness of his voice vibrating on her cheek as he held her face to his broad chest. "Why didn't you tell me?"

"How could I?" she said. "I was in love with you, but you were in love with beauty. I knew you would abandon me if you knew the truth. But, Davian, you must not feel guilty about leaving me now. I have hidden the truth from you, and you must not tie yourself to a woman your eyes cannot bear to look upon."

Davian laughed softly as he stroked her hair. "You haven't

hidden the truth from me; you have revealed it. I have been a fool. Yes, I have loved beauty. I still do, I think even more than ever. But before I knew you, I let my eyes blind me to the depth and breadth of beauty. You taught me that beauty is a truth far greater than mere sight can know. I am drawn to your beauty as a bee is to a blossom, and I don't intend ever to let you go."

"But my scars . . . how can you stand to—"

"Dear, dear Avalessa, your scars no more ruin your beauty than a smudge of flour ruins the face of a fair kitchen maid. If anything, her beauty is all the sweeter because of it. The scar is nothing—a superficial thing of the moment. Your beauty is eternal. When I look at you, I see past the scars to the beauty the Master intended when he formed you. And, if I may be so bold as to say it, he formed you exceedingly well."

Avalessa smiled and protested no more. She could see that Davian's words were not born of pity or duty but came from the center of his soul. She rested against him, thanking the Master over and over that she had chosen to give him sight rather than restore her own beauty. To know that she had sacrificed her beauty for his sight gave her immense joy. It was her gift to him—a gift all the more lovely because he would never know that she had given it. She knew Father Resolaus had been right: she would never regret her choice. She also knew her face would never again be a burden to her. To know she had freely chosen his sight over her beauty gave her a peace about her appearance that would last throughout her life. She had never been so happy. She turned her radiant face up to Davian, and he kissed her warmly and deeply. After a moment he pulled away and held her at arm's length, gazing at her with love and desire.

"We'd better stop this before we forget we are not wed,"

491

he said. "Which is a thing we will remedy the moment we arrive in the land of the Frankens."

Ignatio and Elowynn returned at midmorning. They were astonished to find that Davian had regained his sight. But they could allow no time for celebration. They had sold the horses at good prices and booked passage to Franken on a ship that would sail as soon as it was loaded, which the captain had estimated to be near midafternoon. They thrust their blankets and clothing into four bags and walked the two miles into Souport, both couples hand in hand. They boarded the ship an hour past noon, and less than an hour later the captain gave the order to sail. The crew unfurled the sails to a steady southeastern wind, and the ship moved out into the Narrow Sea. The four passengers were never again seen on the island of the Seven Kingdoms.

Epilogue

A year after the events related in this book, news reached the merchant Renalleo that a talented young sculptor had set up shop in the south of Franken. Reports said the artist was like no other the Frankens had ever known. His work was in high demand, because his stone figures seemed so alive that viewers sometimes swore they saw them breathe. It was rumored that the sculptor had a wife with the voice of an angel who sang songs of surpassing joy. Renalleo determined to find the sculptor on his next journey to the great continent.

When Renalleo met the artist, he was not greatly surprised at his identity. Though he found that Davian now had an agent in the young man who had been an acolyte in Appienne, he worked out an arrangement to solicit commissions in the Seven Kingdoms and the peninsula of Appienne, two countries neither Davian nor his agent could safely enter.

Soon after Rhondale took the throne of Meridan, he levied the first general tax on the entire island. The kings of the Seven Kingdoms were outraged and refused to pay. Threats and diplomatic conflicts followed, resulting in all the kingdoms breaking their ties to the confederation. Though King Rhondale threatened war to force them back into the fold, all knew that with his Hall of Knights decimated by King Perivale's last folly, the threat was empty.

Rhondale's young advisors lacked the skill and experience needed to administer the laws of Meridan, and soon the kingdom's prosperity began to shrivel. Trade slackened, shops closed, and roads both within Meridan and without fell into disrepair. The people began to long for the fulfillment of the cryptic prophecy they could not fully understand and dream of the day when Meridan's glory would be reborn.

Thomas Williams is an author and illustrator. His eight books include fiction, theology, and drama, among them the Gold Medallion Award finalist *In Search of Certainty*, written with Josh McDowell. He owned his own art studio for twelve years and designed and illustrated more than 1,500 book covers for many of the major Christian publishers. He served as executive art director for Word Publishing for fourteen years. His painting of C. S. Lewis hangs in the Wade Collection at Wheaton College. He now writes full-time and provides creative consulting services to book publishers.

Tom and his wife, Faye, have three married daughters and eight grandchildren. They live in Granbury, Texas, near Fort Worth.